Singing

Bright

Madrigals

A Hal Westwood Restoration Mystery

SUMMER 1667

by Jemima Norton

TUDOR GATE
PRESS

LARGE PRINT EDITION

ISBN 978-0-9850753-4-7

LARGE PRINT EDITION

You will find the other books in this series at:
www.jemimanorton.com
www.halwestwood.com

For ordering information visit:
www.tudorgatepress.com

This book is dedicated to:

My brother Terry

1940 - 2013

THE PASSIONATE SHEPHERD TO HIS LOVE

BY CHRISTOPHER MARLOWE

1599

Come live with me and be my love,
And we will all the pleasures prove
That valleys, groves, hills, and fields,
Woods, or steepy mountain yields.

And we will sit upon the rocks,
Seeing the shepherds feed their flocks,
By shallow rivers, to whose falls
Melodious birds sing madrigals.

And I will make thee beds of roses
And a thousand fragrant posies,
A cap of flowers, and a kirtle,
Embroidered all with sprigs of myrtle.

A gown made of the finest wool,
Which from our pretty lambs we pull,
Fair lined slippers for the cold,
With buckles of the purest gold;

A belt of straw and ivy buds,
With coral clasps and amber studs:
And if these pleasures may thee move,
Come live with me, and be my love.

The shepherd swains shall dance and sing
For thy delight each May morning.
If these delights thy mind may move,
Then live with me, and be my love.

Singing Bright Madrigals

July 1667

Family

Sir Henry (Hal) Westwood, 28

> *Guardian of the bride, Justice of the Peace, gentleman*

Sophia (Sophie) Redcroft, 20

> *Hal's & Justin's Ward, widow of Gervase Harcourt*

Mary Armstrong, 29 *Hal's elder sister; Guy's wife*

Guy Armstrong, 30

> *Mary's husband; brother-in-law to Hal*

Ambrose Carver, 30 *brother-in-law to Hal*

Jane Carver, 24 *wife of Ambrose; Hal's sister*

Bess Danvers, 22 *Hal's sister; Justin's wife*

Justin Danvers, 26

> *Lawyer, Joint Guardian of Sophie, Hal's brother-in-law*

Gervase Harcourt, 25

> *Sophie's late husband; elder son of Sir Edgar Harcourt*

Thomas Kingscott, 49 *Margery Kingscott's step-son*

Mary (Molly) Kingscott, 41 *wife of Tom Kingscott*

Margery Kingscott, 61 *Hal's aunt*

Hetta Shearsby, 17   *Hal's sister*

Will Shearsby,19   *Hetta's husband*

Katherine (Kate) Westwood, 41   *Hal's aunt*

Cecily Westwood, 18   *Ned's wife; Hal's sister-in-law*

Ned Westwood, 20   *Hal's brother*

Libby Westwood   *Hal's first wife (deceased)*

Friends

Adam Blackwell, 27   *owner of Bickmarsh Hall*

Cordelia Blackwell, 20   *Adam's wife; Sophie's friend*

Bella Craven   *Simon's sister*

Simon Craven, 28   *owner of Haceby Hall*

Cathy Craven, 24 *Simon's wife;sister of Jack Hollingshead*

Barbara Craven, 52   *Simon's mother*

Phoebe Elgar, 26   *protégé of Margery*

Jack Hollingshead, 26   *kin to Cordelia Blackwell*

Madeleine Hollingshead, 48

       Jack's mother; kin to Cordelia Blackwell

Beatrice Pauncey, 19   *cousin to Bella Craven*

Nick Revesby, 22   *owner of Weston Revesby*

Hugh St John, 21   *Beatrice's betrothed*

Children of the Family

Guy Armstrong, 4,   *Guy & Mary's son*

Nicholas Armstrong, 3 — *Guy and Mary's son*

Katy Armstrong, 1 — *Guy and Mary's daughter*

Basil Blackwell, 3 months — *Adam and Cordelia's son*

Philip Danvers, 3 — *Bess & Justin's son*

Liberty (Berty) Danvers, *2* — *Bess & Justin's son*

Charles Danvers, 1 — *Bess & Justin's son*

Hal Kingscott, 5 weeks — *Tom & Molly's son*

Harry Westwood, 6 — *Hal's & Libby's son*

Francis Westwood, 3 — *Hal's & Libby's son*

Stephen Westwood — *Hal's step-brother*

People of the Town of Chawcester

Susanna Capel, *(formerly Blackwell)*, 38 — *one-time owner of The Greyhound Inn*

Jonas Capel, 58 — *Susanna's husband, a lawyer*

Jenny Calcot, 38 — *Susannah's cook*

Sukey Warren, 17 — *Susanna's maidservant*

Betty Tull, 19 — *Susanna's maidservant(deceased)*

Francis Black, 13 — *Susanna's errand boy*

Elias Keeble, 56 — *constable*

Harry Sambourne, 42 — *constable*

Jem Smith, 38 — *groom at the Greyhound*

Janet Willet, 34	*Jem the groom's sister*
Joe Crumpe, 27	*constable (temporary)*
Saul Watson, 33	*constable (temporary)*
Jesse Hibbet, 39	*bailiff*
Abel Monke, 54	*bailiff*
Eunice Latham, 41	*Justin's cousin &nearest kin*
Rebecca Howell, 18,	*companion and kin of Eunice*
Alice Bracegirdle, 36,	*wife of merchant of Chawcester*
Doctor Phillipe Douay, 37	*Physician*
Marie-Celeste Douay, 28	*Phillipe's wife*
Virginia Douy,	*Phillipe's baby daughter*
Owen, 58	*boatman*
Sally Rose, 26	*seamstress*
Judith Alsop, 19	*Sally Rose's assistant*
Will Guthrie, 30	*carrier*
Ned, 42	*groom at The Ring 'o Bells*
Tansy, 23	*serving girl at The Ring 'o Bells*
Old Harry, 73	*one time groom at The Greyhound*

Others

Farmer Goodacre, 48	*farmer of Chipping Bradbury*
Mistress Goodacre, 45	*his wife*
Blind Wat Jenks, 76	*his shepherd*

Glossary

OED- Oxford English Dictionary

BD Brewer's Dictionary of Phrase & Fable

auguries   to prognosticate from signs or omens

OED 1594

axe to grind   to have a selfish or hidden motive *BD*

brought to bed   colloquial term for having given birth

the Castlemaine   the Duchess of Castlemaine, Barbara Villiers, the mistress of King Charles II

character a detailed report, especially one given to a servant by an employer   *1645 OED*

the Commonwealth   the Republican government in England between 1649-1660

cross-grained   difficult to deal with   *1640-50*

crying for the moon   to crave that which is totally out of one's reach   *BD*

Dissenter one who dissents in matters of religious belief or worship,   *OED 1639*

entailed to settle land or estate on persons in succession so it cannot be possessed by anyone as an absolute owner   *ME OED*

fairings a gift, esp. one bought or given at a fair

flummery a dish made of wheat or oatmeal and milk, hence something insubstantial, nonsensical. *OED 1618*

goodwife the mistress of the house   *ME OED*

jade a term of reprobation for a woman

jointure a sole estate limited to the wife to take effect on the death of a husband.   *OED 1451*

Justice a colloquial term for Justice of the Peace, an inferior magistrate appointed to preserve the peace in county, town, or other district, and to discharge other local magisterial functions   *OED ME*

kirtle a woman's gown, a skirt or outer petticoat,
                                                        OED OE

Lammas August 1- Quarter Day when tenancies begin, payments of rents are due and servants are hired

Glossary

OED- Oxford English Dictionary

BD Brewer's Dictionary of Phrase & Fable

lickspittle a toady, the meanest of sycophants   *BD*

make old bones live to an advance age

mare's nests   to imagine one has found something wonderful.   *OED 1619*

Mop Fair a hiring fair, at which maids carried mops or brooms   *OED 17thC*

Noll nickname for Oliver Cromwell, Lord Protector of the Commonweath

outrider one who rides in escort.   *OED 1530*

physic, physicking   medicine, a cathartic or purge,   *OED ME*

pinchpenny   miser   *OED 1543*

Petty sessions   a court of three Justices of the Peace who dispensed summary justice

Poor Rate an assessment for poor relief   *OED 1601*

ragamuffins   rough, beggarly, good for nothing, disorderly   *OED 1602*

simples   a medicine composed of only one constitu-
ent, specially a herb or plant.   *OED 1539*

slattern   a slovenly woman or girl; slut   *C17*

snivelling one who sniffs to show or pretend emotion.   *OED 1660s*

still in short coats   still wearing children's garments   *1603 OED*

tap   a small room in an inn where ale is dispensed to more ordinary people

tell you to your face / tell you to your head   to
look in the eyes of the person and have no fear of their
displeasure

traps   shortened version of trappings, ornaments,
dress, trifling decoration.   *OED ME*

walls have ears things uttered in secret get rumoured
abroad   *BD*

Chapter One

July 1667

Hal glanced across to Sophie, as Ned and Cecily set off down the avenue on horseback in the moonlight. Sophie was smiling as she returned Cecily's wave, and a moonbeam struck her hair making it glow with an unearthly beauty.

"Come," Hal said extending his hand. "Walk with me. It is a beautiful evening."

"The night air is dangerous," said Aunt Margery, as Sophie turned to him with a smile of delight.

"Not on such a night as this," said Aunt Kate, touching her sister-in-law's arm and shaking her head. "The air is as gentle as a lamb. It is a night for lovers." She took Margery's arm through hers and turned with her back toward the house. "Don't stay out too long or you'll get dew-damped!" she called over her shoulder, to Hal.

Hal chuckled, and hand in hand he and Sophie

strolled under the trees in the wake of the riders.

"I have been thinking," he said, after a few moments of companionable silence. "We should probably make plans for our wedding before we have further trouble with the Dutch. I find I am constantly expecting another disaster, like the raid on our undefended English fleet at the River Medway, to spoil the enchantment of these past few days we have spent together—with a summons to London, or one of the family announces yet another addition to this year's crop of babies."

Sophie gurgled with laughter. "Oh, I think we have a good six months before Cecily will be bought to bed."

"Cecily?" Hal asked quickly. "Is she—?" He stopped to stare at her, then added in a slightly hurt manner: "Ned said nothing to me."

"I would imagine she forbade him to do so. Indeed, no one spoke a word to me either, but she has a look about her. And Ned was filled with such joy, wasn't he?" Sophie replied, detecting the disappointment in his voice and wanting to ease it. "I imagine after all the disappointments they've had, they'll want to be sure."

"Yes," Hal nodded. "Yes, of course, that will be it." Then as he recollected how tenderly his young brother had helped his wife into the saddle, he nodded again.

"Yes, he was very happy wasn't he? Well, that is splendid news to greet my return from London and it gives us a time scale."

"Not one as large as you might imagine," said Sophie. "I'm obliged to remind you of your sisters—Jane, who is due in October—and I believe Mary said something about having a full autumn, too."

"Oh, Mary has a baby every year," said Hal. "They don't seem to incommode her or Guy one bit, but Jane—that is something different. She is a little old to be having her first child."

"Not so very old—and she will be very well looked after by Aunt Kate and Aunt Margery," said Sophie. "Who could have any fear with Aunt Kate by her side? She has helped so many Westwood babes now."

"I could," he replied, tightening his grip on her slender fingers.

She smiled up at him. "I *am* very healthy, Hal," she replied gently.

"I couldn't lose you," he replied starkly. "It was only when I was delayed with the King's affairs and this damned Dutch War, that I realised how much I missed you. I could not contemplate life without you."

She smiled again. "Then perhaps we'd best not marry?"

she suggested mischievously. "For I gather that babies tend to follow on as a consequence."

He hugged her to him. "There can be no question but that we shall be married," he insisted.

She returned his embrace then asked, after a moment's hesitation, "Where do you imagine we will be married, Hal?"

"Where?" he looked at her in astonishment. "Why, here at Westwood, of course!"

"Yes, of course," she agreed quietly.

He had begun to walk on but stopped at this. "Where else?" he asked bluntly.

She shrugged her shoulders, and smiled tightly. "In the church? Alongside Libby's monument?"

"Oh—I see!" He turned to look back at his home, bathed in the glory of moonlight. "I am sorry, that never occurred to me. It just seemed the most natural thing to do."

"Oh, I'd want the feast to be at Westwood—where else, as you say—but, Hal, could we not be married in the Abbey?"

"In the Abbey?" he cried, "In that god-forsaken town of Chawcester? Never! Did I not say I am loathe to set foot in that place again?"

"Yes, you did," she agreed, "but Chawcester was my home. My mother and father are buried there, and Uncle Edmund, and Aunt Hannah."

"Aye, along with most of your acquaintance."

"Indeed, but for dear Mistress Blackwell and Sally Rose, who is making my wedding gown," she agreed mildly. "But Chawcester *is* closer for Mary and Guy. Mistress Blackwell—oh, I can never get used to her new name—Mistress Capel, I should say, has suggested I might wish to be married from my own home."

"Will you be happy to be married from the home of tradespeople?" he asked, in a disparaging manner.

"Indeed, for I am the heir to one, and in truth, I am happy to be married anywhere, if you are to be my bridegroom," she replied placidly. "I merely mentioned that I would quite like to be married at the Abbey in Chawcester. I used to dream of it as a little girl while running in and out playing among the gravestones."

"I had forgotten your parents are buried there," said Hal feeling a little contrite, realising he had not truly given them a thought since the demise of Edmund Benton. He was suddenly ashamed of his introspection.

"Yes, they are both buried in the plot Uncle Edmund bought when my mother died, alongside Aunt Hannah. Uncle Edmund is buried within the Abbey itself, but he managed to get consent for my father to be buried in the same grave as my mother, after he died of the fever in prison."

"Yes, I remember you telling me now. I am sorry it had escaped my memory—well, I suppose it was more that I put it all from my mind after I left," he added truthfully.

"Yes, I know, but don't you see, Hal, if we were to be married there in the Abbey, it would bring it all full circle," she said quietly. "The people of Chawcester would take us to their hearts, and make us one of their own. All the bad gossip would be forgotten. They are to a man so very proud of their Abbey, having raised the money themselves to buy it from the King."

"Yes, I recollect being told that tale when Edmund Benton died," said Hal. "It was the fact that his grandfather had contributed to the sale which meant he could be buried within the Abbey itself." He shrugged his shoulders adding, "I am of the opinion it will just rake up all the old gossip. And you cannot be unaware of an unpleasant incident which occurred there only a few weeks ago."

"You mean the old woman they accused of being a

witch out at Biddington?" replied Sophie wrinkling her nose. "Yes, I heard about it, but surely Biddington is a good few miles away from Chawcester?"

"Almost as far out as Westwood," he agreed, "but that didn't stop a mob of townsfolk storming out there, much as they did at Westwood back during the War. Only in this case they weren't met and repelled by my Aunt Margery and Aunt Kate. At Biddington the mob proceeded to drag a poor old woman out of her cottage and swim her in the pond on the green."

"Yes, your sister Jane mentioned it before your return," shuddered Sophie. "It seemed to have disturbed her greatly, and Aunt Kate was anxious that she shouldn't dwell upon it, so she told me not to discuss it. Therefore I know only the bare facts, which are bad enough. Did the old woman die?"

"Reports vary on that. Some claim she swam down to the bottom of the pond, turned into a toad and hopped away, then they pursued and stoned it," he replied bitterly. "Others say she hid in the reeds and made good her escape after dark and has since left the area. Yet others insist she magicked her broomstick up and took off into the skies. All done on the report of one who claimed that she'd given a foolish trollop a potion to rid her of an unwanted child. The mob terrorised an old woman and may have executed her in the most infamous manner. There are times when I despair of humanity! It doesn't seem to matter how hard we try to uphold the law, and give people the right to a fair and just trial. Evil is only just below the surface and some are only too willing to jump to the wrong conclusion."

"Was it the wrong conclusion?" Sophie asked in some doubt. "Wasn't it wrong of the old woman to give the wench a potion?"

"*If* she did do so, yes, it was wrong, and she should have been brought before a court of law to admit her wrongdoing, and to be sentenced, but we never got the chance to discover the whole truth of the matter. All we know is that she was a local wise-woman—who may or may not have given a slattern a potion—which might or might not have killed her and her unborn child. By all accounts the old woman had never harmed anybody before, and was indeed invaluable to the poor people of the parish, but somebody—probably for their own ends—whipped up a near riot. From what the more sensible villagers said, she was no more a witch than the old dame who used to live near Chipping Barbury. Some of our own villagers used to call *her* a witch, but she never harmed a fly—in fact she kept them in good health. She died only a few years back, much mourned by most of the local population."

"I remember Libby saying the woman taught her a lot about simples, and when to pick various herbs to get the best effect," nodded Sophie. "Yes, I can see what you are saying Hal, but surely there are always trouble-makers in every community? Those who will use the more excitable, foolish members of society for their own ends."

"Indeed there are, and that is why every society has its law keepers. Why it is essential that the law be ad-hered to and mob rule is not allowed to reign," he replied severely.

"Well, I have to say, a walk in the moonlight with you is certainly a different experience," sighed Sophie. "Here I was expecting kisses and perhaps compliments on my beauty and I get a lecture on the judicial system. Certainly life is never dull, with you, Hal!"

He gave an abrupt laugh and complied with her request with alacrity. It was only as they turned about at the end of their stroll, that he returned to the prob-lem at hand asking, "Is it truly your wish to be married from your old home? Don't you think being married in

Chawcester will just rake up all the old troubles, and make us the subject of idle gossip again?"

"Our marriage will do that anyway. Sally Rose says the whole town was full of it as soon as we returned from Lincolnshire with Adam and Cordelia."

"Mistress Blackwell, no doubt?" Hal remarked grimly.

"Mistress Capel, since her marriage," Sophie reminded him. "You have to remember, your arrival in Chawcester, and the events which followed were the most exciting thing to happen in the town since Oliver Cromwell marched through during the war. You were a figure of romance and drama long before you arrived, then once you came, and everyone saw your modish coat and good looks, the town was abuzz."

"Yes, and we left it in a high frenzy!" he replied sharply. "I was in a fever and too ill to care, but as I understand the matter, you were got away to Mary and Guy because the scandal was so great."

"I was *sent* away to Elmley Park because Justin couldn't bear the sight of me. He wanted to protect his sister," said Sophie candidly. "He made Libby send me away, 'in everyone's best interest', he said."

Hal nodded, recollecting those dark days. "I am sorry I was too ill to protect you properly," he apologized formally. Adding, with a heavy sigh, "Well, if it is truly what you want—to be married in the—"

"No, no!" she replied, appalled to see how much he disliked the idea. "No, I don't want you to do it *just* for me. That would rob all the joy from our wedding. If you hate the idea of it so much, then we shall be married at Westwood as you say! Don't you understand? I love you, and I want more than anything to be married to you, as you see fit. The where and when of the wedding are but mere trifles!"

He caught her to him. "It is no mere trifle to be married to me, Miss!" he teased with all the warmth back in his voice. "It is the most important occasion of our lives, and if it is your wish to be married in Chawcester Abbey, attended by all the good gossips of the town, then that is where we shall be wed!"

"And so Aunt Margery shall be told?" Sophie retorted, with a challenge in her eyes, as she withheld her lips.

He smiled wryly, as he saw the trap too late. "And so Aunt Margery shall be told," he agreed in a resigned tone.

"By you?" she added quickly.

"By me," he agreed with a half-laugh, as she surrendered into his embrace.

⚜

Chapter Two

It was the memory of the warmth of her kiss that took Hal in search of his Aunts Margery and Kate the next morning, for he was determined to set all in train for the forthcoming wedding. His period of mourning for his wife Libby was over now. And the term of waiting after Sophie's widowhood had recently been concluded. He also worried that the political situation with the Dutch was growing increasingly unstable, so he thought it might be wise to be married soon, lest there were further delays.

Hal was surprised to find his aunts not occupied by the myriads of tasks, which are the inevitable lot attendant upon the running of a great house. They were sitting in their favourite parlour, laughing and weeping over a letter, which had obviously only just arrived.

"Is something amiss, ma'am?" he asked of his senior

aunt, as Aunt Kate seemed to be lost in the grip of great mirth.

"No, indeed, most definitely not, Hal," Margery replied, wiping the tears from her own eyes. "Kate is just a little overcome."

"So I observe," he said, smiling to see their pleasure. "Am I to conclude you have received good news?" he asked, noting the letter clutched in Margery's hand.

"No, not good news, Hal!" gasped Kate, still laughing, turned to him, her face aglow. "The very best news."

"It is from my step-son Tom," said Margery. "You'll recollect your boys and I spent the autumn with them last year—arriving to celebrate his marriage and not leaving until after Twelfth Night—when you, Kate and Sophie joined us, just after you left your friends at Haceby?"

"Yes, ma'am," he wondered what was coming.

"You'll remember how distressed Tom was—he had not seen his little grandson in a good while—because his son's widow was being most difficult, and keeping his heir from his company?"

"I do indeed, ma'am," he agreed. "I remember saying to you both how I felt sure it had been the pleasure he and Molly had from playing with my boys that had stirred up his grief for his own son, and highlighted his feelings of loss for his baby grandson."

"Well, that is all over now!" Margery cried jubilantly.

"His son's widow has brought the child to visit?" he asked, hopefully.

"No, so much, much, better than that!" Aunt Kate cried, laughing again. "It seems Tom's new wife, Molly, was bought to bed of a baby boy last Tuesday, and both are very well and strong."

"A baby boy—but I wasn't aware Molly was in expectation of a child!" cried Hal.

"Nor were we—and neither were Tom or Molly!" Margery cried in great excitement.

"Yes, he is a seven-month child, but very strong, which is the main thing. Molly had told us all the children from her previous marriage came early. I remember her saying so, when we were discussing your sister Hetta's problems," continued Aunt Kate.

"It must be a seven-month child, Hal," insisted Aunt Margery, "Tom is a gentleman, after all."

"Yes, indeed," frowned Hal as he thought back. "Their wedding was in November—indeed it was their wedding which took us to that part of the world."

Kate quickly explained, "The joke is that Molly was

saying to us how sad she was that plainly she'd never be able to give Tom a son, because she was well past the age of bearing children. She said he mourned so deeply for his lost son, and his grandchild. Margery and I tried our very best to console her."

"I even advised her that certain delicate symptoms she was experiencing, were indeed all the natural course of Mother Nature, and nothing to be worried about for a woman of her age," said Aunt Margery, chuckling, "when in fact they were the signs of incipient motherhood. How Tom will delight in jesting about what he calls my 'midwifery skills' !"

Hal sat down, still rather amazed. "And they really had no idea of any such thing?"

"No, it has taken everyone by surprise," said Aunt Kate, "but they are both very well, both Molly and the baby, and Tom is so very happy."

"Tom cannot believe his good fortune," continued Aunt Margery, reading from the letter she held. "He says, 'not only has the good Lord smiled upon me in giving me the best of wives, he has now made my joy complete in giving me a son by her.' Good Heavens, I must be getting rather foolish in my dotage, for I have the strangest desire to weep with joy."

"That is only natural, Margery, after all, Tom is your son in all but birth. His concerns have been in your thoughts constantly these past five and thirty years," said Aunt Kate.

"Yes, that is very true, Kate. He is like a son to me, rather like Hal here," agreed Aunt Margery, hastily dabbing a handkerchief to her eyes. "The older one gets the more one desires to see one's kin happy."

"And soon we will see Hal happy too," Kate replied soothingly.

"Be assured, both of you, I am not only a very happy man, but a grateful one, too, Especially on hearing Tom's wonderful news. I shall write to him immediately," Hal insisted quickly.

"He says he will write to you, as soon as he has a moment to spare from his beloved wife and baby. Plainly he is in the highest of spirits, but Kate only thinks of the anxiety it has saved everyone," said Aunt Margery, glancing through the letter again. "Had Molly known of the likelihood of a child, how we would all have fretted—indeed you and I would most probably be at her side now. I do hope they are both as strong as Tom thinks, and that she is well attended in her lying-in."

"Tom will see she has the very best of care," said Aunt

Kate, in a soothing manner. "Of that we can be very sure—did you not say he quite doted upon her?"

"True, Tom is like to wrap them both in lamb's wool," agreed Margery, "just as Hal is doing with Sophie."

Hal glanced to her warily, aware a lecture was in the offing. "I beg pardon, ma'am," he said, with an ominous sense of foreboding.

"I was talking to her earlier, and discussing some nonsense which had come to my ears about your wedding taking place in the Abbey at Chawcester. I have no doubt it is nothing but a rumour put about by the gossips of the town, but I advised Sophie to put a stop to it at once. She told me that it is in fact under discussion between you."

"Sophie is quite wrong, ma'am," Hal replied at once. "There is no discussion whether we'll be married at the Abbey in Chawcester."

"Ah, there, Kate, did I not tell you so? I said as much to Sophie, too. I said, 'Hal will be married in Chawcester Abbey, over my dead body!' "

"And what did Sophie reply to that, ma'am?" he asked, with a sense of the inevitable.

"I have to say, Hal, she exhibited more of the sense of levity which I so deplore in you young people. I have tried my best to turn her thoughts to more serious matters, and I would be the first to applaud the way she enters into my concerns for the poor of these parishes. Although, I have to say, she doesn't keep the distance I would like to see exhibited by one at her station in life. I have explained the pitfalls attendant on getting too close to so many of these people, but Kate tells me it is something which will come in time, after some experience."

Kate's lips twitched as she watched the various emotions flitting across Hal's face and unable to stop herself from coming to his assistance she said, "Sophie suggested that the spectacle of the wedding itself was probably enough to entertain the good people of Chawcester, and it wasn't necessary for Margery to add to the festive atmosphere by human sacrifice."

"I am not a fool, Hal," said Margery, as Hal started upon a disjointed apology. "I know the young people see me as a dotard, so I laughed with Kate, as she has advised me to, and agreed it was not an attractive proposition, more a declaration of my opposition to the idea."

"I am pleased to see that you are indeed becoming used to Sophie's manner of using humour to ease what could become an awkward situation," said Hal, thinking how far his aunts had come in their education at Sophie's hands. "But I am sorry to hear you feel so strongly, too. For when I said the matter of our being married in the Abbey was not under discussion, I meant that we are no longer discussing it. Sophie has said she wants to be married at Chawcester Abbey, therefore we *will* be married in Chawcester, at the Abbey."

There was a stunned silence as both aunts digested the news, then Margery laid aside her letter with a sigh. "Well, if you are set upon indulging each and every whim of Sophie's in this manner, I have no more to say," she replied in affronted tones.

"You relieve my mind and ears enormously, ma'am," he said, attempting some of the levity Sophie used to such good effect.

"What is that you say?" she demanded, as Kate gave a snort of laughter. "What did you say? Hal, you know I have grown a little deaf, since last winter. You should be thankful you have all your faculties! Kate, it is no joy to find old age brings enfeeblement in its wake."

"Now that I refuse to believe," Hal said a little more loudly. "I am sorry, but I will not hear such nonsense. You are every bit as sharp as you ever were, Aunt Margery."

"How I deplore these odd expressions you young

people use," she replied. "I know you mean I have a superior intelligence—for which I thank my Maker—but when you have in your possession the whole glory of the English language, why not utilise it?"

"I beg pardon, ma'am," he replied swiftly. "You are, of course, correct. We possess one of the most beautiful languages, and yet we abuse it daily. It is most surely an example of familiarity breeding neglect."

"Indeed it is," Margery agreed, thawing a little in the throes of one of her favourite lectures. "I don't know why speech is so slovenly these days! I only know I can neither hear, nor understand, half of most conversations. I have frequently remarked upon it to you, Kate."

"Indeed you have, Margery," she agreed in soothing tones. "I'll mix you a potion later, to help clear your head a little."

"There is nothing wrong with my head," insisted Margery quickly. "I am merely explaining to Hal, how he'll come to rue the day, if he indulges Sophie's every whim in this fashion."

"Well, I don't think he will, Margery," said Kate reasonably. "Only recollect how Sophie admires Hal. She would never let any harm come to him."

Margery nodded. "It is true, Kate, her devotion and

esteem for Hal is not only admirable, but remarkable. I am pleased to observe it. And as for this nonsense about being married in Chawcester—that is out of the question. Naturally she will be married here."

"No, ma'am, I beg your pardon for disagreeing with you," said Hal firmly, "but the matter is quite decided, and I will have no further dispute. Sophie and I will be married at the Abbey in Chawcester."

"Are you sure of this, Hal?" Kate asked, as Margery looked very displeased. "You do dislike the town so."

"It is Sophie's wish," he replied, in a tone to end discussion on the matter. "It is the only home she knew as a child, and all her loved ones are buried at the Abbey."

"Of course," said Kate quickly, "how easily one forgets how alone the poor child is."

Aunt Margery, who had obviously been turning the matter over in her mind said, "Well, I suppose if she is married from Elmley Park it wouldn't be so very bad. Kate and I could remove there, and give Molly the benefit of our advice on the preparations."

"But you'll be needed here, ma'am," said Hal swiftly, as another domestic pit opened before him. "I'll need you and Aunt Kate to organise everything here for the feast, and celebrations which will follow the wedding."

"What? You'll travel all the way back here to Westwood, just for the feast!" Margery cried in shock.

"It is no more than six miles, ma'am, and the roads are quite reasonable at this time of year," said Hal.

"Yes, but it is four miles from Elmley Park to the Abbey for Sophie, and then if she has to travel six miles back here, she will be exhausted," said Margery.

"When have we ever seen Sophie exhausted?" Kate laughed at the thought. "Why, she came down from Cousin Tom's house with us last winter, in quite the most appalling weather, and didn't show the slightest sign of fatigue, though you, Cordelia, and I went straight to our beds."

"As indeed was sensible," said Hal smiling in recollection, "for Adam and I dozed the evening away. Anyway, ma'am, Sophie won't be staying at Elmley Park. She will be married from her old home in Chawcester."

"You cannot mean she means to be married from Mistress Capel's house?" asked Aunt Margery in horror. "From the home of that rascally rogue who calls himself a lawyer? Why, Mistress Capel—agreeable though she maybe—was herself an innkeeper!"

"Although I must agree Jonas Capel is not to my taste either, ma'am, he is considered locally to be a man of some probity and substance," replied Hal mildly. "As for Mistress Capel she—like Adam—chose to pay the debts her husband left by honest toil, in the only way she could. It is greatly to her credit that she is now a wealthy and respected woman, and the only connection Adam has left to him. You would not think well of him, I am sure, if he abandoned the nearest thing to a mother he's ever had? I know that Adam and Cordelia will be staying with Sophie and Mistress Capel for the wedding, and as I mentioned earlier, it is, in fact, still Sophie's house—and one of the finest in Chawcester."

"Indeed, it would be considered something of a slight by the people of Chawcester if Sophie was married anywhere else," agreed Kate. "You'll remember Master Benton's beautiful old house, Margery, you have often said how much you admire it."

"One can admire a house for the architecture and craftsmanship without being obliged to be on familiar terms with its inhabitants," Aunt Margery replied with a disparaging sniff. "Surely you cannot be unaware of the gossip surrounding Mistress Capel, Hal? And that unpleasant fellow she married? Nor the disgraceful behaviour of the people of Chawcester in hounding a poor old woman to her death for foolish superstition."

"I am not unaware of these facts, ma'am," he replied stiffly. "As a Justice of the Peace I am obliged to be aware of any misdemeanors that happen locally. "

"Indeed," agreed Kate, anxious to avoid a dispute. "I recollect you mentioning it earlier Hal, but only stop to consider, Margery—for I do believe Hal is correct. You and I should remain here at Westwood. We can organise everything for the celebration feast so much more easily if we do. After all, Madeleine Hollingshead has said she'll be making a visit soon, and she'll need time to talk privately with you about chosing Jack's future wife."

"Madeleine and I have been in correspondence ever since the winter, Kate," replied Aunt Margery with some hauteur. "That matter is all settled."

"Settled!" Hal cried, in laughing dismay. "How can Jack's future bride be settled without Jack even being aware of who it is?"

"Jack doesn't need to be aware of anything," replied Aunt Margery firmly, thawing slightly. "He'll be presented with two, possibly three, options of a suitable bride sometime soon. Jack is a sensible man. He is not like your foolish wards, Hal."

"Poor Jack!" Hal replied with feeling. "A suitable bride!"

"Jack Hollingshead is his own man," Kate remarked, as Margery gave an impatient sigh. "He would never allow himself to be pushed into anything."

"No one is speaking of pushing, Kate," replied Margery swiftly. "I know better than to think of pushing a man like Jack Hollingshead into matrimony. He is aware, so Madeleine insists, of time's relentless march. However, he is now ready, he claims, to take a bride as all his contemporaries have done."

"It is a great shame that your step-son Tom is not likely to attend my wedding now." Hal, who had been briefly reading his cousin's letter, added humorously. "He wrote only last week saying how much he and his Molly were looking forward to attending my nuptials, and asking if I would be pleased to forward him with a detailed list of how all my guests are related, and indicate not only people most likely to be murdered on that august occasion, but all of my chief suspects."

Aunt Margery looked displeased at Hal's levity, but had mellowed so much that she merely frowned a little as Kate chuckled. "You cannot comprehend how pleased I am, Hal, that you and dear Tom have become such good companions. I believe I have in the past expressed some anxiety about the odd friendships you have formed, and I lay the blame for that wholeheartedly at the feet of your father—for those years in exile in France appeared to have given you a taste for low company. But now, when I see you with Tom, Jack Hollingshead, Simon Craven and that young scamp Nick Revesby, I know you will never go far astray."

Hal hid a smile. "Thank you, ma'am," he replied politely. "I am pleased to relieve you of that anxiety, but in this changing world one finds oneself making friendships with many folk one might not have met before, and do you know, I think society will become the better for it."

This was going too far for Aunt Margery. "I am not sure I agree with that, Hal. Before the war we met only the best families. One would never have dreamt of sitting at table with tradespeople."

"But how often these days, Aunt, have the best people been pressed by circumstances to *become* tradespeople? And many are making a success of it! Only think of how my own sister Mary's husband, is one such case. Is Guy not a perfect example of what we speak, a gentleman, forced by changing fortunes, using trade to his advantage?"

"Guy always displays the character of a gentleman,"

Margery replied swiftly. "Guy may have been forced by circumstances to improve his fortune by putting his money into trading, as indeed many of our great families now do, but Guy does not serve in his own shop."

Hal grinned. "No, ma'am, and that is just as well, for Guy is not the most patient of men, and neither does he have a head for figures. If Ambrose didn't assist him with his affairs, I am pretty sure his venture wouldn't be half so profitable."

Kate laughed again. "Now that is very true, Hal. What a boon Ambrose has become to the family—Justin, too," she added as an afterthought. "Indeed, Margery, upon reflection, Hal is correct. Society has been improved by being more open. Do you not remember how it was when Henry was negotiating Hal's marriage with Libby's father? That poor man felt himself to be so very much out of his depth. He was so unsure of himself, that if my Henry had not been such a gentleman, he could have driven a very hard bargain indeed."

"Whereas, Libby's brother, Justin thinks nothing of abusing Uncle Henry's nephew, as if he were little better than a tinker," agreed Hal with a rueful smile.

"Indeed," said Aunt Margery, "and that sort of behaviour proves exactly what I say. Many may think that they have achieved the status of a gentleman, but sadly their behaviour belies the fact."

"Well, whether that's so or not, Bess and Justin will be at the wedding. Bess said she wouldn't miss it for the world," Kate insisted rather desperately.

"It is my intention to summon both Bess and her husband Justin to discuss this matter before the ceremony," announced Aunt Margery. "This nonsense has gone on long enough. There is no doubt we were all saddened by the death of his sister Libby. She was a good and faithful wife to you, Hal, and we all grieve at your loss, but this vendetta of Justin's against Sophie has reached ridiculous proportions."

"I do not think it would be wise to try to discuss the matter with Justin, ma'am," replied Hal uneasily. "Recollect how very bitter he has become of late."

"You, Hal, plainly think it is part of your penance to bear with his intolerable manners, but I will not tolerate them a moment longer, and I have no hesitation in telling Bess of my decision," insisted Aunt Margery.

"Poor, dear Bess has a difficult enough time of it with Justin anyway, Margery. She does not need his failings pointed out to her. Better to say nothing to her. It is not long since she left her bed for her last lying-in."

"No," sighed Margery. "Neither it is, the poor dear, I had forgot. Whatever else his faults—and they are many—Justin has raised a brood of healthy children."

"I rather think that is because you and Aunt Kate are so assiduous in attending the lying-in of any of your kin," said Hal. "We do realise, as a family, how fortunate we are to have such devoted care, even though it seems to me you are kept very busy indeed. "

"That is the task set by the Lord for us old women," replied Kate. "Just when you think you are of no further use in your life, your nieces start bearing children, and you discover you are useful again. Never fear, we'll be there for your future babies, too, Hal."

"Yes," nodded Margery thoughtfully. "I must say, Hal, you've chosen a fine, healthy, young bride as mother of your future children. Indeed you have chosen a better wife for yourself than your Uncle Henry did for you."

"I rather think my uncle was somewhat constrained by the need to provide me with a fortune, ma'am. For myself I couldn't fault his choice. Libby made me an admirable wife, who always put my interests first. I would that I could have loved her more."

"I never heard her complain, Hal," insisted Kate, trying to reassure him. "She was devoted to you."

"Yes, ma'am," he agreed, "she was totally devoted to me—and I used her ill."

"No, I won't hear that!" snapped Aunt Margery. "You have always been the epitome of a gentleman, Hal. No woman could ask for more."

Hal laughed and looked embarrassed by such fulsome praise. "Remind me to tell Sophie so, ma'am!"

"Sophie is well-aware of her good fortune," said Margery. "I remarked upon it to her the other day, and she agreed with me entirely. She said she had never expected to be so very happy, and confessed she was often filled with anxiety—for she was well aware that the gods don't like to see mortals happy. I chided her, as you might imagine, for talking such pagan nonsense, and reminded her that the good Lord looks after those he has chosen as his handmaidens. And do you know—she agreed with me, then thanked me for my words, which she said were very sensible. I have to say, Hal, the improvement in her character since she returned from the Eastern Counties has been remarkable."

Hal glanced away to avoid the gaze of his other aunt, and wondered how quickily he and Sophie could leave Westwood to take up residence in Chawcester in preparation for the wedding. Surely this new-found accord between his senior aunt and his beloved would not be of long duration. "Indeed, ma'am," he agreed swiftly, and made haste to leave their presence before levity could overtake him.

Chapter Three

"So, Sir Henry, how is it with you?" asked Phillipe Douay as he glanced shrewdly to his guest, then took a seat in the parlour, his sharp eyes taking note of his friend's demeanour, once the first glad cries of greeting and good fellowship were done.

"I am as well as can be expected for a widower about to embark on another marriage—especially a marriage to Sophie," Hal replied with a smile.

"Yes," agreed the Frenchman. "I met with her yesterday. You are to be congratulated, *mon ami*, I was stunned by her beauty. She was always a pretty maid, but now?" He kissed the tips of his fingers to express his admiration.

Hal smile wryly. "My Aunt Margery is not with you on either head, my friend, but please, tell me of your adventures. I could not believe it when Sophie told me you were back in Chawcester. How are your wife and child? And how is it you are back in England? I do hope the journey from Virginia was not too fatiguing for them. Was the colony no better than France?"

Phillipe grimaced as he poured them both a cup of wine and came to take a seat opposite. "Ah, my Marie Celeste, she is in good health, and little Virginia, she never ails—she is a sturdy one, that child," he paused sipping his wine. "Alas, you are right, the settlement didn't suit us—and that was before we were put on alert against the Dutch raids. Why is it, *mon ami*, the English can not tell one nationality from another? Once again we were outsiders—Frenchies—considered only just a bit more trustworthy than the Dutch, or the savages in the forests."

Hal looked dismayed. "I am grieved, Phillipe. I did hope that in a new land, one dedicated to freedom, all men might be equal."

"Certainly all Englishmen are supposed to be so," he agreed with a smile. "And I cannot deny they were polite enough to our faces, especially if they had the flux or the ague, but there was no real meeting of minds, such as we have, no true friendship."

"Most settlers are non-conformists by inclination,"

said Hal thoughtfully. "And I suppose if there is an extension of the war with the Dutch they would be uneasy, but I have observed they are not the most cheerful of companions. Most certainly that scoundrel from Virginia my Aunt Kate nearly married, Sir Richard Harrison, was not."

"Having attended upon his wife, I can well understand. That was an odd affair, Hal, was it not? Are you aware that Harrison went by a different name in the Virginia settlement?"

"Yes, he was obliged to change his name that he might inherit from his kinsman. I believe he went by both names for a while, but in truth Sir Richard Harworth-Harrison proved to be a bit of a mouthful, so he dropped the Harworth."

"Yes, his wife Mistress Harworth was most displeased when she heard about it from the captain of the next vessel which arrived after her recovery from the fever," grimaced Phillipe. "She was much grieved, and appeared to think her husband's continued absence was an attempt to escape his responsibilities back in Virginia."

"As to that, I could not say," frowned Hal. "As far as *we* knew he was recently widowed. Indeed, he claimed to be so, and I do believe he thought that was the case at first, when he began courting my aunt. His crime was in not informing my aunt, when this proved to be an error. I had hoped that you might be able to send me word of his arrival back in Virginia, so I could be sure we were well-rid of him, but I calculate your passages must have been at a similar time. Who knows? Perhaps your ships passed on the ocean. Either way, I am glad you survived the journey, and I wonder, in more private moments, if his intention was never to do so."

Phillipe frowned. "What? Do you suspect that he would deliberately take his own life? Surely no Christian would do such a thing! Is it not much more likely he went overboard in an accident? Is your respected Aunt greatly grieved?"

"More, I think, by his failings than his death," replied Hal dispassionately. "We all found ourselves in a difficult situation, but I tell you this, I am never more thankful that I went personally to get my aunt out of that disastrous entanglement, for I greatly fear such was his temperament that he might have attempted to persuade her to take the same option. He was a difficult man to admire—a curious compound of impossibly high ideals, which were so obviously doomed to wretched failure. And each failure, even as it galled him, appeared to further convince him that he was pursuing the Lord's chosen path. Yet that faith which drove him did not seem to give any comfort. It was a most unsatisfactory affair, and my aunt is still much shocked and deeply grieved. As for my suspicions, the magistrate in me finds it convenient that he went overboard in a relatively calm sea, close to an island within possible striking distance of the coast of Virginia."

Phillipe frowned. "Surely to think of taking a chance like that in a vast ocean denotes a mind strangely disturbed? And what future could he have, alone and friendless in a region more renowned for cut-throats and pirates, than law-abiding citizens?"

"The late war taught us nothing, if it did not demonstrate that in desperate conditions the trappings of respectability are but skin-deep," replied Hal dispassionately. "Many who now grace the Court at Whitehall have left behind a chequered career. My own father was one such—and Prince Rupert another. How many of those who nod and bow in St James Park are clothed in the outward conventions of respectability, yet still conceal the heart of a pirate?"

"That I cannot say, being but a humble medical man

in a small country town," Phillipe replied, although he looked troubled by the thought.

"My point is that even in a small country town the instincts of men are the same. Most go about their business in a law-abiding fashion, but beneath the surface run all sorts of tensions that we know nothing of," replied Hal.

"Which is probably just as well, for acquaintance with one's fellow man does not fill one with great enthusiasm for the future of mankind," sighed Phillipe.

"There are troubles here?" Hal asked quickly.

"No more than any town in the country," the physician replied swiftly. "The same petty squabbles such as are enacted throughout the land, I have no doubt."

"No doubt, but I have often noticed, Phillipe, how acute your observations are. If there is anything I should be aware of, please tell me at once. I am here because Sophie very much wants to be wed in the Abbey, but I tell you in truth I am every bit as uneasy about it as my Aunt Margery."

Phillipe looked grave. "If your respected aunt is uneasy, then my reservations increase threefold. Mistress Kingscott may not admit my existence, but I have a healthy regard for hers."

Hal's eyes were suddenly sharp. "And your point is?"

"There is much unrest in the town and muttering in the taverns. This war with the Dutch has increased prices and old political leanings are being aired. Any honeymoon period enjoyed after the return of the King is long gone. Reports of life at the Court of St James are circulated by gossips, much embroidered no doubt by idle tongues, and those who have a connection with the Court are being tarred with the same brush."

Hal nodded thoughtfully. "Thank you, Phillipe, I have understood the warning. And once again I am lost in admiration of your command of the English language. You have a far finer understanding of colloquial idioms than my Aunt Margery."

"No, Hal, I admit my understanding of them, indeed, in my profession it is essential I know them," replied the physician with a laugh.

Hal smiled in acknowledgement of this truth. "How is it for you here—a Frenchman, who abandoned them to seek his fortune in the New World—and then returned to Chawcester?"

"I am fortunate in that no English physician appeared in my absence. They were left to the mercies of Master Jesse Cresswell, who is now the mayor and has even less time to devote to his clients. How I shall fare when there is an alternative, I cannot say. In the meantime, my strange and deep longings for my adopted home have been assuaged and my poor wife is coming to terms with living in England which, luckily for me, is more preferable to being on board one of your brother-in-law's ships."

Hal chuckled. "Guy doesn't own the ships. He merely commissions them to carry the goods he and his partners trade, but it was useful for you to find passage with them."

"Yes, by the time I had cured the captain of his headaches, and removed the rotten teeth of at least half of the crew, we had docked in Bristol, and transferred to a river boat, which brought us here. Chawcester, it seems had been left to the tender mercies of my good friend Cresswell, who welcomed my return with open arms."

"I see you are even back at your old lodgings at The Sign of the Golden Key." Hal glanced about the spacious apartment curiously.

"It had remained untenanted since our departure, so I wrote to the owner, who fortunately had no hesitation in granting me a lease," said Phillipe.

"That was good fortune, for your departure was rather abrupt," agreed Hal. " 'Tis lucky he held no grudge."

"The lease was paid in full, and I have never known Sophie be anything other than a good business woman."

"Good Heavens, do you tell me the owner is Sophie? She said nothing of it to me!" Hal replied amazed.

"Yes, she said you appeared to have little interest in your future wealth," the physician replied with a frown.

"Sophie's money has been tied up in a legal tangle for so long since her disastrous marriage and widowhood. I have never cared to discuss it with either her—or Justin, come to that. Usually when she and I are together we find more pleasant things to talk about—that is if we are not trying to discover the latest murderer," replied Hal with such tenderness the Frenchman smiled.

"So, Hal, all your doubts are past, are they?"

"I don't know that I'll ever be without doubt about the mischief Sophie will somehow be involved in, but I do know, that I missed her like a physical ache, in the time we were apart last year." He grinned suddenly. "I am certain that however much she can—and almost certainly will—exasperate me every day of our lives together, I'd sooner spend my hours being infuriated, than face the empty void of life without her."

"I have to say, the town, which it seemed to me had

sunk into a torpor of boredom, came alive within a few hours of the rumour of your wedding. It will surely be at a fever pitch by the time the ceremony takes place," replied Phillipe with a grin.

"Talking of ceremonies, will you do me the honour of being one of my groomsmen?" Hal asked. "My brother Ned, will be escorting me to church. Cecily tells me he has the wedding band and had mislaid it three times already, so I must remember to purchase another. You might hold that for me, Phillipe, for it would mean much to me for you to stand as my friend, especially as you do have a genuine affection for Sophie, which Ned, try as he may, does not."

"Poor Ned, it would ever be thus," added Phillipe wisely, having given his gracious acceptance. "Any wife of yours would be his enemy."

"No, indeed you are mistaken,"said Hal quickly. "Ned was, I think, so very fond of Libby. He feels—as do many of my family—that I betray her with this new marriage."

"What nonsense, Hal! The reason Libby was so acceptable to Ned was because you didn't love her," Phillipe cried sapiently. "With Sophie he can have no doubt of the depths of your affection, or hers for you, which makes him feel he has become an outsider in your life."

Hal frowned. "That cannot be! Ned is full-grown now. He has Cecily and the baby—when it arrives—will make his happiness complete."

"*Naturellement*, he does, but his love for you has been ingrained for so much longer. You are his elder brother, his hero, but once he sees how happy you are with So-phie, he will be happier himself."

"I sincerely hope all goes well with his baby," replied Hal with feeling. "Now what is it you are not telling me, Phillipe? What is the gossip? You say Chawcester was sunk into a torpor. Has nothing happened in the past two years?"

"Gossip is rife, as ever," replied Phillipe, with a wry twist to his mouth. "Things have happened, it would seem, but little of import, so the townsfolk have taken to gossip as a way of enlivening their dull existence. Mostly it is Dame Rumour, and her friend, Count Eru-mour they indulge in. It is ever so with small-minded people."

Hal smiled at his friend's mastery of his adopted lan-guage. "Who do the gossips have their claws into now?"

"Whytheir claws are in your old esteemed friend from our finest inn, The Greyhound, Mistress Blackwell—or

Mistress Capel as she is known these days."

"Mistress Capel?" Hal repeated in dismay. "Now why should such a universally respected citizen be a source of local gossip? My Aunt Margery will be most displeased, for Sophie is staying at Mistress Capel's home for the next few days! What is the gossip about?"

"As far as I know, nothing of great import," Phillipe replied in soothing tone. "A mere *bagatelle*, Hal. Mistress Capel is universally esteemed, as you say, although her husband is not popular."

"Lawyers seldom are," observed Hal. "Especially those who eagerly make capital out the suffering of others."

Phillipe nodded in agreement. "Indeed, I am convinced the affair is no more than gossip."

"Yes, you seek to relieve me, Phillipe, but I would sooner know what is being said, so I can think of a way to sooth Aunt Margery, before she and Sophie are at loggerheads again."

" 'Tis said Capel has set up a mistress," he said bluntly.

"Is it so?" Hal asked in surprise that so unremarkable a thing should cause comment.

"One of his maidservants," added Phillipe.

"Oh dear, tasteless, but no more than one would expect from such a fellow as Capel."

"Mistress Capel didn't greet the news with well-bred decorum," murmured Phillipe.

"Ah! No, well, I can see that she might not. Come, Phillipe, the round tale if you please!"

"It would seem—and this part is but hearsay—it would seem, Mistress Capel, burst in on her servants demanding to know, and I quote, 'Which of you sluts is my husband's whore?' "

"Oh dear! Pray God nothing of this comes to my Aunt Margery's ears! His answer?"asked Hal, with foreboding.

"Betty, the maid who wasn't there, was in my chamber, trying to persuade me to give her a potion to rid her of her unwanted child."

Hal looked displeased. "You refused, of course?"

"Indeed, *mon ami*, I refused," replied Phillipe sharply. "I was trying to persuade the foolish woman God's will be done, when Mistress Capel, came bursting into my chamber, thrusting aside my wife, who tried to restrain her. I make allowances for the good woman's anger. Mistress Capel is mostly a gentle soul, and she is not an old woman. But two of her previous husbands have been older men. I think perhaps she had hopes of a child of her own. Perhaps it was the failure of these hopes which sparked Mistress Capel's rage, or perhaps the insult in contaminating the sanctity of her home, I know not, but like so many placid, good-natured women, her temper had been greatly inflamed."

"She reached the wretched maid?" Hal asked.

"But for my interference, she could well have physically abused the wench—perhaps even worse than that, for the trollop mocked her roundly."

Hal shut his eyes in dismay. "And the outcome?"

"Disaster!" the physician replied. "Mistress Capel, held off by me loudly threatened the life of the wench, her husband and the whole town of Chawcester, including myself, if I didn't release her from my restraining grip immediately. In view of her great rage, I dismissed the unfortunate maid Betty, and she made off whilst my wife and I calmed Mistress Capel with a tisane. Then the wench went to see an old woman in a nearby village, and obtained a potion, which successfully rid her of not only her child, but also her own life."

"God rest their souls!" Hal sighed. "This took place whilst I was London. Did the town not form a mob, and go after the old woman, intent on violence? Aunt Kate told me it is thought that the wise woman hasn't been seen since. When exactly did this occur, Phillipe?"

"It was back in the spring, a few weeks after our return. Marie Celeste was convinced we'd be ruined and no client would set foot through my door, but this being Chawcester, the reverse was true."

"They invented ailments to give themselves the opportunity to gossip?" he suggested.

"I prefer to think trivial illnesses were used as an excuse to come here," he agreed.

"And you treated them?"

"I treated the problem they presented with, and reminded them that a physician or apothecary with a loose tongue would be of no interest to anyone. No one would like tales told of boils on their fundament."

Hal laughed. "That surely is threatening behaviour."

"No, *mon ami*, it is good business practice. The physician with a discreet tongue can only be truly appreciated if one suffers an embarrassing ailment."

Hal nodded, "So everything has settled down now?"

"Settled? *Non,* Hal, life here doesn't settle down. Life is a boiling kettle, always something will lift the lid and spill over into the flames."

"Pray God it doesn't within the next few days before my wedding! So, Mistress Capel and her rascally husband are now reconciled?"

"Reconciled?" Phillipe considered the word as if it were new to him. "No," he said at last, "not that, I think, perhaps more disinterested."

Hal pulled a face. "Sophie said no good would come of their marriage, and I was inclined to agree with her, although Justin says he is a competent lawyer."

Phillipe cast him an sapient look. "How goes it with you and your brother-in-law?"

Hal flashed a smile which didn't reach his eyes. "Oh, well enough, provided we are not often in company."

"I find Justin is not liked in Chawcester. The townsfolk talk of harsh treatment and little leniency in rent payments," said Phillipe.

"Chawcester folk seldom like any not actually born here. They are pleasant enough to your face, but will happily assassinate your character behind your back—but then there is no difference between here and Adamsholme, or London, come to think of it! As for Justin—he has grown harder and colder. He looks a disappointed man." Hal was silent for a space. "He *is* a disappointed man. I would that I could help him."

"It all goes back to his father's death?"

"Indeed, Libby left everything to me, even though we had agreed otherwise. I had always insisted that money be kept aside in trust for her brother Justin, once he could be brought to accept it. "

Phillipe frowned. "This was agreed between you? Does Justin know the decision was Libby's?"

"He was at that time my man-of-law. He knew my feelings. It was Libby who made the alteration just before her death. Why, I do not know."

"Perhaps to keep you yoked to the same plough?" suggested Phillipe frowning over the conundrum. "For surely if her money had gone to Justin there would be no need for you to ever meet him again."

"But that he is married to my sister Bess," shrugged Hal. "No, Justin was mortified that his marriage to my sister Bess caused his father's fortune to go to Libby. My father had refused to pay the dowry for Bess because theirs was a clandestine wedding, so Bess had no money. Justin's father refused to acknowledge their match, and but for my interference they would both have fared ill. I had hoped we could persuade Justin to take Libby's inheritance, but he refused it. The root of his enmity is he feels he has been cheated by everyone."

"I feel for him, Hal, but he could not hope for a better brother-in-law. The man is a fool to shun and irk you."

"I find it difficult to be civil to him these days," agreed Hal. "It seems his intention is to be objectionable."

"Hmm, I begin to see now why you ask me to be your groomsman!" the Frenchman remarked humorously. "A brother who doesn't care for your bride, a brother-in-law who doesn't like you, an aunt who cannot approve of your choice, and a town already restless, and famous for bearing a grudge—I can see this is going to be a memorable wedding!"

Chapter Four

Meanwhile, Justin was nearby pacing the floor of a very fine old merchant's house. The invitation to meet his Cousin Eunice had come as a surprise, but as she was one of his few personal clients, he could not afford to offend her. He did not however, have valuable time to waste dancing attendance upon her, and as she was late, his temper, already irked by the prospect of the imminent marriage of his foolish brother-in-law, grew shorter.

Minutes ticked by, and he was about to make his departure, when he heard footsteps below and the slam of the outer door. He advanced to the head of a very finely carved staircase and looked down just as his cousin reached the first step.

"Ah, there you are, Justin," she remarked, as she paused, stick in hand. "I see you are early."

"Cousin, I'll come down to save you the journey up."

"Don't be a fool!" she retorted as she toiled up the first flight of stairs. "There is no house down here, only the shop. I've come to inspect my latest purchase."

Silenced by surprise, his courtesy returned and he hastily ran down to give her his arm as she ascended to the next floor.

"Well, I see you do have some manners, then," she remarked as she paused for breath on the spacious landing. "Your brother-in-law, Sir Henry, when in Chawcester last week, turned back on his errand and personally escorted me home with upmost courtesy, because the river was rising after all the rain."

"I don't doubt it. Sir Henry is ever the one for the pretty, meaningless gesture," he replied acidly. "You have lived here all your life. You know the rise and fall of the river better than he."

She paused for breath, and looked about her up towards the magnificent carving and fine old dog-leg stairs, which spiralled away to the next floor. "Yes, it was a courtesy. Only he knew it and I knew it! You begin to sound more and more like your late father. He was a bitter man, too," she remarked bluntly.

"Most likely he had cause. I am thankful he died before Libby did," he replied. "Have you truly bought this house, ma'am? It will be the death of you. Surely you don't think to climb these stairs on a daily basis?"

"No," she replied, "I intend to get you to do that for me. I have just bought the place for you and your family. It is time Chawcester had a decent lawyer."

"You have bought it for me and mine?" he asked in amazement. "But we live in Adamsholme!"

"Aye, in a cramped few rooms above your chambers, just as your father did," she agreed.

"If it was good enough for him, I am content," he replied acidly.

"Of course, your father was at least his own man," she agreed affably. "He wasn't owned lock, stock and barrel, by another."

Justin gritted his teeth. "My father had better fortune than I."

"He did not! He lost nearly everything that was precious to him—save you and your sister!" she replied sharply. Come, let us move into the parlour. It has a splendid view of the High Street." She continued, as he escorted her along the corridor, past several handsome chambers. "No, your father had bitter fortune. His wife never had the connections yours does, and he was forced to leave her in a cold grave in that savage land Virginia. He had but two things to love and he lavished all his care on them."

"Love?" he echoed the word incredulously.

"Did you ever want for anything as a child? Were not both you and Libby the apple of his eye?" she demanded. "There now, isn't this a most handsome chamber?"

"Indeed," he agreed, pausing to look about him at the elegantly panelled room with leaded windows looking out over the junction of the High Street and the London Road. "This is a most handsome property, Cousin. You've invested your money well. You should get a sound return in rent for it."

"In this instance I am not looking to get a return for my money," she replied tartly. "I am looking to the future. I cannot get about as I once did and I feel isolated out in the country. The town will suit me better. I want to settle my affairs, and intend to settle them on you—once I've found a suitable husband for Rebecca."

"Rebecca?" he asked, startled by her words.

"Rebecca Howell," she said tartly. "You met her last year when you escorted me to her father's funeral. She is kin of my late husband, and has made her home with me these past six months, since her maternal grandmother died, leaving her with very little. I'll take that chair over there, if you'll be sure it is sound, Justin."

Hastily he tested the ancient high-backed chair for soundness and helped her to it. "It appears to have four somewhat uneven legs, ma'am, and you are very much a feather weight. I am confident it will pass muster."

She groaned as she sat. "It could bear a cushion, but it is a grand old chair, probably older than me."

Justin made the semblance of a smile. "You don't look a day older than when we first met, ma'am."

"I remember it well. Near five and twenty years ago. You were a whey-faced scrap, in your sister's arms," she replied and shook her head. "Your eyes even then, huge with misery. No, you didn't smile then, no more do you now. Your brother-in-law is the master of the pleasant mien, with his air of gentle concern and courteous phrase. He beats you hands down every turn. What are you going to do about it?"

Justin, who had turned away impatiently at her words, whipped back and snapped, "What can I do? As you say, he beats me at every turn! Everyone is beguiled by his charm, his looks, his money!"

"Ah, so finally the poison spills! To heal a boil, one must lance the poison. What has Sir Henry done to you, to earn such ill-will towards him?"

"How can you ask? You know he killed Libby!"

"I know no such thing, but you are a man-of-law, so present your case."

He turned from her, goaded, his hands clenched in fists, then spun back to her, his face a mask of fury. "I cannot! God knows, I've tried—I've tried everything I know, but can find nothing to accuse him of!"

"Except perhaps, happiness, and the ability to charm others?" she suggested. "Enumerate his crimes for me, that I may judge for myself why you so hate him."

He stood rigidly for a few seconds. "I don't hate Hal," he sighed. "Dear God, I loved him so once. He dazzled us both, don't you see? Libby and I, we both thought him a god. You don't know him. When you are his friend, it's like being part of a charmed circle, but if you lose his trust, you are cast into the outer darkness."

"And there is no way back?" she asked with sympathy.

"No route *I* can take. He has me in his thrall and I cannot escape," he replied bitterly.

"And Mistress Redcroft?" she frowned over his words.

His mouth twisted with bitterness again. "Sophie Redcroft is a heartless jade! I pray she'll subject him to the misery I endure. "

"Do you?" she asked again, and the silence length-ened against the muted sounds of the street below.

"No," he replied sullenly, as he opened a window.

"The noise is not unpleasant," she remarked.

"No worse than Adamsholme," he agreed.

"It is a handsome house. I would like you to move your family here. This is my gift to you, Justin. You'll lose the clients from Adamsholme so you'll have to start again, of course. I assume Ambrose Carver will take control there."

"He already does, in that he acts for Hal," replied Justin wearily.

She nodded being well aware of this. "Well, you shall have my business which isn't inconsiderable, and the town could do with a better lawyer than Capel."

"I can hardly charge you fees, ma'am," he replied sharply. "You are kin, and I'll be indebted to you."

"On the contrary, I'd be indebted to you," she con-fessed. "I have so enjoyed having young Rebecca with me. I hadn't realised how stale my life had become. One needs young people about one, if one is not to sink into miserable old age."

"You will live here with us, ma'am?"

"That was my plan," she admitted. "Do you object?"

"In the face of such generosity, how could I object? It is more I worry that my children can be very noisy."

"I imagine they are," she agreed with a chuckle, "but they always strike me as good-natured, well-mannered boys. They will be sent to school as soon as they are of age, I assume?"

"Well, yes, Pip is due to start taking lessons soon, as he is plainly ready for them. He can go through his primer in no time."

"Chawcester has a school, although that is for later on, but I have been to see it. The master doesn't drink, and the boys don't look beaten. In the meantime, Rebecca can help Bess with his schooling," said Eunice.

Justin frowned as he realised his household would be swelled by the addition of another young woman. "I see you are well prepared, ma'am, but I am concerned that there is not enough work for two lawyers in a small market town."

"Perhaps," she replied, "but I know Capel isn't trusted by many. I know of people in the area who would be glad of a sound man, who is within an easier distance than Adamsholme, or Maucester." Then as he nodded thoughtfully while watching the comings and goings in the street below, she continued, "I think I told you I've been wanting to settle my affairs for sometime, and I have had this house in mind, for I have always admired it. Now I see my way clear. It was far too large for me on my own, but if it is the home of the sort of man-of-law Chawcester needs, a man of integrity, it makes sense. You are here often enough as Clerk to the Magistrates. Bess will be closer to her old home, and her sister Mary, and Ned and Cecily, and young Henrietta and her husband are not so very far away. She and Bess were very close, I think?"

"Indeed, ma'am," he agreed. "All you say is true, although the difference between here and Westwood, is perhaps five miles or,—"

"Five miles on a wet night is a long way," said Eunice.

"Bess never travels after dark, but I take your point."

"Perhaps with his sister resident in one of the best houses, Sir Henry might visit more often, too," she continued relentlessly.

"Certainly he would be able to stay over with us at the Petty Sessions," Justin agreed thoughtfully, "rather than taking rooms at The Greyhound, which has gone sadly downhill since Mistress Capel departed."

"Much better all round that he be lodged in a private house," she agreed, pleased to see he was considering the matter. "And of course, your dear Bess will be so much better than I at getting young Rebecca settled."

"Rebecca settled?" he repeated blankly.

"I mean to see her well-married," she replied in a determined manner. "I shall give her a good dowry, for she is an excellent young woman, well-educated, gentle and kind. We just don't move in the right circles for her to meet the sort of young man she needs, but Bess does."

Justin hesitated, "Bess moves in those circles, but I don't as a rule—and not easily."

"More fool you then," she replied roundly. "That must be an inheritance from your maternal grandfather, a stiff-necked old fool that he was! I have seen you in company with Bess and her family. They make no difference in their manner. It is you who does that. You are stiff, sullen and give the impression you are bored."

"It is not easy with Margery Kingscott looking down her nose at me!" he retorted.

"Mistress Kingscott looks down her nose at everybody, including—so I have heard—Sir Henry himself!"

"Not so much since he became Sir Henry," he observed wryly. "Whilst I'd not go so far as to say she approves of Hal, she views him with a little more tolerance these days, probably because he eschews my company."

"Sir Henry doesn't eschew any company in which he finds a welcome. The gossip is that he's with the French apothecary, and he has spent more than an hour in his company already—bets are being laid if he'll return to take dinner with him and his wife! I have no doubt if Sir Henry found you less embittered, he'd spend more time in his sister's house."

He flung his hand out to indicate the chamber and demanded, "Is that what you are seeking? Am I to be obliged to invite Sir Henry Westwood into my fine new home, in pursuit of a match for your protégée?"

"I make no demands, you young fool—save that you wake up and see your own best interests," she replied sharply. "I do this because I want to. I would be obliged if Bess could introduce Rebecca to some better company than she will find in my small circle, and honesty obliges me to admit my aim is to secure her an invitation to the dinner party being given by the Armstrongs at Elmley Park on the day after tomorrow. But it is no part of an exchange, any more than my advice to you to give up on this enmity you have for your brother-in-law, who, by the way, just happens to fast becoming one of the most influential men in this part of the world! Come, you say you favour plain speech," she added as he looked affronted. "What has your vendetta against Hal Westwood profited you?"

"Nothing," he replied tersely.

"And on the loss side?" she countered.

There was a sullen silence. "Much," he admitted.

"Much misery, too," she agreed with sympathy. "Come, Justin, you weren't meant for such gloom. Take heart and put your life into new order!"

He smiled at her briefly and agreed, "Your generosity will certainly put my affairs in better order."

"Well, I am not that generous," she said with a half laugh. "Recollect I shall be living at bed and board with you. In fact, you must consult your wife before we agree to anything."

He smiled more fully. "When has Bess, bless her, ever raised an objection to anything I do—other that quarrelling with her brother?"

"Then it is probably high time you obliged her in ceasing to do so," she suggested.

"I don't know even where to begin," he sighed.

"You might make a start by offering him your congratulations on his forthcoming marriage when you next meet," she encouraged sapiently.

He laughed, "By Heavens, the shock would kill him!"

"That's as maybe, but I am serious in this, Justin," she said firmly. "It has long been in my mind to say it. So whilst I'm gilding the marchpane, for everyone's good, you must end this bitterness between yourself and your brother-in-law—after all he *is* wedding *your* ward. This is the very time to do it."

He turned to stare at her, taken aback by her forthright manner, and curiously touched by her concern. As a motherless child, the only gentleness he had known as a boy came from his sister and this acid-tongued lady. He knew she had his best interests at heart.

"You echo the words of my dear Bess, ma'am," he admitted reluctantly. "Only last evening she gave me the gentlest of lectures on my stubborn nature, which provokes me to cut off my nose to spite my face."

"Your choice of wife was one of your more sensible decisions, Justin, although it cost you dear. Yet Bess tells me Sir Henry has tried on more than one occasion to get you to take your father's money."

"Blood money! Recollect I had the administering of father's Last Will and Testament, so I know he left every penny of his fortune to his second wife—that trollop and her bastard, an unborn child! Then after she was murdered his fortune reverted to my sister Libby, his own 'sweet and dutiful daughter'."

"Libby *was* a sweet and dutiful daughter and a sweet, dutiful, loving sister, too," said his cousin tartly.

"Indeed, and an adoring wife," he retorted. "Much good it did her. She died miserable, alone and weeping for her husband."

"She didn't die alone. She was attended by her loving family. I was there, Justin. She was surrounded by the love of her family!"

"But not her husband!" he cried angrily. "She would forgo all of us for one glimpse of her husband, and where was he?"

She sighed heavily. "When you get to my age, Justin you will soon come to realise that raking over the past serves little purpose. Do you think one so proud as Sir Henry doesn't rue each day that he wasn't by his wife's side as she lay dying? You know him well. Hasn't most of his life been spent in trying to establish some order from the chaos of conflict after the war? To prevent the lawlessness of a few, so the many may live their lives in peace and prosperity. Why do you persist in blinding yourself to his virtues because of one error? Did Libby ever censure his conduct? Did she level one word of blame or accuse him of abandoning her?"

"You know she did not!" he cried angrily. "You know she persisted 'til the very end in saying that he would not have left her alone for so long if he hadn't thought it necessary. She said it wasn't his fault that he didn't come—it was hers that she had neglected to send for him in time. Even as the breath left her body she whispered, 'Tell Hal it is all my blame'."

Cousin Eunice sighed. "Yes, I was as near to her as you were, Justin and I caught her last words, 'Tell Hal I will always love him, and it is my blame that he didn't know.'"

"She was a sainted woman, and now he is about to marry that—that—"

"Your ward, Sophie, who is a good and generous young woman. Remember how tirelessly she worked to save your life when you were taken up for the murder of that woman whom you had made your mistress?"

"She only did that to make it impossible for me to accuse her," he snapped.

Mistress Latham glanced to him sharply. "Do you truly believe that, Justin? Don't you think it is time you laid aside this play-acting pretence that you can see no good in either her, or your brother-in-law? Can you not see how you are beginning to believe your own half-truths, and lose your own sense of justice in a mindless resentment of your brother-in-law? I used to so admire your integrity. I would be sorry to see it a casualty of your grief."

He returned her look, taken aback by the truth, suddenly very ashamed of his words. "No, I do not believe her to be a devious woman, but don't you see, they are both the same, they cover everything in a cloak of goodness yet still pursue their own selfish course."

"Which one of us doesn't do that?" she asked with a sigh. "You accuse them of nothing but being human beings with faults. I cannot find either guilty and neither can you—and that is what rankles so."

He turned from her to hide his disquiet, for her words echoed not only his wife's, but his own conscience. "There is some truth in your words," he admitted, "but it is so very difficult to forget the past."

"No, it is impossible to forget the past," she replied roundly, "but it is just that—the past. One must make a conscious effort to move forward into the future and not nurse a sense of grievance as an excuse for one's conduct."

Justin drew in his breath, recollecting that his cousin was every bit as formidable as Hal's Aunt Margery in her own way, and the only answer was tacit submission. "Well, ma'am, you are giving me the chance to do so, and I give you my word I'll do my best not to let you down in the future."

Mistress Latham nodded, getting to her feet, well pleased with her progress. "I'll leave you and Bess to remove yourselves into this house in your own good time, and then I shall join you. If Bess needs any help, send word to me and I'll send Rebecca to assist her."

"I can't begin to thank you for your generosity, Cousin Eunice," he said quickly, seeing the interview was at and end. He took her hand, helping her into an upright position and bestowed a kiss on her faded cheek. "Bess will be amazed, indeed I am myself. Thank you, ma'am, not only for this magnificent gift, but in that you still have a care for me."

"Blood is blood," she replied, "but don't forget I expect your help with Rebecca. After all, if you have been Sophie Redcroft's guardian, assisting me with my charge should be simplicity itself."

He smiled ruefully. "Save my dearest Bess, I find females difficult to understand, but I will ask Mary Armstrong for an invitation for Mistress Howell. "

❖

Chapter Five

Cordelia Blackwell hesitated in the doorway of a handsome dining parlour, and smiled nervously at her host, who was sitting at the table, with a dish of gruel before him and a sheaf of papers spread around it.

"Good morning, Master Capel," she said uncertainly, "I do hope I don't disturb you. It is so very kind of you to give us lodging here."

Jonas Capel looked up at her from the scrutiny of his own crabbed handwriting, his face set in lines so grim she was reminded of the stone carvings of saints. " 'Tis none of my affair, Mistress Blackwell," he replied coldly. "My wife arranges everything in her house, or rather, I should say, in Mistress Redcroft's house."

"Oh, indeed! Pray, don't let me disturb your work" replied Cordelia, wishing she had waited for her husband Adam to join her at the table.

"As if you could disturb him!" Mistress Capel cried, entering the chamber flanked by her serving boy and a sour-faced maid. "Jonas Capel, get those grimy ledgers from my table this minute! Good Heavens, what will Mistress Blackwell be thinking—that she is to break her fast with uncouth heathens?"

"No doubt she views us all as heathens! Coming, as she does, from foreign parts!" he snapped, snatching his papers into a bundle, and scraping his chair back across the polished floor, as the servants began laying the board with breakfast.

"I do beg pardon for my husband's manners, Mistress Blackwell," cried Mistress Capel, her cheeks reddening in anger and shame, as he stomped from the chamber, muttering under his breath.

"Mistress Capel, pray do not apologise," said Cordelia quickly. "I am only too aware of how we trespass on your generosity. Perhaps it might reassure Master Capel if he knew I have been taking instruction from our Rector at home, and I have been received into the Church of England. In truth, I am neither Catholic nor French," she smiled as Mistress Capel grew redder and more flustered. "Even after so short a time in England, I can see how strong feelings can still be."

Mistress Capel's mortification was complete. "Oh, Mistress Cordelia! I don't know how to apologise," she cried. "I am so ashamed that my dear Adam's wife should be so insulted at my table! I do not seek to excuse him, ma'am—indeed, I don't, but he was for Parliament in the last war, you see, and to have everything they fought for upturned as it has been when the old order was restored. It has been very difficult for him and given him such a hatred for foreigners and such."

Sophie entered the chamber adding, "Hatred of anything and everything! My dear, ma'am, pray, don't distress yourself, but wasn't he ever a mean-spirited, cross-grained fellow? My own father was for Parliament, too, but I do not recollect him ever being such a tiresome, intolerant man. I suppose he was more other-worldly than anything. I know father used to infuriate my dear Uncle Edmund with his ideas that the good Lord would provide for his faithful souls! I recall Uncle Edmund sitting at this very table, and crying out in anger to him, that the Lord hadn't seen fit to put shoes on my poor bleeding and blistered feet, nor stop my mother from dying in a ditch from starvation, so he presumed the Lord expected him to do so instead." She smiled sadly at the recollection of those departed. "Now, that was a dear, sweet man, Cordelia. I only realise how much I miss Uncle Edmund now that I'm in his house again."

"Aye, we gave him little peace in his last days, didn't we?" Adam remarked as he entered the chamber. "Poor Master Edmund Benton—he would have been so pleased to see me married to Cordelia, and you, Sophie, about to marry Sir Henry."

Sophie smiled as she gave Mistress Capel a quick hug. "I pray you, ma'am, dry your tears. This is a time of rejoicing. Adam shall seek out Master Capel and explain—"

Adam interrupted, "I shall seek out Master Capel and tell him *plainly to his face*, that if I and my wife choose to accept my step-mother's invitation to stay with her for a few days I don't expect either of them to be in tears for the duration of the visit—or he'll answer to *me* for it. That man is an intolerant coward and a bully, Susanna! How have you allowed this behaviour? You never let my father have his head that way."

Mistress Capel gave a snort of laughter which ended her tears. "Your father, Adam, was a darling, and far too sharp for the pair of us! He never did a thing he didn't want to, yet you and I both made excuses for him as he drank himself to death."

Adam sighed bleakly. "Aye, some wounds, ma'am, go too deep to ever be healed."

"I didn't know your father was wounded, Adam," said Cordelia as they finally sat down to eat, served by the boy.

"Aye, he took a wound to his heart," he replied accepting a mug of ale, as the boy loaded his plate with beef. "It cut deep, and although none could have tried harder than Susanna to heal it, it was broken and could never be made whole again."

Sophie said with admiration, "It is amazing how much more pragmatic you've become, Adam. Only two years ago you were very much like your father—bewailing your lost heritage, cross with Uncle Edmund for refusing to allow us to marry, furious with Guy Armstrong for buying your estate. Now here you are a married man with a beautiful bride, a baby son, your own property, which you are constantly improving—a gentleman of means, no longer tied to an inn."

"We all have much to be thankful for," agreed Adam. "Although I do wish your lot were better, Susanna. It can't be easy for you living with Jonas Capel."

"Oh, we jog along," replied Mistress Capel, tight-lipped. "He's just not an hospitable man, I'm afraid. He sees a guest and a deficit in the same light."

In the pleasant company of her guests, Mistress Capel found some relief from her woes, and was soon on the way to forgetting the unpleasantness in plans for the day. Her guests talked of the supper and dancing to be held that evening at Elmley Park, and Adam tried to persuade Sophie to remain with them there for the night.

"No, Adam, I shall return here. Mary has enough guests already, and Hal has to be in Chawcester tomorrow. I'll ride back with him tonight, and see my dressmaker Sally Rose in the morning. We have some business to attend to together, and the final fitting for my wedding gown."

"It is so then, you and she are partners in business," observed Mistress Capel.

"Not exactly, but I try to help her as much as possible. She and her children suffered so when her husband, Wat, died."

"I hear that eldest lad of hers is a handful. He'll need putting to something before he brings her to grief."

"Yes, Willy Rose is a handful," replied Sophie thoughtfully. "I was wondering about sending him to school, for he is a bright lad, but he is a little young yet."

"I pity the schoolmaster that has the teaching of him," said Mistress Capel. "Better to apprentice him—Jonas is ever looking for a bright lad to run errands."

Sophie grimaced. "I don't see them dealing together, anymore than I see young Willy Rose as a clerk. He seems to have an abundant capacity for mischief, and very little else."

"As you say, he is young yet, but such young men may be often best served in the Army," said Adam.

Sophie laughed. "He is definitely too young for that and I fear for the realm should he attain any high position—and his own health, for his father Wat Rose the best baker in Chawcester, was still a drunk, who met a bad end."

"What does Sir Henry think?"

"I try not to trouble Hal with my problems, not when I can contain them," replied Sophie.

"He needs a firm hand, a father figure," said Adam. "If he continues to give Sally trouble, tell her I'll take him back to Manor Farm with me. I need a likely young lad, and I'll see he keeps out of mischief."

Sophie agreed, "So you would. That is a very good solution Adam, thank you. The farm will give him a chance to work off his high spirits in fresh air—he'd never dare disobey you. Then when he is a little older we can consider where best to place him. Will you be happy with that Cordelia?"

"If Adam is happy, then so am I," she replied. "I never forget how Sir Henry took me in. I would still be saying my prayers in a French nunnery, but for his generosity. I have much to be thankful for, and am happy to help another at any time."

Breakfast continued with an air of happy accord, then the women dispersed to their tasks, quickly becoming involved in admiring and overseeing the ablutions of Adam's baby son.

Although Adam had put his anger aside, it was not forgotten so he sought out the lawyer Capel in his office, a small chamber with a separate entrance that opened directly to the street. Jonas Capel looked up irritably as Adam entered, hastily shutting the ledger he was perusing, and crossing his hands over it.

"Yes? Can it be that you wish to consult me? I thought you hangers-on of Sir Henry Westwood used Justin Danvers as a matter of form?" he snapped with barely-concealed hostility.

Adam was determined not to be provoked and struggled with his temper. "Yes, I dealt with Sir Henry's brother-in-law in the matter of Cordelia's property. Though I can't say I cared for his manner, any more than I do yours. Is incivility part of the training in becoming a man-of-law?"

The attorney snorted and shrugged his shoulders. "Don't let me keep you. If you need a lawyer to flatter your vanity, then be off to London. They specialise on flummery there," he retorted.

Adam fixed him with a hard stare. "I have come neither to consult you, nor to be insulted by you, but to tell you plainly to your face, that if you continue to make either my wife or my step-mother unhappy you shall answer to me for your conduct. I knew you for a bully when I was a child running about the alleys of Chawcester, but you shall not continue to bully or berate me, or mine, any longer. This is not your house, merely your lodging, and you will keep a civil tongue in your head—or I'll make sure you are unable to speak for sometime."

"Ha, you threaten me with violence!" he cried. "In my own home, you seek me out and threaten my life!"

"I wouldn't lower myself to threaten your skinny little

neck," replied Adam, with impatient contempt. "I'd no more kill you than I'd crush a fly. You are not worth the effort. I merely mean to teach you some much-needed manners!"

"Ho, Adam Blackwell, the gentleman, is it?" he sneered. "Model yourself on Sir Henry Westwood, do you? Yet another of the raff-and-scaff, the dregs of Royalist rag-a-muffins come back to lord it over us common folk! I remember you when you served ale in the tap of The Greyhound—not so high and mighty then!"

"Anymore than a snivelling little tinpot lawyer's clerk, who's managed to pull himself from the gutter by marrying a good lady," Adam retorted. "That's the trouble with small towns. Everyone knows you, and your secrets! I have nothing to be ashamed of. My father lost everything fighting for his King, and then drank himself into an early grave. I inherited his debts, and had no choice but to work with his widow Susanna to pay them off. Good fortune has shown me the way to a better life for me and mine, and I am glad of it, but I have never pretended to be what I am not. As an innkeeper I grew used to determining the manner of men. Don't consider me a fool now I no longer sell ale. You were always a mean, snivelling, pinchpenny I knew even as a child, set on making as much profit from others' misfortunes as you could. Nothing has changed."

"And I knew you for a bitter fool, with his heart set on a wench determined to claw herself to better things. She cared nothing for you! Does your foreign wife know she is but second best? Does your wonderful Sir Henry know his bride-to-be is damaged goods?"

"Take care you don't swallow your own spittle and die of poison!" Adam snapped. "For your information, my wife is probably more English than you are, and I'd have a care before maligning your betters! Sir Henry can afford a better lawyer than a country attorney! He is as well aware of what constitutes slander as you are, and will know how to deal with it on his bride's behalf!"

Mistress Capel hastened into the chamber. "Adam, Adam, what is going on? Please stop! You can be heard half way down the street!"

"Your pardon, Susanna, I was merely instructing your husband in manners befitting a gentleman," Adam replied calmly.

"Manners of a creeping lickspittle!" sneered Capel.

"Jonas Capel, you hold your tongue!" Mistress Capel cried angrily, seeing the wanton provocation. "I'll not have your foul moods put us all to the blush! Take yourself off to the ale-house and conduct what business you have there. I will not have you contaminate the very air of my home!"

" 'Tis my home! You wed me at church door, woman. Everything is mine now!" he snapped.

"This house is mine," interrupted Sophie, called hence by the furore. "Mistress Capel lives here at my behest. You pay no rent on it, Jonas Capel. It is no concern of yours, but a private arrangement between Susanna and me."

Capel thrust back his chair, and snatched up his papers. "Aye, you three hang together, don't you? You take care you don't hang on the gallows that way! This isn't the end of the matter, Susanna! I am your husband. You'll do as I say, or it will be the worse for you! Get out of my way, you overgrown oaf. I need some air."

"You take care someone doesn't help you to it by slitting your throat!" snapped Adam as Jonas Capel shoved his way out of the chamber. "By Heaven, Susanna, I knew the fellow was a disagreeable bully, but do you have to put up with this sort of thing often?"

Mistress Capel, who had sunk into a chair, shook her head. "He is much put out by me having you all here, of course, but he is becoming increasingly bad tempered, so that clients are going elsewhere, and I begin to go in fear of irking him."

"Pray, don't fret, dearest Mistress Capel," soothed Sophie, crouching beside her to cradle her in her arms.

Adam viewed her tears with dismay. "But Susanna, you never gave way to my father like this, even when he was drunk! Why, you kept us both in line and never allowed any leeway!"

Mistress Capel smiled up at him through her tears, and hugged Sophie hard. "When was the need? Your father was the sweetest of men sober, and your faults were that of untried youth. Yes, I was firm with you both, but you were fond of me, and I loved you both with all my heart."

"Truly, we both adored you, Susanna. My father used to say you were the best thing that ever happened to him. He loved you far more than my mother, I think, most certainly too well to abuse and threaten you. How can you tolerate Capel's demeaning manner?"

Mistress Capel wiped her eyes and squeezed Adam's hand. "I grow too old and weary to fight," she sighed. "His constant ill-humour wears away my courage."

"You shall come and make a visit with us, Mistress Capel," said Cordelia, who arrived with her baby to see what the noise was all about. "Once we've seen Sophie

safely wed to Sir Henry, we shall pack up your things
and carry you off to Old Manor Farm for a rest."

"What a splendid idea, Cordelia," said Adam, seeing
Mistress Capel's eyes light up. "Susanna will be company for you whilst I tend the harvest, although I don't
know that baby Basil will allow any of us much rest."

"Oh, the poor little sweeting only has the colic," said
Sophie, cooing at the child. "Mary's babe was exactly
the same. Aunt Kate will find you a new wet nurse,
Cordelia, and all will be well. It will be so nice to have
you nearby. Mistress Capel, we shall have such merry
times this summer."

"Perhaps Sir Henry may have different ideas, Sophie,"
said Adam with a smile. "He might want his bride to
himself."

"Hal loves good company. We shall have the rest of
our lives together," she replied. "Now, I have much to
do today, and there is supper tonight at Elmley Park, so
I'd best leave you in peace and be off to see Sally Rose."

❧

Chapter Six

Sometime later Sophie turned down one of the many alleys off the lower part of the High Street, and followed the twists and turns until she came to a yard not far from the river. The gate opened onto a barren strip of beaten earth and there, at a long trestle table, covered by a fine linen sheet, sat a dozen young girls sewing busily.

The eldest stood up, hastily unpinning the cloth from her gown, whilst the others viewed Sophie with undisguised curiosity, nudging and whispering. "Mistress Redcroft?" she asked quickly. "Sally is expecting you. Will you come this way, please?"

Rather surprised, Sophie followed the girl to the sagging porch of an old weaver's cottage, then up a twisted stair to a chamber under the eaves. The whole length of the room was brightened by windows called weaver's lights. Here, another group of slightly older girls sat at a cloth-covered trestle, stitching a brocade gown.

A small, thin woman, jumped up from the head of the table in delight, and hurried to embrace her. "Mistress Sophie! Oh, you are a sight for sore eyes!"

"Sally!" Sophie returned her hug with enthusiasm. "How goes my wedding gown?"

"All is in hand, Mistress Sophie," she replied briskly. "Judith, are the petticoats nearly ready?"

"But for the hem, Sally," she replied. "For you said it were better to pin it in place for the final fitting."

Sally nodded and pointed to the brocade laid out on the table. "I decided to fit it to you, Mistress Sophie, and then finish it off."

"It will be completed in time?" Sophie asked anxiously.

"Even if I have to follow you up the aisle of the Abbey church itself, to set in the last stitches," replied Sally, with a half-laugh.

Sophie viewed her pale face with concern. "You look weary, Sally. Have my wedding clothes been a great trouble to you?"

"No trouble at all, my dear Mistress Sophie, I enjoy making anything for you. It has been everyone else who has been troublesome. I vow every old biddy and spinster in Chawcester has suddenly decided, they'd like a new gown for the occasion of your wedding. We have been run off our feet from dawn to dusk, since the news of your wedding to Sir Henry was announced. I hope you are expecting a crammed church!"

Sophie looked aghast. "Oh dear, Sir Henry did say he hoped we'd almost pass unnoticed!"

Sally laughed. "Nothing passes unnoticed in Chawcester! If someone kills a mouse at breakfast, news of their infestation is on the streets before they are aired, and its ancestry settled by noon! There could hardly be more interest if the King himself were coming!"

"Yes, that is something to be thankful for," said Sophie, unwisely. "Hal was in London last week because of this war with the Dutch. The King sent for him and threatened to come dance at our wedding. Thank Heavens there is so much afoot in the country, *that* is not to be thought of!"

Sally looked astonished, and too late Sophie recollected Hal had warned her to be circumspect in discussing anything to do with London and the Court.

"Well," said Sally, "Your wedding has been very much to my advantage, Mistress Sophie. I have never earned so much money, and as you see, I've had to employ more girls temporarily. They come from the poor house each day. And I tell you to your head, I am glad to be able to give them a square meal, as well as their wages. Thank Heaven the weather has held, too, so we are no longer all squeezed in up here."

"Are they good seamstresses?" Sophie asked, glancing through one of the windows to the table of maids diligently stitching below.

Sally sighed and came to stand beside her. "Yes, for the most part none are bad from malice, poor things. They are barely fed, and two have the cough so bad they can do little but the roughest work. But that one—do you see the little dark-haired girl—and the one next to her with the nut-brown hair? They both have real talent. If only they had the chance, they could become very skilled."

"Could you take them on as apprentices if I paid their indentures?" Sophie asked thoughtfully.

Sally seemed rather taken aback. "Well, I suppose I might be able to. Judith has nearly finished her apprentice time now, but I—"

"I'll give you a sum for their upkeep, too," interrupted Sophie, as the dressmaker hesitated, calculating ways and means. Then as Sally raised her eyebrows in astonishment, Sophie smiled. "Call it my wedding gift to Chawcester. Uncle Edmund used to take a new apprentice every year, and so shall I, if you are agreeable, although, if you are going to add girls, you might need to take larger premises."

Sally stared at her, struggling to keep up with all the new ideas then said thoughtfully, "Well, there is another weaver's cottage to let next door, with a good storeroom attached. I suppose I could take the lease on it with some of the money I've made these past weeks."

"No, I'll take on any lease," said Sophie swiftly. "For my other guardian, Mr Danvers, has finally got back most of my dowry from my late husband's family. I'll talk to Hal about it. We should probably set up some sort of formal partnership, Sally, but he'll know what is best to be done for us both. In the meantime," She took some coins from her purse, and handed them to the stunned dressmaker. "Take these and send out to an inn for some hot food, so they can all be really well-fed. And I'll send Doctor Douay to physic those two girls with a cough." She frowned suddenly. "Hal must know something of the poorhouse and its Board of Governors. I will discuss it with him."

"The Board of Governors!" Sally snorted her contempt. "That is usually made of clerks from the Abbey and members of the town council. None of them would even know what hunger is. They are not like to worry themselves over a few dying girls!"

Sophie nodded her understanding but said no more on the subject. Then a girl arrived with her arms full of fabric so she hastened to step out of her gown, and try on first the silken petticoats, and then the brocade gown, which was caught up with pins until such time as Sally would sew on the jewelled clasps.

"See here is the lace, as you sent last week, Mistress Sophie," said Sally placing the foamy collar and sleeve edgings in position.

"Yes, it was sent by Mistress Hollingshead, who went to Nottingham for it personally," Sophie replied. "Wasn't that kind of her to take such trouble? It is such beautiful workmanship."

"I have never seen anything finer, like cobwebs gathered with the dew still on them. I have never touched better, and this brocade is wonderful," agreed Sally as her fingers lingered on it.

"Mistress Kingscott knew a warehouse in London, and Hal's brother-in-law collected it for me on his last visit. Everybody has been so very kind. Mary's husband even got me some Spanish leather for my shoes."

"Yes, my friend Guthrie, the carrier took it to a shoe-maker in Maucester, who dyed it perfectly to match the brocade. I had my doubts about it, but he said he could do it, and see how perfect they are. He's a clever man who makes a fine shoe. Guthrie is a comely looking fellow, too."

"Oh, ho, do I detect the beginnings of a romance?" Sophie laughed as she tried on the shoe, knowing how susceptible Sally was to a handsome man.

"I've no time for that sort of nonsense, not with the way you demand bride clothes. I cannot believe you had a whole new set made. You said you never wore any of the last set I made for your marriage last year, and it took me months to make them!"

"I am sorry, Sally, but I just couldn't bear to!" said Sophie, looking ashamed. "They were all so tainted for me. The smell that arose from my baggage made me want to vomit. Once I was safely away with Cordelia at Bickmarsh, I burned the gown that I wore for that wedding. We took it out into the stable yard and made a bonfire of it. Everything else you made I gave away."

Sally leaned forward to embrace her. "You are such a darling, Mistress Sophie. So good and kind, always trying to help those less fortunate than yourself! I pray marrying Sir Henry won't change you, or take you away from us! Where would I be but for your help? In the poorhouse like those desperate wenches, that's where!"

Sophie found herself blushing. "As if I'll not always need a new gown! And you know how lucky I've been, Sally, my father for all his book learning, was the next best thing to a pauper. In my early years I wandered about the countryside with him and my mother whilst he preached. We got more kicks than good food, and but for my mother's uncle, Master Benton, we would most probably have ended up in the poorhouse, too. I try never to forget how good he was to me. It is my eternal shame that I was so ungrateful and full of my own importance during those last dreadful days before his death. I thank God we were on good terms on that last ride home with him from Elmley Park. We laughed about Uncle Edmund setting up his own coach, when he complained about his bones aching. Little did we know that the poison was already working its way through his body."

"There, there, Mistress Sophie, don't weep no more! Only think how pleased he would be to see you wedding Sir Henry!"

Sophie summoned a watery smile. "Yes, he would be

pleased, wouldn't he? He once said someone like Sir Henry would be the very husband for me," she agreed. "Returning to Chawcester, and staying again in his house, has brought back a host of memories. Every way I turn I see his ghost."

"Now, now, less of this maudlin talk!" scolded Sally. "Plainly you are overtired! We've much to be thankful for, both of us! I always think Chawcester must be chock full of ghosts, what with the monks and the soldiers from that great battle, not to mention those men when Sir Henry fought over you!"

"That wasn't in Chawcester, thank Heaven! That vile, vile man and poor Hal so cruelly wounded!" She shuddered again, recollecting tempestuous times.

"And last year, little better," remarked Sally, busily pinning the hem into position. "That other wedding of yours sounds like a perfect bloodbath!"

Sophie shivered, then took a firm hold on her emotions. "Yes, it was, rather, but what are we at, recalling all these appalling events? 'Tis my wedding day Tuesday and I intend to be very happy, with no more looking back to the past! Now, that's my wedding dress organised," she added, as Sally got wearily to her feet. "Thank you so much, Sally, I do so love it. I know you have worked very hard on this, but what about the gown I am to wear this evening for supper at Elmley Park? Have you had time to finish that?"

"Oh, that was quite simple. Judith and I finished it days ago! I am also anxious, as green, you know, is very unlucky," said Sally, helping her from the voluminous folds of the wedding gown.

"No, only females who can't wear green say that!" Sophie laughed, as she stood in her petticoats. "Anyway, it is not really green. Sir Henry gave me a necklace of turquoise and pearls, and I bought the silk to match the necklace."

"I have to say, it has made up well, but it is so very plain. Did you not want lace at the neck or sleeves?" asked Sally as she unfolded the gown and held it up for inspection.

"No, just the simple frill as we discussed. Yes, that is quite perfect. I have brought the necklace with me, and you shall see. Ah, me, I am so glad to have my money again and some finery. All my clothes had gone almost threadbare, with my dowry being caught up in that legal squabble for so long. And I would not borrow from Sir Henry. Ah, but look to the time! The afternoon is fast slipping away, and I shall be in such disgrace if I am late, for we ride to Elmley Park with Cordelia and Adam."

"How is Mistress Blackwell? It was good of her to order a gown from me, but I am concerned that she will not like it, for I had no chance to fit it to her. Will she come tomorrow that I may adjust it?"

"Yes, for I have said I will sit with baby Basil, who is a little fractious at present. Adam says it is Cordelia's fault for choosing me as god-parent. He says he is screaming the devil out of him! Poor baby! He is a big lad, and plainly has Adam's constitution, so I think the nurse's milk isn't strong enough for him. I know my arms will ache when I hold him at the font for his baptism."

"Is Mistress Blackwell recovered from her lying-in?" Sally asked, as she tied the bodice into position. "Mistress Capel were saying as how she has lost all her French ways, and speaks English like us now—Oh, Mistress Sophie, that colour suits you so well! Oh, how lovely! And them there are turquoises are they? Well, I never did see such a pretty thing!"

Sophie blushed at the rush of praise and glanced to the rather pitted looking glass hanging on the wall, which showed enough of her reflection to satisfy her. "It shows the necklace off to perfection. I do hope Hal is pleased! Good Heavens, Sally, that cannot be the Abbey clock chiming out four o'clock, can it? Sir Henry will be waiting for me with the horses. I must go at once! Will you pack up my old gown for me to take now? If he sees me dressed ready for the supper, perhaps he'll not scold me for tardiness!"

"My dear Mistress Sophie, ride in that lovely silk you will not!" Sally cried, scandalised at the thought. "It will take but a moment for you to step out of it and put on your old gown! I'll fold this myself," she added as she began ruthlessly unbuttoning it. "I promise it shall not crease! I know you'll not want to arrive for a supper in your honour, and sit all the evening smelling of horses!"

It was some twenty minutes later, that Sophie hastened up the High Street, to find Hal standing with the horses and talking politely with Mistress Capel. She sighed, "I know, I'm late, you may scold me as you will."

"I am sufficiently dazzled," he replied wryly, "and Mistress Capel has had your bag brought down and strapped to your horse. We have only to add your latest acquisitions, and mount up to be on our way. With luck we can catch Adam and Cordelia before they get there. Is that hat suitable for riding?"

"No, but it is very becoming, don't you think?" she countered, as he grasped her slender waist to lift her into the saddle.

"What? You expect a compliment on your beauty when you keep me kicking my heels waiting on you?" he asked as she bent to pat her horse.

"If a woman don't get compliments a-plenty before the wedding, 'tis certain plain she'll get none after," remarked Mistress Capel dryly.

Hal grinned and kissed the face so invitingly close to his own. "Your beauty is, as you well know, incomparable. Now, thank Mistress Capel for her time and trouble, and let us be gone, or we'll have my sister furious because we are late."

"Dear Mistress Capel, did you collect my small jewel pouch too?" she whispered as she clasped her hand in thanks.

"Indeed I did, and a warm cloak for coming home tonight. I'll wait up for your return," she replied.

"There is no need," said Sophie quickly. "I know my way about the house well, so I shouldn't disturb you."

"Bless you, child, you'll not disturb me. I never sleep

well anyway," Mistress Capel returned. "Now, you be on your way, and enjoy yourselves."

"Madam, your servant," said Hal, as he swiftly mounted his own horse and bowed low over the saddle. "We'll take great care not to be late on our return, and I promise to escort Sophie into the house myself."

"Come, Hal, or we'll be late," called Sophie saucily, turning her mount about. "Perhaps, we might manage a gallop once we are clear of the town."

"Not in that hat you'll not," he retorted. "It will come off at the first puff of wind!"

Mistress Capel watched them with a sad smile on her face, as they rode the length of the street laughing and squabbling together. Their gentle, affectionate mockery was all so familiar to her. Adam's father had ever used that bantering, soothing tone to her, and though years might have passed since his death, she found she still missed him sorely.

As they took the right hand fork in the road and jogged through a hamlet on the way to Elmley Park Sophie said, "I am glad of this chance to talk to you about the poorhouse."

"The poorhouse? Good God, Sophie, just how expensive were your bride clothes?"

She laughed. "Less expensive, I swear, than most. I didn't think I would get my dowry back so quickly."

"True, so I deduce we are not destined for the poorhouse immediately then? Thank Heavens! So why the sudden interest?"

"You know that Sally Rose makes all my gowns."

"Yes," he agreed, frowning. "Do things go ill with her? I thought both Mary and Cordelia were going to her for their gowns now. Are her charges too low? Is that the problem?"

"No, she is successful, too successful right now, perhaps, for she has been worked off her feet and has had to get girls in from the poorhouse to help her."

"I see, yes, that is often done. Those at the poorhouse deemed fit for work are hired out at harvest or apple picking time."

"Fit for work—sturdy beggars—wasn't that the phrase? Only some of the girls—some as young as eight or ten—are far from sturdy. All are frail, and two in particular, have the cough. They are so ill-fed it is all they can do to lift a needle! I got Sally to send for Doctor Douay, and I gave her some more money to get decent food for them all," she replied hotly.

"Try as the governors do, there are always some cases of neglect," he sighed. "I believe the food is better if they go out working."

"You feed the poor souls while they are working, then return them to the semi-starvation which is their usual lot?"

He acknowledged the truth of this and frowned. "The governors are—"

"The governors are fat clerics from the Abbey and smug tradesmen—all with well-filled bellies!"

"Thank you, I was one of their number for a short time. Which of your descriptions applies to me?"

She smiled provocatively, "Well, you certainly are not fat—so far—so perhaps you are merely complacent!"

He raised his brows. "Thank you, I am relieved to know I am not fat. Tell me, have you ever been hungry—

"Not for many, many years," she replied more soberly. "Not since I was a small child, and my mother was dying. I suspect she fed me and neglected herself."

Hal nodded his understanding. "I, too, was frequently hungry when we were in exile in France. There was never enough money to feed us, unless my father had been lucky at dice. My sisters were younger and needed good food as they grew. It was that which made me sure they at least, had to go home to England. I spent weeks disputing the problem with my father, and eventually I persuaded him to let me take them back to Aunt Kate and Uncle Henry. He finally consented and I travelled to Westwood—as my father would surely be arrested if he had gone and he was too bitter to do so. It was a difficult time, I didn't know if I'd ever see my sisters again. The bit of money my father had reluctantly handed over meant we ate little on the journey. It rained all the way. We arrived, soaked to the skin, cold and hungry. My uncle, such an astute man, had a warm fire and hot food and Aunt Kate—well, I don't have to tell you about Aunt Kate, but she had warm clothes and even ribbons for the girls. My first sight of Westwood since I was a small child was as a haven of blessed peace. I never understood how other Royalists spoke of home with such longing until that day when I sat in the Hall at Westwood and listened to the silence. To just sit there and know we weren't going to have to cheat and lie and wrangle for our next meal. To have others treat you with respect rather than contempt. Believe me, Sophie, I never forget those times, and I try my hardest not to be complacent."

She leant across the saddle to squeeze his arm. "I am sorry, Hal, I never realised how bad it was for you. You've never mentioned it before."

"No," he agreed. "I don't talk of it. There is little purpose in doing so. Whilst we lived it, we endured it. But having seen what life could be like in a settled home, I was more than willing to give up exile and do anything to return."

"You are talking of your arranged marriage?"

"Most marriages are arranged, my love," he replied softly. "Few people are as fortunate as we are. Most are obliged to marry at another's command. We are both financially independent and marry as we wish."

She smiled and reminded him. "We weren't always independent of the wishes of others either."

"No, we have been very lucky."

"Yes," she nodded soberly. "I am conscious of that, and it makes me even more determined to assist Sally where I can, if possible. I know you can help me with this. I want to become a legal partner in her workshop, so that I can protect her—"

"Tell me," he interrupted hastily, as she began to outline some of the ideas in her head, "Are we to discuss Sally and the poorhouse all the way to Elmley Park?

I give you my word, I'll consider your ideas and have as many answers as you require as soon as I am able, but I had thought, as chance has given us the opportunity to ride alone, we might take time to discuss some more personal matters. It seems to me there has been precious little time or privacy since we announced our wedding."

"I know! It seemed when we were merely getting married at an unspecified time no one much bothered us. Once we decided upon a date, there have been endless things to do. But even so, we must ask ourselves, is it right for us to waste our time in heedless pleasure whilst other are sick and starving?"

Hal pulled both horses to a halt. "Merciful Heavens! I promise I'll send a gift of a good meal to all the inmates of the poorhouse to celebrate our wedding, and the same to Sally Rose on the condition that we leave looking into any other abuses at the poorhouse until after our wedding. And by that I do not mean the very next day! I'll assist you to the best of my ability with the question of a loose partnership between you and Sally Rose, but again, after a decent interval. In the meantime, am I expected to grovel in the dust to earn a kiss?"

"Oh, you mean that kind of personal matter! Oh,

Hal, as if you even need to ask!" she laughed softly.

"What? Am I to play the thief and steal kisses?" he asked, leaning across to do so.

"You cannot steal that which is freely given," she replied accepting his kiss. "Love isn't rationed out. It is constant, enduring."

"Enough of your words, pretty though they are," he countered, and they paused embracing in the evening light until the rumble of a cart gave warning of company, and sent them on their way, still laughing, to Elmley Park.

Chapter Seven

Hal stood in the dining parlour of Elmley Park, smiling as he viewed those assembled. His eyes lit on Sophie, who looked magnificent. He approved not only of her taste in choosing a gown so deceptively simple, but also the jeweller who had persuaded him to buy the turquoises and then set them so artfully.

Then he observed his brother-in-law, Justin over by the table and moved to join him, asking pleasantly, "Who is that young woman talking with Bess and Sophie? Didn't I see you and Bess arrive with her earlier?"

Justin, who had paused to refill his goblet with wine, glanced across the crowded parlour to where his wife was introducing a slender young woman with reddish gold hair. He replied coldly, "A relative of my Cousin Eunice. Her father died last year and her mother has recently remarried a much younger husband, who, gossip has it, finds the daughter more attractive than the mother, so now Rebecca is no longer welcome in her own home. She has come to live with Cousin Eunice, who is enlisting the help of Bess in the search for a husband for her."

"Not too arduous a task, one feels," remarked Hal, as all three women laughed together. "She has a good air, and smile. Has she any money?"

"Other than a modest dowry provided by Cousin Eunice, none whatsoever. So she can hold little interest for you!" he snapped.

Hal glanced to his bitter face. "Other than the usual interest taken in a stranger in our midst, I have no interest. Recollect, this is a celebration to mark my forthcoming marriage."

Justin half turned away. "You forget, I am aware of your last marriage. I know how fickle your affec—" He stopped himself and visibly took a hold of his anger. "I beg pardon, as you say, this is a celebration, and I have yet to wish you joy of your new bride."

This was said with rigid formality, and a low bow as he moved away, leaving Hal to stare after him with a mixture of bemusement and indignation, as his brother Ned came to join him.

"Justin doesn't improve, does he?" Ned remarked

with a grimace, his face looking strained and anxious, and suddenly that of a man, no longer a boy.

Hal forced his face to relax into a smile as he turned to his brother. "He was attempting to be unusually polite, although it seems to have cost him dear," he replied lightly. "Tell me, how is Cecily faring? I do hope this wedding won't be too difficult for her."

"She is well enough, although I am heartily glad she'll be with Mary and Aunt Kate for a while," he replied, with all the anxiety of an expectant father. "She barely eats enough to keep a mouse alive. I thought women were supposed to eat for two at such a time."

"Does she feel ill?" Hal asked, viewing his sister-in-law's pale face with concern.

"She says not, but the merest thing affects her. The dogs brought in a dead baby rabbit last week, and she wept about it the entire day."

"She will be better for being amongst the other women," soothed Hal. "You are right, it will be good for her to be with Aunt Kate, who will know at once if anything is amiss—and Mary too, has a brood of babies. She'll know how to keep Cecily cheerful."

"But Mary never has any trouble. Why, she dined with us the evening before her last, and then rode home with Guy, who sent word the following morning to say she was delivered of a baby girl before breakfast."

Hal laughed. "They certainly are blessed with a healthy family. Ah, we go into supper at last. Thank Heavens! I am ravenous after the ride here."

The meal passed much as those at Elmley Park were wont to, for Guy and Mary were an hospitable couple and Mary, given a free hand, ordered her domestic affairs well. The food was delicious, and the wine, thanks to Guy's connections, excellent.

Indeed, the entire company was very much in a holiday mood, and enjoyed gently teasing the prospective bride and groom. Most of those attending were either family or friends arriving to celebrate the forthcoming wedding, so everyone was known to each other and as a consequence there was much laughter. Hal, glancing about the table at one point, could scarce believe the change in his circumstances since his arrival in England as a penniless exile only a few short years ago.

Towards the end of the meal Guy, who was sitting next to a late arrival, called down the table, "Hal, before the dancing begins, allow me to introduce you to my neighbour, Mr Julius Langley, recently returned to this part of the world. He is eager to meet you."

Hal bowed elegantly with a faint frown, as the name, if not the face stirred a recollection. He cast a quick, appraising glance in their direction, then moved his seat to be nearer to them.

"So, at last I get to meet Hal Westwood," laughed the man merrily, as Hal looked puzzled, for try as he may he could not place the face. "I spent several months with your father back in—well it must have been in the late '50s—and he spoke of you constantly." Julius turned to include Guy in the conversation. "Yes, the name was so constantly in my ears that if it hadn't been for the fact that your father had once saved my life in battle, I might have been moved to choke him. It was 'my son Hal is the most handsome,' 'my boy Hal is the tallest,' 'my lad Hal speaks French like a native,' 'my son Hal has the very' —"

"I beg your pardon for him," interrupted Hal, as others seated nearby began to smile. "How very tiresome it must have been! My father was ever convinced that anything of his must naturally be of the very best."

"A device to remain cheerful in difficult times, and, by God, those where grim days," agreed the man pleasantly, as everybody else laughed at Hal's wit.

Hal nodded, "I recollect something of them myself."

"We were all casting about, looking for a future that didn't involve abject poverty or unpleasant death," said Julius Langley in a reminiscent vein. "Richard Cromwell, had succeeded his father, Oliver, and it looked as if none of us would never get back home to England. Temporary exile, whilst we waited for old Noll Cromwell to die, had been a possibility, but if it was to be longer well, something had to be done."

"What was your decision?" Guy asked, knowing what actions Francis Westwood had deemed necessary, and the resulting distress and horror it had involved for his wife Mary, who still occasionally suffered nightmares.

"I took ship for the New World, along with some companions. I lived there for some years as a settler, beating an existence from the soil," he grimaced. "I must confess it was not my idea of living. It was damned hard toil, day after day—and skirmishes with the natives on a regular basis, the only form of diversion! And what was worse, the same old problems which had led to the war, imported to a new land."

"So you came home?" concluded Hal.

"I came home," he agreed. "If I must work the land like a peasant, better to do it amongst my own people. A cousin had died and left me a small property in Herefordshire, and of course I still have the ruin that was my home across the river."

"It fared ill?" Hal asked knowing the answer.

Julius agreed solemnly. "It fared ill. It was given into the hands of a fellow who had never turned the soil, it seemed. A petty clerk, who squeezed the last bit of worth out of it, sold off all the beasts and left it a ruin."

"My father found his estate in a similar state," said Hal, in some sympathy. "My uncle had managed to buy it back from the Court of Sequestrations, thinking it was for the best to at least retain it by paying the fines, as he was compelled to do. My father's continued fighting meant that he could never find the money to repair or restore it. It was a great bone of contention between them, and never truly resolved."

"It wasn't until Hal married his heiress that restoration could be thought of," said Guy.

"Oh, your bride is an heiress, as well as a beauty. That's a rare combination," said Julius Langley, glancing further down the table, to where Sophie was laughing with Cecily and Hetta.

"Not this bride, although Sophie is an heiress, too."

"How do you come to be such a lucky dog, Hal?" Guy asked, as the thought occurred to him.

"My first wife died some eighteen months ago," Hal explained to the newcomer. "She was the sister to Justin Danvers, who I saw you talking with earlier. I don't know how lucky that makes me, Guy, but Mistress Redcroft, my betrothed, is certainly an heiress, yes."

"Well, if they are that thick on the ground round here, perhaps I'll try my luck," said Julius Langley affably. "I, like you, Sir Henry, was widowed—oh, some two years ago now. I lost both my wife and children in a bout of fever."

As both men expressed their condolences, Julius Langley smothered a sigh, and nodded. "Aye, I talk lightly of it, but it was a crushing blow at the time. That is why I came back home. Working in a strange land is difficult enough, but once there is no longer a reason, why try?"

"Guy, come lead the way, it is time to be dancing," said Mary, coming to join them, as the servants opened the doors into the Long Gallery, where a group of fiddlers were already tuning their instruments. "Come, Hal, this is a celebration of your wedding. You must lead off the dance with Sophie!"

"I shall do so with alacrity," he replied as other musicians started playing. "Mr Langley, your servant, it was good to exchange reminiscences of my father."

"Sir Henry," he replied bowing, and turning quickly to his host and hostess, he added, "Mistress Armstrong, direct me to the nearest heiress if you will. I mean to mend my fortune, and I am convinced it must be you who is behind the success of your brother in marrying one heiress after another!"

"Indeed no, Mr Langley," replied Mary in surprise, "my uncle, Henry Westwood, arranged Hal's first marriage, and Sophie herself arrange this second one."

"In the face of your Aunt Margery's opposition," added Guy. "When Sophie makes up her mind to something, we lesser mortals are but chaff swept along in her path."

"Is it so?" his companion asked, glancing along the gallery to where Hal and Sophie stood, arm in arm, feet tapping, waiting for the other dancers.

"Sophie is a lovely young woman, Guy, and both she and Hal are deeply in love—anyone can see that," said Mary sharply, as others came to form a dance and the musicians struck up.

"Alas, so there are no more heiresses. It would seem I have arrived too late," Julius Langley laughed.

"Well, there's the young female your Aunt Margery has in hand, Mistress Phoebe Elgar, but you say she is intended for Jack Hollingshead. And there is that pretty lass, Rebecca Howell, who it seems, is like to inherit from Justin's Cousin Eunice," said Guy.

"There is no such likelihood, Guy," said Mary swiftly. "Eunice Latham told me she was settling a decent marriage portion on her. That is all. The bulk of her fortune will go to Justin when she dies, but Eunice is not an old woman. She may yet remarry herself."

"I don't think so. Eunice Latham has been a widow a good while now. She is not really the marrying type," replied Guy with a grin.

"Come, matters improve," laughed Julius Langley. "Suddenly there are three females to choose from, and to my mind there is no such thing as a woman who won't be married, just the absence of the right man for her. For myself, I favour an older lady, if she is still comely."

Mary smiled, taking the observation lightly as intended, "Alas, I cannot introduce you to Mistress Latham today, but I have no doubt she will be at the wedding. Mistress Elgar by now will surely be dancing with—oh, now that isn't right!" cried Mary in comic dismay. "She is supposed to be partnering Jack Hollingshead. Aunt Margery sent specific instructions!"

"Well, Jack has taken to the floor with Rebecca Howell," chuckled Guy. "He has no intentions of obeying instructions. Now the cat will be amongst the pigeons."

"Perhaps I might be permitted to ask you to partner me, ma'am. Then you might relate to me all the gossip, so I know who is who? That is, if your husband has no objection to my partnering the loveliest lady in the chamber," suggested the newcomer.

"Oh, Guy seldom dances these days," said Mary, looking gratified. "Although, Guy, you'd best go and ask Mistress Elgar to dance to make her feel better."

As Guy went off reluctantly to bow over the hand of the affronted Mistress Elgar, Mary—as light on her feet as ever in spite of her pregnancy—swung into the music with her guest.

"Your family seem well settled in these parts, ma'am," Julius remarked politely.

"Well, it is our home territory, so to speak. Hal and I were born not far from here at Rushley Manor, although neither of us actually recollect it, leaving as we did as small children, to live out our early years in exile."

"Ah, yes, the lot of so many of us," he agreed. "Did you all remain in exile?"

"Yes, for some years, then my father remarried, and

our new step-mother brought all of us back to England to her family home where Ned was born. Then when she died at Hetta's birth, Father came to take the rest of us away with him, leaving only Ned and the baby with their grandparents. Unfortunately, when their grandfather died, that estate was entailed to a cousin, so Ned and Hetta went to live with our Uncle Henry and Aunt Kate at Westwood, and eventually when father married again, we were all reunited, except for Hal, who remained in exile with Father."

He nodded his understanding of the difficulties suffered by families parted by conflict, thinking of his own exile. "I know it well, the going from here to there, always beholden to another for a place to lay one's head. Never having anywhere to call home, never truly fitting in, always the poor relation."

"Oh, I hated it so, but Aunt Kate and Uncle Henry were never like that. At Westwood we were all made to feel most welcome."

"Until Guy came along to whisk you off to his home," he said in admiration of the elegant surroundings.

She was silent for a few seconds, looking troubled. "No, I couldn't remain at Westwood as the others did. My father had arranged a marriage for me that took me into the county where you have a property. Guy is my second husband. For nearly four years, I was married to a man older than my father, who abused me for not producing the heir he desired. His death was the saviour of my sanity. It gave me the opportunity of a new, better life with Guy." She made visible effort to return to cheerfulness. "Tell me, are you settled in your new home, or do you hope to return here?"

"When I meet such charming company I am sorely tempted," he replied. "I came merely to look over my old home and calculate what it might take me to restore it. The farm I have in Herefordshire is comfortable, but doesn't draw me like my old one. Alas, it would appear I cannot hope to make much progress at present. It is sadly ruinous, but perhaps one day—hence the need for an heiress."

Mary smiled, for the latter was said with wry humour. "Then you should visit London, sir, for that is where most heiresses go, to Court to find a husband."

"Aye, as do the tricksters and fraudsters! Thank you, I'll try my luck here first. I am too old for the merry dance of London."

"Yet you dance so well, sir," said Mary, for her companion was older than her husband by some years.

He smiled down at her. "I confess it has always been a pleasant form of exercise for me, coupled as it is, with good company. Are you pleased by your brother's choice of bride, ma'am? You mentioned Mistress Redcroft arranged the marriage, yet surely she is of no great age and unmarried?"

"Sophie is—Sophie. My brother met her a few years ago, when he came to Chawcester to look into the curious death of her guardian's journeyman. Though Hal, was married, Sophie, in the manner of wilful young ladies, fell in love with his handsome face. Then when her guardian was killed a few days later, Hal and his brother-in-law found they had been named as her guardians. Sophie burst into our family life rather like a tempest, and there seemed no stopping her. As Guy said, 'she sweeps all along in her path.' Yet in spite of everything which has gone before—and it is too much to speak of here—we have all come to love her. Her kindness is well-known, although occasionally overwhelming."

"Certainly your brother appears more than content with his lot," he observed, as Hal suddenly laughed in reply to a remark by his partner.

Mary glanced across to them and sighed a little. "He is the happiest I have ever seen him and I pray with all my heart he remains so. He is a good brother, who has had great care for us all, better by far than what my father ever gave us. He deserves contentment."

"Amen to that for us all," Julius agreed. "Would you oblige me with an introduction to your prospective sister-in-law presently? She sounds a surprising young woman."

Mary assented a shade doubtfully, and made haste to change the subject, then as the dance came to a close, led him to meet her sister Jane.

Chapter Eight

Guy, meanwhile, was struggling to converse with his partner Mistress Elgar. "I see you have the advantage of me, ma'am, in that you are skilled in the art of dancing," he said, with a merry smile. "I am rather out of practise I fear, being an old, married man."

The handsome young woman smiled upon him graciously. "I have had the advantage of the finest dancing masters, sir. It is mostly a matter of practise, I find."

"Indeed," he agreed, narrowly missing her foot and finding to his dismay, that he was beginning to breathe rather heavily. "Exactly what I fear I lack."

She smiled with aloof dignity. "I have no doubt, sir, you are a very busy man. I understand you have a very fine estate here."

"Yes," he agreed, looking more cheerful at the thought. "It is beginning to look more as it should, but it has taken a lot of work and a vast amount of money to bring it about. I don't like to say anything before Adam Blackwell, but I think his father had been letting it go for years before the war ruined it."

"Adam Blackwell?" she enquired. "Oh, that rather large young man," she nodded as Guy pointed him out. "I think I met his wife earlier on."

"Cordelia, is a nice little woman. Quiet, but she has only recently left her bed from childbirth."

"I believe Mistress Kingscott told me of the circumstances surrounding her return to England," replied Mistress Elgar, shaking her head. "One can only feel for a small child abandoned in a convent in such circumstances. What an ordeal for her, and what a wonderful recovery she has made."

Guy looked surprised. "I think Cordelia was genuinely fond of the nuns. I imagine if as a child one grew up in such circumstances, one would know no difference. She says they treated her very well, and she still corresponds with them. Indeed, they sent some beautiful clothes for her baby, so my wife tells me."

The woman nodded and smiled remotely, so Guy was forced to search his head for another topic of conversation. "You are not from this locality, Mistress Elgar?"

"No, my parental estates are further north, near Nottingham."

"I've not been that far north since the war," he remarked. "My mother took me to Nottingham to be with my father when the late King raised his Standard in '42. That signified the beginning of the war— not that I understood, mind—I was still in short coats. But I remember her trembling in fear, and how I wept when the soldiers marched by, with the guns, the noise and confusion, and how my father laughed at us both. It was the last time we saw him in any great health. He was wounded at Edgehill, and never truly recovered, although he took to the field at Worcester, and I went along with him, to look after him, and so was able to bring him home to die."

The young woman looked disturbed, but made haste to say, "It was indeed a tragic time for our country, sir. So many lost their lives, and fortunes, too."

"Aye," Guy nodded grimly. "In many ways I was glad my father died, for we lost nearly everything during the reign of the Commonwealth. At one point I had but two farms left of my father's estate, neither of them producing sufficient to support a family. Then an uncle died, and left me his holding, which had a house, so matters improved a little and then I began to remake my fortune."

"You are to be congratulated, sir, on your fortitude," she replied.

"Fortitude doesn't come into it," said Guy bluntly, with a grin. "It was good, old-fashioned desperation."

Mistress Elgar curtsied as the music finished, and Guy bowed in heartfelt relief. "Come let me introduce you to a new partner more suited to your steps. Here is Jack Hollingsworth. He is from your part of the world. You'll have a lot in common. Jack, well met, allow me to introduce Mistress Elgar, as your partner for the next dance, and I can take Mistress Howell off to find a new partner."

Jack surrendered his partner's hand a shade reluctantly, and bowing dutifully led Mistress Elgar onto the floor—much to Mary's relief—whilst she hurried off to find partners for any who lacked them. She sent Hal to rescue Guy, whilst Sophie joined the next set and smiled amicably upon her new partner then asked politely, "You are a newcomer to Chawchester, sir?"

"No, I recollect it well, I find. I used to come to market here many years ago, when I was a child. It hasn't changed a great deal," said Julius Langley.

Sophie smiled, "No indeed, it never changes. It has an enduring quality. Am I to suppose you have been in exile, sir?"

"In the Low Countries and then more latterly in the Virginias. Whilst in France and the Low Countries I had some acquaintance with Francis Westwood, Sir Henry's father."

Sophie nodded. "Sir Francis, he died a few years back, in France. I never met him."

"I knew both him and his French wife, Jacqueline," continued Julius Langley. "We shared a dreadful lodging in Paris for a few months."

Sophie cast him a speculative look, and would have asked more about Hal's step-mother, but he forestalled her by asking, "Did I hear our hostess say you were lodging in Chawcester with a Mistress Capel?

"Yes, she is an acquaintance of mine from childhood, when she was known as Mistress Blackwood and owned The Greyhound Inn."

"Ah, I see, and her new husband—he was perhaps a friend of your former guardian?"

"Jonas Capel? No, he was never a friend of Uncle Edmund," said Sophie, puzzled by his questions. "I think he may have been forced to use him once on a legal matter, but he had low opinion of him. I recollect him saying Jonas Capel wasn't fit to lick the boots of my uncle's man-of-law in Chawcester."

"Indeed?" her partner remarked, as he led her faultlessly through a complicated dance.

"Uncle Edmund was convinced Capel hadn't the probity of Master Hornby, for they were contemporaries, you understand? To Uncle Edmund, Jonas Capel was not Chawcester born and bred, so he wasn't a reliable sort of a fellow."

Julius Langley smiled a little. "I see your former guardian was a man of decided judgements, but what do you think of Mr Capel? Does he administer your affairs?"

"No, he does not," replied Sophie, quickly. "I think it was to prevent that occurrence, that Mr Danvers and Sir Henry were chosen as my guardians. The control of my fortune was put into their joint hands. Mr Danvers is Sir Henry's brother-in-law and a very capable man-of-law. He has taken very great care of my affairs."

"Whilst Sir Henry took great care of you, it would seem," he remarked slyly.

"I have these past two years nominally been in his guardianship, and made my home in his house, but I came under the supervision of his wife, until she fell ill, and then his aunts," replied Sophie, her eyes searching his impassive face. "Forgive me, sir, but you ask a good many questions. To what end?"

He met her eyes and smiled ruefully. "Oh, pure interest," he replied evasively. "I was absent from my homeland for close on fifteen years. Everything is so very changed. I find it hard to understand."

Sophie nodded, but was still a little wary. "Sir Henry said he found it difficult, too, when he first returned. So much of what we learn we absorb as children. For those brought up in an alien land, England must be difficult to understand. Like you, Sir Henry hated exile, and has never been happier since he came home."

Her partner nodded, "There is no pain to equal it, save that of the loss of loved ones."

"And you have suffered both," she observed, seeing it in his face. "I am sorry, sir, for your losses."

He glanced to her, moved by her sincerity, and smiled a little. "Thank you for your kindness Mistress Redcroft, but I see I must look to the future. I cannot deny my heart is yet sore, for the death of my wife and children, but I must face facts. I need to remarry to recover my estates." He smiled, and his tone went from sombre, to lightly teasing. "I was told you were an heiress, and I thought to try my hand at cutting out Sir Henry, until I saw you dance together, and realised I would never stand a chance."

Sophie laughed, liking him the better for his audacity. "Yet you dance splendidly, sir, and will surely find a new partner very soon."

He joined her in a genuine laugh. "Reports do not lie, Mistress Redcroft, you are indeed a forthright young woman and a most charming companion. Sir Henry is to be congratulated."

"Well done, Guy," said Mary, coming to rest at his side, as he paused to drink a glass of wine after his exertions. "You managed to get Jack dancing with Phoebe Elgar. She is destined to be his bride."

"Not if I am any judge of the matter," replied Guy, bluntly. "He wasn't overeager to take her hand, and even now is more concerned with marking the progress of his former partner, Mistress Howell, than giving his ear to Mistress Elgar's improving discourse."

"Rebecca Howell? Oh, that will not do. She has only a marriage portion, you know," said Mary, looking anxious, as indeed Jack appeared to be giving only half an ear to his partner's words.

"His mother and your Aunt Margery can plot as they

wish. Jack Hollingshead is his own man," remarked Guy with a grin.

"Well, I don't know about that," said Mary. "Look how he was prepared to marry Cordelia, before he'd even met her, just to get back her father's estate."

"Yes, but he didn't marry Cordelia, did he? Thanks to Sophie!" Guy countered. "And since that date he has assisted Hal to settle Nick Revesby's and Bella Craven's affairs. By now he will have acquired a taste for high romance. Besides, Mistress Elgar is the image of your Aunt Margery forty years ago."

"Yes!" Mary sighed in dismay, as she acknowledged the truth of his observation. "There is that self-same un-approachable demeanour, isn't there? The same belief that in spite of all *you* say, *she* knows best."

"I suppose that could just mask a bashful manner," suggested Guy, with surprising insight. "But her aloof-ness will be enough to put most men off."

"Now that is unkind," said Mary indignantly. "She is a little haughty, I grant you, but— oh Jack, now that is naughty!" she exclaimed as the music came to a close, and Jack cleverly passed his partner Mistress Elgar onto Julius Langley then deftly retrieved Mistress Howell, bearing her off to obtain a drink of refreshing cordial.

"Yes," Mary sighed. "One can see Hal's influence all too plainly. What am I to tell Aunt Margery?"

"That was very neatly done!" Guy said in admiration. "I have to say Jack is a quick learner! As for your Aunt Margery, feign ignorance. I always do."

"Do you think this Julius Langley a man of good character?" Mary asked bluntly, as the he fell into easy conversation with his new partner.

"He is intent on restoring his fortune, one way or another—much as I was when I met you," he replied, watching the others' progress.

"Sweetheart!" she cried, laughing. "How could you be termed a fortune hunter? When you first met me I was married to Sir Edward, and fast loosing my grip on sanity. A fortune hunter would never have given me a second look, even if I had a penny of my own, which I did not."

"The first look was enough for me," he replied. "Once I'd seen your lovely face, I knew my fate. It was you and no other! Although, I did in the back of my mind, note that you had sisters."

She laughed, "Just in case Sir Edward proved to be an octogenarian?"

"No, I knew from his wild behaviour both on and

off the hunting field he'd never make old bones! If the drink didn't get him, hunting would," replied Guy, adding, "Only think of him dying as he did!" He shuddered, though it was a warm evening.

Mary nodded and smiled, "Thank Heavens that is all in the past! I would that Cecily carried this baby easier, but she and Ned look so happy tonight, don't they?"

"Indeed," he replied with a tender smile, as he glanced to his younger sister. "I asked how she was, and wished her joy, but I knew she already had it. She tells me our baby and theirs must be good friends, and that as Ned wants a son, you must produce another daughter, so they can be married later."

"Well, I wouldn't mind a companion for my sweet little Katie," agreed Mary, "but there can be no marriage between such close kin. Ned and I are half-brother and sister, and you and Cecily are full brother and sister. It would be very foolish for our children to marry."

"Aye, even though you and Ned had different dams, you both had the same sire. I'd not thought of that."

"Don't say anything to her about it, though," warned Mary. "At this stage of a pregnancy women get odd fancies. Ned tells me her spirits are unequal."

"Only in pregnancy they get odd fancies?" he asked.

Mary ignored this, speaking severely, "The dance will be over soon. I must have a few words with Cordelia, who is looking a little fatigued so pray, find a new partner for Mistress Elgar." She hurried off, leaving Guy to pair Mistress Elgar with Adam.

By then Hal was leading Mistress Howell to the floor. "May I congratulate you on your forthcoming marriage, Sir Henry, and wish you every happiness" she remarked as the music began.

"Thank you, Mistress Howell, I feel certain I will get exactly that—every happiness" he replied quickly.

"I understand Mistress Redcroft is your ward, sir, so then you'll have the felicity of knowing her character well. Those of us with less certain futures envy her the boon of knowing her future husband."

He smiled again and nodded as he exchanged greetings with other couples in the dance. "As a widower, I am in the position of experiencing that type of marriage. I met my first bride, Libby, a mere thirty-six hours before the wedding."

She nodded, "Tell me, sir, if you will, what were your first thoughts?"

Hal smiled, "I was a penniless, rather conceited youth and was making a marriage to a young woman, whose father wished to buy her a position in society. My first feeling was one of sheer, selfish relief, that she wasn't crooked or ill-favoured."

She nodded, "And your second?"

"That my poor bride was even more terrified than I was!" he replied with a smile. "Thereafter, I had no clear thoughts, only a desire to set her at ease, so that the forthcoming ordeal might be lessened for both of us."

"That was a generous impulse," she remarked. "I wonder how many other suitors share it?"

"You must understand more of the situation, Mistress Howell. This marriage was to bring me back from exile, and help restore the fortunes of my family by making me my uncle's heir. I felt that I owed dear Libby a vast debt of gratitude, and it was up to me to make her comfortable with the arrangement."

"And was she? Was she comfortable in your marriage?" she asked thoughtfully.

"Not always," he replied candidly. "I've already told you I was young and conceited. Mostly I did my best, and pray God, mostly I succeeded."

"You speak of comfort, of concern, of a desire to set her at her ease, all kind, generous thoughts—yet you make no mention of love," she said quietly.

"No," he replied softly. "I don't. Yet I tell you in truth, ma'am, I held my first wife in great affection and esteem."

She lifted her eyes to his, her expression hard to read. "Affection and esteem? Could a wife ask for more?"

He thought he caught an undertone of mockery in the question. "That I cannot answer, Mistress Howell. I was married for more than five years. My wife bore me several children, of which two survive, Harry and Francis. I tried to live my life as most honest men do, honouring my wife, my children, my home, my life. In that time from being a youth, with nothing, I inherited an estate from my uncle, with all the responsibilities thereof, the care of my sisters and brother, and eventually, a title and another baby brother from my late father. As I recall the matter—apart from the tragic deaths of our babies—we were mostly happy. I never heard my wife complain."

"I beg pardon, sir," she said hastily, suddenly aware she had transgressed. "I meant no disrespect to you, or your wife."

"But you are aware of the gossip," he said sharply. "You live in Chawcester, so you must be aware of the gossip."

She smiled uneasily, "It would appear the empty heads like to rattle."

"Then you'll be fully aware that I met Sophie before my wife died, and fell in love with her. You see, I make no denial, but I assure you neither Sophie or I murdered Libby," he said bluntly.

Relieved, she realised he very much favoured plain speech. "My Cousin Eunice assured me of that, too, Sir Henry. She was emphatic about it. She says she knows you and she knows Sophie, and that neither of you have a wicked or ungenerous bone in your bodies. Indeed, Libby was, in fact, a distant connection of mine and I heard she always thought you the most perfect man in the Kingdom."

Hal laughed. "If dear Libby had a fault, it was her inability to see any faults in me," he replied with a loving smile.

"I don't somehow think your future wife will be so blinded by love, sir," she replied, warming to him.

He gave a snort of abrupt laughter, "Sophie? Most decidedly not! She sees my faults with glaring clarity, and she has no doubt about telling me of them, yet still she loves me!" He smiled again as she swept past them in the dance.

"As you love her?" she asked.

"As I love her," he agreed.

"Then again, I wish you joy, sir," she said.

"And I wish you joy, too, Mistress Howell, when your time comes, as it will, I think, soon."

She returned his smile, but looked troubled. "I can only pray, sir, that I am blessed with equal felicity."

Their dance came to a convenient end and they parted amicably, as the dancing continued unabated, until the evening drew to a close.

❧

Taking advantage of the moonlight, Sophie and Hal, bid their hosts farewell then set off back to Chawcester. As they rode under the bright sky of a summer evening Sophie said, "I saw you dancing with Mistress Elgar. Was she to your taste?"

"She is pleasant, although a little high in her notions. Like a younger version of Aunt Margery, I would think. I can see why Jack Hollingshead prefers Mistress Howell, who has a great deal of charm and common sense."

"Yes, she never lacked a partner the whole evening, did she?" Sophie replied, casting him a glance. "I talked with her before the dancing began and liked her manners, once she got over her shyness."

"It must have been difficult for her, a stranger suddenly thrust into our society. Yet as you say, she showed to advantage. As I understand it, her circumstances are not entirely happy, and so Justin's Cousin Eunice, is looking for a husband for her."

"I rather think that will be a task for Bess," frowned Sophie. "Though where she'll find the time, I am at a loss to understand."

Hal nodded. "What with her children and her husband, Bess is kept very busy, but I imagine Eunice Latham merely wants her to mix with people Bess knows. Mistress Howell is engaging, and pleasant, given the right company, she'll find her own husband."

"That is to be hoped, for her sake," agreed Sophie.

As they continued, meandering along through quiet leafy lanes Hal said, "So, I saw you dancing with Mary and Guy's new neighbour. He seemed to keep you amused."

Sophie glanced to his face, half hidden by the brim of his hat, in surprise. "He has a certain charm. He told me he had heard I was an heiress, and thought he might like to present his suit and cut you out."

Hal's brows rose a little irked by the other's vanity, as

he asked, "At so late a date? He must have great faith in his charm!"

"Not without cause," she smiled provocatively.

Hal glanced to her sharply, and could see little but the shape of her chin, neck and shoulders in the moonlight. Then guessing she was teasing, he gained control of his jealousy. "Indeed, he is a man of great charm. Mary was similarly taken in, and singing his praises."

She met his eyes, puzzled. "Taken in?" she repeated.

"My dear," he said, in the blandest of tones. "The man was a friend and companion-in-arms of my father. I'd give you odds of ten to one the fellow is a complete rascal!"

"Oh, Hal, I thought so, too, but wanted to tease you! Why do you never rise to my bait?"

"Alas, because you always cast your fly so plainly," he replied, laughing at her dismay. "Come, give me a kiss, then we must hurry back to Chawcester before the gathering clouds make our way more difficult. I am certain in my mind, Mistress Capel will not sleep a wink until you are safely back under her roof."

⚜

Chapter Nine

A loud scream, followed by a wailing sob woke Sophie from a sound sleep. In a moment, the past came flooding back in a jumble of odd recollections. For a moment or two, she lay, blinking in the early morning sunlight, thinking all that had passed before had been naught but a dream, for here she was back in the bedchamber of her childhood.

Then came another, louder wail, and the sound of running feet. Still half asleep she was out of bed, and running with bare feet, along the shining boards of a long corridor to the best bedchamber where Uncle Edmund had lain dead. It was not his pain-filled grey face, which confronted her as she catapulted through the open door, but the ashen one of Mistress Capel, who was pointing rigidly at the body of her husband, as she screamed. Sophie took command of the situation after stumbling over the maid who lay prone in the doorway. "Is he dead?" Sophie cried.

She addressed the sturdy boy from the kitchen as he stood open-mouthed. "Francis, pick that maid up! What ails her? She cannot be dead too!"

"No, Mistress Sophie," Francis replied, with every sign of great enjoyment. "When the Mistress screamed Sukey and me come running. She took one look at Master, swooned and fell down!" The boy grabbed Sukey the maid and thrust her upright against the doorpost, then heartily slapped her cheek for good measure.

"Dear Mistress Capel, I fear your husband has died in the night," cried Sophie, coming to put an arm about the shaking shoulders of the shocked woman, who shuddered and swayed at her touch.

This forced Sophie to take command of the situation. "Francis, quickly, run downstairs and call to Cook, if you please. Bring back a pail of water to throw over Sukey. If she doesn't get to her feet and start to help me at once, I vow she'll be out of the house this very day! The last thing your mistress needs at this time, is a wench who gives herself airs! Come, get up, girl!" ordered Sophie as Sukey wailed.

Turning about as the boy departed swiftly, Sophie

coaxed Mistress Capel from the chamber, with the girl tottering shakily in her wake. "Come, my dear Mistress Capel, we must leave this sad sight, and lock the door, too, just in case there should be anything amiss." Still supporting the half-fainting woman, she dropped the key into a bowl of herbs, which stood on a chest beside the door, then turned to find the boy racing up the stairs with an ewer, spilling water in his wake.

"Now, Francis, have a care! You are slopping water all over the stairs! Put that down, and run to fetch a cloth and mop it up. Heavens above, the stairs are quite treacherous. Did you tell Cook? Good, now you must away to the Constable, for this is a sudden death, so, the authorities must look into it. Sukey, take that cloth from Francis, and carefully dry the stairs, whilst Mistress Capel and I go down to the parlour. A nip of brandywine will help her over the shock. And don't let me hear any more of that sniffling, Sukey, or I'll see you turned off from here without a character, this very day!"

Having thus dealt strong-mindedly with the servants, Sophie supported her hostess to a handsome parlour, then firmly shut the door on prying eyes.

"Dear Mistress Capel, are you ill?" she asked anxiously, as she set her in a chair at the head of the table.

Mistress Capel shook her head wordlessly, and took a sip of the brandy Sophie hastily poured into a pewter mug. Her hand shook violently, and she choked on the fiery liquid, but managed finally to speak. "No! no, but it is such a shock!" she gasped as she looked up into Sophie's concerned face and tears filled her eyes. "I came down to breakfast, and wondered where Jonas was. You know how he is such a stickler for punctuality. We live by those Abbey bells! It seemed so odd that he wasn't sitting here, drumming his fingers on the table with a face like thunder, because the bell had rung the hour as I came down the stairs."

Sophie nodded, poured a thimbleful of the spirit, sipped it and sat down beside her, covering Mistress Capel's trembling hands with her own. "So, he wasn't dead when you rose up to dress? He was taken suddenly, yet you heard no sound?"

"I heard nothing," she replied quickly, and took another sip of the brandy, making a face at the taste. "I don't sleep in the same chamber as Jonas. I haven't done since—since I found out about his slut! I moved my things to the chamber overlooking the river and mill."

"What slut?" Sophie exclaimed in surprise.

"You must have heard the gossip," Mistress Capel's

face turned dull red in embarrassment. "I thought everybody in these three counties had heard the gossip!"

"Everybody but me, dear Mistress Capel."

"Don't call me that! I vow I detest the very name of the man!" she cried passionately.

"I must confess I will always think of you as Mistress Blackwell, and have had to mind my words ever since I arrived."

"I'm Susanna," Mistress Capel said dully. "Susanna, that's what my beloved—Adam's father—used to call me—and I'll have no other. Not my father's name, nor that of my first or second husband—but certainly not, most definitely not the name that of that black-hearted villain I made the mistake of wedding last year!"

"Mistress Cap—Mistress Susanna, please mind what you say," cried Sophie, taken aback. "I know you were disappointed in the character of Master Capel. Indeed, I must confess I was amazed when I heard it said you were marrying him, for he was not a man held in universal esteem when I lived in Chawcester. Uncle Edmund used to say—"

"Yes, yes, I know," she said quickly, "but when you and Adam, both went away, I felt so dreadfully alone. My marriage to Jack Woolley was over almost as soon as it began, with him being took with the cough, before we'd even had time to wear out our bride clothes. I don't know, somehow the light seemed to go out of my life, when I lost my baby within weeks. You marry, you think to raise children, only I never did, you see, not any of my own. Adam was like a son to me, and believe me I was so pleased to see him go back to his rightful place in the world. I kept hoping he might persuade you into marriage, but then, when he and Mistress Cordelia made a match of it, I thought him lost to me, living as he did all those miles away in Lincolnshire. Jonas Capel had been so very attentive to me, helping with Jack's will, and then he began to pay court to me," she paused to take a further sip of the brandy, and laughed bitterly. "Aye, what man isn't agreeable when he has money in his eye? He brought me posies and ribbons, took me on walks in the moonlight by the river. It was like being a girl again!" She laughed then began to sob. "You'd think a woman of my age would have had more sense!"

"Hush, hush," Sophie came to put her arms about her. "Never you fret! Weep, that's right, weep away all the pain."

"It was that bitch, Betty, my maidservant!" exclaimed Mistress Capel through her tears. "She were an idle slut, always hiding away in corners, sniffing out gossip, and so full of guile, she was. And such airs before men! I told Jonas I'd not keep her unless she mended her ways, she'd unsettle them all, but he said he'd have a word with her, and make sure she behaved herself!" She began to sob again, tears falling faster, "Well, he had more than a word with her, didn't he? The next thing I know, she's parading herself about the house as if she owns it. And when I told her to get back to her work, she said I'd best ask the master what he had to say! That's when Cook told me about her having Capel's baby."

A knock came upon the door and the boy Francis entered, looking wary. "The Constable is downstairs. Cook's giving him a mug of ale, and says you are both to eat this gruel, before you think of having him up here. She's sweetened it with honey, and she doesn't expect to see it downstairs again."

He put a small dish of gruel before each woman, and Sophie put a spoon into Mistress Capel's hand. "Do eat, ma'am. Cook is right, trouble grows on an empty stomach. Francis, do step down to The Greyhound, and fetch Sir Henry Westwood to me, if you please. Tell him—and this is important, so heed me well—tell him: 'Mistress Sophie needs you immediately on a matter of great importance!' Have you understood that?"

The boy repeated her message perfectly, adding, "I am away to fetch him, but you'll need to get the Constable up here quick, like! That Sukey is spilling the beans, and old Constable Sambourne is not so slow-witted that he won't be thinking to save himself trouble by accusing my Mistress of murder."

Sophie and Mistress Capel exchanged horrified looks. "Oh, dear God! Send the Constable up immediately, Francis, then be off to get Sir Henry! Mistress Susanna, I must away to get a stitch on my back, before he and the Constable are come. Do, I beg you, say not one word to him. Have hysterics if necessary, but say nothing! I'll be back in a trice."

Chapter Ten

Sophie heard the Constable's ponderous step on the lower stairs, as she fled to her chamber, scrambled into her gown, twisted her hair into a knot and flung a scarf about her neck. She snatched up several handkerchiefs and her shoes, then hurried down to the parlour arriving in the open doorway to see Mistress Capel dabbing her eyes with a damp handkerchief, and Constable Sambourne standing uncomfortably by the table.

"Oh, Mistress Capel," she cried, "I pray you, don't give way to your grief so! Here, take these kerchiefs, and I'll call Sukey to bring the Constable a mug of ale, whilst you try to compose yourself a little."

"Thank you, Mistress Redcroft, but Cook gave me a mug of ale in the kitchen. I need to keep my wits about me, if what they do say is true. It be so, do it? Master Capel be dead?" he asked.

Sophie spread her hands wide. "Who among us can tell for sure? I was about to send the boy for the apothecary, but it looked to us—poor females that we be—as if he might indeed be dead."

The man nodded, his eyes going slowly from one to the other. "I'm thinking I might take a look at the—at him myself—if that be agreeable to you, Mistress Capel?" The Constable looked at them uncomfortably.

"Stay!" Sophie commanded, as Mistress Capel looked up, her eyes still streaming. "Is that not Sir Henry's voice I hear on the stairs?"

"Aye, and that there Frenchie, too," agreed the Constable, in a disgruntled manner.

"Ah, how clever of Sir Henry to summon Doctor Douay! I was about to do so myself. He is so much more obliging than Master Cresswell, who since he became Mayor, seldom tends any but his immediate circle."

"Aye, well happen we're a healthier town since he's been Mayor," Constable remarked sourly, as Hal, looking unshaven and as if he had thrown his clothes on, entered the chamber hastily, followed by the Frenchman.

"Hal!" Sophie hurried to clasp his hands, as his worried face sought hers. "Thank you for coming to our aid so quickly! And you too, dear Doctor Douay."

"What is amiss? You are unharmed? Both of you?" Hal cried, his eyes going to Mistress Capel, who sat weeping. "Is Mistress Capel ill?"

"No, well, only in that she is shocked by finding her husband," said Sophie. "Master Capel needs Doctor Douay's assistance, though, I fear he is past any help now."

"Master Jonas Capel—is dead?" Hal asked in dismay.

"I am no physician, but he looked so to me," Sophie replied frankly.

"I shall go and see, *mon ami*," the doctor said at once, opening a small bag he carried. "Sophie, hold this under Mistress Capel's nose. It should stop the inevitable hysterics." He handed a small phial to Sophie, and turned in the doorway. "Do you come, too, Hal?"

"If Sophie doesn't need me." Her watery smile and nod relieved him of his primary concern, and in the doctor's wake he waved the confused Constable before him out the door. "Go on, Sambourne, this is not a day for precedence, neither shall I bite you!"

Left alone, Sophie uncorked the phial and waved it under the nose of the weeping woman, who gave an abrupt snort, then fell to coughing and spluttering.

Sophie hastily corked the foul-smelling mixture and said, "I am so sorry, my dear Susanna, but you must try to get some control and still your tears a little. Recollect, I, too have been in the position you now find yourself. I cannot impress upon you how important it is to mind what you say."

Mistress Capel, her eyes and nose streaming, stared at her in dawning horror and gasped, "You think this—is murder? Not a natural death?"

"Pray God fasting, it is not!" Sophie said quickly. "But you know the gossips of this town! There is already a scandal to fuel anything untoward. I do not accuse you of anything, ma'am, but I am begging you to weigh every word you say."

Mistress Capel nodded, her head clearing a little. "As God is my witness, I did not kill him," she said calmly.

"So I know, ma'am, but you said you were angry with him. Did you not threatened him and his doxy a few weeks ago? If you did, there are many here who will remember it, and will be glad to say so! That is why it is so important for you to be careful of your words before uttering them. Any thoughtless remark will set tongues wagging tenfold! There will not be one of the gossipy inhabitants of this town who won't be able to recall, in lurid detail, every word you've uttered in your anger."

"And repeat it with all manner of embellishment!"

Mistress Capel agreed, her face suddenly white with fear. "Oh, Mistress Sophie, what am I to do?"

"Don't be afraid," Sophie replied swiftly. "Sir Henry is here and he will see justice done. Once he is convinced of your innocence he will protect you. But you do understand how careful you must be? No more hysterics now, and think before you utter another word! I remember after my bridegroom died, I frightened Hal and Justin, by saying I thanked God for my release. You see, I had come to have doubts about my husband in the weeks leading up to the wedding. He seemed to become more and more unpleasant each day that passed, and none gave heed to a word I said—and in my distraught state, I gave no heed to how I might incriminate myself. I just uttered the first words which came into my head."

Mistress Capel nodded in understanding, but before she could speak, the door opened to admit Hal.

"Pray allow me to console you on the loss of your husband, Mistress Capel," he said gravely. "As Sophie surmised, Master Capel is indeed dead." His searching glance took in the widow and noted she had gained some composure. "I do hope you can answer some of my questions, ma'am. I don't need to tell you it will greatly aid our enquiries if you can do so at this time."

The mildness of his tone reassured Mistress Capel. "I will do my very best, Sir Henry," she replied, her lips trembling.

"Hal, would you care for a mug of ale, some breakfast?" Sophie asked, realising from the sketchiness of his attire, that he had virtually leapt straight from his bed.

He smiled faintly. "A mug of ale would go down well," he agreed. "I awoke this morning with rather a thick head. Too much of Guy's wine last evening, I fear—and probably too much dancing."

"Pray, do not be afraid, Mistress Susanna," soothed Sophie when Susanna rose to her feet. "I shall call Francis. I will not leave your side, I promise. Hal, come, take a seat, I will be but a matter of moments."

Hal handed his hostess to the table and came to take a seat alongside her, but waited until Sophie returned to her place, before saying kindly, "Now, Mistress Capel, as you know, we were all at Elmley Park last evening, and didn't return until quite late. We met only for a few moments, when I escorted Sophie home. Was Master Capel already at home and abed?"

Mistress Capel looked up from her tightly clenched hands, her lips trembling again. "Sir Henry, you have been in Chawcester a few days, so I expect you know all the gossip. Master Capel and I have—have had a few differences." She hesitated, and as Hal made no reply, only nodding gravely, she added, "Last evening, as far as I know, he was at the tavern with his friends. Normally in such a case, he would return home a little after half-past-ten by the Abbey clock, then retire to bed."

"It would seem Master Capel was a stickler for the time, Hal," said Sophie, as the door opened to admit the boy Francis and Sukey the maid.

"That is all to the good," replied Hal. "The closer we can identify his movements, the more easily we can discover exactly what has gone forward." His glance strayed to the servants, as they furnished the table with food, placing a mug of ale and a pot of sweet-smelling chocolate, before Mistress Capel, and a side of beef and a fine, white loaf before Hal.

"You, boy, did you attend your master last evening? What manner of mood was he in?" he asked as the lad brought him a mug of ale.

"Young Francis would be abed by that hour, Sir Henry," said Mistress Capel. "He is a growing lad and needs his sleep. Everything would already be laid out ready for my husband, but he was not a fine gentleman like yourself, who had a man to wait upon him."

Hal laughed. "I am not such a gentleman as to require a valet to attend upon me," he remarked, sipping his ale, as Sophie poured a dish of chocolate for Mistress Capel. "Usually one of the maids brings me some warm water to wash in, and the rest I shift for myself."

Mistress Capel took a tentative sip of the chocolate, and looked surprised. "Why, this is good," she remarked. "I had never tasted it before, but bought some from the grocer for Mistress Sophie and Mistress Cordelia."

"I am told it is a favourite of the ladies at court," said Hal, as Sophie also took a cautious sip of the dish she had poured for herself. "I observed the water jug, still full in the bedchamber. So, who put out the water for Master Capel?" he asked, glancing enquiringly to the girl, whose eyes darted from one to another.

"It was me, you honour," replied Sukey promptly. "Since Betty was took, everything falls to me because the mistress won't have another girl in the house!"

"I see," said Hal. "That must mean you are kept very busy. . . ?" He hesitated over her name.

"Sukey," she snapped sullenly. "And yes, I am *very* busy, for that there Francis spends all the day buttering up Cook and the Mistress!"

Hal nodded as Mistress Capel was moved to protest. " 'Tis as well your mistress has you to rely on, for lads can be idle. I know, I was one myself a few years ago." Hal agreed, winking at the boy, who was helping him to a large slice of roast beef. He nodded again as the lad sliced a chunk of fresh white bread. "Thank you, I'll talk to you both again, later if I may. Now, the good lady who is your excellent cook, has she been with you long, Mistress Capel?"

"Since my marriage to Jack Wooley that was, I don't know if you'll remember him, a local farmer and live-stock dealer. I married him after Adam and I sold The Greyhound. You'll remember, Sophie, how he died of the cough within six months of our wedding?"

Hal nodded as Sophie assented, then waited until the servants had departed, taking the opportunity to eat the excellent bread and beef before adding, "Well, ma'am, I'll not deny I have heard rumours of a dispute between you and your husband—and not just from servants and scandal-mongers. Doctor Douay, the physician, was witness to your anger with the wench in question, and to the rather wild threats you uttered in your fury."

"Sir Henry, I don't deny I was filled with such rage that day, at the insult to me and my home! But it was nothing more than that, sir, words and fury!" she sobbed.

"Indeed, ma'am," he replied thoughtfully. "Doctor Douay is of the opinion that those who scream their anger and distress are less likely to kill than those who contain it and allow it to fester. For myself, I must keep an open mind, and deal with the facts presented, so if you'll forgive me, I must continue to ask you questions."

Mistress Capel nodded her understanding. "I *didn't* kill him, your honour," she insisted firmly.

Hal smiled wryly. "I am here as a friend, ma'am. Summoned by my betrothed. I hold no jurisdiction at present, but if you'd care to tell me the facts, I will present them to the relevant authority, and also to a man-of-law, who will assist you in presenting a case to support your innocence, should the need arise."

"Do you think it will, Hal?" Sophie asked anxiously, cutting him some more bread and beef, and taking a small slice for herself.

"Given the circumstances of so public a scandal, those in authority don't usually trouble to look much further than the end of their noses," sighed Hal. "This is why we must deal in hard facts, Mistress Capel. Tell me, when was the last time you were in company with your husband?"

"At breakfast yesterday morning, and only briefly, sir," she replied, after a moment's thought. "You were there—Sophie, and Adam and Mistress Blackwell, too."

"Indeed I was," agreed Sophie, and Hal groaned inwardly. Aunt Margery was going to be furious about all this. The family was inextricably mixed up in the scandal, and she'd blame Sophie for it.

"You spent no other time with him throughout the day, or evening?," he asked hopefully.

"No," she replied. "I had a fitting for my new gown with Sally Rose later on—after you and Mistress Sophie departed for Elmley Park—and then I had a bite to eat with her. For Mistress Sophie had given Sally money to send out for food from The Greyhound. Jonas had said he was dining at The Ring o' Bells, hard by the Abbey. That is the tavern where all the legal people gather."

Hal nodded, being aware of this. "So you saw him at no time during the day or evening?"

"I passed him on the stairs before supper time, Sir Henry. He been in to wash his hands, and change his linen, for I found his shirt and neckcloth thrown on the floor, and the dirty water still in the bowl," she replied, frowning at the recollection.

"And did you have any words with him?" he asked.

Mistress Capel watched him anxiously. "He said doubtless I'd been out spending his money on useless finery again, and I replied I had only spent that which was mine by right. To which he said everything was his by law, and that if I didn't curb my spending, he'd find a way to do it for me."

Hal looked grave. "Is there justification for his words?"

She looked up, her eyes wet with unshed tears. "I was a widow, sir, when I married Adam's father. That dear, sweet man did his best to drink The Greyhound dry— which was all my husband had left to me—and I never grudged him a penny of it, for he was ever the gentleman, he was. Adam and I worked hard in the years after his death, to clear our outstanding debts, and when we split the profits from The Greyhound, I was left comfortable enough. Then I married Jack Wooley, who had a tidy fortune himself, and he—being taken as he was, within six months of our wedding—I inherited all his money. That was when I made the biggest mistake of my life, and married Jonas Capel."

She broke off, as Sophie looked at her in horror, shaking her head, then added, "For I'll not deny it, Sir Henry, I was sadly mistaken in my husband's character. I knew he was careful with money, and thought that a good thing, after my dearest—Adam's father—but I didn't know Jonas was mean. Mean enough to count the eggs in the pantry twice a week, mean enough to insist we drank second skimmings milk, mean enough to drive my Cook distracted, it seemed to me. Adam told me he was mean before the wedding, and I didn't heed him, but I am not a fool. I entered into a contract, for better or worse, I was stuck with it. He was my husband, and I owed him a duty as wife, but I did *not* kill him."

"How did he die, Hal?" Sophie asked quickly.

"Until Phillipe returns I am not sure, Sophie," he admitted. "On the face of it, it could be a natural death, but I am most anxious, in view of the rumours of discord between the dead man and Mistress Capel—rumours I might add, it would seem the servant girl was pouring into Sambourne's ears from the moment he arrived at the house. Although, to be fair to both, he said he knew of them anyway. Taking all this into account, I think it makes sense to investigate the affair properly, lest in a town of busy bodies such as this, rumours are given the credence of truth, merely by being repeated. Many a person leads a life of despair because of unfounded rumours."

"Aye, and I know the source of them rumours," said

Mistress Capel grimly. "Sukey is kin to Betty, that slut that was with Jonas. She has been at pains to be difficult and unpleasant these past weeks, since Betty died. I've been minded to dismiss her many a day, but I thought it best to keep her under my eye, rather than letting her go and take her tale even further afield."

"You are probably wise," sighed Sophie. "There is no malice like that of a dismissed servant."

"She shows no loyalty to you, Mistress Capel?" Hal asked carefully.

"No," replied Mistress Capel in a mortified tone. "Polly, my own wench, has been with me these past ten years, but the chance came for her to be wed to a farmer back in her own village. I was pleased for her, so I gave her a dowry on her marriage, and Jonas took on this Betty and her kinswoman, Sukey. He said they had been together over Chipping Barbury way, and came with a good report."

"Did he?" Hal looked surprised, and made a note of this in his book. "Were they hired at the Mop Fair?"

"No, it weren't that time of year. They just arrived one day. I think perhaps they are kin of one of his drinking cronies. I must confess I never took to either of them, but then I sorely missed my Polly. My Cook Lizzie Burton has been with me five, six years this Michaelmas, and Francis, the boy, is her nephew." she replied, in exhausted tones.

"Yes, I see, thank you—" Hal nodded and stopped talking, as the door opened to admit Doctor Douay.

"So, Hal, I see you sit at your ease, whilst I labour!" he cried at once, in mock indignation, then recollecting the circumstances, he turned to the lady of the house. "Mistress Capel, you have my condolences on your husband's demise. Tell me, if you please, had he consulted any other apothecary recently?"

"Not to my knowledge," she replied. "Since you left Chawcester, sir, we've not been served well. For when Master Cresswell became Mayor, he saw only those he chose to."

The physician nodded. "But he made no complaints, your husband of his health? He had no symptoms you noticed?"

"Saving the headaches, sir, as I told you last month."

"Ah, the headaches, Mistress Capel, I recollect now."

"Master Capel always had pains in his head," she said slowly. "Ever since we've been married, and before that too, I believe. I think perhaps it was the poring over books and papers by bad light. Often he'd be laid low with them, especially if he was in court with a tricky plea. Sure enough, later that evening, he'd take to his bed with pains in his head, and bring up his supper, needing cold compresses and hot bricks all night long."

The physician nodded his head wisely, leaving Hal to ask, "Well, do you have any conclusions, Phillipe?"

"I have several ideas, but none I'd care to advance, without further reflection."

Hal mastered his impatience. "Can you tell whether foul play was involved or not?"

The French man sighed. "I cannot be sure, you understand—and yet—I am inclined to say something is amiss. I cannot say the where or the why without further investigation. I thought I might have his body taken to my home, if Mistress Capel has no objection?"

Mistress Capel dropped her head into her hands. "Trouble to the last," she whispered. "Even in death he is going to be trouble. No, sir, I have no objection."

The physician raised an eyebrow and looked at Sophie. "Perhaps Mistress Capel may need a tisane?"

"Mistress Capel has been answering Sir Henry's question in the most rational manner, but she is growing weary, I think," agreed Sophie.

"I am relieved to hear she has remained rational, but

I'll make her a tisane. I think that she should sleep, once Hal has finished his interrogation. I shall go to the kitchen, ma'am, and teach your cook my methods, for you'll need the steadiness over the next few days."

"But will you not break your fast with us, Doctor Douay?" Much to Sophie's surprise, Mistress Capel expressed no concern at his intentions. "I can easily get the boy to fetch another pot of chocolate, if you don't care for ale."

"*Non, merci* madam, do not bestir yourself. I am becoming an Englishman. I'll take bread, beef and ale, like Sir Henry."

"Perhaps I should go and assist him," said Sophie as the physician departed. "How good is your cook at making tisanes, Mistress Susanna? She is probably much harassed at present."

"She is a most capable wench, Mistress Sophie. No, don't you trouble yourself. She has a soft spot for Doctor Douay, since he cured her corns," said Mistress Capel, fighting the desire to weep again. "Oh, I was so happy, when you and Adam and dear Mistress Blackwell said you were coming to stay with me! And now it is all ruined. You'll all have to go away again because of all the shame and the scandal!"

"That we will not!" Sophie insisted quickly, before Hal could speak. "Why, that would be like saying we thought you guilty! No, we shall all remain, just as if nothing untoward has happened. And it hasn't—other than a rather tiresome fellow has died."

"Sophie, take care what you say!" said Hal quickly.

"See, Mistress Sophie? Sir Henry, doesn't want you to get involved with me and my problems!" Mistress Capel cried, laying her head in her hands. "And who can blame him?"

Hal sighed as he cast her a resigned look. "I rather fear we are involved, Mistress Capel. Sophie has, as usual, put her finger on the problem. If we all depart to avoid any scandal, we, by implication, condemn you. And whether his death is natural, or not—whether the culprit is apprehended, or not—you'll always remain under suspicion, as the wife who disposed of an unpleasant husband."

As she sat up with a horrified look on her tear-stained face, he glanced at her ruefully, then said, "Cost each of us what it may, we have no choice, ma'am. There will have to be a thorough investigation, but oh, please God, over and done within this week as I will be married on Tuesday next!"

Sophie returned his look. "Then we'd best bustle about, for there is much to be done!"

"Indeed," he agreed. "Bess didn't say last evening if Justin was returning to Adamsholme, did she?

"Justin?" Sophie repeated the name warily. "You think to ask for his help?"

"He is a capable man-of-law," replied Hal, with a sigh. "Chawcester hasn't had one."

"Bess said they are visiting Justin's Cousin Eunice today, as she and the boys are staying there before our wedding ceremony at the Abbey then going on to Westwood for the feast. After that they will move into the house here at The Cross. I didn't ask about Justin. I assumed he would be going back to Adamsholme later today."

Hal sighed. "Then I must seek him out. Pray God he is in a civil mood, when I find him. I must also question your people here, Mistress Capel, with your permission, before I ride out to the farm your servant girls came from, and hopefully find their former employer.

"I'll go with you," said Sophie at once, "I'll probably get more out of the servants than you will."

"No, Sophie, I think you should remain here, with Mistress Capel. She needs you far more than I do," insisted Hal firmly. "And there is the wedding to be thought of. Everyone is already gathered, or on their way. Our wedding really must go ahead, come what may."

Chapter Eleven

Once Mistress Capel was persuaded to take Doctor Douay's concoction and rest in her chamber, Hal sought out the servants for their accounts of what had gone forward in the house. He first listened to the boy's excited recitation of what occurred, then the Cook's shocked but more accurate account, and finally he came to the sullen maidservant.

"Mistress Sukey," said Hal being careful to keep his voice neutral, "I understand you and your cousin were very close, almost like sisters. I am sorry for your loss. You must miss her companionship a great deal."

The girl eyed him uncertainly, as if unable to fully comprehend his words. "Aye," she said with reluctance.

Hal nodded. "Had you been companions long?"

She looked suspicious and frowned heavily. "She were my cousin. I lived with her and her Mam when mine were took with the cough, about ten year back. Mam died in a cottage out Binney way," the girl replied shortly.

"I understand. So your aunt took you in when your mother died? You came from out of town, did you?"

"Aye, my aunt were dairy maid to a farmer at Binney, but he took sick and died, so we all had to leave after the farm were sold. We found another place, then my aunt got sick, and we went to yet another farm after she died. But the work there was hard, and the food poor, and Betty said we'd never get anywhere stuck with clods, so we came to Chawcester Mop, near two year back now, looking for work, and met up with a cousin of Betty's on her dad's side, who were an attorney's clerk. He said he could get us settled like."

"Ah, and he introduced you to Master Capel, did he?" Hal frowned over this history.

"No, he never did," she cried angrily. "Nothing but lies we had from him, lies and leading us on. He never knew no attorneys, though he were happy enough to sell us to any of his pals as would pay! So Betty up and went to the constable, and we ended up on a farm again, even further away from town, with nowt but farmhands wanting a tumble in the hay for nought."

Hal frowned. "Did you not seek recourse to the farmer or his wife?"

"Farmer? He were worse than the hands," she replied bitterly. "He'd grab you and then beat you once he'd taken his pleasure."

"The farmer?" cried Hal in shock.

"Aye, Elias Dimpney ! A devil he were, and that wife o' his no better!"

"Did you make no compliant to the Constable about his behaviour? Where was this farm? Is it local?"

"No, it were way beyond Chipping Bradbury, it were. That's why we went to the Fairacres, because we heard they were good folks, but then Betty fell for Tom Fairacre, and that caused such a to-do. The mistress said we were whores and sent us off without a penny or a character, so we were out again. Only this time my cousin came up with Master Capel wanting a new wench, so we came here. Now Betty is dead, and Mistress will send me off as soon as she can!"

"Mistress Capel is a good Christian woman," said Hal firmly. "Provided you carry out the tasks she gives you to her satisfaction, and show her some loyalty, I am confident she will do no such thing."

The girl frowned over his words and admitted reluctantly. "I don't often know what she means. If I have time I ask Cook, but the mistress don't like me."

"Your mistress has had many problems to deal with lately, some attributable to your cousin, but she is a good-hearted woman. Show her your support and she will not treat you ill, I am confident of that," Hal repeated with some emphasis.

The girl looked doubtful but said nothing, so Hal continued to ask questions. "Now, tell me if you can, what occurred on the night of your master's death?"

The girl looked blank then hesitated, "He died?"

Hal smiled faintly. "Indeed, it would seem so, wouldn't it? Now can you tell me what happened? When did he come back to the house? Was he in a good mood when he did? Was it your task to attend on him?"

"No, that were the lad's duty, but as ever, Francis sloped off fishing so it were left to me to fetch Master's water."

Hal shook his head. "Ah, these young lads, always unreliable, I'll be bound."

"Aye, but he butters up the Mistress, so he do. She thinks he can do no wrong."

"Yes, Francis has a ready tongue on him, I noticed. So, he'd gone leaving you to do his tasks, had he?"

"Aye, Mistress now, she thought Francis were abed, but he'd put his pillow under the cover, and he didn't come in until after the master had gone to bed."

Hal looked thoughtful. "But earlier, when your Master came in to change his clothes—what time was that? Do you remember?"

"Early evening, I think I heard the Abbey bells ringing the half hour, so it were half past six. Master saying they were to sup at seven," she replied.

"Was he in a good mood?" Hal asked, thinking they were finally getting somewhere.

"He didn't throw nothing," she replied thoughtfully, "but he'd been like a bear with a sore head ever since the news broke of your wedding."

"My wedding?" Hal looked surprised. "What had my wedding to do with him?"

She shrugged. "Mistress said as how Mistress Sophie would come on a visit. Master don't like no visitors. He said visitors made the Mistress be spendthrift."

Hal nodded his understanding. "Mistress Sophie isn't one to impose upon her friends. If she were to stay here, as she has done, she would have settled terms with your mistress."

"Mistress wouldn't have none of that," said the girl

quickly. "She told him straight as how they'd lived here rent free these last few years, and that no doubt once Mistress Sophie were married to you, things would change smartish! She said as how you weren't no fool, and you'd expect a fair rent on any property you owned."

"I shall not own the property. I shall merely administer it for my wife. In all probability, it will remain as her jointure, or be settled upon any daughters she may have," he replied absently, his mind racing ahead. "So, did your Master take a drink, or eat anything before he left for supper at the Inn?" He asked, tacking this question on in the hope she wouldn't think before answering.

"Nay, he were supping with his cronies, there'd be plenty of both. He mostly comes back from the tavern unsteady on his legs, and it ain't from what he's eaten!"

Hal nodded. "So he took nothing in the way of food and drink here that evening?" he asked, in some relief.

"No, Your Honour, not a thing passed his lips, but the physick he took regular like."

"Physick?" Hal repeated. "Doctor Douay said nothing of this earlier. What physick was this?"

"Oh, it weren't one of his physicks, no, we don't hold with the potions that there Frenchie gives out. Why he charges a weeks wages for 'em, so he does. None of us folk can afford them. We goes to Ned, the groom at The Ring o' Bells. He's been curing folks for years, and not many die as wouldn't have done any right."

Hal nodded, well-aware of the many unlicensed quacks or healers who preyed on the poor and, it seemed, finished off their fellows with impunity, or as luck dictated. "Had your master been taking this physick for long?" he asked.

She leered unpleasantly. "Well now, that'd be telling! Got it from Mother Sandwell she did."

"*She* did ? Whom do you mean? Mistress Capel? Was Sandwell not the name of that unfortunate woman they swum as a witch recently?" frowned Hal.

"Nay, Sandwell weren't no witch!" cried the girl quickly. "She be kin of ours way back. Betty got it from her!"

"When you say way back, how long ago?"

"I ain't no witch! I just know her as kin!" cried the girl in panic.

"Do not fear!" Hal said gently, seeing her terror. "I do not call you a witch, but I am interested in how this old woman was treated so ill, when she appears to have tended the local people hereabouts for many years."

Some of the terror and suspicion cleared from her face, and she shrugged her ample shoulders. "I don't know about that. One minute everyone used to go to her, the next, a mob springs up, calling her witch! She and my grandam were sisters, I think, or they could have been cousins. Most folk is cousins round 'ere."

"Ah, so she was kin of yours, in some measure?" he concluded. "Yes, that makes sense, and she gave your cousin a potion for Jonas Capel, yes?"

"Aye, it were just to get him along a bit. He were getting creaky at the knees, so to say, and Betty said she'd get something to liven him up a bit, so he weren't such hard work in bed."

Enlightenment dawned on Hal. "Ah, yes, now I understand, an aphrodisiac of some sort?"

The girl shrugged her shoulders. "It were a potion, Betty called it. Ned, the groom said like as not it were what he gave to the horses to pep them up when they were worn down, so it should give old Capel a bit of life!"

Hal nodded in some relief. "Of course, well, that was helpful to your cousin. So Ned, the groom at The Ring o' Bells uses the same potion on his horses? He gets it from the old woman they swum as a witch?"

"Nay, he makes his own potion for the horses!" the girl cried impatiently. "She taught him how to do it! Ned is good with simples and he being kin to her, she taught him them there recipes! Ever since she run off after the swimming to-do, Ned has made everything."

"But of course, there is always another to fill a place vacated. So is Ned now the local witch?"

"Nay, he's the groom at The Ring o' Bells!" she cried in exasperation. "I don't know why they think you are so clever. You don't know nothing!"

Hal laughed abruptly. "Indeed, I think you must be right, Sukey. Now listen and heed me well, for this is important. You must show loyalty to your mistress, for if you do she will keep you on as her servant. Do not gossip about her to any—kin or no. Keep a silent tongue in your head and all will be well. Do you hear me?"

"Oh, aye," she said resigned. "I know how to keep quiet. Do you want me now, or am I to come to The Greyhound later?"

Shocked to silence Hal stared at her in astonishment, suddenly understanding how badly she had been treated all her life, used as a convenience, threatened and abused. The girl began to untie her apron.

"No, don't," he cried, partly in horror, but more in

shame that she should accept her degradation with such unthinking compliance. "Sukey, if you could choose, what would you do?"

"Do?" she repeated blankly.

"If you could choose anything in life, what would be the thing you would like most?" he asked.

"I'd like a new gown. And to go to the Mop Fair with a few pennies to buy some fairings."

He nodded. "But how would you like to live your life? Where were you happiest?"

She stared at him bemused, as if she had never considered it. "On the farm," she replied slowly. "The sun were warm, and the May blossom smelled so sweet, that Walt climbed the tree to get some for me hair."

"Was Walt your lover?" Hal asked softly.

"Happen, if the plague hadn't come," she replied. "The spots appeared two days later, and he were buried by the end of the week."

"You were lucky to survive then."

"Happen," she shrugged. "You don't want me then?"

"No, Sukey. I have a love and hold true to her. She is to be my wife in a few days," he replied gently.

"Mistress Sophie is a pretty lass, and has plenty o' pennies," she agreed.

"Would you like to work on a farm again, if that could be arranged—with a decent master, and a good mistress who would treat you well?"

She frowned at him as of doubting such a thing existed. "Happen," she shrugged.

"I'll see what can be done," he said. "In the meantime, please remember what I said about your Mistress and try to assist her in this troublesome time."

The girl nodded and frowned as she considered his words. "I am to go to the country?" she asked.

"If that is your wish," he answered.

She stood thinking, then nodded. "I'll best get back to work then."

⚜

Whilst Hal was making a careful record of all he had been told, Justin, stopped at The Ring o' Bells to slake the thirst, which comes after a night of festivity. Whilst there he decided to linger and pick up any news of what was afoot in the town, which was about to become his new home.

He had been to the inn many times before. It was a favourite of clerks and lawyers, being as close as it was to the Abbey, where most of the legal work was required. He sat for some time drinking ale, and reading papers. After a while he took an early dinner and considered visiting his Cousin Eunice again, before making his way back to Adamsholme. Then he overheard some of the gossip going round the tavern. He listened carefully to some of the more lurid tales already doing the rounds and then, having paid for his food, hastened away.

Chapter Twelve

As Hal was about to depart in search of information, the lad Fancis came running to tell him there was a man waiting to see him in the chamber where Jonas Capel used to meet with those seeking his aid. Hal laid aside his hat and went along, wondering who in the town hadn't heard of Capel's demise.

Justin looked up defensively as Hal entered the dusty, untidy chamber. "I've come to offer my services," he said a shade too quickly. "The gossip on the High Street is that either Susanna Capel or Adam Blackwell murdered Jonas Capel in an effort to rid the world of a scoundrel. You find me here because I don't want to intrude upon Susanna Capel."

It was on the tip of Hal's tongue to make a sarcastic reply about Justin not wanting to be civil to Sophie either, but he mastered that impulse, then asked with a shade of curiousity, "What service is it you offer?"

Justin shrugged. "What service do you require? Foot soldier? Defending counsel? Devil's advocate? Any, or all three if necessary. I know you would probably rather have Ambrose, but I have the advantage of being to hand."

"Ambrose is still in London, but I'd rather *your* brain, given the choice. You have a skill which cannot be taught."

Justin narrowed his eyes. "The common touch?" he suggested. "Or natural cunning?"

Hal smiled. "More sheer intelligence, I thought, when not clouded by resentment."

Justin smiled back reluctantly. "I have no quarrel with either Susanna Capel or Adam Blackwell, and the case against either is good. They have both made public statements of their intention to kill Jonas Capel within the hearing of witnesses."

"As, indeed, we are all guilty of speaking in a fit of fury at sometime in our lives," replied Hal evenly.

"Hopefully some of us are more circumspect," replied Justin dryly. "But, yes, I agree, that is no proof of intent. However, Constable Sambourne is easily convinced, and doubtless would have been here to arrest

Mistress Capel, but for your presence—and the gossip, which reports Adam Blackwell as threatening only yesterday morning 'to wring Capel's skinny neck', within the hearing of several witnesses. This has, of course, confused the Constable's poor mind entirely, until some bright spark put it into his head that it might be a conspiracy. So he is now dementedly rushing hither and thither, trying to prove so excellent a solution to his problem. The only good news is that the Baliff Jesse Hibbet, has gone off to Kent for the wedding of a godson, and won't be returned in less than a sen'night," he added as Hal gave a groan of dismay.

"Is there not another Baliff?" Hal asked.

"Abel Monke is laid up with his gout, it seems."

"So, we are left with Constable Sambourne again. He has the merit of being biddable, if nothing else. So if we can get this all resolved before the wedding—"

"All will be well?" suggested Justin cynically.

Hal decided if he was to work closely with Justin, he would have to become deaf and blind to his sneers and snide remarks. "It is a good opportunity to get this affair wrapped up before his return," he agreed smoothly. "Thank you. I'll be glad of your help."

"Well, it will probably be the last time we jog along

in harness," said Justin hesitantly. "My cousin Eunice has bought the house at The Cross for Bess and me."

Hal had already heard rumours. "What good fortune! That is extremely generous of her," he said politely.

"Well, she intends to make her home with us, and Chawcester needs a decent man-of-law."

"Indeed it does, especially now. So you will abandon Adamsholme?"

Justin shrugged his shoulders. "I have never felt the same about the place, since my father married that woman. I wasted a good part of my life there. It holds too many bitter memories."

Hal looked grave as he glimpsed the depths of Justin's bitterness. "I am sorry that you feel so disappointed, and that I shall be losing so able a lawyer, but it is wonderful news for you, Justin. I wish you every success."

Justin glanced to his brother-in-law, with irritation. He had forgotten Hal's ability to rise to the occasion. Was he ever caught out in wishing others to fall foul of fate? If so, he hid it admirably. "Well, I was meaning that we wouldn't be competing with each other."

"Indeed! In fact, it would be to our advantage, as kin, to form some sort of alliance. I know how vital the happiness of Bess is to both of us."

"Bess *is* very happy at the news," said Justin quickly.

"She must be," agreed Hal. "The house at The Cross is very handsome indeed, and your Cousin Eunice is an agreeable companion. Phillipe Douay looked at it on his return and said it reminded him of his grandmother's house in France, but it was beyond his pocket. However, he will be a close neighbour."

"Yes, Bess was pleased that he and Marie Celeste will be so near at hand. But come; to work. Your wedding is only days away. We cannot afford to waste time in idle chatter. What would you have me do?"

"I have questioned all the servants, especially the maidservant, Sukey but she is hostile to almost everyone in the house, and seems to have suffered a rather unpleasant existence of late. I could not get much information from her—other than that most of the locals get any physick they need from the groom at The Ring o' Bells. As a man of law, you will no doubt be familiar in that tavern, whereas I, should I set foot in the place would stand out like a sore thumb. So if you are agreeable, you could see what you can find out there later. You might also ask why Jonas Capel hired those girls, for it seems they came recommended by one of his drinking companions, who may be kin of some sort."

"Betty Tull, and her cousin Sukey Warren?" Justin asked, making a note.

"If you have been in Chawcester for more than half an hour, you'll no doubt be aware that Jonas Capel got the serving wench Betty with child. To whit, the said wench who, having been refused a potion to do away with the child by Doctor Phillipe Douay, promptly took herself off to an old wise woman in one of the villages, who complied with her request and managed to kill both Betty and her child. That led to a near riot, after a mob gathered. I am not yet in possession of all the details, but it seems somehow the crone escaped and—in the manner of witches—disappeared."

"Yes, the usual garbled version leading to the invariable outcome," Justin agreed. "So Betty and her bastard brat were disposed of? Yes, I shall be discreet. I have every reason to go to that tavern where the legal profession gathers to exchange gossip. Am I not in search of a clerk to assist me in my new office?"

"And, much more to the point, are you not known to be very much at odds with both me and my new bride? So hopefully the gossips will be much more forthcoming with you, than they would ever be with me," sighed Hal.

Justin nodded, frowning. "At odds occasionally, perhaps," he said awkwardly. "You frequently irritate me—but no, I was never against you, Hal."

Hal glanced at him and replied slowly, "I am glad to hear you say that. I think I had come to realise it, but I'm relieved you'll give me a good character, Justin."

Justin made a wry face as he got to his feet. "Indeed, how could I do otherwise? The only trouble I have is, that your good character is unconscious. It comes from a natural goodness of heart. You don't have to struggle with a baser nature, as I do. Do you make this house your headquarters? Or are you still staying at The Greyhound."

"Only nominally, in that I sleep there overnight. Leave any messages here with Sophie. She can be trusted not to make a fuss. The more I am here in this house, the longer Sambourne will hesitate to arrest Mistress Capel."

"And Adam Blackwell—is he still here?" asked Justin.

"He and Cordelia were to be travelling back later today, but I'll want him to remain here as protection at night. If somebody killed Capel, it is for us to find the suspects. In the meantime, I plan to make a visit to the farmer near Chipping Bradbury, who previously employed both the wench Sukey and her cousin, Betty," replied Hal. "Perhaps that will hold the key to it all. Would you care to accompany me? I value your insight."

It took some time to collect Justin's horse from the Inn's stables, and discover from the lad in the yard the way to their destination, a small village in the fertile valley on the way to Chipping Barbury. Conversation was a little stilted between the brothers-in-law, and Hal was only too glad to arrive, but a little disconcerted to find everyone was about to sit down to their main meal of the day. A hearty invitation to join them could not be declined, and he was soon seated between his host Farmer Goodacre and his wife.

Hal glanced across to Justin, who sat on the opposite side of the long table set out in the yard of what was obviously a prosperous farm. All along the length of the table men, women and children were eating with great gusto, having been working since cockcrow. With yet another eight hours or so of good weather before them, they would continue working until the last glimmer of light. Hal felt awkward, for he knew well their visit was disturbing the working rhythm of the day, yet what choice did he have, but to interrupt these good people during hay making.

"I am aware you must be cursing me, Master Goodacre," he said, with the courtesy which won him friends wherever he went. "I am a farmer myself, and know how much my visit must incommode you, but alas, these things must be investigated."

"Indeed they must, Sir Henry. The law is the law. And if it weren't upheld by the gentry, the likes of us wouldn't be allowed to farm in peace. No, it would be back to the bad days like the last war, when thieving soldiers could come—aye, from either side—and run off your best beasts and trample down your corn. You couldn't say them nay or they'd slit your throat."

"I grieve to hear you suffered so badly," replied Hal. "Thank Heavens for peace and the return of law and order."

"God save the King! And damnation to all Dutchmen!" cried the man, and all raised their ale and echoed him, much to Justin's amazement.

"I am happy to see you are all such good, loyal subjects," said Hal quickly, surprised by the display of loyalty. "When I am next in the presence of His Majesty,

I will tell him of this occasion, and he will be greatly pleased to hear of his loyal countrymen here in the shires. "

"Not that I cared for his father, mind," continued the farmer, and a general growl of assent went round the table. "Him and his Frenchie wife, causing all the mayhem they did to honest Englishmen. 'Twas a disgrace! But his son, well, he seems to be a different sort of man, one perhaps prepared to listen."

"The King is most anxious to know how his beloved people feel," replied Hal swiftly. "That is why I am charged to go amongst my neighbours, and listen to their grievances, and report back to the King, in a general way, about the state of our country. He never again wants us to get into the position where we would take up arms against each other."

"Aye, but will 'ee do anything about it?" asked Mistress Goodacre, as weather-worn and rotund as her husband, as she grasped the nub of the conversation, and tossed it back to Hal, in a manner which made Justin grin.

Hal turned the full charm of his smile on her. "Madam, I won't insult you by pretending he can do a vast amount. Like us all, he is beset by those around him, by lack of money, by the war with the Dutch, but he is mindful, just as we are, of the past. He knows he owes his allegiance to his people, just as they consent to give theirs to him."

"Not all of us give our consent," said a man bent with age, who sat near the foot of the table with his eyes showing an injury and a dog curled against his legs. "Some of us aren't so simple as to believe the words that come from Lunnon, prettily parcelled or no. Some of us remember the lies of the past."

" 'Tis old Wat Jenks, your honour," said the farmer quietly. "He were blinded in the war. He's got a bit of sight back, and with the aid of his dog, tends the flocks. 'Tis said he can hear a fox two fields away."

"He can hear you sucking up to the gentry, that's for sure!" the old man snapped, and all those around him laughed. Hal joined in, and the farmer, after a second, did, too.

"I may be gentry, Wat," said Hal, "yet I knew want and hardship in the war, just as you did, and I didn't even have the comfort of being with my own people. I recollect sitting under the hedge in the rain in France many a day, and wondering when we'd next see food. I tell you to your head, Wat, that frequently the only reason I ate was because my father was better at dice than most men. It was not the youth I'd choose for my sons, but then it wasn't the youth my father chose for me, and all our experiences teach us something."

"Aye, so what did you learn, my fine lord?" asked the old man bitterly.

"That I hadn't inherited my father's skill at gaming, and that I loved my country so much, I would do anything to get home."

"As we all do, Sir Henry, and you mind your tongue, Wat Jenks!" the farmer's wife scolded. "You put us all to shame with your ill humour! The gentleman has been very patient with you, but I'm not minded to listen to your moans and groans no more, so if you can't hold your tongue, take yourself off from my table. None of us had it easy during the war. But the past is the past! Isn't that so, Sir Henry?"

"I devoutly hope so, ma'am," he replied.

"I heard you asking Goodacre about them wenches, Betty Tull and her cousin Sukey Warren," she continued in an undertone. "They weren't with us above a season, your honour, for I tell you to your face, we didn't suit. Kin they be, of one of them lawyer's clerks in Chawcester, and him known for being a sly, underhand fellow. It must be a family trait, I am thinking, for I found them both unsuitable for farm work. I suggested they went to Chawcester, for I can get good honest wenches from the villages about here, who haven't got ideas above their station. That there Betty wanted to be a lady's maid she said—in Lunnon! I told her she were crying at the moon! She were no more fit for Lunnon, than she were for the Bishop's Palace!"

The farmer nodded. "They were trouble, Sir Henry, as I told you straight off. I had my doubts at the Mop Fair, but it were back near harvest time—what, more than a year back, I'm thinking, and we were short-handed, so I thought they might serve."

"Aye, they served all right!" his wife snapped. "They served near every man on the farm! I have never had such sluts in my employ! Aye, and never will again! They had the whole yard in uproar by time the winter were done, with fighting and drinking over they!"

"Aye," the farmer said looking harassed at the memory. "And not above coming back, either! I caught that Betty in a hayrick with our own lad back in the spring, and him not more than fifteen! He'd met up with her in Chawcester on market day, and she'd followed him back, with not so much as an ounce of shame. It earned him a beating, and I threatened to have her up before the courts, if she set foot on my land again."

"She cursed us all, she did, that whore," said the Mistress Goodacre, anger returning at the memory. "And now 'tis being said she did the same to Susanna Blackwell, her as used to be landlady of The Greyhound! Though, whatever she were a thinking of, wedding that slimy rogue of a lawyer, Jonas Capel, I do not know."

"Aye, now Jack Wooley, he were a fine man," said the farmer nodding. "I'm sure we all wished he and Mistress Susanna well. Aye, that were a tragedy, for sure, him being took within a few months o' the wedding!"

"And then Mistress Susanna loosing her baby straight away after! That would be the grief, it would," the farmer's wife nodded sagely. "Poor woman, she surely has had her fair share of trouble, one way and another."

"And more yet to come," agreed Hal, "for the other wench, Sukey, is whispering that Mistress Capel has reason to dispose of her husband. Thus, you see me and my brother-in-law here to seek your word on the character of these wenches."

"Well, there's no character to be had," said the farmer's wife roundly. "Trollops they were, the pair o' them! And these fools all sniffing after them like they were bitches in heat!" Her scorn included the whole table, most of whom ducked their heads and got on with their meal. "You tell Mistress Susanna I'll speak up for her in a court of law, so I will, and tell whosoever wants to know, that Betty Tull got what she deserved!"

As Hal and Justin rode back to Chawcester, Justin said, "The only trouble I see with the farmer's wife's testimony is it would hang Mistress Capel like as not."

Hal gave a short laugh. "True, but I liked her robust honesty. Give me a female who speaks her mind like Mistress Goodacre anyday—and the vernacular she uses shames the devil—rather than these wenches who won't tell you the truth, or use words to twist it."

Justin grunted and made a wry face. "Aye, robust honesty indeed. God knows farmhands work long hours, but how do they consume so much food at this time of day? If I had to sit over my papers now I'd be asleep in five minutes."

"It is as well we have a good ride before us. It will aid our digestion," laughed Hal. "Interesting comments from the farmer's wife—a shrewd woman, I thought."

"Indeed," agreed Justin. "So it probably wasn't Capel's child anyway, for 'tis plain this Betty was next best thing to a harlot."

"Aye, and the cousin by accounts little better," remarked Hal thoughtfully, wondering how best to deal with the problem. "Yet when I spoke to the wench, it seemed to me she was more sinned against than sinning."

"The worst aspect I can see is that neither of the wenches exhibited any loyalty to Mistress Capel," said Justin in disapproving tones.

"That is a common enough occurrence. Obviously any loyalty they had was to each other," agreed Hal.

Justin sighed. "Aye, it is ever thus. You don't think she might have killed Capel in retaliation for her kinswoman?"

Hal considered the question. "But if he wasn't the father of Betty's child, which seems possible after what we heard, then why kill him? Surely convincing him he might be the father was her only protection from being sent to the poorhouse. No, her grudge seems to be against her mistress, and who knows what lies Jonas Capel may have fed those wenches. I imagine Mistress Capel is pretty exacting. Years of experience at The Greyhound have given her a nose for idle maidservants."

Justin nodded. "True, but you said your Frenchie friend thinks somebody might have disliked Capel enough to do him an injury."

"Well, by all accounts he wasn't a pleasant man, and lawyers, by dint of their profession can accrue dislike. They are always present at the great events of life, marriages and deaths, and if there is an inheritance to be had, there are always a few who consider their claim the greater than the actual recipient's."

Justin narrowed his eyes at this bland remark. "What is your opinion of the cousin? You have met her?"

"I have spoken to her and she certainly holds a grudge against her mistress, but she is of limited understanding, sullen and ill-favoured. She is the sort who would happily carry a grudge forever and a day, but I don't see her killing her master. She had too much to lose."

"If she is of limited intelligence would she comprehend that? I cannot for the life of me see why Capel took them into his home. Mistress Capel was much more experienced in taking on servants, and there must have been others available."

"I can only think this Betty knew how to flatter a fellow like Capel. It is obvious from Mistress Capel's words theirs was not a happy marriage. Presumably the wench took the opportunity to exploit the situation. But you are right, Justin, why he took them into his home is a much more fruitful line of questioning. Why take them, when there are servants to be had with better characters? Mistress Capel was so much more capable of picking a good, hardworking wench."

Justin grunted adding reflectively, "Well, whilst you see what further information is to be had, I'll find out what is being said at The Ring o' Bells." He hesitated, adding a shade uneasily, "It may be that I am required to traduce your name a little, in the course of these en-quiries. Please understand I do so only that I might get the sort of response we require."

Hal hid a smile. "Traduce away and be welcome. We need to solve this problem with speed, and if calling my name into disrepute will aid matters, then do so. The sooner the truth is discovered the better for us all."

Justin grunted, and they parted at The Greyhound, Justin to take the pulse of the lower town at The Ring o' Bells and Hal to oversee the stabling of his horse.

⚜

Chapter Thirteen

Justin took his mug of ale from the reluctant pot-man, drew out his sheaf of papers and began to peruse them, giving half-an-ear to the various conversations going on around him, in the stuffy, overcrowded inn. The men engaged in a game of dice he gave little heed to, beyond mentally cursing them for their raised voices, as he tried to keep track of other conversations. Whilst the two older men discussing the rise in the price of barley held little interest, the soldier trying to secure the offices of the pretty maidservant was a more fertile matter, until his eye caught two young men he had never seen before. He therefore deduced they were newcomers to Chawcester, who were so deep in conversation as they ate their food they scarce noticed anyone.

He ordered supper from Tansy, the red-cheeked maid and kept a covert eye on the men, who sat at a table across the chamber from him. Justin could just distinguish their voices, and realised it was the lack of the local burr which marked them out as strangers, indeed, their accent was not of any locale he had heard. Shuffling his papers, he shifted slightly on the bench in order to get a look at them. At once it became obvious they were in some way related, for even though one had darker hair than the other, there was a similarity in the cast of their countenance which suggested brothers—or at least kin—and their clothes were similar. They were neither lawyers, clerks, or minor clergy of the Abbey, not yet even the middling sort of tradesmen of the town who made up the clientele of the inn for the most part.

Justin hesitated trying to place them and for a few moments he was irked by his failure to do so. It was an important part of his occupation, to be able to place his fellow man exactly in their social position in life, yet these two youngish men presented an enigma, for they did not slot into any of the usual sorts of people he would expect to encounter—not by the way they dressed, nor their behaviour. For although their clothes were respectable, they did not sit easily in them. They were not the garments habitually worn, more likely Sunday best clothes pressed into use for every day wear.

The darker of the two was older by some years, being perhaps in his early to mid-twenties, whilst the younger, still had some of the tow-haired sheen of youth upon him. And it was he who was by far the most uneasy about their situation, for he looked about him constantly, anxiety showing in the way he poked at his food, and drank deeply of the ale in his cup, turning angrily on his companion who tried to sooth him. All at once he cried out, "What then? Are we to wait here twiddling our thumbs whilst our father's killer goes free?"

The elder hushed him immediately, looking about to see if anyone had overheard, refilled his mug and glanced to Justin, who now had his nose in his papers and his ears at the ready.

"Nay then, Zeal, catch thy tongue. There be no need for hot words, not if we don't want to be discovered."

"How will we be discovered? No one knows us here, Persy," protested the other.

"Aye, 'tis so, but they all know each other. See how as they come in and they hail each other, and how they all look at us. Stand out like a pair of jack rabbits in a field of Indian corn we do! Livery said it would be difficult, so we must think on something to account for us being here."

"Livery is better than us at thinking things up," protested Zeal.

"Aye, but I heard tell that him we want to find is getting wed here—this very week! Aye, and when I stood at the tap to order supper, some were complaining as how the town be filling up with strangers come to his wedding. All we have to do is let them think we are servants of these people, and they'll notice nothing of us."

"Aye, it might serve, but I do wish Livery were back from the North. Do you think he'll find the fellow as cheated father?"

"If it be possible, Livery is the man to do it. Meantime we must do as he told us. Watch out for this Sir Henry Westwood."

This made Justin sit up sharply, and as his action caught the other's eye, he quickly covered his movement with a groan and winced, grimacing in their direction. "Been sitting too long over my papers," he remarked glumly. "Best take my supper now, and seek out my bed. Tansy!" He hailed the busy maid servant, who made haste to bring him his supper.

Justin nodded to the men, who were now covertly watching him, as she plonked his dish before him. "You strangers to these parts?" he asked them agreeably.

"Aye," they replied uneasily, in unison.

"The town doesn't get many strangers," Justin nodded. "Set in their ways they be."

"You're not from round here then?" the man called Zeal asked, with an air of relief.

"Not far away, Adamsholme, but it could be the moon as far as Chawester is concerned."

The men chuckled. "Aye, 'tis like our set—village," said the younger.

"Have you come far?" Justin asked, pausing in his supper to drink from his ale.

"A fair stretch," the elder replied quickly. "You've heard there is to be a wedding?"

"I believe I've heard it mentioned," Justin replied. "A fuss about nothing, I dare say. These things usually are. You will be guests of Sir Henry Westwood, I take it?"

The men laughed uneasily. "Nay, then, we're with Sir Simon—Hollingsby—and his wife."

"Ah, no, I am not familiar with 'em," said Justin truthfully. "I have only recently taken up residence here."

" 'Tis an agreeable town," the man called Persy, said quickly.

Justin smiled. "Most people say so. I am sorry let me introduce myself. I am Justin Danvers, a lawyer."

The unspoken question hung in the air as the men looked at each other, disconcerted. "We are brothers," said the elder, quickly kicking his companion's shin. "Persistance and Zeal—Smithson!"

"Ah, you'll be of a Puritan persuasion, as were my parents," remarked Justin pleasantly. "I was baptised Justice, but it proved something of a handicap for a lawyer, so I go by the name of Justin."

"Aye," said Zeal before his brother could speak. "There isn't much a man can do with Zeal, but we call him Persy, and our other brother is Livery, short for Deliverence."

Justin grinned. "A difficult name to live up to!"

"Not for Livery! He will get things done, come what may!"

"Is he in the employ of Sir Simon Hollingsby, too?" asked Justin.

"No, he—he's employed in the north, Lincolnshire way, for a Mr Revington, or some such name," said the elder quickly. "Zeal, happen we should be on our way back to the inn, just in case we are called for. Good evening, Mr Danvers, 'twas a pleasure to make your acquaintance."

"Good evening, Mr Persy, Mr Zeal," replied Justin.

Then, as they beat a hasty retreat, the girl came to collect their platters. Justin remarked, "Pleasant young men, Tansy. Are they here for the wedding?"

"Nay then, Mr Danvers, you'll know better than that. As if the likes of they would be at Sir Henry's wedding! Dissenters they be, I've heard 'em at their prayers!"

"Being at prayers doesn't make them Dissenters," said Justin thoughtfully.

"No, but they don't go to our Abbey, and it's the most beautiful in all England," she replied with the fervour of a local. "They ain't from round these parts, of course."

Justin nodded, "No, I think they come from further afield, but I just couldn't get a handle on their accent."

She nodded. "It will be some foreign place, beyond Bristol even, probably, like Somerset, or I know, Devon most likely! A man came up river from Gloucester, a couple of year back and not one of us could understand a word he said. And he came from—now, where were it?" She paused screwing up her pretty face in concentration, "I know, Bideford! That'll be it, Mr Danvers. They be West Country folk, for sure!"

"Most likely, Tansy! Yes, Western folk, surely," agreed Justin with a smile. "Only don't tell them I asked after them, will you, should they come in again?"

"Surely they won't be back again, just passing through so they reckoned. Though mind, they have been here two days now."

Justin nodded as her name was bellowed from the kitchen, and continued to eat his meal, his mind racing over what he had heard, wondering why they were seeking Hal. It was obvious their knowledge was sketchy, for their errors were glaring, yet even given the simple mistakes they had made, there was still enough content to make Justin turn his steps toward The Greyhound and leave a message for Hal.

"Hal, are you finally returned?" Sophie called down the staircase as he hesitated at the foot.

"Yes," he replied hastening upstairs.

"Is Justin not still with you?" she asked, looking past him.

"No, he has gone on to The Ring o' Bells, but he may join us soon," he replied catching her hand and drawing her close with a kiss. "Why?"

"See, Mr Langley has called to express his condolences to Mistress Capel," she said brightly. "He has been so kind keeping company with us, seeking to raise Susanna's spirits. Mistress Capel has just recommended Justin as a man-of-law to him, now that her husband is no more. And we thought to perform the introduction at once."

Hal followed her into the parlour frowning a little over her words. "Sir," he said directing a bow to the guest.

"Ah, Sir Henry, you are returned. I trust your errand prospered," said Mistress Capel anxiously.

Hal smiled reassuringly at her. "I was fortunate to find some of the information I sought, ma'am," he replied. "It would seem you are not alone in your estimation of your serving wench. The farmer's wife told me she had no hesitation in dismissing both her and her cousin. And furthermore she states that she will go into the witness box to swear they were sent from her employ for lewd behaviour with many members of their workforce."

Mistress Capel looked dismayed. "Why, Jonas insisted they came to him with good characters!" she exclaimed.

"Characters given them by their kinsmen, I'll be bound," nodded Hal.

"Possibly, I regret I am not familiar with all my late husband's acquaintances, but stay—here is Mr Langley come calling. He was a companion of Master Benton, we're you not, sir?"

"I knew of Master Benton," Julius Langley corrected her swiftly, "for this was many years ago, when I was but a callow youth, visiting the town with my father before the war. I doubt he knew of my existence."

"Dear Uncle Edmund," sighed Sophie. "I wonder what he would make of Chawcester today?"

"I believe it is as it has ever been. As I understand it small market towns are much the same everywhere," said Hal.

"Not in the New World, they are not," said Julius Langley with a laugh. "Chawcester would pass as a bustling metropolis in the Americas. Why, I travelled to Jamestown once and felt quite giddy from the number of horses and carts I met up with." This was said with a wry, comical smile and had the desired effect of making not only Sophie, but also Mistress Capel giggle, so that Hal, who had been marking the strain showing in both their faces was forced to feel a sense of obligation to the man, for managing to banish, if only for a short while, the anxiety which vexed their minds.

"Then you'd not care for London these days, Mr Langley," he said in more cordial accents. "The volume of wheeled traffic has become incredible, and the sneak thieves and footpads incorrigible."

Langley smiled in reply. "It was ever thus, I suspect. I recollect my father shaking his head over it on his return from London before the war. No doubt my grandfather did so, too."

"At least in his day many travelled by boat. The Thames seems ever awash with craft, but this is no time for reminiscing. I regret, Mr Langley, that my esteemed brother-in-law has stepped out to a nearby tavern in pursuit of further information, and I cannot vouch for his return at anytime soon. May I assist you by suggesting he waits upon you tomorrow forenoon at your own abode?"

"I am, like you, staying at The Greyhound," Langley replied swiftly, "so if it would suit Danvers to visit me there at that time, I'd be obliged."

"I am certain he would be happy to do so," agreed Hal. "He and I are well acquainted with the Inn, as we have used it frequently in better days, when it was run by our esteemed hostess."

With this pointed dismissal Julius Langley had to be

satisfied, and he was soon seen out by a servant. Hal recounted to Sophie and Susanna in more detail all he'd learned from the farmer and his wife. Then when they had discussed it again, decided he'd best seek out Justin at The Greyhound before he fell in with the newcomer.

Chapter Fourteen

Sophie and Mistress Capel continued with their tasks, while discussing which carriage would convey guests to Westwood after the wedding, but they were soon interrupted by the sound of heavy footsteps on the stairs, then Adam's face came round the door.

"Is is so?" he cried in shock. "Is what the boy says true? Jonas Capel is dead?"

"Oh, thank Heavens! You are back from Elmley Park," Sophie exclaimed. "Yes, it is true, Mistress Capel found him this morning."

"Killed so the lad said," Adam continued in shocked tones. "Cordelia has gone off to see the baby is safe, even though the girl said he was sound asleep in his cradle."

"Yes, I looked in on him just before Hal arrived back," said Sophie. "The baby was his usual bonny self."

"Where is Sir Henry? What has he to say to this? Susanna, I am very sorry this trouble should be brought upon you." He hastened across the chamber to envelop her in a bear hug. "What does Sir Henry say?" he repeated as Mistress Capel, sobbed softly into the folds of his coat.

"It seems difficult to establish exactly what has happened, but Hal suspects foul play. Phillipe, Doctor Douay, is still unsure as to the cause of his death."

"But how did he die?" Adam asked in confusion, as if unable to take in the enormity of what had occurred. "Presumably there wasn't a knife in his heart, or the marks of a man's hand about his throat?"

"No, neither of those," shrugged Sophie shaking her head. "He was just—dead."

"Just dead?" Adam repeated the words uneasily, his handsome face marred by a deep frown. "Was there a forced entry to the house? Was it a robbery? Had he caught the thief out?"

"No," said Sophie. "Nothing was taken and no robbery. He was just found dead in his bed."

"Dead in his bed," Adam repeated the words, his grave voice echoing his concern. "Why that must mean those in this house are suspect!"

"Yes, and no," sighed Sophie. "Mistress Capel had left the door unlocked lest you, Adam, and Cordelia should take it into your heads to return early. She knew how uneasy Cordelia had been about leaving little Basil with his nurse overnight, and she thought you might be here before first light."

"Well, thank God for that much mercy anyway!" Adam exclaimed. "At least you and Susanna aren't the only ones under suspicion!" He smiled down at his step-mother. "You are pretty sharp, Susanna. I had the greatest difficulty in stopping Cordelia from returning with Sophie and Hal last night. Thank Heaven Phillipe Douay had given her a sleeping draught, when she began suffering with night terrors after Basil's birth. I poured a little of it into her wine, she slept like a baby, and awoke feeling so much the better for it."

"Yes," said Sophie slowly. "Which means, of course, Adam, you have no witness to your movements last night."

"Me?" he asked blankly.

"You and Jonas Capel quarrelled loudly yesterday morning and half of Chawcester heard you," Sophie reminded him. "Now by the time that nosy maid Sukey, has finished telling everyone, the other half of the town had heard all about it care of the gossips."

"Why should I kill Jonas Capel?" Adam cried, exasperated by the truth of her observation.

"To be revenged upon him for his insults, or for his treatment of Susanna. Who can tell what another may think?" she replied helplessly.

"Am I truly under suspicion?" Adam asked appalled, as he suddenly saw the danger he was in.

"No more than Susanna or I," she replied with a sigh.

"This is all stuff and nonsense!" Adam grew more angry, "I can see Susanna might be under suspicion. His lack of consideration for her is common knowledge, but you, Sophie? That is just malicious gossip!"

"Recollect my bridegroom died on our wedding night only last year, and Sir Henry's wife died shortly before that," she replied quietly. "Hal has said nothing, but I can see how very anxious he is."

"This is all nonsense just Chawcester gossip!" cried Adam angrily, suddenly seeing her point. "I dare say there are at least thirty people who would be happy to see Jonas Capel dead!"

"Unfortunately, a great many fewer people had the opportunity to kill him," remarked Hal, entering the chamber. "I beg pardon for walking in on you, Mistress

Capel, but your maidservant was nowhere to be seen, so I took the liberty of ascending to your parlour, to point out, Adam, that the windows are open and your voice can be heard almost as far as The Greyhound!"

Adam shot the windows a glance then hastened to close them, whilst Sophie went to open those which looked out over the garden. "There, that is to the good, for there is a breeze from the river," she remarked, in an attempt at cheerfulness.

Hal looked round at the assembled company, his face grave. "I don't have to remind you all to keep a watch on your tongues, because Sophie has just done so, but I do have to remind you how the slightest remark can be twisted by those who have a mind to." He hesitated, and then added reluctantly. "I am not sure what is afoot here, whether it is merely the foolishness of the natives, or a malicious campaign by someone in particular, but Justin reports all manner of wild rumours are in circulation about Capel's death, and regardless of whether it was a natural death or no, the speculation as to *who* his killer is is rife!"

"But surely it was a natural death! He was not an old man, 'tis true, but he never struck me as being robust," Adam remarked, as Cordelia, satisfied her son was safe and well, entered the chamber. "Why Susanna, you've often said how he was forever ailing with a headache, sniffles or the ague!"

"There is no reason to suspect it wasn't a natural death," agreed Hal, as Mistress Capel nodded, with a sigh. "Other than the fact that he was not a man universally admired by anyone, it would seem. Cordelia, my dear," Hal continued, turning to her swiftly. "What do you say to removing to Westwood with young Basil? The air there is more agreeable for the baby. And the town is very noisy. Sophie could go along with you—"

"I will not leave Susanna, Hal," Sophie interrupted him quickly, before the bewildered Cordelia could reply. "No more will I run and hide."

"Sweetheart, none suspect you," he replied advancing on her and catching her hand to draw her close, whilst Mistress Capel nodded at once that she should go.

"To please me, will you not go with Cordelia to Westwood, or to Mary, where I know you'll be safe?" asked Hal.

"Even to please you, Hal. I *cannot* abandon Susanna," Sophie replied, holding on tightly to his hand and looking up into his face earnestly. "Much as I love you, and want to please you by doing as you wish me to do, I cannot believe you would have me abandon a good friend to ease your fears, when I'd much rather be with both you and Mistress Capel. No, Susanna, say no more, Hal knows I would not leave either you or him."

He caught her to him, hugged her, and kissed the top of her head. "No, I knew you wouldn't, but thought it worth trying to persuade you. I would feel so much happier if I could get you all away to safety." He kissed her again and reluctantly released her adding: "When I got back to The Greyhound, Jack Hollingshead's servant had just arrived to say that the Cravens, Mistress Pauncey and her daughters and Hugh St John, who is Beatrice's betrothed and Nick Revesby are expected later at Elmley Park. It seems the men have formed a plan to leave the womenfolk in Mary's care, then come into Chawcester and take lodgings at The Greyhound. Jack says it was agreed between them that so many visiting at the same time would make Mary's life very difficult, and they wanted to be here in town, especially as young Hugh St John wanted to meet you, Sophie, to thank you personally for your kindness to Beatrice Pauncey."

"Well, if you think they will be comfortable at The Greyhound," began Mistress Capel. "You know I would by far prefer you all took up residence here."

He laughed. "But for the fact of laying our heads on pillows at The Greyhound, we seem to spend all our time with you Mistress Capel, and very comfortable you make us, too, but I am anxious that the strain on you is too great. I would that I could take you to Westwood, but it would be very remiss of me to flout the law, which says we must remain here until the facts of Capel's death are established to the satisfaction of that law."

"Which, as law abiding citizens, we all agree to, but for the fact that it might take Sambourne a month to discover who killed Jonas Capel, if he ever does," sighed Sophie.

"That is why we shall do it for him," insisted Hal swiftly. "We are to be married within the next few days, so we have only that much time to discover who killed Capel, and bring the miscreant to justice."

"Put like that, it is but a simple task, Sir Henry," said Adam wryly. "What would you have us do?"

"If I cannot persuade the women folk to go to Elmley Park, then I must ask that they do not go about the town unaccompanied," he replied promptly. "Mistress Capel, I beg you won't take this amiss, but I want you to remain here, so that it might be thought you are under house arrest by the population at large, and so

lull who ever did kill Jonas Capel into a false sense of
security—if indeed he was killed—and it is not just a
rumour put about by the foolish. However, until Doctor Phillipe Douay can come to a conclusion as to how
Capel met his death, we must all do out best to discover what is afoot here. Cordelia, you will not want to
leave your baby, so you can keep company here. Adam,
do you have any former acquaintance in the town who
might be able to give you information? Those who used
to sup ale at the tap in The Greyhound, perhaps?"

Adam looked thoughtful. "Those I'd trust are few and
far between, but there is the odd one or two, perhaps."

"It would seem quite normal for you to seek them
out, and ask after their families," said Hal, thoughtfully.
"It might well be seen as a politic gesture, from one who
has much improved his status in their eyes, perhaps?"

Adam nodded. "Perhaps—although equally, with
Chawcester folk, it might be thought I've come back to
parade my good fortune. One can never tell how it may
be seen."

"It is a risk we have to take," Hal agreed, nodding.
"It is always difficult to say how folk will respond. You
could be welcomed with open arms, as Justin expects
to be, when he traduces my good name at The Ring o'

Bells, or it could be your former acquaintance won't have heard of me."

"Not heard of you? Sir Henry, why, all Chawcester knows of you," said Mistress Capel who did not quite follow the conversation. "Wasn't there such a to-do when 'twas heard that you were off to visit the King at Whitehall? And that were nothing to the fuss when you returned from France to join your uncle at Westwood."

"Was there?" Hal sighed. "Yes, no doubt there was a lot of talk and precious little of it to my benefit I'll be bound."

"The gossip was mixed," Sophie smiled at the recollection. "It ranged from your being a returned exile, full of fancy foreign ways, dressed in French clothes on the one hand—to a young hero come to help his uncle, on the other."

"Which tells us everything about gossip —wildly inaccurate and deeply prejudiced," returned Hal swiftly.

"Yet essentially, the truth," grinned Adam. "Don't I recall you telling me of the dashing young man dressed in the height of fashion, who had come to help his uncle, Mr Westwood, and one day take his place at the Petty Assizes, Susanna?"

Mistress Capel blushed. "I believe I may have done,

Adam. Good Heavens! How long ago it all was, and how foolish is makes me seem!"

"My dear Mistress Capel, we all appear foolish every day of our lives. So much so that I wonder the good Lord has any patience with us at times. So that is agreed is it, Sophie? If you won't go to Mary at Elmley Park, you women folk must all stay within this house for the better part of our time here, or if you must go into the town, you'll take either Adam or I as an escort?"

"Yes, or I could take the boy Francis with me," she agreed reluctantly.

"No, Sophie, you'll not take the boy with you," said Hal firmly, "Adam or I, or at a push, Simon Craven, or when they arrive, Jack Hollingshead, or even Nick Revesby, may be your escort. Although Nick, is too easily led in my opinion, his admiration of you appears to know no bounds."

"Why, Hal, you sound as if you are jealous!" Sophie cried in mocking tones. "True Nick is young and dashing, but he is devoted to Bella."

"Indeed he is, but it would seem all our acquaintance from that part of the world are fulsome in your praise, regardless of the reckless nature of your behaviour," returned Hal, half-laughing, and aware as he spoke he was but adding fuel to her remarks.

"Now that I find hard to believe," she retorted. "Next you'll be saying Jack Hollingshead thinks me a pattern card of virtue."

Hal sighed wryly. "According to Guy, Madeleine Hollingshead is in despair, for Jack has refused to countenance any of the matches proposed for him by either herself or my Aunt Margery. It seems he has announced he is looking for a bride with some spirit."

"They will quarrel constantly," Sophie said bluntly. "Jack might think he wants a bride with spirit, but if he had one he'll instantly set about trying to master her."

Hal smiled. "Perhaps that is the attraction," he suggested. "Either way, Jack's marriage plans can be shelved until a more convenient date. It is our marriage that is to be accomplished at present. Mistress Capel, I hope you will not be too discomposed if our acquaintances call upon you? I suggested we hold a meeting here a little later in the day. There are things we need to discuss in privacy, which alas, is just not to be had at The Greyhound."

"Indeed, Sir Henry, I shall be honoured if the gentlemen call. I'll away to discuss dinner with Cook."

As Hal began to protest Sophie said, "No, Hal, let

her go. Believe me she is much better occupied. It gives her less time to dwell on her fears, and feeding gentlemen has been her life's work."

❧

A short time later Adam announced he'd take a stroll down to The Greyhound to see Jem, the groom, whom he knew well from when he and Susanna ran the Inn. He turned under the arch into the yard, in the wake of several visitors, and made haste to seek the sanctuary of the stables, were he hoped to find his former acquaintance. "Jem," Adam nodded to the man as he ducked his head and followed him into the stables at the rear.

"Mr Blackwell," replied the groom with distant politeness.

"How are you, Jem? And how is you sister Janet?"

"Aye, her be good enough," he replied gruffly, " 'Tis that there lad o' hers that is trouble."

"What, young Joseph? Why, I thought him a bright lad," said Adam frowning. "He had such a way with beasts, just as you have, Jem."

"Aye," the groom nodded gloomily. "I had him lined up to follow on from me, so as I could keep an eye on him, but he's had his head turned, that's what."

"His head turned? By a lass? Surely not—he can only just be out of short coats!" exclaimed Adam.

The groom chuckled, as was Adam's intention. "Nay then, he's seen thirteen summers, aye, and would nigh on reach your shoulder, I'll be bound! Nay, 'tis no lass, least ways I do surely trust not. No, 'tis the crowd he's fallen in with. Them as live down the back of the moorings, hard by the river. Janet is that put about by it all."

"I am sorry to hear you say so. Your sister, Janet is a good woman. She deserves better. Can nothing be done?" This was said with such kindly interest, that the groom's stiffness relaxed.

"Aye, well, truth to tell, we don't know which way to turn. You know well, as how I've stood like a father to the lad, Master Adam, since his father that scoundrel left Janet to fend for herself," he confided. "I was all for giving the lad a good beating, but you know Janet's soft heart. But 'tis spare the rod and spoil the child, to my thinking. I don't know how many beatings I had off my father, when he used to come home drunk night after night."

"Aye, I remember it well, Jem—and how you never saw a penny of your wages," agreed Adam. "But I don't know that a beating would help in these circumstances. Likely he'll just get all the more defiant, and Janet would be more greatly distressed. She is fond of a growing boy. I remember well how she used to feed me up with her oatcakes."

Jem chuckled as some of his anxiety faded while talking to Adam. "She used to marvel at how many oat cakes you could pack away. 'A growing lad needs plenty of fodder,' she used to say, and I reckons her oatcakes made you the man you are today."

"Indeed they did, and I'd like to call on her to show her my son, if she wouldn't object."

"Wouldn't object? She'd think Christmas had come early!" he cried in delight, at this kind attention to his sister. "She's been bending my ear ever since word broke you were back from the Eastern Counties, asking if I'd set eyes on you, and wanting to know all the gossip about your rich French wife."

"My wife is as English as you or I, Jem. She just had the misfortune to be abandoned in France by her father, who was killed—how we are not too sure, but it seems possibly in a failed attempt to get the King back home—although it sounded to me more likely in a tavern brawl. Either way he left her at a nunnery in France as a baby and never went back for her. Sir Henry discovered her when he was searching for his baby brother."

"Aye, we heard tell of some of that outlandish tale, and how Sir Henry brought her back to England, and set about finding her kin. It seems he be a fine, upstanding gentleman, do Sir Henry. Not many would have taken the lady in as he did.

"You are right, Jem, and you can imagine how grateful I am personally to him for bringing Cordelia home, and what's more, forgiving us for our runaway marriage. His aunt had organised a match for her, but Cordelia was too unused to life outside the cloister to be happy with it, and Mistress Sophie guessed we would suit better, and so she helped us."

"Aye, I'll be bound she did," the man chuckled. "Mistress Sophie and her ways are well known in these parts. She be a caution, she do, but a sweet lady and never too proud to stop to talk, neither—just like you Master Adam. And Janet would be that pleased to see your lad, if your wife don't object."

"Cordelia would be delighted to meet any who have helped me in the past. Though whether Janet will be so happy to meet young Basil is another question. The lad has such lungs on him, as you wouldn't believe."

"Do 'ee now, do 'ee?" the groom chuckled in delight at the thought, shaking his head. "You just wait until I tell Janet as how your wife will be calling with thy lad! She'll turn out the cottage from top to bottom, so she will. She'll be that pleased to have the lady visit."

"Cordelia wouldn't want her to go to a lot of trouble," said Adam quickly. "Recollect she was raised in a small nunnery and is not used to fancy ways. She says she's had more to eat here in the last few years, as she had in the previous sixteen."

"Aye, poor lass! Starved her did they, the Frenchies?" cried the man shaking his head

"I think it was more the plainness of the food she was thinking of," said Adam hastily. "The nuns were very good to her, she says, even though her father never paid them a penny for her keep. She was very pleased Sir Henry made the nunnery a handsome gift when they left. But that is just like Sir Henry, he always does the pretty! And those nuns never forget to write to her regularly. They even sent beautifully-worked clothes for little Basil, when he was born."

"Aye? Well, they be women of God after all then," replied the man, still shaking his head over foreign ways. " 'Tis nice to think they've not forgotten your little lass."

"Nor she, their kindness all those years," said Adam. "Jem, I've been thinking as we speak, and I am wondering if perhaps when we leave, after Sir Henry's wedding, we should take Janet's young lad Joseph with us."

"Master Adam?" Jem asked looking up quickly.

"Well, if you are concerned about the company he keeps here in the town, perhaps a spell in the country might be the place for him. If he is half as good with beasts as you are, I could well use him on the farm—and it would keep him out of mischief. It is a grand place the Old Manor. I've been working on it for a bit now, and I am getting things straight, but I could do with a lad to help. It looks like I might have Sally Rose's lad, too. He's another who needs keeping out of mischief. And you know, a bit of responsibility might be just what young Joseph needs. They'd be company for each other, and you can be sure I'll take great care of both of them."

"Why, Master Adam, you make me ashamed of myself. I've been having such black thoughts," cried the man. "I been thinking here's Master Adam, back from the East and never set foot in the town as raised him, now he's got a fine fortune and a new wife! I should have known better. Of course you'd be working at getting your old place back in working order again."

"It's taken some work, I can tell you Jem! It were in a sorry state, and I can't abide how folks let things go. It isn't anything like Elmley Park, and no doubt my father would be turning in his grave to see me struggling behind my own plough, but needs must, until better times come."

"Aye, and you were never one to be afraid of hard work, Master Adam, not from a little lad, you weren't."

"No, praise the Lord I've a strong back and a good right arm, and I wasn't raised to fancy ways. But, tell me, what do you say to these rumours running in the town about Mistress Capel?"

"I say they are wicked lies, Master Adam, and so I tell those who come slinging mud about," Jem replied.

"Are there many of those folk, Jem?" Adam put the question quickly.

"A fair few, and not one without an axe to grind. Those who were refused ale on account of their drunken ways, those who never dared set foot in the place and were jealous of her success—aye, and those who were glad to see the back of that grasping husband of hers, so they be slinging mud first, to get their accusations in, so to speak."

Adam nodded, "Aye, so we thought, but this could turn nasty, Jem. Sir Henry is growing anxious. Now he wouldn't want you to run into trouble. He knows you have to live in this town and it's a place which has long memories, but it would be a great help if we knew the names of any trouble makers, and the reasons for their discontent."

The groom looked wary, glancing about the deserted stable. "Walls have ears, Master Adam," he muttered.

"Aye, I dare say they do," he agreed, "but if you could think about it, and perhaps when I come to visit Janet with my wife and baby, we can talk again?"

Then as another groom entered the stable, he added, "Well, I am pleased to see that hock of my mare has less heat in it. Thank you for your care. I quite thought I'd have to hire another to go to Sir Henry's wedding."

"I heard tell as how there were to be a fancy carriage procession back to Westwood Hall such as Chawcester is never like to see again," the other man muttered.

Adam frowned, "I expect there will be two or three, to take the ladies back from the Abbey," he agreed amicably. "Mistress Armstrong from Elmley Park, Sir Henry's sister, has offered my wife a seat in her carriage, and no doubt Sir Henry's aunts will travel in one too—and the bride and groom—not to mention a few of the guests. How else would the older ladies travel?"

"Much as other folk do, on their own two feet," suggested the man with a shrug.

"It is plain you aren't a married man," observed Adam. "Walk several miles through the dusty lanes and ruin their finery? Why the men's ears would be afire!"

Jem gave a chortle of laughter at the thought, and after a few seconds, the man reluctantly joined in, so that Adam could make good his escape and return to Mistress Capel's house.

Chapter Fifteen

The following day Margery smiled at her newly arrived guests with some satisfaction. These were the sort of people she was proud to welcome to Westwood. So much more satisfactory than some of the people Hal habitually invited to his table. She was fully aware that the world was a different place these days but she, for one, was happier with the old ways.

"I do trust you are not too fatigued by your jollifications the other evening, Mistress Elgar?" she asked graciously.

Mistress Elgar smiled a tight smile. "Thank you, ma'am, I did not find myself so overburdened with partners, but it was a very pleasant occasion."

Margery glanced to Kate and Jane, and then to Madelaine Hollingshead, a little disconcerted by the reply. "Were there insufficient partners then? Surely not, I was under the impression my niece, Mary, had invited half the county."

"No, there was a wealth of men to dance with," replied Madeleine, glancing uneasy to her protege. "But you know how it is at such an event. Often in the melee it is difficult to secure the best partner. One has to perhaps, be a little less nice in one's notions, and dance with everyone."

Kate looked up from her mental calculations of what had to be accomplished that day. "Yes, in the country it is generally so," she agreed, giving their guest a kindly smile. "As a rule the wheat separates from the chaff naturally."

"I am greatly relieved to hear it," replied Mistress Elgar with some hauteur. "For one who led me out in a dance was a great, lumbering fellow, a farmer of some sort, one supposes, who had no skill at dancing, and even less at conversation."

"Adam Blackwell," sighed Aunt Margery recognising the description. "Yes, not entirely the best partner for you perhaps, a but good man."

"Adam always finds it difficult to be at Elmley Park," said Jane, rising to the defence of one who was considered almost family. "Elmley Park was Adam's family home. Unfortunately it was lost to them in the war, when those rascally Puritans stole it from his father, who was injured fighting for the King. Adam was but a boy at the time, and he still feels the loss greatly. I suppose it is only natural that he wouldn't be his usual cheerful self when he considers that, in a previous time, he would be master of a great house, instead of the smaller manor he now inhabits with his wife and child."

Madelaine turned to her companion and explained, "Adam married my kinswoman, Cordelia Sandys. You recollect me telling you the story of how she was lost in France for the greater part of her life? Indeed, none of us even knew of the existence of a child of my husband's cousin, Basil Sandys. As a family we were on opposing sides during the war and all connection was severed between us. Cordelia's mother, who I gather was the daughter of an impoverished Royalist supporter, sought refuge with the nuns when her husband did not return. Sir Henry found Cordelia quite by chance, when he was seeking his youngest brother, who had also been abandoned in France, after Sir Henry's step-mother died in childbirth."

"Yes, I do recollect the sorry tale, ma'am, and how you lost valuable land from it," nodded Mistress Elgar.

"Well, yes, in the beginning when I received the letter from Mistress Kingscott, I must confess, I was a little less than pleased by the outcome of events, but now that we know Sir Henry better, and have come to love Cordelia, we are happy that she has found joy with a good man," said Mistress Holligshead, looking uncomfortable.

"It was a difficult time for you, Madelaine," said Margery, swiftly. "I remember when I wrote to you, although our acquaintance was slight, I knew enough of your character to realise you would want a wrong righted. Hal—Sir Henry—is so inclined for justice that he takes actions which occasionally ruffle feathers. None was more amazed than I when he returned from France after his wife Libby's tragic death. Then, to be followed within days by an acquaintance escorting Cordelia and his baby brother—for their nurse, who had been sent with them, fled. They were left to take ship from Calais and fortunately both are stout characters, so no harm was done. They arrived safely and in the weeks which followed, we began to search for Cordelia's kinsfolk."

"Which was a good thing for us all, Margery, for thanks to Sir Henry's actions we have become friends," said Mistress Hollingshead. "We have gained a cousin we never knew existed, and she has happily married the man of her choice, thanks to the intervention of Sophie. Jack and I had it in our minds that a match with Cordelia would be a solution to the problem she presented, but in the end she found happiness with Adam Blackwell. And Mr Blackwell and Jack are now in agreement over the land Cordelia owned, so 'all's well that ends well,' as the poet says."

"It is very gracious of you, Madelaine, to call Sophie's actions intervention," said Margery with a sigh, "especially when a better name for it would be havoc."

"I think we all recognise that Sophie has the very best of intentions, though she does create havoc—and it does give Hal the opportunity to put everything to rights," laughed Kate. After a moment or two, Margery and Jane joined her, whilst Madelaine nodded ruefully and Mistress Elgar looked at them in some amazement.

"I am sorry, my dear, you must think us silly women. If you don't know Sophie, you'll never understand," continued Madelaine Hollingshead. "Sophie is—"

"Sophie!" Kate concluded.

A little put out by the warmth she sensed for the absent Sophie, Mistress Elgar replied, "I met Mistress Redwood and she seemed quite ordinary to me. I thought her rather pretty, in a somewhat rustic sort of way."

There was a stunned silence, for the barb in her reply was unmistakable. Then Margery said carefully, "Yes, she is a lovely young woman, not just in the conventional way, but in that her sweet face reflects her nature. She does her upmost to help others as Kate says, occasionally precipitating a little confusion and chaos in the process, but always she has the very best of intentions. I must confess when I first became acquainted with her I didn't value her as highly as I do now, but in these past few months it has become plain to me she is the perfect wife for Hal, in that she brings him joy past measure."

Kate clasped her sister-in-law's hand and bestowed a smile upon her. "We are so happy that they will finally be married, and so cross, Madelaine that you should have witnessed their agreement to marry, whilst we did not."

Madelaine smiled at the recollection. "What a Christmastide it was! Good Heavens, we were near dead on our feet from worry and a lack of sleep, by the time Sir Henry arrived. Then came the grief for poor Mistress Pauncey and her daughters. It was a house full of people too, for my poor daughter Cathy, to deal with, for the guests had all been gathered to witness Bella's wedding.

Her groom was an older man, with a child for each year of his previous marriage. It was plain that Bella was not greatly enamoured of the match, so it was no real surprise when she and Rosalind went missing. The weather was dreadful, so we were out of our mind with worry, as you might imagine, Margery. Just when we were all at our wits end Jack insisted we needed Sir Henry, who was staying with Margery at the home of her step-son. I knew that in spite of their differences, Jack had come to admire Sir Henry. None of us wanted to intrude upon him, but Jack insisted Sir Henry would solve our mystery and so it proved. He is such a clever man, and so determined. I think everyone of us was delighted when he claimed his reward before us all, telling Sophie he had us all as witness to her agreement to marry him, and that he would hold her to it."

The amazement of Mistress Elgar was obvious in her voice, "She had to be coerced into marrying him? Sir Henry is a wealthy man—of some standing I understand."

"Yes, he is all that, but he is also the best of men," said Margery. "I have known many fellows in my time, but Hal *is* the perfect gentleman."

"I know Jack models himself upon him," agreed Madelaine. "Only the other day he had a problem with one of his tenants, and I heard him say to his steward, 'No, give him a little longer. It has been a hard time for him, as Sir Henry would say.' "

"That is quite a tribute, Madelaine. I shall tell Hal of it," said Kate. "He is always so patient with his people, as he says he's known what it is to be hungry, without a home, or hope for the future and that is not something he would wish upon another man."

"My brother, Sir Henry, went into exile with my father, Sir Francis, and they were many years in France." Jane explained to Mistress Elgar. "We younger children were much more fortunate and came here to Westwood, to a loving family."

Mistress Elgar finally showed some interest in the conversation. "France? At the court of King Louis? Now there is a place I'd like to visit —Paris or even London! They say it has become quite modish these days!"

"I really couldn't say. I cannot abide the noise and bustle," replied Margery, a frown furrowing her brow. "Hal says it gets worse on each occasion he goes there."

The envy was apparent in Mistress Elgar's voice, "Does he often go to Court?"

"Only when summoned by the King," replied Kate, taking out a tablet, and consulting it, with a view to beginning what would be for her a very long day.

"The *King* summons him—personally?" asked their guest in awed tones.

"Well, I don't know that he does it personally. I imagine he has a secretary, but Hal knows it is a command he cannot refuse. He was summoned there only the week before last, about this trouble with the Dutch, and the burning of our fleet. He was of the court in exile, of course, and he and the King are of a similar age. His father, Sir Francis, was often charged with tasks for the King." Margery frowned suddenly, glancing to her sister-in-law, as if the notion had only just occurred to her. "Hal seems to continue the tradition."

"Well, Kate, do not hold back. Give us our allotted tasks," cried Madelaine, who had observed Kate's glances, and noted the anxiety flitting across her face. "You do not imagine we came to Westwood to be idle, do you? I know from experience these sort of occasions don't organise themselves."

Kate smiled ruefully. "Indeed they don't!" she agreed. "From tomorrow we have several guests arriving, indeed, aren't Mr Craven and your daughter and their little ones coming with Bella and Nick Revesby from Elmley Park?"

"I don't think they will arrive any time soon," replied Madelaine. "Mary—Mistress Armstrong—was eager for them to remain there, so they could get to know each other, and she wanted to keep the number of children underfoot here to a minimum."

"Rather a pointless exercise," observed Jane dryly. "Bess arrives with her boys today, and Hetta and Will thereafter, so poor Aunt Kate will be driven to distracted in attempting to sooth Will's fears for Hetta, and Hetta's fears for her baby."

"The tragedy of Hetta's child-bearing is ever in both their minds," said Kate, smiling at her forthright niece. "They only require reassurance. Neither she nor poor Will have had an easy time since their marriage."

"I do believe Sophie mentioned how tragedy seemed to stalk them. Didn't your Hetta's husband lose both his parents in the plague?" Madelaine asked sympathetically. "He was struck down by it, too, yet recovered."

"Thanks to Hetta's devoted nursing, yes," agreed Jane. "That was when she lost her first baby. There have been two more lost since then, which makes her very uneasy."

"If only she were more calm, she would carry the child full term," insisted Margery. "Are you aware of the glad tidings from my step-son Tom Kingscott, Madelaine? His wife Molly has just given birth to a son! A seven-month child it would seem, but Tom writes that he is thriving."

Madelaine smiled. "Indeed we were all pleased at the news, and had we been able, we would have visited to bring you tidings of his progress, but Tom was anxious that Molly should have complete rest, although she herself had told me that she has never had any trouble bearing children."

"Tom is so delighted by the news. When his son died after a fall from a horse, his daughter-in-law remarried a kinsman taking his grandson away with her, and he felt his world had ended. Now here he is just a few years later, a father again," said Margery, her delight obvious. "No doubt his daughter-in-law will permit his grand-son to visit now."

"It is ever thus in families," agreed Madelaine with a sigh, casting a doubtful glance to Mistress Elgar, who was extolling the delights of a visit to London to Jane's distracted ears. "So, Kate, you do not say, what is the campaign plan? I often think this part of a wedding is the most enjoyable, provided there are enough hands to attend to it."

"Jane has very kindly turned over her part of the

house—in the old wing that was damaged in the war, and only recently made good—to those with children, as it has access to the garden, so their high spirits can be exercised in the fresh air," said Kate. "So I would advise any of a nervous disposition to avoid that area of the house. Other than that, I need to discuss the final arrangements for the feast with Cook, and do something about this choir that Hal asked me to arrange."

"Choir?" Madelaine looked at her rather askance. "Do you mean a church choir?"

"No, for recollect they are being wed at the Abbey, which has a very fine choir. No, this is all to do with a jest between Sophie and Hal. It seems when he asked her to marry him he quoted a poem to her, in which the lover describes the delights he has to offer." Then, as Madelaine cast her another odd look, Kate grew flustered. "Indeed it is no more than some flummery or other he has in mind. I am not sure, but I think he had been reading something by Marlowe, so Sophie said."

"Christopher Marlowe?" All at once there was a trace of a Puritan about Madelaine, and Margery raised her brows in a disapproving manner.

"You recollect, Margery, how Tom is ever adding to Hal's books." Kate turned to her in appeal. "He gave books as gifts at Christmastide, when Hal stood as his groomsman."

"Indeed I do, but I thought he had given him another of Shakespeare's plays? Yes, I recollect now, he was having a jest with Hal and gave him *The Taming of the Shrew*. I remember him saying it might serve to aid him in his courtship," nodded Margery.

"And Christopher Marlowe's poems," said Kate, "I remember him reading them to us. I rather think you had dropped into a doze, Margery, but it is that lovely one about singing melodious madrigals."

"Well, I suppose there had to be something good about the fellow Marlowe, but reports made him a drunkard at the very least," said Margery haughtily.

"If not worse," agreed Madelaine.

"Hal wants me to arrange some maidens and shepherds to greet their arrival back from the Abbey. You know they are to all come here in a cavalcade? Well, if it can be arranged he wants shepherds and maidens, singing bright madrigals to welcome his arriving guests."

"Melodious Madrigals, surely?" asked Madelaine.

"No? Oh dear, I don't think this is going be possible!" Kate shook her head anxiously, thinking if she couldn't even explain it, how could she possibly hope to arrange

all Hal had asked her to do. Desperately she turned to
them in appeal, "It seems Sophie thought the poem was
called *Singing Bright Madrigals*, and so they call it that
now. They have a foolish jest between them, you know,
as lovers do?"

"Yes, Kate, old though we undoubtedly are, we do
recollect having a foolish jest with a lover," smiled Madelaine. "Do we not, Margery?"

Margery looked taken aback, and then the faint-
est of smiles curved her thin lips. "Yes, yes I do—not
that Thomas Kingscott had any truck with the likes of
Christopher Marlowe," she added hastily.

"His son Tom must take after his mother then," said
Kate. "For he is such a kind and gentle man. Your husband, Thomas, terrified me, Margery, on the one occasion I met him."

"Thomas did not have an easy manner about him,
but he was a good man at heart," said Margery loy-
ally. "Also, Kate, you met him when he was worn down
by the fighting. To him it was a terrible thing that our
country had come to such a pass. I do believe the dreadful war took us years to get over," she added with a sigh.

"Indeed it did, Margery," said Madelaine. "Jack's father took no injury from the battles he fought in, but

the heart seemed to go out of him. I recollect his return after Worcester. He was in essence a broken man. We may have fought on different sides, but in a war between one's own people, nobody wins."

"It was *such* a long time ago," sighed Mistress Elgar, bored by the turn of the conversation.

"And nothing to do with this joyous occasion," agreed Kate swiftly, making a mental note to keep her from Margery's company. "Well, if you would truly like to assist me, Madelaine, Jane and I are about to walk to the village to hear the church choir, and see if they would like to be our shepherds. It is a pleasant day, so perhaps Mistress Elgar might might like a little fresh air, too."

"If Mistress Hollingshead is to accompany you, Aunt Kate, I would be better employed in overseeing the chambers being prepared for Bess and her boys. Perhaps, Mistress Elgar might like to take a turn in the gardens? It is a lovely day," said Jane.

Mistress Elgar looked as if wandering about the gardens might be more to her taste, and so, in short space of time, they set off, leaving Margery to discuss menus with the cook and await the arrival of Bess.

The day was indeed fine with a gentle breeze, and the

walk gave them time to speculate on the likelihood of an untrained village choir meeting Hal's requirements.

"Besides which," sighed Kate, "what shall we do for maidens? I do wish I had kept my tongue between my teeth, but Hal looked so harassed, that I asked what I could do to help him. He seemed to have an impossibly long list of things to accomplish, all of which have probably been abandoned in the face of Lawyer Capel's untimely death."

"Well, what will be, will be," Madelaine said comfortably. "I dare say they can be married without a choir of maidens and rustics."

"Oh, indeed," agreed Kate, "it was just something Hal mentioned in passing, but he takes such great trouble for others, and his wedding to Sophie is so important to him. You wouldn't believe the odd things he has bought her, and the wonderful jewels. There's a rope of pearls the size of pigeon's eggs, and amazing emeralds and rubies! He is so kind and patient with us all, that I feel I would like to do this for him—and for Sophie. I am aware it is something and nothing, but one's desire to accomplish any of his expressed wishes is always uppermost in my heart."

Madelaine acknowledge her words with a nod "Yes,

you are right, Kate, they both worked tirelessly trying to find Rosalind. And tried even harder to make Nick Revesby and young Bella happy. If we can do some small service for them on their wedding day, it is only fitting. Let us turn our minds to it, Kate! I am sure we can find a few young people from the village to sing."

Chapter Sixteen

Justin found Hal still closeted in the parlour with Sophie and Cordelia. When the nurse brought Cordelia's baby and Mistress Capel joined them, he took this opportunity to take Hal to one side.

"You have discovered something?" Hal asked in an undertone, as the women exclaimed in delight over the child.

"I hardly know, yet there is something curious more than anything. I also ran into your French friend, who says he will wait upon you presently," he replied, softly.

"Come, we will do better in Capel's office, if you have anything of import, then we can look out for Phillipe." replied Hal. The women were so engaged in admiring the baby, that their absence wouldn't be noticed.

Hal lead the way down to the cramped chamber and was about to close the door on eavesdroppers, when

Adam appeared at the foot of the stairs. "Is this a council of war?" He asked the question lightly, but Hal could see the look of concern in his face.

"We've come to talk privately, away from the ladies for fear of alarming them—and because Doctor Douay will be joining us presently, hopefully with news of what killed Capel. Come in and be welcome, Adam," he replied cordially. "Every additional mind helps. I must explain that Justin and I rode out to see the farmer who employed Betty the servant who died, and her cousin, Sukey who is still a maid here. The farmer's and his wife's discourses gave us pause for thought. And Justin, who continued making enquiries at a local tavern, has come to report his findings. I am going to confess at once that I have not got any further forward in my investigations."

"I imagine you have been more agreeably occupied," said Justin, in an attempt at pleasantness. "I, however, took my supper at The Ring o' Bells."

"You'd not be out of place there," Adam nodded his understanding.

"No," agreed Justin. "I saw many familiar faces and picked up a lot of gossip and rumour, some of which is vaguely unsettling, but perhaps you can enlighten us,

Adam, as you lived in Chawcester for many years. Is the local population usually so very militant and vocal, or is there some agency behind it? I mean, I know the average fellow loves nothing more than a good grouse about almost anything, but are they usually so volatile?"

"Certainly this has always been a town for rumour and surmise," replied Adam thoughtfully. "Its situation on the river, and being close to the border, means there is a constant coming and going of strangers. When Susannah and I ran The Greyhound we were at the hub of it, so to speak, but it rather passed over my head most of the time. I suppose I had so little experience, I thought all towns were so. Then when Cordelia and I were at Bickmarsh Hall, we saw so few people, the only things which concerned us were on the estate. It is only now as we have come back here, that I am struck by how much tittle-tattle exists on the streets."

Justin nodded. "I am trying to stand back and make a clear judgement. I am obviously more familiar with Adamsholme, and believe me that can be a viper's nest of scandal-mongering at the best of times. You must remember how it was when I was accused of murder?"

Hal nodded, a little bemused, for Justin had seldom voluntarily mentioned that time, or acknowledged his part in it. "Indeed I do, it was the same when my uncle was murdered, and my father held in the prison at Maucester. I am afraid most of my experiences of towns like this were in France and the Low Countries, and I had—unconsciously, I suppose—expected those of England to be superior. Hark, is that Phillipe's step? Adam, would you mind opening the door?" Adam did as he was bid, ushering in the physician.

Hal waited as greetings were exchanged, before saying, "Phillipe, we are discussing the rumblings of trouble in the town, but we'll hear your findings first, if we may?"

"Indeed, Sir Henry, I shall be glad to do so," replied the French man bowing to each in turn, before taking the seat indicated by Hal. "I have spent a great deal of time in examination of the body of Master Capel, and found some curious medical anomalies, but these had no bearing on his death, which I am still inclined to think may be irregular. I can, however, give you no proof of this. All I can say is that I have an instinct that he was somehow killed, but cannot say how."

Hal looked disappointed. "So we cannot say categorically one way or the other?"

"No, *mon ami*, I would that I could."

"Well, in that case, Susanna can have nothing to fear," said Adam in obvious relief. "If you cannot find proof, then it must be a natural death."

"One would like to think so, *monsieur*," agreed the physician. "Certainly I shall make a report with this, my final conclusion."

"And yet?" asked Justin, as there was a short silence.

Phillipe smiled thinly. "Yes, *monsieur*, but without any proof one way or the other …and yet." He shook his head. "I daresay a dozen people die every day, who might have been killed. It would have been good in this case to have said he had some disease, if only to have scotched the rumours that abound in the town."

"Ah, you have heard rumours, Phillipe! What is being said?" Hal cried at once.

"It is the usual nonsense, Sir Henry. I have never known a death without there being speculation as to who is likely to benefit. Idle heads make for much malicious gossip. It has always been and will always be so."

"Are we to deduce then, that all towns are hotbeds of rumour and speculation?" asked Hal anxiously. "I know London is, but that is a city, and the capital of our country, where the rich rub shoulders with the poor, and it seems to me the devil takes the hindmost.

But surely, out here in the country, in the heart of England, there should be more order? Are we to decide this is nothing more than a little local difficulty, which will fade as soon as something more interesting appears?"

"I might be inclined to agree, Hal," said Justin.

Adam interrupted in a soothing manner: "I wouldn't be surprised if it wasn't all forgotten by the end of market day. To my mind the townsfolk often manufacture a drama, to have something to gossip about around The Cross and in the taverns. However, there is definitely something afoot that centres around you, Sir Henry. I haven't been able to discover who or what is at the back of it, but I've heard your name mentioned, and then someone nudges the speaker, and they all glance my way and begin to discuss the barley harvest, or whether the river will flood if the rains come down from Wales."

"What can I have possibly done to offend them?" Hal frowned. "Sophie insisted they'd be pleased if we were wed in the Abbey, and other than the wedding, I have little to do with this place."

"And therein lies the problem, most likely," said Adam, thoughtfully. "In most circumstances you seldom set foot on the town unless it is the Sessions, or you are attending a special service at the Abbey. The locals would say you set yourself too high above them." He blushed suddenly. "I mean no offence, Sir Henry. I was thinking out loud."

"I think it is about time, Adam, we acknowledged the connection between us. You call me Hal, as most of my family do," said Hal mildly. "And I take your point, but Sophie uses the services here in town, and thanks to her agency, so do my sisters and Aunt Kate."

"Yes, but that is only what they would expect, and they don't carry the prestige of a title. To have Sir Henry patronise their wares is a totally different thing," remarked Justin cynically.

Hal looked surprised. "But I have never purchased anything locally," he protested. "When I first arrived, my clothes were those my father had purchased in Paris at, as he told me repeatedly, great expense—most likely to the tailor, for I doubt my father ever paid a bill there. Since then, I usually buy any requirements in London."

"Indeed," agreed Justin affably, as the others chuckled. "In fact, if you didn't, they would be greatly disappointed, for you bring them all the latest in fashion, though that doesn't stop them grumbling that you are too high to stop your carriage in the High Street to buy a pair of stockings."

Adam chuckled again, interrupting Hal's indignant reply that he only ever rode in a carriage if he was escorting his aunts. "No, Sir H—Hal, that is a Chawcester saying. I don't know if I understand these people myself. I suspect you have to have been born here and go back at least five generations to become one of them, but they don't like outsiders, not truly. They'll tolerate them, and possibly eventually respect them, but you'll never actually *be* one of them."

"That is not something I aspire to," replied Hal tartly. "I merely want to get married in the Abbey, in accord with Sophie's wish, without the accompaniment of a full scale riot, if that can be achieved."

"As usual, Sir Henry, you have gone to the heart of the problem. Can we control a riot if need be?" Justin's mockery had the slightest edge to it, and made Adam glance to him warily. Adam exchanged glances with the physician, as all became aware of the tension between the two. They waited for the next attack from Justin.

Hal was deep in thought and did not reply, then asked suddenly, "You said it was the ones you didn't recognise which gave you pause? Which ones?"

"Ah, I had forgotten how nothing ever escapes you. You may be tempted down a byway, but you always return to the point," replied Justin.

"Never mind the flummery, it ill becomes you—tell me!" Hal snapped. "You know me as well as I know you. I must find the truth, but must you *always* plant barbs as you go?"

Justin looked faintly piqued, yet embarrassed at this acute assessment. "My patron, Cousin Eunice tells me to succeed I must amend my manners to resemble yours, Sir Henry. Thank you for the salient reminder."

Irritation flickered across Hal's face. "Plain dealing, Justin! I am Hal. You are Justin. This is Adam. This is Phillipe. We are kinsfolk—friends. So no more sparring and no more jibes—just the truth."

Adam waited for the explosion, but none came. Justin sat silently for a few seconds, and then said mildly, "I only hesitate for fear I am making something of nothing. I said, did I not, that it was the ones I didn't recognise, that gave me pause?"

"Strangers?" Hal asked.

"Indeed, and not just those coming in for market day. I asked Tansy, the wench who waits at the tables at The Ring o' Bells about them. You understand I eat there occasionally, when I have cause to be in Chawcester and know the wench, who is not one to gossip, in the usual run of things. She, like me, was puzzled by their accents."

Hal's attention, which had been distracted by Justin's barbs was caught again. "Oh, from really a good way out of town, not just from one of the villages?"

"Yes, we speculated upon it, idly, as one does with those one has but a passing acquaintance with, for I did not want her to remark on it to them, and perhaps put them on their guard."

"And your conclusion?" Hal asked quickly, as again Justin hesitated.

"Tansy insists they are foreign—and not in the usual local tradition, which says everyone not born in the town or surrounding villages must be foreign—but truly so, in that they come from another county."

Adam grinned. "Chawcester can't pronounce worse than that. To not be born within sound of the Abbey bells means you are forever an outsider."

"Where did they come from?" Hal asked, irked by the senseless local jest and becoming more certain something was afoot.

"Further west was the conclusion we came to, on account of their accents."

"Welsh?" Hal asked sharply in irritation.

"No, it wasn't an accent so easy to pick up as Welsh. She said, 'Not West Country, real foreigners, further away than Somerset. She said 'possibly from Devon that land of legend.' "

"I am sorry, but does this have any bearing?" asked Hal impatiently, as Adam chuckled, becoming convinced this was just part of a local jest. "What if they do come from Devon? How does that affect us and the situation here?"

"I do not know this Devon place, but why should it be of such interest?" asked Phillipe, looking puzzled.

"It may indeed have nothing to do with it," agreed Justin in a soothing manner, "but I got into conversation with two young men—in an idle sort of manner, you understand, as one does—and they had some interesting, but puzzling things to say."

Hal's attention was caught. "I am looking for something out of the usual run of things, Phillipe," he explained. "So, Justin what was so out of the ordinary?"

"Well, it was more what they got *wrong* rather than anything else," replied Justin as Hal exuded impatience. "For example, they claimed to be servants of guests coming to the wedding of Sir Henry Westwood, servants of those folk from the Eastern Counties."

"With Simon Craven or Jack Hollingsworth?" Hal asked in surprise. "Jack has been at Elmley Park since the beginning of the week, and has brought only his groom and his mother's maidservant. I know because he told me so, saying he felt they intruded upon Mary and Guy. And Simon and Nick have only just arrived!"

"Indeed, Bess has acquainted me with the arrangements for your wedding on several occasions, and I have a dread feeling at some point I shall be obliged to pass muster, and know all the intricacies of what appears to resemble a military campaign. I merely observe these men were not good servants, in that they couldn't quite get the names of their employers right. They spoke of Sir Simon Hollingsby, and a Mr. Revington."

"Hollingsby and Revington?" Hal asked quickly. "But they surely couldn't get names of their employers that wrong? That is most suspicious!"

"Is it?" Adam asked. "Perhaps they are newly taken on? Sent ahead perhaps to—no, it doesn't make any sense, does it? If you are a newly-acquired servant the very first thing you learn is your patron's name, if you wish to keep your position."

"Indeed, the very first thing you learn is how important your master is, for his status enhances yours, in the world of a servant," agreed Justin. "It struck me that if one were to arrive in a small town, and wished to pass without comment amongst the locals, claiming to be the servant of a bona fide visitor would give you access to information and allow you to pass unhindered amongst those who are genuine guests at the wedding."

There was an abrupt silence, as they digested this information, then Adam asked bluntly, "But why?"

"Ah, that is another question," agreed Justin. "One perhaps Hal can answer?"

Hal opened his eyes wide and looked bemused. "Nothing springs to mind," he replied slowly.

"Yet you have been involved in solving several murders in recent years and seen the murderers bought to justice. Does it not occur to you that you might in due course, become the target of enmity? I think a link with the Eastern Counties and that business you were embroiled in at Christmas might have some bearing," said Justin, a shade sourly.

Hal replied dismissively, "There was no murder, so we could not invoke the law. It was a matter settled between us privately, to save a mother further grief."

Adam interrupted quickly, to avert a quarrel between Hal and Justin. "I have been talking to my old friend

Jem at The Greyhound, who was head groom when Susanna ran it, and is still there today, although he says he is getting too old and suffers with the rheumatism. He says that the town is much the same as ever, afire with gossip—what with the barley being good and your wedding—and that for the most part it is nothing but idle chatter and a sprinkling of malice. Few folks liked Jonas Capel, it seems. He was said to be mean and underhanded, and it would appear that Jem, at least, has an affection for Susanna. I can't deny there is a little muttering about her mixing with her betters, but I expect they say the same about me, too. Sophie they regard with a mixture of awe and pride, as most of us do, I suppose," he added, with a grin for Hal. "I felt there wasn't malice intended, just the usual idle gossip." He hesitated, adding uneasily, "I think for the most part, Sir—Hal, they hold you in high esteem, with just a tinge of envy."

Hal frowned. "I do not understand why they consider me at all—other than as a Justice of the Sessions."

"Then you are being naive," Justin insisted sharply. "When you formed part of the Court-in-Exile, did you not discuss the King?"

Hal frowned over the question. "My father constantly

monitored the comings and goings amongst us, though to call us a Court-in-Exile makes it sound so much more grand than it was. To me we were more a loose-knit mob of wandering soldiers and ne'er-do-wells."

"But the affairs of the King were discussed?" asked Justin.

"With endless tedium," agreed Hal.

"And you are their Lord of the Manor, therefore everything you do is of interest to them."

"I cannot see it," replied Hal. "Granted I have given cause for gossip over the years. I can see that my return to be my uncle's heir, and my marriage to Libby would have been of mild interest, but since that date I have tried to keep myself to myself."

"And you have failed in the most singular manner in doing so," Justin retorted, with laughing disbelief. "Do you really think that your rescue of Sophie, and the duel you fought was keeping a low profile?"

"No," Hal admitted tersely. "I could hardly fail to know we were a nine-day-wonder, but since that unfortunate occurrence I have tried to pass unnoticed as much as possible."

"Do you truly think that every man-jack doesn't know you go regularly to Court, and that you are often in the

King's presence? That you are one of his inner circle?"

"No, for I am not," Hal said firmly. "I am merely one of his sounding boards—one of many men all over the kingdom who bring him news of the countryside. The King is no fool. He knows his father's greatest errors were a result of his lack of understanding of his own people. His intention is that he should always have his finger on the pulse of his subjects. If there is any dissension in any part of his realm, he should know of it, almost first hand—and the cause—that the matter might be redressed immediately and concord be restored."

Justin looked surprised at this information. "Does he think that can be achieved?"

"He is determined upon it," replied Hal firmly. "The King is very aware he rules by the agreement of the people, not by any right. To know what is in the hearts of his subjects therefore, is of vital importance to him."

There was an abrupt silence as they digested his words. "Do you tell me that you report to him the doings of this part of the country?" Adam put the question slowly, as he tried to keep pace with what he was hearing.

"No—and yet—yes—in essence," he glanced to Justin who had given a small, abruptly silenced hiss. "It is nothing so definitive," Hal continued slowly, "and most certainly nothing sinister." He glanced to Adam, who was frowning and Phillipe's bland expression. "As I have said, he has no desire to lose touch with his people, as his father did. He does not consider he has a God-given right to rule this country. He understands he can only do it with the people's consent, but he also knows he can only do so if he has accurate information. Hence he has a network of men whom he has cause to trust, who periodically give their opinion on what the country is thinking. 'Gossip from the shires,' he calls it."

"And probably pays as much heed to it," snapped Justin.

"Never make the mistake of under-estimating the King," Hal insisted seriously. "He is a highly intelligent man. He has studied the history of our country, and he listens to the opinions of everyone he sees. He may not always agree with them, but he heeds their words. Just because he chooses to rule in an easy—to those who don't know him—light-hearted manner, does not mean he doesn't know exactly what is afoot all about him."

"He has fooled me," cried Justin cynically. "I see a pleasure-seeker who would rather dally with the Castlemaine and Francis Stuart than attend to his ministers."

"You see what you choose to believe," replied Hal swiftly. "You consider the return of the monarchy a backward step, so therefore it must be an inferior rule to that of Cromwell."

"I don't know that I approved of Cromwell anymore than I do the King," replied Justin candidly. "I approve of the rule of law, and any who seek to uphold that law. Therefore I support any who can do so, provided it doesn't include involving us in wars every few years."

"No doubt the King would be interested to know how you would deal with the Dutch," replied Hal swiftly. "I'll beg leave that I may take you with me on the next occasion I go to Court, so you can give him the benefit of your advice."

Phillipe spoke quickly before they could come to blows. "Pardon my interruption! As a mere Frenchman, might I suggest you postpone your interesting political discussion to another time, whilst we deal with the matter in hand?"

Hal hid a smile. "Indeed, Phillipe, as a 'mere Frenchman,' you may, for I suspect this is a discussion which will be at the heart of our relationship for years, Justin."

"The discussion of the local situation is more pressing in the short term," agreed Justin, shortly. "Adam, you are very quiet, yet, you lived here for many years. Are we sitting on a powder keg?"

"Possibly," he agreed thoughtfully, "but I don't see anyone approaching with a taper. Chawcester loves a drama. It is meat and drink to them, but they don't truly care for a drama to escalate. In my opinion we all had enough excitement these past years."

"So, where does that leave us?" asked the doctor, glancing from one to the other. "Me, I am a stranger here, and a Frenchman. I am also a physician, and so have some armour, but I also have a family, which it is my duty to protect."

Hal nodded. "Yes, that has been on my mind, too, Phillipe, but that is a problem easily solved. Should there be any chance of danger, then you must be called to Westwood, on account of my aunts' health, and as it is so close to the wedding, it would be natural for you to take your wife and child with you and remain there."

Phillipe nodded, pleased his friend had his best interests at heart, then added wryly, "I see, *mon ami*, you think to tip us—as your saying goes—from the frying pan into the fire!"

Hal smiled. "Better the frying pan of Aunt Margery's disapproval, than the fire of a riot, I think."

"Are you sure?" asked Adam with feeling. "I think I'd sooner face a riot."

Hal laughed. "Come, Adam, you are making great progress with Aunt Margery. Not only are you and Cordelia settled well within her circle, but you have produced a son and heir, and are making good your estate."

"So, what is our conclusion?" Justin asked, impatient with such light heartedness. "Is there likely to be trouble before the wedding? Can we hold it back, do you think, until after the 'great event'?"

Hal shrugged his shoulders, not deaf to Justin's sneers. "I think we can wait a little longer before turning tail and fleeing," he replied coldly.

Justin nodded. "That being the case, I am for my bed. If matters are not resolved by tomorrow, I will take up residence in my new abode, which has the merit of being at the heart of the town, so that I may monitor the coming and goings."

Chapter Seventeen

The next morning Hal entered the parlour overlooking a pretty garden to find Sophie with Cordelia, her sleeping baby and Mistress Capel.

"Mistress Capel," he said rather loudly, as if in warning, "Constable Sambourne has called bringing further news, I fear, of another accusation levelled at you—one of witchcraft."

"Witchcraft!" Sophie cried, as all three women stared at him in various degrees of dismay.

"I am sure I don't need to impress upon you, ma'am, the gravity of such a charge, and the necessity of dealing with it at once, before the content becomes common gossip on the streets of the town. I therefore propose to bring Samborne up here at once with your accuser, and let him confront you with this nonsen—matter."

His look widened to include both Sophie and Cordelia. "I don't know if either of you wish to remain here.

Would you rather absent yourself from this interview?"

"I'll stay!" Sophie interrupted him sharply. "I cannot believe you would even give credence to this, Hal!"

"I am Justice of the Peace, Sophie. I am obliged to look into all sorts of affairs. My personal views must be put aside until the case is examined in the prescribed manner."

"I'll remain, too, ma'am, if you will permit," added Cordelia quickly, guessing Adam would wish her to.

As Mistress Capel gave her a tremulous smile of thanks Hal said, "I applaud your loyalty, my dear, but a word of caution—it is widely known that you were brought up in the Catholic faith by French nuns, and to the stupid and the ignorant that is often considered suspicious. We must ask ourselves if it would not be more sensible to stand aside in this instance and not court trouble."

Cordelia replied firmly. "I am a practising member of the Church of England, the faith of my father and his before him—and have been so ever since my return to this country of my forefathers. I shall be taking communion with you all at your wedding, Sir Henry."

Looking frightened, as the true gravity of her situation began to sink in, Mistress Capel said, "If Mistress

Cordelia is minded to stay with me, Sir Henry—and you have no qualms about Mistress Sophie remaining, I would be most grateful for their support."

"Indeed, ma'am," he replied quickly. "I agree the more we present a rational, united front, the better for you, but I am obliged to give everyone a hearing."

"I would expect nothing but justice from you, Sir Henry," she replied, trying to stop her voice from shaking fearfully. "I am obliged to you for your kindness."

Hal nodded and with a quick reassuring smile for them all, went to call down the staircase to the constable waiting below, "Sambourne, pray ascend, and bring Mistress Bracegirdle with you, if you please."

"Alice Bracegirdle!" Mistress Capel exclaimed in fury. "I might have guessed it! As silly a—" She broke off abruptly as Hal shook his head at her, then the company waited in silence as Constable Sambourne stomped panting up the stairs in the wake of Mistress Bracegirdle, the wife of a leading merchant of Chawcester.

They entered the room to an icy silence. Mistress Bracegirdle, a plump, over-dressed goodwife of the town, took the seat Hal indicated, whilst Sambourne took his station by the door.

"Now," said Hal, "I want it understood this is a

purely informal discussion to determine as to whether Mistress Bracegirdle is desirous of bringing a charge of witchcraft against her neighbour Mistress Capel or not." He turned to Mistress Bracegirdle, "Before we begin, ma'am, I must emphasise to you the gravity of your charge, and explain to you that it is this very gravity which means we must discuss it at once. I do hope you understand?" Then, as the woman began looking apprehensive he added, "In that case, pray tell us, in your own words, if you please, the tale you relayed earlier to Constable Sambourne."

The woman, a stout, self-important contemporary of Mistress Capel, wriggled uncomfortably in her chair. "Well! It be like this. We were a talking, Susanna and me, one day a few weeks back—"

"A few weeks back?" Hal interrupted as he sat down at the table and took up a pen to make notes. He looked up, his quill poised over the ink pot, and asked, "How many weeks?"

"Well, now, it were—it were about the time the news of your wedding broke, Sir Henry—or no, perhaps it were a day or two later. When did we meet up at that there apothacary place, Susanna?"

"Last Wednesday fortnight," replied Mistress Capel,

after a moment. "I'd gone for some headache powders for Jonas, and you said you needed a salve for your itch."

"Aye, that be it," Mistress Bracegirdle agreed, her cheeks flushed, and she looked put out by her neighbour's indiscreet description.

"I see," nodded Hal gravely. "Last Wednesday fortnight, the first week in July?" Then as she nodded uncertainly, watching him commit her words to paper, he added: "Tell me, why did you wait until now to report so serious a matter as a suspicion of witchcraft?"

She looked stunned, clearly not expecting such a question, "Well, Jonas Capel hadn't died until now."

Hal nodded, and made a note of the day and date, and her disingenuous reply on the sheaf of papers spread out on the table before him. "Pray, proceed with your explanation, ma'am," he said coolly.

The woman grew flustered at this officious command. "Well! It were when Sambourne were asking if anybody knew anything about Susanna and Jonas Capel," she said quickly, tripping over her words, as three pairs of feminine eyes glared at her flushed face with varying degrees of dislike and resentment. "I felt it were my duty to tell him of what had passed between us."

"As is your duty to relay it now, ma'am," Hal agreed.

Mistress Bracegirdle, having been given sanction to gossip, hurried on. "Well, I asked Susanna what were amiss with her, to be at the Frenchies place. And she said, it weren't her, she was as happy as a grig, being as Mistress Sophie were back at Westwood Hall and about to be married to you, Sir Henry, and that Mistress Blackwell had safely given birth to her baby boy." She paused to nod in Cordelia's direction, with a simper, and was rewarded by a cold state in return. "Then Susanna started on saying about how Capel was driving her to distraction with his vile temper," she gabbled hastily, wishing to have the conversation, which was veering out of control, over and done with. "And we agreed as how men as a race were cross-grained old miseries—saving your presence, Sir Henry—and I told her 'as how Bracegirdle were stricken with the gout, on account of the port wine he drinks with Churchwarden Thomas, and how I had the itch—' "

Mistress Capel interrupted angrily, "And I asked if it were that new handsome young journeyman of yourn, who'd given it you, and put a spring in your step!"

"If you please, Mistress Capel, allow me to ask the questions of the witness," said Hal in a reproving tone, anxious there should not be an unseemly furore.

As the merchant's wife fixed her erstwhile friend and neighbour with a glare Hal asked, "Was there anything further said, Mistress Bracegirdle?"

"Aye," she replied, taking a deep breath in preparation for launching her assault. "I said as how 'it were common knowledge that Capel were tupping her girl Betty, and the cousin, too, like as not,'—and Susanna said 'she knew that, she weren't deaf nor blind and that Capel should watch his step, or she'd settle him once and for all!' "

"I see," replied Hal, pausing to make an exact note of her words. "Did she indicate in what manner she envisaged achieving this end?" he added absently, his attention on his words.

The woman wrinkled her nose in a puzzled manner glancing to the constable, who shrugged and shook his head looking confused in reply.

Hal glanced up, surprised at her hesitation, when she had been so voluble before, and seeing her incomprehension, re-phrased his words, "Did Mistress Capel leave the discussion at that—or did she say how she would stop her husband's seduction of her maids?"

The woman nodded her understanding, and paused for dramatic effect, her gaze sweeping the chamber to include them all. "She said—she said as how Mother Sandwell over at Biddington used to have such as would put a stop to his gallop! She said she'd put a powder in Capel's broth to keep him from lifting their kirtles and she'd teach him how he'd best keep his breeches on in future!" she announced in excited tones.

"I see," said Hal gravely, once again making a careful note of her words. He glanced up again, fixing the merchant's wife with a piercing look, then added, "And you took these words to mean—

"No, Mistress Capel," he interrupted Susanna as she started to break into indignant speech. "Pray let Mistress Bracegirdle continue. I shall give you the opportunity to speak yourself in a moment,"

Then as Mistress Capel fell silent, her face much flushed with agitation, Mistress Bracegirdle added in satisfied tones, "Well, I though as how she'd got a potion from the old woman to stop his wandering. But when I heard as how Capel were dead, just like that, without ever being ill and Sambourne were asking folks as how they might have heard anything, well, I thought what she said should be known!"

"Yes, I see," replied Hal with cold formality. "Thank you for such a public-spirited gesture—"

Mistress Capel interrupted furiously, trembling from head to foot with mingled fear and anger. "You know right well, Ally Bracegirdle, I meant no such thing! You evil-tongued old biddy! You knew I had no more intention of going to Mother Sandwell than I had of flying! You know full well that it were all said in jest!"

"Mistress Capel, pray keep silent," Hal said sharply, as Sambourne's eyes narrowed at these words, and Mistress Bracegirdle bridled at the insult.

He turned back to the woman. "Is this the sum total of your accusation, ma'am?" he asked directly.

"It is!" she replied defiantly, glaring at her neighbour. "If wrong has been done, I have a right to say so."

"Indeed, Madam, you do, if the law agrees a wrong has been done," Hal replied calmly. "This being so, I shall read your testimony back to you, that you may be sure I have not misunderstood your words, before you sign the affidavit: 'Mistress Capel, whom you met by chance on a visit to the physician's house in Chawcester High Street, announced her intention to you, of consulting Mother Sandwell, a local woman, commonly named as a wise woman, who has some knowledge of herbs, and who has recently been swum by some disaffected villagers as a witch. It is my understanding the woman is reputedly gone from this area, but previously was believed to have not only the power to supply potions to cure minor ailments, relieve toothache and procure the miscarriage of unborn children, but to also curtail the wandering inclinations of married men. Mistress Capel, you claim, said she would, or had, obtained one of these potions, from the said woman, which she would put into her husband's broth.' Have I transcribed your words correctly, ma'am?"

"Yes, I—I think so," she replied, rather flustered, by the long words and formal language.

Hal looked up to meet her eyes and fixed her gaze. "You do understand the ramifications of this testimony, ma'am?" he asked patiently. "You do realise you will be require to swear this to be the truth, on oath, in a court of law, as a true and exact account of what passed between you."

"Well, I might not—have the words—exactly," began the woman awkwardly, "but it were something like that, weren't it, Susanna?" she turned to her neighbour in appeal.

"It were nothing like—" she sputtered.

"Mistress Capel, you are enjoined to keep silent!" Hal interrupted swiftly, as Susanna grew angry again.

"Mistress Bracegirdle, I have your words written here. At this moment, they are just that words—an account of gossip between two goodwives of the town. However, once you affix your signature, this becomes a legal document, and the full force of the law rolls into motion. Are you desirous of adding your signature to this document? Or would you prefer to have a few hours to further consider the matter? I can tell you there is no great hurry. Dr. Douay has not yet finished his examination of the body, and early inspection has ruled out poisoning as a cause of death."

Mistress Bracegirdle looked surprised, "Oh! Sambourne's been saying as how Capel were surely poisoned by Susanna!"

"Plainly Constable Sambourne has better information than either Dr Douay or myself," Hal replied sharply as he glanced to the man coldly. "It would seem he also fails to comprehend his position as a minor official. Fortunately the law has a remedy in such cases, and it could well be that Mistress Capel can herself bring a case of slander against Sambourne. You had better report to me later, Sambourne, and explain how you come to be in possession of such important information and yet have failed to communicate it to me."

"I didn't say he was poisoned, your honour!" the constable protested, looking appalled as he turned to glare at his witness. "I just said it were odd, as how Capel upped and died like that!"

"What is odd is that an officer of the law has been gossiping and hastening to bring a spurious accusation with very little evidence against a recently widowed woman!" Hal glared sharply. "I shall be discussing your conduct with Keeble once he returns to his duties." Then, recollecting that it was unfair to berate one so lacking in mother wit, he turned back to Mistress Bracegirdle, but before he could speak, the constable interrupted again.

"If it please your Honour, I never said Capel were poisoned," he repeated quickly. "All I were saying was that this be the fourth husband Mistress Capel had taken. And they all seem to have met unfortunate ends."

"Unfortunate ends?" Hal repeated the words icily, well aware how insidious gossip like this was. "For whom?"

"Well, Sir Henry, there were him as owned The Greyhound, he were took first—"

"Wasn't that some years back?" Hal frowned.

"Indeed it were, your honour," cried Mistress Capel

in amazement. "Back when old Noll Cromwell won at Worcester, and the soldiers all came rampaging into town, looking for the Prince—King Charles as he is now. They drank The Greyhound dry, they did and Will—my husband at that time, William Deene—he were furious for he never got a penny for any of it!"

"Worcester!" Hal exclaimed looking amazed. "Back in 1650?"

"Indeed, and he were in his dotage then," Mistress Capel confirmed.

"Then there were the fine gentleman from Elmley Park, a Mr Blackwell, that she wed," interrupted Mistress Bracegirdle, with a snide smile.

"Blackwell were my husband for a good few years," said Mistress Capel, as tears filled her eyes. "Of all my husbands he were the best—and Adam will swear to it. We both did our best to wean him from the brandy."

"Then there were Jack Wooley, only the year before last," said Sambourne, nodding his head. "He were dead within six months of being wed to you, Susanna."

"Master Cresswell said he had the cough. Jack brought up blood, he did," cried Mistress Capel, as tears coursed down her cheeks. "I nursed him until the last breath left his body, poor man. I held him in my arms as he struggled to breathe his last. I loved Jack with all my heart."

"It didn't stop you wedding Capel though, did it? And well within the year!" sneered Mistress Bracegirdle nastily.

"No, it didn't!" snapped Mistress Capel angrily. "No, fool that I am, I believed all Jonas Capel's lies! When he said 'if only I'd wed him I'd never have another care,' I thought he meant he'd care for me, instead of which he was only talking about my money! That's all he ever cared about—my money!"

She turned to Hal, sobbing, "You know me, Sir Henry! You've stayed at The Greyhound when I was landlady there. You know I am not beautiful, nor clever like Mistress Sophie. You know I am just a silly woman who should know better—but that doesn't mean I don't dream of being loved! All my life I've been pulled that way and this. Married off at another's convenience, to man after man! I was in my thirteenth summer when my father was swept away in a flood. They didn't find him for three days. We were destitute, and there were ten of us, so my mother had no choice but to sell me off to the landlord of The Greyhound. It could have been worse, but he was a kind man, and didn't beat me. I nursed him for years right through the war, learning the trade, then when Adam's father won the Inn off him, I was happy to marry him, for he treated me like a lady, he did—and so too did my next husband, Jack. It broke my heart when he were took. We'd been wed but a few months and then I lost my baby. That's when Capel came calling. All smiles and so helpful, and I thought perhaps finally I might be able to find some happiness. But I was wrong, he didn't want a wife and a family. He wanted money—just money. So, yes, I've had four husbands, but I am a Christian woman, once the knot is tied, so am I, for better or for worse!"

"Pray, Mistress Capel, do not distress yourself!" Sophie cried, hurrying to her side. "Come, ma'am, this has been such a troublesome day. You need a period of rest and reflection. Sir Henry, have you finished with your questions?"

Hal glancing to Mistress Capel sobbing on Sophie's shoulder, nodded in resignation, and as they left the chamber, he turned to the constable and his companion.

"I need to make it very clear to you both, that this accusation is now part of the enquiry into Jonas Capel's death. You do understand that, don't you?" Then as both nodded mutely, their faces showing little comprehension, he added slowly, carefully enunciating every word. "This means the matter is now sub-judice, and neither of you may speak of anything which has been discussed here today—not to each other, or to any other person—except when this should come to a court of law. Everything you have said here today is inviolably confidential and I expect it to remain so. If I hear of any rumours of this matter abroad in the town, I will therefore know of their source, and either—or both— of you can expect a penal sentence, should that occur."

They both looked shocked at the gravity of his words, but once again they nodded, making haste to depart.

Hal followed them to watch their descent of the staircase, and then crossed the chamber to the window, to mark their progress down the narrow street.

"I do trust I haven't worried you, Cordelia," he said over his shoulder. "I fear in my attempts to contain a dangerous situation I may have appeared very severe."

"Yes, Sir Henry," she replied quietly.

"Obviously the ban on discussion doesn't apply to you. I know well I can trust your discretion."

"Indeed, sir," she agreed.

"I would that I could have a similar reliance upon Sophie and Mistress Capel," he added with a sigh.

"Would you like me to go and try to get them to understand your desire for discretion?" she asked.

"Do you think that could be achieved?" he asked candidly.

"I think if I tried to convey it, there might be less friction than if you do," she replied a little tentatively. "What is it you fear, sir?"

He glanced to her, his face uncharacteristically worried. "I fear mob rule, a riot," he replied succinctly. "I fear they may try to take Mistress Capel, much as they did that poor old woman they swum as a witch, and then we will all get caught up in it!"

She met his eyes then replied quietly, "Yes, of course! I'll see what can be done," before hurrying away to find Sophie and Mistress Capel.

Mistress Capel was attempting to trim the hat she intended to wear for Sophie's wedding with a hand which shook visibly.

"Do tell me Sambourne has gone," insisted Sophie as soon as Cordelia appeared. "I don't know how Hal has the patience to deal with such a fool of a man!"

"Hal *must* deal with him," replied Cordelia. "We must

deal with the office, whatever our feelings for the man.”

“I can’t credit the sheer malice of Alice Bracegirdle!” cried Mistress Capel, who was still angry and disturbed. “And all because Jack Wooley came courting me, instead of her. You know she’d made a play for Jack before she wed Alderman Bracegirdle?”

“I never knew Mistress Bracegirdle had a yen for Mr Wooley,” gasped Sophie in astonishment, as she paused to admire little baby Basil, who was gurgling happily.

“Well, he were widowed about the same time as she was,” sighed Mistress Capel, abandoning her hat in favour of the baby. “My Jack were a lovesome man, when all’s said and done. I don’t know what possessed me to think of wedding Capel after my Jack.”

“Loneliness is a dreadful thing,” replied Sophie thoughtfully. “Most likely, if you’d not been so sad, you’d never have thought to take Capel as a husband.”

“Probably not,” agreed Mistress Capel, with a sigh and a frown. “Although he were different before we wed. Why is that do you think? Was it something I did?”

“I shouldn’t think so. Did you quarrel often?”asked Sophie, as she sat and Cordelia began humming a lullaby.

"We quarrelled most days," said Mistress Capel with a sigh, picking up her maltreated hat again.

"What about?" Cordelia asked curiously.

"Money, mostly," replied Mistress Capel reflectively. "Capel were a regular skinflint, just as I told Sir Henry. He'd skin a flea, he would, for its hide and tallow."

Sophie chuckled, "Come Susanna, let me trim your hat. You'll never get it straight whilst you are in such a pother."

Cordelia frowned as Mistress Capel gladly surrendered the broad-brimmed hat and the recalcitrant feathers. "Why did you quarrel about money so much?" she asked. "Adam says you were left a wealthy widow when you sold The Greyhound. Did you give Adam too much money, to help us purchase our land?"

"No, Adam and I split it fair and square, as we agreed," replied Mistress Capel at once. "I tried to give Adam more, but for all that his father let money slip through his fingers, Adam likes plain dealing, so he does. He said if he found he were desperate for money he'd come back for a helping hand, but I knew he'd cut off his hand first, before he'd take help from anybody. Remember, I wed Jack that year, too. And Jack left every penny of his fortune to me, having no chick nor child of his own. I don't know the exact figures. 'Tis funny, I can reckon a bill of fare, but once it gets into big numbers my head gets all muzzy. But I knew I'd want for nothing all my days. That was when I was fool enough to fall for Jonas Capel's lies. He used to tell me the sums of money I had and that frightened me, so he offered to take care of it all for me. And then he said he probably ought to take care of me, too. Take care of me! Once we were wed it was plain he'd wanted nothing but my money! And then he started getting meaner and meaner. Why, he held me to account for every penny spent in the house, as if I were a servant! Sir Henry says he'll look into my finances for me to see I've not been cheated. He says Jonas might well have been charging me fees for the handling of my affairs, like the lawyer he was, rather than a husband. Thinking on it, 'tis most likely, for the more I saved, the less money there seemed to be."

"Sir Henry is most anxious, Susanna, that you understand how dangerous Mistress Bracegirdle's accusation is," Cordelia continued gently. "He has sent her and Constable Samborne away with a dire warning about gossip, telling them that if one word of this accusation gets out into the streets, he will send them both to prison, but I think he has little faith in their discretion."

"Samborne has no discretion," said Sophie bluntly. "He wouldn't even know what it means. And I know Mistress Bracegirdle will find it difficult to keep her tongue between her big horse teeth."

Mistress Capel gasped, and then began to weep anew saying, "My Jack used to say he'd sooner a mare to wife, than Alice Bracegirdle—or Alice Cowell, as she was known back then. Sir Henry is right, I know I must take care, Mistress Cordelia, but I am so afraid. I don't know what to do. Will they throw me into prison, do you think? I never gave Capel a thing, other than the powders Doctor Douay gave him for his headaches—and only when he asked for them, I swear. It were all banter. You know how it is with neighbours—you meet them somewhere, at the Abbey or in a shop—and you exchange the time of day, talk about the weather and the latest gossip. I know I complained about Capel. Well, he weren't a man you could could get close to, but I never meant him no harm. He just used to rile me so with his mean, penny-pinching ways."

Sophie abandoned the hat and came to hug her friend. "Do not worry, Susanna! Sir Henry will protect you. I'll not leave you, and neither will Adam. They'll not take you off to prison whilst we are with you."

"Sir Henry wishes us to go back to Westwood," said Cordelia tentatively. "He says he cannot vouch for our safety if the townspeople decides to take matters into their own hands."

Sophie nodded, "Indeed, you and baby Basil must go, Cordelia. It is the only sensible thing to do. I shall remain here with Susanna."

"No, Mistress Sophie, Sir Henry is right, everyone should go to a place of safety. Not that I think Chawcester would run mad. The folks round here, they might get drunk and break a few windows, but Capel wasn't popular with most people. It is right that you should go to Westwood with Mistress Cordelia."

Sophie frowned, "Susanna, if there's no proof that you had a hand in Master Capel's death, then there is no reason you shouldn't come too, surely? Then if things don't improve, I suppose we'll just have to be married at Westwood as Aunt Margery wishes." She gave a little sigh. "After all, it's the marriage itself that is important, not the wedding place. I just did so want to be close to Uncle Edmund and my parents when we wed."

Cordelia sighed, "At least you'll have some kin at your wedding, Sophie. Adam and I just had two servants, but it was still special."

Sophie smiled, "Yes, you are right Cordelia, the where isn't really important as is the ceremony itself. As long as Hal and I are married, that is the important thing. I just didn't want to be wed alongside Libby's memorial in the parish church at Westwood."

"From what I have heard of her, she would be wishing you both every happiness," suggested Cordelia.

Sophie smiled. "Libby was one of the sweetest people I've ever met. When things were bad after Hal left and went back to France with Doctor Douay, she protected me and wouldn't let any of the family censure me. She said that Hal must have had his reasons for going away, and that it was in no way my fault that he'd left. I felt she was the only friend I had at that time." She sighed. "An Abbey wedding was a lovely dream. One I've had in mind since I was a child visiting my mother's grave. I used to sit there and tell her how the bells would ring out joyously and the Abbey would be full of candles with the choir singing—and how I would marry a fine gentleman, who would love me, and keep me safe. I am so very, very close to achieving my dream!" Tears glistened in her eyes, then she shook herself suddenly saying, "How foolish of me!" and hurried from the chamber. ❧

Chapter Eighteen

Later at The Greyhound, as Hal sat writing a letter at the table in his chamber there was a hesitant knock on his door. Irritation flickered across his face, for he wanted peace to finish his task and dispatch it in case help should be need. "Enter!" he called irritably, then sat with his quill in his hand, waiting as the door opened to reveal the constable.

"Sambourne, is aught amiss?"

"No, Sir Henry, I escorted Mistress Bracegirdle back to her house as you bade me and I stressed your words, sir, that she weren't to gossip to nobody about nothing," the Constable replied, in ingratiating tones.

"And have you any faith in her ability to keep a still tongue in her head?" Hal asked impatiently.

The man's forehead creased as he tried to decipher the meaning behind the words, so, Hal was forced to translate suscinctly, "Will she keep her mouth shut?"

His brow cleared miraculously. "Oh, aye! Oh, indeed, she were powerful scared of your warning, Sir Henry! She said she won't mention nothing to a soul."

"That directive applies to you also, Sambourne. You understand that, don't you? You cannot discuss this with *any* other person."

The constable scratched his head in confusion. "How am I to ferret out what's going on then?" he asked after a long pause.

"Ferret out?" Hal exclaimed quickly. "No! We are in a difficult situation here, Sambourne. You may make discreet enquiries, as to the likelihood of Mistress Capel visiting the herbalist at Billington, but I very strongly emphasise the word discreet."

Again the silence, as the man looked more confused. "You want me to go tomorrow?" he asked hopefully.

Hal mastered his impatience with the man's slow wits asking, "Sambourne, what is our task in this town?"

"To arrest wrongdoers, and to bring them to justice—that be you," he replied promptly.

"Yes, that is our ultimate task," agreed Hal, "but before we do that?"

There was a lengthy silence as the man cast about in

his mind for the words which would bring him favour in the eyes of the Justice. "Remember to collect a cudgel?" he put the suggestion without any real hope.

"Certainly a cudgel is useful, when confronted by a mob," agreed Hal, "but surely not necessary if you are merely asking questions."

Sambourne shook his head. "You don't know them as live out at Riversmeet, just below the ferry," he replied, "They are trouble, they are! I allus take a cudgel, and I always take anyone who are game for a fight with me, if I am to go to Riversmeet.

"No!" the word exploded from Hal and the man took a step backward in trepidation. Hal took a firm hold on his impatience, and tried to speak calmly. "Listen carefully Sambourne! Our task is to keep the King's Peace. It is as simple as that. We—you and I and all other peacekeepers—are here to do exactly that. To make sure there is no trouble in the town and surrounding areas. Now, I know you are over-worked, that your superiors are absent, or in bad health, but that means we must work more effectively. We don't need to be running off after false trails and mare's nests, which exist only in the fevered imaginations of foolish females. We must deal with the here and now. Trouble—fighting in the town mostly—but if it is possible, you may ask questions of those you trust about the likelihood of Mistress Capel lately visiting the village of Billingham."

The man nodded slowly, working his way through Hal's words. His brow knitted again as he licked his lips and, casting Hal a doubtful look said, "You don't think she, Mistress Bracegirdle, were telling the truth then?"

Hal smiled, relieved he was beginning to see the light. "I think she is a lonely woman, who has little to occupy herself and she sometimes allows her thoughts to run off in foolish directions," he said with slow deliberation. "I cannot acquit her of malice at present, but I am certain she is jealous of Mistress Capel's position at the heart of events connected to my wedding. And as Mistress Bracegirdle is not, there is no doubt she thought to take Mistress Capel down a peg or two."

Sambourne nodded his comprehension thoughtfully. "Aye, she were full of malice about Susanna, which were odd, as I thought they were thick as thieves at one time! But then it were the same last time, when Jack Wooley upped and married Susanna—Mistress Capel, I should say. Mistress Bracegirdle were that sour about it all, sneering at them both Jack and Susanna."

"Ah, now you are starting to think like a Justice! You

begin to look behind what is said and done, for the reason it was said and done," Hal said with relief.

Once again there was the pause, as the man thought through the words, then his brow cleared, and a smug smile of satisfaction flitted across his broad face. "Aye, I can do that. Think like a Justice and look behind what is said and done."

"That's the idea," agreed Hal. "Don't take everything at face value. Look for the hidden meaning."

The man nodded sagely and said, "Hidden meaning," as he rolled the words around his tongue.

Hal had a moment of doubt, but was too anxious to get his letters written and sent off, so he put it aside and contented himself with asking, "Do you have that clear in your mind now, Sambourne? I am writing to my fellow Justices, asking for them to be ready to come to our aid if need be. I just require that you keep the town peaceful for the next few days."

"Aye, Sir Henry," nodded the Constable. "I'll keep the town quiet and think like a Justice."

"Good fellow!" Hal exclaimed, then had another moment of doubt, but thrust it aside as he took his leave.

❖

After Hal's correspondence was complete, he set off at dusk to return to Mistress Capel's house and take supper as bid. He followed his instincts, which had been fretting him all day, and turned to walk through the dark alleys behind the High Street, where the sun never shone. As he traversed the narrow back lanes he heard the scuffle of footsteps near the turn and was instantly alert, wary of walking into a trap. He stepped nimbly into a shadowy doorway, and glanced behind him. Nothing appeared to move in the shadows, but insidiously the sound of light footfall moved nearer. Then, a sudden break in the clouds revealed the sharp face of Francis, Mistress Capel's lad who ran errands and generally got under everyone's feet.

"Why do you follow me?" hissed Hal, as the boy jumped in consternation.

"Beg pardon, Sir Henry, but Mistress Sophie said I were to follow you, if you left the Inn alone," he cried.

Hal glared at him in disbelief. "Follow *me*?" he repeated in astonishment.

"Yes, sir, at a distance. Just in case aught befell you," he insisted in dismay. "She said if anything happened to you, I was to run back for help. If you please, Sir Henry, I only did it to—to—"

"Set her mind at rest," supplied Hal as the lad's face furrowed in anxiety, then cleared as the words, which had failed him were supplied. Francis grinned. "Mistress Sophie is such a good sort of lady," he explained. "When my sister got childbed fever she sent that there Froggie to her with physick, so that she were soon better, and didn't die like my other sister. She allus has a care for us servants—and she do worship the ground you walk upon. If aught befell you—her heart would break, so it would, Sir Henry." He uttered these words with a finality, which plainly showed they pleased him.

Hal laughed, slightly embarrassed at the ingenious reply, then remembering he was trying to pass unnoticed, put his finger to his lips. "As would mine if aught befell her," he agreed on an undertone. "So sauce for the gander, is good for the goose. I can see your days are to be filled by following either me or her."

The boy's brow furrowed again. "I am to follow Mistress Sophie, too?" he asked slowly, as sense hit him.

"Whither she goes, there thou goest," Hal agreed.

The boy grimaced. "Her won't like that," he observed candidly.

"True," Hal agreed affably, "but you wouldn't like my heart to break now, would you?"

"No, Sir Henry," he replied soberly. "For you are a great gentleman, who has a care for so many people. I reckon those as do, be lucky to serve you."

Hal suppressed a snort of laughter. "I see Mistress Sophie has been priming you. Come along then, if you are to dog me, stay closer and listen for any footsteps."

The lad nodded, and they set off at a fast pace until they emerged into a courtyard further down the High Street, then they hurried across to a solid gate in one of the high walls which surrounded it. Hal glanced over his shoulder and, reassured they were alone, turned the handle and entered another smaller yard behind The House of the Golden Key. He crossed the square then nodded to the boy. "Stay here and listen out for any sound. If you hear trouble knock on this door," he murmured in an undertone. "I might require your assistance presently."

After a few moments the door was opened by the physician, who took in his visitors at a glance. "Trouble?" he asked succinctly.

"Not yet," replied Hal affably, as he stepped over the threshold.

"Does the boy enter?" he asked glancing to him.

"No, he is there to listen," replied Hal, adding to the

lad, "Make sure you stay alert!"

Francis nodded, and Phillipe with a shrug, ushered his guest past the kitchens and into his back parlour.

"I have come to see if you have reached a conclusion about how Capel died. And to tell you I want you to go to Westwood, Phillipe," Hal announced without preamble. "I think it will be safer if you take your family. Give out the word that my aunt, Mistress Kingscott's health is giving cause for concern, and that your wife needs rest before her baby is born."

Phillipe raised his brows. "Hah, I forget, very little escapes your notice, does it?"

"No, I have a host of sisters who seem set upon re-populating the county," he replied with a grin.

"Why do you fear for us? I am a physician," asked Phillipe thoughtfully.

"You are also a foreigner. If this were a French town on the verge of trouble, who would they turn on first?"

"Foreigners and usually their traditional foe, the English," he agreed slowly. "But I am their physician. Only a fool turns upon a man who can cure what ails him."

"I would think that is one of the reasons you've not been troubled so far," replied Hal. "I am serious about this, Phillipe. Things could turn very ugly. I do also have some anxiety for my aunt and this is a method of my obtaining your covert opinion of her health."

Phillipe nodded. "On the other part of your mission, I must fail you, I fear, Sir Henry. I have examined Capel's body as best I can, but I can find no cause of death to suggest murder. It would seem he died because he ceased breathing."

"A smothering?" suggested Hal.

"Often in such a case there could be some colouring to the face, but there was nothing. I am sorry, Hal, I know it would be better for us all of we could announce a definitive cause, but there isn't one."

"The truth is what we require, Phillipe, if the truth is that he just died, then he just died."

"Unfortunately the truth will not stop the rumours, or the trouble which is threatening," said Phillipe wryly.

"No, and such rumours as abound suggest a hidden agenda, although at this stage I cannot see either the who or the why," replied Hal thoughtfully.

"Which in itself is unusual," agreed Phillipe. "I find the locals usually transparent in their dealings."

Hal nodded, looking weary. "I am hopeful of getting Adam to take Cordelia away and Sophie, too."

Phillipe laughed, "Come, Hal, do not stop at that!

Why not ask the moon to leave the sky and go to West-wood?" Then as Hal smiled he added, "If Mistress Blackwell would permit, there will be room in my carriage for her and the baby, too. For it would be better if Master Blackwell remained. He is of the town and understands it well. As for Mistress Sophie, there is absolutely nothing you could do to persuade her to abandon Mistress Capel, so don't waste your time on it, *mon ami*. She will stay here to make sure you are safe."

"And I would be so much more at ease if I thought *she* was safe," replied Hal.

"Oh, I have misunderstood the matter, have I?" Phillipe cried in mock astonishment. "Your intention in marrying Mistress Sophie is for a life of peace and domestic ease?"

Hal nodded in recognition of his companion's wit. "I will get Adam to bring Cordelia and the baby here as quickly as possible. You'll want to be on your way as soon as you are ready."

"One moment, Hal. I have a duty to the people of this town, too. Do not forget there has been talk of the return of last year's plague. Indeed, I am surprised you don't use those rumours as a reason to shut the inns and put a ban on meetings," said Phillipe quickly.

"I have not done so because this is England, and such a move, without a single dead body, would probably cause the riot I am so anxious to prevent. We fought a long and bitter war, Phillipe, to prove that high-handed methods must only be applied in times of extremis."

Phillipe shrugged his shoulders. "In France they would bring out the troops, shoot a few men, then all go to the tavern. However, we are not here to discuss politics. I have sick people who depend upon me. I must give it some thought."

"Then do so at once, Phillipe, for time is of the essence," replied Hal sharply. "Who amongst those seeking your aid could not manage without you?"

Phillipe, who had raised his brows at Hal's tone, took time to review his patients. "At this moment, I have several females of the town, including the creature who has accused poor Mistress Capel—who I trust will no longer be seen in town after she made her foolish accusations. She sent for me and sought my advice earlier, about the terrible pains in her head and breathlessness."

"Is she sick?" asked Hal swiftly, his attention arrested.

"Not to my mind, more filled with anxiety at the results of her folly. I gave her a purge," he replied with a grin. "I told her to her face she had over-excited her humours by her foolishness, and that complete rest was essential to her future well being."

Hal grinned briefly, then said, "Do have a care, Phillipe, the town is like a powder keg. Do you have any serious cases in hand?"

"Several others I can do nothing for, but help to ease their departure from this world in due course. And perhaps two others who require regular care, but I have been training up a lad, who could apply salves in the immediate future."

"Then what is your objection to leaving at once?" asked Hal impatiently.

"None, save that it has a theatrical appearance, and I don't care to appear to be running from trouble. I shall call for a coach tomorrow morning, pack up my family, and announce to any who care to listen, that your respected aunt requires my attendance, and that we will remain with her until your wedding."

Hal looked thoughtful and agreed, "Surely that is how you would normally behave, but I'd sooner have you, your wife and child safe this night."

"Hal, you have a dozen servants at your beck and call. We have but the one girl and it will take us until dawn to be ready. You know my Celeste, if she is going to Westwood, she will have everything just so."

"I could send for some to assist you," suggested Hal.

"Wouldn't that defeat the point and tell the good people of Chawcester exactly what is going on?" asked the physician. "No, Hal, leave us to our own devices. We will leave early in the morning, as I said, and all will be well. Do you remain?"

"I shall see this through, if humanly possible. I don't care to be worsted by the rabble, for that is what is going on here. The ordinary folk of the town don't care greatly one way or another where I get married. If anything, they are quite pleased about it. It is the troublemakers causing this unpleasantness which I am concerned about, and I want to know who ultimately is at the back of it all."

Phillipe was suddenly aware there was more to his unease than usual. "You think there is one person behind it? Have you any suspicions?"

"None which bear scrutiny. However, I cannot linger, Phillipe. Fare thee well! When I see you at Westwood I'll be a married man."

Phillipe grasped his hand. "Fare thee and your bride well, too, *mon ami*. I will have great care of your Aunt, if she will permit it, and pray tell Adam to bring Madame Blackwell to us as soon as she is ready to depart. I think it would be as well for us not to drive up to Mistress Capel's house."

Hal agreed, and promising to have Cordelia and her baby with them by first light, he departed swiftly, proceeding back to The Greyhound to spend another night disturbed by bad dreams.

Chapter Nineteen

Sophie pulled up the hood of her dark cloak and slipped out into the alley followed by the boy Francis. She hesitated in the shadows, then put her finger to her lips at the sound of voices coming from the High Street. They waited until the sounds had almost died away before stealing out into the half-light of dusk. Her destination was no distance away. She crossed the cobbled street and hugged the shadows of the buildings until they came to another dark alley.

A little further down the High Street was a tavern, the open door spilled bright light in a golden glow, amid the noise of raucous voices. Without hesitation they slipped into another alley and followed its length to a silent, deserted courtyard. Taking a diagonal course back on themselves, still following one after the other, they came out in an open piece of land, then crossed another courtyard to Sally Rose's weaver's cottages. Lights still shone at the upper windows, and figures bent wearily over their work were visible through the thick glass. Sophie crossed the uneven surface with the boy by her side, as he darted uneasy looks about him.

"Nearly there," she said with a slight smile.

"Sir Henry will skin me alive," he hissed. "Only yesterday he told me as how you weren't to go outside the house until the town settled down a bit."

"With luck we'll be back before he even notices we've gone. Hush now! Here is Sally's cottage."

She didn't trouble to knock, but entered into the shadowy lower chamber, where a few weary girls, who had sewn all day, were stretched out snatching a few hours sleep on mattresses. After warning him in an undertone, not to disturb them, she left the boy then ascended the unsteady stairs with the light from above.

Hearing low voices and the grumble of a dispute, she hurried into the large workroom to find Sally, still sitting over a pile of fabric, whilst a large man leaned over the table at the other end insisting, "I tell you, Sal, I don't like the look of it!"

Sal shook her head wearily, "I hear what you say, Will, but I ain't gonna get this chance again," she replied, pausing, as her body sagged with exhaustion. "I've made enough money since Mistress Sophie came back to set me up—Mistress Sophie, what be you doing here? Sir Henry said as how you weren't to come again, but I was to send word and he'd fetch me to you himself! Oh, Mistress Sophie, he will be right angry will me that I have you here!" she cried in consternation.

"Seems to me Sal, as how you can't stop the young lady," said her companion reasonably.

"Oh, Mistress Sophie, this be Will Guthrie, him as used to splash me with water as soon as I set foot near the river when we were little 'uns together," said Sally by way of an introduction. "He's a carrier. He takes goods back and forth."

Sophie nodded cautiously, subjecting the man's pleasant, open face to a quick scrutiny. She liked what she saw, but such was her heightened sense of danger, that she still hesitated.

"Will is trying to get me to leave the town and go out to my Ma's place," Sally explained. "He says it ain't safe for one who is known to be associated with you and Sir Henry to remain here, but I've been a telling him that I can't let all my ladies down. They want their gowns ready and waiting before your wedding."

"Sal, there ain't like to be no wedding, if things don't calm down," said the man anxiously. "Saving your presence, my lady, but the streets out there are uneasy."

"Sir Henry is aware of the situation, and is taking measures to bring it under control. But Master Guthrie is right, Sally, if there should be trouble, you will be at risk, and like as not your customers won't get their gowns, in that case," agreed Sophie.

The man instantly warmed to her. "There now, Sal, the lady ain't so daft, it seems. She says the same as me."

"Will Guthrie, 'tis plain you'd be no use fetching and carrying for the gentry!" cried Sally horrified at his lack of tact. "Mistress Sophie, I do apologise for him!"

"Don't apologise for me, Sal, I'm only saying what is true," said the the man quickly. "I mean no disrespect to the lady, nor indeed to Sir Henry, who is reckoned a fair man, but some folk in the town seem set to cause a stir—and it's you who'll be at the rough end of it all!"

"He is right, Sally," Sophie interrupted without compunction. "Why do you think I've come out to see you in defiance of Sir Henry? It is vital you and your girls get away like the French doctor did. You must pack up all your things and go to the great barn at Westwood. I have written a letter, which I want you to take to Aunt

Kate," she handed over a note to the seamstress. "Mistress Westwood will see you are provided with food and have some men set up sewing tables in the barn. You'll be in the heart of Westwood lands and safe. After all, most of your customers are of the Westwood family and friends, so you'll be nearby for any final adjustments. Later if things calm down, someone can bring you back here on Monday before the wedding. Only think, Sally, if things were to get out of hand, you could lose all your hard work and everything to the marauding rabble or a fire!"

Sally, who had been about to dispute the matter, looked appalled at the thought, and her companion, quickly added his arguments to Sophie's. "Aye now, there's the truth, plain and unvarnished, my lady!" he said regarding Sophie with approval. "Haven't I been saying the self same thing this last hour or more! This ain't the time, Sal, for stubbornness! It's the time for using the sense the good Lord gave you, and getting the hell out of here until it quiets down!"

"Mistress Sophie, I do beg pardon!" Sally cried appalled at his familiarity with Sophie.

"Sally, this isn't time for any pretty speeches and fine manners," said Sophie quickly. "You don't have time. I don't have time. I must be back before Sir Henry misses me and starts searching the town, thus precipitating the trouble we all fear. Mr Guthrie, I am assuming if you are a carrier, you'll have transport?"

"My cart's in the yard, not a stone throw away," he replied instantly. "It will take me less time than a cat takes to wash it's whiskers, to pack all this up, and be gone, once you give me the word, Sal."

"But what about my girls?" Sally worried indecisively.

"Take them all," said Sophie. "The fresh air will be better for them anyway, and if you leave the doors of the great Westwood barn open the light will be enough. Or you can all go outside in the day. The weather is set fair—so Owen the boat man told me yesterday. He said the water will come down from Wales by Sunday, and then it will be dry and sunny for a week."

Will Guthrie began to pick things up and put them into baskets. "Bustle about, Sal, it ain't long 'til dawn this time o' year. Best to be gone from the town soon as we can."

"I'll go and stir up Judith and the girls," said Sally suddenly galvanised. "I tell you it will be something of a relief to get out of the town. It's been like sitting on a powder keg these last few days."

"I'll come down and help," said Sophie. "It will be better if the girls quietly slip away a few at a time."

"Get them to go out through to Widden Wood, and wait until they are gathered there. They'll be all the safer if we travel in a body," Will added, hastily picking up various half-made garments then gathering them into the big cloth that had covered the table.

"Sally, before you go, can I have my wedding gown?" Sophie asked anxiously. "I shall rest easier if it is to hand."

"Indeed, Mistress Sophie, I was to bring it to you tomorrow. It is all packed ready," said Sally, turning back distracted, to pick up a cumbersome package. "I'll carry it to your house for you."

"No, I've brought the boy Francis. He'll carry it for me. I want you gone from here, Sally, as quickly as possible, and with no one the wiser," said Sophie following her down the ramshackle stairs to the room below, where Judith was already waking the other girls.

"Hush now, remember, this must be accomplished as quickly and as silently as possible," Sophie added, as the sleepy girls began to chatter. "Be as silent as mice until you get clear of the town. No talking now, and each of you shall have a silver penny and plenty to eat when you get to the great barn at Westwood. Shh! Silent as woodland creatures, or you'll disturb the birds and arouse folk as you pass."

Within minutes Judith led the first party towards the woods, followed by the others under the care of an older girl. Sally and Will carried the bundles to his cart, and silently harnessed his horse. Within half an hour all was ready.

Sophie, who had done her fair share of fetching and carrying, gave Sally a quick hug and turned away, whispering over her shoulder. "I am leaving Sal and her girls in your charge, Will Guthrie! Make sure they are safe at Westwood, if you please."

"I'll bring you word tomorrow morning, Mistress Sophie," he replied, as he lifted Sally into the cart and settled her down amid the mounds of cloth. "I'll see them safe. Never you fear!"

"I'll give you something to fear, Will Guthrie, if I have to press every one of these gowns again!" cried Sally in a furious undertone. "Do you know how many pins are in this lot, and needles, too? You could do me an injury."

He grinned and winked at Sophie as he climbed into his cart. "Don't you fret now, my pet! I promise to put salve on any injury you get with my own fair hands! Good night, Mistress Sophie." Then he raised his whip in salute to Sophie and the cart rumbled out of the yard and along a narrow lane.

Sophie stood watching, with the boy beside her. "I do hope the noise doesn't disturb anyone and no one looks out and sees what is going on," she whispered anxiously, as they turned back across the open space.

"This be a town, Mistress Sophie," Francis replied comfortably. "They be used to noise and bustle. No doubt the carter's neighbours often hear the creak of his cart and jingle of the harness. This time of day they'll all be busy at their suppers," he grinned cheekily. "I wouldn't mind getting back to mine. Cook has made a pie full of broken meats with a golden crust on it."

"Yes, I could smell it as we left the house," replied Sophie, as her mouth watered at the recollection. "Now to get back home and inside the house before we are discovered missing."

The journey back to the house, was accomplished as quickly and as silently as the outward one. In no time at all they were back in the kitchen, where the boy was saved from a scolding, once the cook understood he'd gone as escort to Sophie on an errand.

"I have just been to collect the gown I shall wear for my wedding," Sophie explained, aware that the girl, Sukey was in a scullery within hearing distance. "Sally is so full of work, she was feared it might be crushed. May the boy carry it upstairs for me? I am sorry to have taken him on an errand, but Sir Henry was anxious I shouldn't go into the town alone. And he is so busy, that he couldn't go with me himself."

"Aye," agreed the cook, looking harassed. "Sir Henry is in the master's old chamber, talking with a gentleman. It seems some other gentlemen will be arriving from the Eastern Counties, and might decide to join him. Mistress Capel wants supper prepared for them all, just in case they do."

"Just let me take this upstairs and put it safe in my chamber, and I shall be back down to help you in a trice. This is a lot to put on you when you are already shorthanded." Sophie offered, feeling guilty as she saw how hot and harassed the woman was.

"Well, the boy is back now, and he can begin by fetching the vegetables from the cellar. There are peas to be shucked, and wine to be decanted. I must say it is good to be able to make some decent food again. Since the mistress wed that old skinflint Capel I've done nothing but scrimp and stretch to save on food. It's a joy to be able to put a decent dish before a gentleman without Jonas Capel calculating the cost."

Sophie nodded, "I'll just take this to my chamber, put on an apron, and be back down to help. I'll wager you a shilling, Francis, that I can shuck peas faster than you."

Chapter Twenty

And so it proved, within half an hour the guests arrived. Hal found his anxieties began to slip away in talking with them and laughing over time spent together last winter. By the time they sat down to a table laden with delicacies provided by Mistress Capel, his good humour was restored.

"So, Nick," he said, as they paused between servings. "You've come to see how we soft West Country folk get married, have you?"

"Indeed we have," he replied promptly. "Have we not, Bella? I said 'Bella, my love, this is an opportunity not to be missed! If anybody can be married in style, it will be Sir Henry and Mistress Sophie!' "

"Nick!" Bella protested. "Indeed Sir Henry, we owe you and dearest Sophie so much we felt we had to be here for your wedding. So we teased poor Cathy and

Simon, until it was agreed they'd make up a party. And then Mistress Hollingshead and Jack were to come. Before we knew it, we were all coming. I do hope we don't trespass upon your good nature, Mistress Capel! So many of us to feed and at such short notice!"

Mistress Capel shyly shook her head.

"Susanna is thrilled to meet you all," said Sophie. "She has heard your names forever on our lips and now will be able to put faces to them. And her cook is only too pleased to be able to show off her skills again. I don't think she has had such a task in a long while, Susanna. When I went down to the kitchen, just before everyone arrived, she was sitting weeping into her apron. I thought it was all too much for her, but she stopped long enough to tell me she shed tears of joy. She is so happy to make decent food again, and not those slops the Master Jonas used to demand."

"Forgive me, Mistress Capel! In our excitement, we forgot to express our condolences on your sad loss," said Simon, looking concerned.

"Thank you, sir," Susanna bowed uncertainly. "It has been a bad time, and I don't know how I would have borne it, but for Sir Henry's help, and the comfort of having Adam and Sophie with me."

Adam arrived, and took a seat opposite Jack, who asked, "Cousin Cordelia has gone ahead to Westwood, has she?"

"Yes, the town is getting a little unruly. Our neighbour, the physician was leaving to attend upon Mistress Kingscott, so I persuaded Cordelia to take our son Basil to Westwood, out of the heat and bustle," he replied. "Speaking of which, it occurred to us that we might have Basil baptised whilst everyone is here, if that can be arranged. Cordelia and I would be greatly obliged if you would be one of his godparents, Mr Hollingshead. Sir Henry has already consented, as well as Susanna and Sophie. We thought a blood relation would be most appropriate, as he has so few."

Jack Hollingshead looked momentarily taken aback, then recognised the offer of an olive branch. "I am honoured, Sir, and I pray I may not be found wanting in my tenure. In such good company, I am sure to be ably assisted. Please allow me to introduce you to my cousin, Mistress Beatrice Pauncey and her betrothed, Hugh St John. I think you have met Mistress Bella, sister to my brother-in-law, Simon, and Nick Revesby, the gentleman she is betrothed to."

Adam bowed to each in turn. "Names familiar to us

all. Mr Revesby, you are to be doubly congratulated on regaining not only your fortune, but also a lovely bride. Mr St John, Mr Craven, hopefully our better acquaintance will be achieved. Mistress Bella, your story kept us all intrigued and we were grieved, Mistress Beatrice , that your sister lost her life. I do hope your mother and younger sister are recovering from their loss."

"Thank you, sir," Beatrice replied softly. "They are making a stay with our half-brother, who is married to Hugh's sister. I am reminded, Sophie, to give you my mother's best wishes for your wedding. She says you deserve to be very happy."

Sophie smiled. "How kind of her! I do hope she is recovering from poor Rosalind's death?"

Beatrice smiled uncertainly. "I hope so, too, Mistress Sophie."

"Come," said Bella, "this is a joyous occasion, we mourn those lost to us, but not at Sir Henry's and Sophie's wedding."

"Should we achieve such a happy event," said Justin, a shade sourly.

"We *shall*," said Hal with an edge to his voice, "but not necessarily in this town. As Sophie protested he added, "I am sorry, sweetheart, but we must face facts.

If the mood in this town doesn't improve, then we must not put our guests at risk, so we'll gladden Aunt Margery's heart and return to Westwood. It is the marriage which is important, not the place of the wedding."

Sophie reached out to clasp his hand. "Indeed, Hal, you are right, but may we not give it another day or two?"

"My love, we are to be married on Tuesday. There are only a few days left," he replied, returning the pressure of her hand. "Is it to be an unseemly rout?"

"Nothing you do, Hal, is ever unseemly," she replied. "If we are compelled to leave, we'll do so in a huge procession, so they'll know they missed the most important event of the year."

"If we depart, we'll do so in small groups, at night," he replied. "'Tis plain you've never lived the life of a vagabond in France, my love."

"I have not, but if that is where we are bound, so long as you are by my side for the adventure, I care not," she retorted.

He laughed with the others at the table, adding, "Oh, Sophie, you make me feel my age!"

"Now that I cannot conceive," cried Jack, "Please tell us more. What was it like to live in a Court in exile?"

Hal smiled uncertainly. "No tales I'd care to repeat in mixed company, Jack, but on another occasion, perhaps. I say only this, I am in total accord with the King about going off on my travels again."

"Were you in London when our Fleet at Sheerness was attacked by the Dutch Navy, Sir Henry?" Simon asked, looking grave.

"I was waiting to see the King at the time, as he had sent for those concerned with the Muster of Troops, to report on how measures were working. Some of us hurried down to Chatham in time to see the Dutch coming up the river. It was not a sight I ever expected to see."

"Did you see the *The Royal Charles* being towed away?" asked Nick in dismay.

"To my grief I did, and *The Unity,* and the fire ships, which set alight the remainder of those ships laid up," replied Hal gravely. "We can but thank our stars that at least the docks at Chatham survived, so now we can rebuild those ships the King ordered scuttled."

"But where will the money to rebuild be found?" asked Simon. "Will Parliament be recalled, think you?"

Hal smiled tightly. "I am not privy to the King's thoughts. I merely take orders and make reports."

"And receive honours," said Justin, silkily.

Hal glanced to him, with a warning in his gaze, but it was too late, for Sophie cried, "Yes, Hal has been given a great honour. The King has made him a lord. He is to be my Lord Westwood."

"Is it so, Hal?" Nick asked in delight. "Good Heavens, Lord Westwood, I am so pleased for you."

"It is still not generally spoken of," said Hal, with some hesitation. "I am not entirely sure, that is to say, there are still matters to be considered."

"What is there to consider?" Adam asked bluntly. "The King has given you an honour. Only a fool would not consider it. Most of us would grab it with both hands. Oh, I beg pardon, Sir Henry—my lord—"

"Yes, exactly," said Hal, as they all laughed. "Amongst friends I am Hal, if you please. As for grabbing it with both hands—" He sighed. "The truth is I have little choice, one cannot offend one's King."

"Why would one want to?" asked Jack curiously. "Your family have always been King's men. Why would you even consider anything else? Surely it is not just an honour for you, but a recognition of the support your family has given the Crown?"

Hal smiled wryly. "Yes, Jack, if only I could be sure of the form that support took. My father was not known to possess the finest of scruples."

"Who would have during those difficult times?" Simon remarked thoughtfully. "I dare say if we examined in detail the actions of any of our antecedents we might not be pleasantly surprised. It is not for us to judge our ancestors. A man can only be in control of his own conscience."

"See, Hal, what sense our friends speak!" cried Sophie. "Did any of you truly have any choice over your conscience during the war? You all grew into a set position, the decision was already taken long before the conflict arrived. None of us truly have any choice, family ties, love, affection, each took us one way or the other."

"Indeed," agreed Bella. "Those of us who came later can only marvel at the courage shown by our families. I do not know that I could exhibit such stoicism in a like position."

"I don't know that courage came into it," said Hal, glancing to Simon. "It was more a matter of dealing with the situation as one found it."

"Return of the King to England! Surely that must have been everyone's hopes and desires?" Nick cried, taken aback by this rather prosaic attitude.

"Yes, it was," agreed Hal. "Only we had no clear idea if it would actually happen. It was naturally talked of continuously during exile. It was, if you will, the stuff of dreams. Yet I swear when we all set sail, it was still a matter of doubt for many of us. The King seemed sanguine about it, yet he had lived his life making the best of very little. He was surely among the first Princes of England to know what it was like to suffer privation. His advisors, like him, had few illusions. There had been so many setbacks and reverses. Few of us could rid ourselves of the thought at the back of our minds that it might just be a trap." He frowned over the memories which he seldom called to mind these days. "I was, as I said, quite young, but not too young to remember the tension as we sighted England. The gathering excitement as we realised the quayside was packed with cheering people. Followed by the procession through the streets, again packed with people cheering and calling down blessings on the King, and the wild drinking in the taverns and inns." He smiled suddenly at the recollection. "I remember asking my father how anyone slept in England, it was so noisy."

"Were you and my father part of the triumphal procession into London?" asked Nick.

"I made up the numbers in the hindmost," Hal grinned. "There was little triumphant about us. I was bedraggled and had out-grown almost everything I owned. I remember father taking one look at me, and deciding my place was with the servants in the baggage train. He said if he could win enough at dice, he'd buy me some clothes in London."

"And did he?" Nick asked quickly.

"My father had funded our exile by gambling," replied Hal with a grimace. "By the time we got to London, he had won enough money to have tailors bowing and scraping in the yard of our inn. Then later he sent to France for the clothes for my first wedding."

"He had won a fortune?" asked Hugh St John, who had been listening open-mouthed.

Hal frowned uncomfortably. "My father won many fortunes in the course of his life-in-exile, and lost them too. It was, to say the least, a precarious existence, yet one he greatly enjoyed. I did not. The uncertainty, the vagabond ways were not something which sat well with me. It seems I was more like my Uncle and namesake. I preferred the settled life of running an estate and farming. It was a matter of great disappointment to my father, when I gladly accepted my Uncle Henry's offer of becoming his heir, and living with him and dear Aunt Kate at Westwood."

"Now *that* I can understand," said Bella, "Your Aunt Kate is, I do believe, a favourite with us all. I shudder to remember how that dreadful man took her hostage and how courageous she was."

"And how cowardly her betrothed was," cried Nick. "We were speaking of it only the other day, were we not?"

"When one considers what could have occurred," Simon nodded shuddering. "That you managed to cut through our confusion and grief and set near everything right again, Sir Henry, is much to your credit."

"I take no credit for any of it," Hal replied swiftly "I grieve that we could not manage to save your sister's life, Mistress Beatrice."

Beatrice nodded, as her betrothed clasped her hand in sympathy. "Pray do not grieve, Sir Henry, not when you and Mistress Sophie are about to wed."

"No, Hal," Sophie insisted. "We are about to be married, so we must put aside our grief for those who have gone before us and embrace joy!"

"I will gladly embrace all the joy you represent, my love, once we get these next few days over with, and

when are on our way back to Westwood," Hal replied
swiftly. "But let us not talk of problems this evening!
Let us enjoy our good company, for we are fortunate
to find ourselves among friends. I give you a toast: To
absent friends and peaceful times!"

Chapter Twenty One

"So Constable Sambourne, what news do you bring us of the mood in the town?" asked Hal the next morning. Having summoned the man from his favourite tavern, they met by Justin's suggestion at his new home, the house by The Cross.

"All be well, your honour," he replied. "I were telling Alderman Chudleighly as how everything were settling down now, and as how we can rest easy."

"I think you are a little too sanguine, Sambourne," replied Justin sharply. "I hear nothing of such optimism in the taverns. Quite the reverse, in fact."

The man looked affronted.

"Tell me, Constable, did you go out to Billington?" interrupted Hal, before Sambourne and Justin could get into a dispute.

"I did your honour," he replied quickly. "My cousin,

Josiah lives out that way, so I took a stroll last evening to visit his cottage, companionable like, and asked his thoughts on what happened there back in the spring."

"Was he a witness to those events?" Justin asked.

"No, Mr Danvers, his cottage is a mile out of the village, but he knows everyone, and all their gossip. He said it were all down to some fools from Chawcester, who came out there, to get even with another fellow who had cheated them in a game of quoits. And then that Mother Sandwell set about them, telling them to be off back to Chawcester and leave the fool alone. He said it turned from being a bit of horseplay, into something nastier after she screamed curses at the men. It were then they started to call her a witch and decided to swim her, still in jest, so to speak, but it all went awry."

Justin interrupted, "Yes, we have both read the official report. It was a scandal that there was no one in authority there to put a stop to those events."

" 'Tis a small village, your honour," replied the man, defensively. "Josiah said by the time the constable were summoned from the next village, it were like a parson's picnic on a Sunday—no sign of anyone. They'd never had trouble in that village afore."

"To get back to the matter in hand, Sambourne," Hal

interrupted, before the other two could get into an arguement. "Did your cousin ever recollect seeing Mistress Capel visit that village?"

"He did not, Sir Henry," replied the constable quickly. "He knows Susanna, on account of how he were pig man to the farmer who used to supply The Greyhound. He said he took sides of bacon to her often in the old days, and she'd give him a mug of ale, and talk with him about the country, wistful-like. He said he never set eyes on Susanna Capel since last Michaelmas, when she bought some bacon at the market in Chawcester and they'd talked over the old days, and about how Adam Blackwell had got his self married."

"Not exactly conclusive evidence," remarked Justin.

"But good enough; It is within the bounds of credence," said Hal. "The man knows the accused, and most definitely did not see her, nor hear tell of her being there. Depend upon it, if Mistress Blackwell had been to see Mother Sandwell, somebody would have seen her doing so, and it would have become part of the gossip of that village. If you are still unhappy, then Sambourne can go back there, once this present trouble is done with, and waste his time taking the depositions of as many of the villagers as he can find."

"I am only thinking ahead," said Justin mildly. "If this does blow up into something we cannot contain, if we do have to call in the militia, and anyone is killed, it will be we three who have to explain our actions."

Hal glanced to him, acknowledging the truth of his words nodding, "Sage advice, thank you! You are correct. We must follow the rules laid down for us. But well done, anyway, Sambourne! You used your wits and didn't allow any local malice to colour your account. However, Mr Danvers talks sense. Once this trouble is over, it would be best if you went back to Billington to take official dispositions of all those caught up in the trouble, just to make sure."

"I'll go with you," said Justin. "I have not set up much here in the way of business yet. It will give me something to do, once your wedding is over. Anything will be better than staying in the house whilst my cousin and Bess get everything settled to their satisfaction."

Hal nodded, making a note to send some servants to help Bess. Then turning back to the constable asked, "Did you discover anything further, Sambourne?

"My cousin said as how they is all shocked at the thought of Susanna Capel being taken up as a witch. He said Mother Sandwell weren't no witch neither. But it were some groom from an ale house by the river as set the up that rumour about her—on account of him thinking he made better simples than she."

"Now that does have the ring of truth," Justin sighed. "The pity of it is that an old woman should lose her life because of the loose tongue of a drunken groom."

The constable stirred himself and said, "Mother Sandwell ain't dead, Mr Danvers. 'Tis said in the village she swum to the other side of the pond and hid in the rushes 'til they'd all gone, then packed up what were left of her traps. Maybe went to live with a cousin in Swaddlestoke over the far side across and down river.

Hal stared at him in astonishment. "Gone to live in Swaddlestoke? Why have you not said so before? Do you have any proof of this? Where in Hades' name is Swaddlestoke?"

The constable shrugged his ample shoulders, surprised anyone would not know. "We don't hold with folks across the river. They don't be aught to do with us, across the river they don't."

"But it is only a few miles away, as the crow flies," said Hal sharply. "Whether you hold with the people there or not, it is your duty to seek out the truth!"

"Not across the river it ain't. It is a natural border.

We live here. They live there. We don't hold with 'em. Foreigners, they be, with webbed feet, like as not."

"Sambourne, you are the representative of the law. A woman in your jurisdiction has gone missing. Mother Sandwell did not walk off the end of the Earth. If she has crossed the river it is your duty to go after her, and find out how she fared."

"Cross the river?" he cried in dismay. "They is different folk over there! Why, I might never be seen again! They say as how you may never get back. I ain't ever been told afore as how I had to cross over the river!"

"Well, I am telling you now, on this day, you must cross the river and seek out Mother Sandwell, to find the truth of what occurred. If she is well and settled, then that is to the good, but if she took harm that day, then I expect you to come back with names of those who treated her badly, that justice might be seen to be done," insisted Hal.

"Wait, Hal, is this the right time to send our one remaining constable away?" Justin asked, as Sambourne looked horrified. "Would Sambourne not be better employed in keeping order in the increasingly unruly town?"

"Sambourne knows the woman," replied Hal. "It is

not that far. If I swear-in two men now, as temporary constables, they can surely hold down any trouble until Sambourne returns this evening."

"Cross the river and come back, all in one day!" Sambourne cried, aghast.

"Yes, I can see you think you will need a week to recover from the exertion," replied Hal sharply. "We are living in troubled times, Sambourne. Hire a horse, take the ferry and cross the river within the hour! Do you hear me?"

"The river be in flood!" Sambourne stared in horror.

"As I understand it the river is in flood best part of the year. You must be accustomed to it by now. Be off with you now and report back to me this very evening," ordered Hal.

As the constable started for the door in high dudgeon Hal called, "Wait! Who often acts as temporary constable when the need arises? I shall need to swear them in."

Sambourne looked glum. "There ain't many as would take the trouble," he replied reluctantly. "Not since we had the plague. Old Harry's son were took. He used to help me when Old Harry went slack in the knees. Will Guthrie the carrier will lend a hand, if he be here, but he ain't. There's some young 'uns about, but I don't know that they would be much use in time o' trouble."

"I saw some younger men by the river yesterday," said Justin. "I'll go and see what I can find, I'll be needing a likely young fellow myself to give me a hand."

"A good idea," agreed Hal. "I'll try asking Adam. He knows most folk in Chawcester and we'll meet up again later, Justin."

❖

Sophie hurried down to meet Hal when he called on her at Mistress Capel's house later that day. She was full of the news of Cordelia's early departure with the physician and his family. Baby Basil seemed fretful so Cordelia was pleased to go with them to the peaceful air of Westwood.

Sophie asked Hal when Jonas Capel could be buried.

"It is thought he died a natural death, but no one truly believes that—or so Jem, the groom from The Greyhound tells me,"Hal replied.

"It's an unwritten law in Chawcester not to give credence to any official explanation," said Sophie, with an attempt at humour, though she appeared anxious.

Hal, who was still suffering from his restless night,

nodded and asked what were her plans for the day.

"Well, I was going to escort Susanna to pay the coffin maker and make arrangements for the funeral, but Adam has said he will attend to it for her. He doesn't want Susanna to leave the house, as there is still a feeling of unrest in the town. He is going to see about the burial. It won't be at the Abbey, as Jonas Capel was a member of a sect that has a chapel in a back street by the river, near to where all the troublemakers gather."

"I don't know that one could call a sect troublemakers," said Hal mildly, hoping to make her smile.

"Oh, and the gossips say—so the maid tells me—that Doctor Douay left town at first light, heading for Westwood, where your Aunt Margery lies near death."

"How they do love drama, the people of this town!" remarked Hal. "So my Aunt lies near death, but I still remain here?"

"On account of your adoration for me!" Sophie replied with a saucy look, which relieved him of some of his anxiety. "It seems they are expecting us to hurry and hot foot it to the Abbey to be wed immediately, lest she die and spoil the wedding."

"That idea is appealing," he agreed, thinking how lovely she looked. "Would you be bitterly disappointed?"

"No, but is Aunt Margery truly ill? Did you sent Doctor Douay to see her, as they say?"

Hal glanced about to see if they were overheard. Giving her a meaningful look he quietly replied, "I am more concerned for the health of Phillipe and his family."

She nodded, "That's what I said to Adam earlier. So Aunt Margery is well enough?"

"According to Aunt Kate, who sent a note over this morning. She is greatly enjoying her visitors, and she and Madelaine Hollingshead have their heads together in a plot to get Jack settled with a wife before our wedding is over," he replied. "So I rather think the townsfolk are to be cheated out of that particular drama."

"Poor Jack! He has all my sympathy," said Sophie wryly. "I know how it feels to have Aunt Margery determined to see one settled."

"Yes, I have no doubt she counts us one of her failures, whilst I think we are a success," he replied, taking her hand and kissing it. "Are you sure this isn't all becoming too much for you? Would you not rather go back to Westwood, too? I can find another woman to remain here with Mistress Capel."

"No, I do not want you to do that," she replied quickly. "Susanna is already anxious and it would frightened her so much more if I were to abandon her now."

"I will not abandon her. Neither will Adam, I assure you," he replied quickly. "I would feel so much happier if I knew you were safe from harm."

"I know you would, but I don't want to leave either of you. If I were at Westwood I would only fret all the more about what was going on here. We only have to last out a little longer," she replied. "Once we are finally wed, I shall be easy."

"There is only a short while to go now," he agreed soothingly. "Once we get past this evening, when traditionally the taverns and inns are full, the worst should be over. Tomorrow they will all be in church or chapel, which surely must give them pause for thought."

"It might be as well to have a word with Constable Sambourne," said Sophie. "Has he anyone to assist him if there should be trouble tonight?"

"He is not yet back from Swaddlestoke unfortunately. But Jem from The Greyhound is holding the lock up, and I am seeking more help for this evening. I'll step out and find Justin again and see what else can be done. I need to speak to him anyway. If necessary, I can swear-in a few temporary constables to cover the next few days." He glanced to her uneasily. "You will remain here with Mistress Capel, won't you? You'll not think of going about in the town by yourself."

"No, I will not when you and Adam are so against it," she replied calmly. "We have many things to do before the wedding. Then once we are wed Susanna is going to make a stay with Adam and Cordelia, so I suggested she may as well go on to the Old Manor from Westwood. I've been keeping her mind from her problems by getting her to plan what she might need, so it could be packed up ready to go with us when we leave."

Hal nodded. "It will give her something else to think about."

Sophie met his eyes. "The departure of Cordelia and the baby affected her greatly. She understands the necessity of their leaving, but feels bereft."

"We shall not abandon her," he repeated swiftly. "I have given you my word upon it."

She smiled up at him. "Thank you, I knew you would not leave her, but Susanna has learned through bitter experience not to put her trust in many."

He sighed. "Poor woman, I do feel for her, but Adam will not betray her either. He has said that once we can be sure there is no charge to answer, he'll take her from here, and she can stay with them. I think, in fact, he intends to take several people from town back with him."

"Yes, he is taking Sally's eldest lad, and Jem, the groom from The Greyhound's nephew, not to mention Jem himself and his widowed sister, if they are willing. Adam says he is sure his harvest will be good, and that the price of corn is rising because of the war with the Dutch, so he can afford to take on more help."

Hal nodded. "No doubt Jack Hollingshead will have brought him the rent from Cordelia's property. I understand they too are confident of a good harvest, and Adam surely could do with some assistance." He hesitated, adding, "It looks as if things might improve, but we must still be aware that the ways of a mob cannot ever be predicted. So do be mindful of what has been discussed. Do not take any foolish risks, if you please."

She nodded and sealed her agreement with a kiss.

❧

Chapter Twenty Two

Hal took a walk before breakfast the next morning out beyond the Abbey, to mark how the meadows had disappeared and the river widened into a huge lake around about the mill. The flood waters were lower the next morning, as predicted. He paused down by the ferry, to pass the time of day with an old acquaintance, Owen the boatman. Hal passed a package to him, with swiftly whispered instructions to carry it down river to the authorities, should trouble break out within the next few days. He also asked Owen to collect Constable Sambourne from across the river.

The boat man took the package discreetly, nodding, all the while assuring Hal in a loud voice, that he need have no fear for his wedding, the water would go down with the tide as it always did, time out of mind.

Hal thanked him gravely. The old man repeated best

wishes for his nuptials, leaving Hal to retrace his steps.

Hal stopped at the lock-up to see how the temporary constable had fared overnight. Jem, the groom from The Greyhound, looked uneasy, but admitted it had been quiet enough, adding that he still had a feeling a storm was about to break about their heads.

Hal nodded, "Yes, I don't like the atmosphere abroad on the town today either. I am pleased to have persuaded Mistress Cordelia to leave town with Doctor Douay and his family, but I do hope your sister wasn't too disappointed by not meeting up with her and the baby."

"Well, I'll not deny it, Sir Henry, that she were," admitted the groom, ruefully. "She'd turned her cottage out from top to bottom, she had. Made us all put on our Sunday best, and cooked enough food for an army, let alone one lady."

Hal smiled, "Yes, the ladies do like to do things in style, don't they? I am sorry she is disappointed. I know Cordelia was unhappy about it, too. I wonder, would it help at all, if your sister Janet—indeed all your family —came to Westwood for the wedding feast? Then she could see Cordelia and the baby there."

The groom stared at him in astonishment. "Come to your wedding feast, Sir Henry—me and mine?" Then as Hal nodded, smiling slightly in encouragement, he cried, "Well, I never! We are to go to Sir Henry West-wood's wedding! Janet will never stop talking about this!" Then as the full import of the invitation sank in, he added in mock-horror, "Oh, by all that's holy, she'll make us all wear our Sunday clothes—or worse, she'll insist we have new!"

"No, there isn't time," soothed Hal chuckling. "You are to tell her, Sir Henry apologises for the lateness of the invitation, and begs that she take no trouble with her attire, but just to come as she is, and be welcome, to my home."

The groom closed his eyes committing the words to memory, whilst Hal took the opportunity of his silence to say, a shade anxiously, "To return to the matter at hand, there is still no sign of Sambourne. I've spoken to Owen the boatman, who says he'll go across to collect him as soon as the high water has come down. Owen doesn't see an end to the water rising until the tide turns lower down the river."

"Aye, 'tis usually so. Recollect old Sambourne didn't set off until late in the day. The roads will be washed out now, and none of the boatmen upstream will risk bringing him back with water that high. I doubt me we'll see him afore supper time, if not tomorrow."

"I'll try to find someone to assist you, Jem, although the town looks peaceful enough at the moment."

"Aye, 'tis the lull afore a storm," he repeated, in more cheerful accents. "My young nephew is a coming along with my breakfast. Happen I'll keep him by me. He'd be useful to send word to you if trouble starts to brew."

"A good thought, Jem. Do that. I'll pay your wages both. Although I admit it will be a miracle if we get through this day without some trouble."

Jem darted him a doubtful look then asked, "So the French doctor left in a carriage at your command, Sir Henry?"

"My Aunt Margery's health is giving us some cause for concern and I asked him to call on her and as he was going to Westwood anyway, he took his wife and baby along with him. I would hate to think I might have to cancel the wedding at this late date," Hal replied.

The groom nodded his head uneasily. "They say as how the Doctor reckons old Jonas Capel just upped and died, and that Susanna Capel didn't kill him."

"So Doctor Douay told me. Capel was not a young man after all, and not in very good health either."

"Susanna is well-liked in Chawcester. I don't know

what possesses some folks, I surely don't. Seems they just like to think up some scandal, to liven up market day."

"You could be right, Jem. They do say empty vessels make most noise," Hal agreed.

The groom grinned. "Aye, they surely do, and Chaw-cester has its fill o' empty vessels!" He nodded then dropped his voice. "The thing is, Sir Henry, there's those who don't believe that Jonas Capel died a natural death. There's them as say they wouldn't believe anything that there Frenchie doctor says, and those who say he's in your pocket anyway. Even fools here will remember you spent years in France, and are next best thing to a Frenchman yourself, with your fancy foreign notions."

Hal half laughed. "Next best thing to a Frenchman? They do know how to insult a fellow. Now you hold firm, Jem, and we'll see this trouble through. Sambourne will be back soon. Hopefully with Mother Sandwell's testimony that she has not ever seen Mistress Capel."

" 'Tis this coming evening I fear most," said the groom apprehensively.

"I agree with you, but we can still pray for a miracle," said Hal in bracing tones.

"Thank you for having spoke to Tom Thorpe up at The Greyhound, Sir Henry. He stopped by here last evening, to see how I was getting on, saying as how he were pleased I'd stepped into the breech, and how we all had to stand shoulder to shoulder in these difficult times."

Hal grinned. "I must confess, Jem, I 'buttered him up,' as my young brother would say. I told him how I'd mention his name to the King when I make my report, and how men of substance, like inn-keepers such as himself were the backbone of the country."

Jem grinned, showing an odd assortment of teeth. "'Tis said he has plans to stand for the town council. Happen he'll expect your support, Sir Henry."

"Provided he is on the side of right, Jem, and stands with us, I will be happy to do so," replied Hal mildly.

"He won't get in on his own, that's for sure," said the groom, as Hal turned to go. "He be from the Forest, he do. None of us hold with they from the Forest. That's what did it for Susanna, when she sold out The Greyhound to Tom Thorpe from the Forest."

Hal frowned, turning back. "Why?"

Jem frowned with him. " 'Tis across the river, is the Forest," he replied. "Chawcester folk they don't hold with them across the river."

"So I have heard," Hal nodded, then frowned again.

"Why should the river make such a difference or cause such a divide?

The groom shrugged. "Always been that way. Happen because they is border folk?"

"Perhaps," Hal nodded. "Yet they are in the same county as you, and are essentially the same people. This needs thinking on, Jem. Perhaps we need a fair, or a feast day, when they are made welcome in the town."

"Surely some will come to celebrate your wedding, Sir Henry. 'Tis said you'll be opening the taverns," he added hopefully.

"Most likely I will," he agreed. "Provided there is no bloodshed. It wouldn't do for a Justice to allow blood to be spilt, now would it? So, if we can have agreement on no trouble, I'll readily open the taverns for making merry on my wedding day. Pass the message round Jem, when you can."

Jem nodded, his spirits lifting. "I told Constable Sambourne as much. 'Sir Henry, will do the pretty, Sammy, provided you keep a lid on the trouble,' I said."

"Provided he is back from across the river in time," Hal agreed.

"He'll be back. Owen the boatman is to fetch him along about supper time. It don't do to keep Owen waiting for his supper. If you be late, he'll wait there until you hove into view, then he'll row away as you get close. I've known them as have had to leap into the water and clamber aboard when they were late. He charges extra for that, too, he do."

Hal chuckled at the novel way the boatman had of making his customers keep time and took his leave, feeling slightly reassured as he went back to see how Sophie fared.

Chapter Twenty Three

Sally Rose stood before the Great Barn at Westwood her courage failing her after the sleepless night and the fear of being pursued. "I don't know what to do for the best, Will," she confessed. "I do know Mistress Westwood. She is a sweet lady, who came to me to have a gown made for this wedding, in spite of me being nothing but a country seamstress. I don't know Mistress Kingscott, at all. I've see her pass through the town in a carriage occasionally, but she is said to be a fearsome high lady. They say even Sir Henry doesn't care to offend her."

"I guess she be a mortal, like us all, Sal," Will replied laconically. "Have you delivered the gown to Sir Henry's Aunt Westwood?"

"Where has been the time?" Sally cried, close to tears. "She bade me to keep it until she sent for it."

"Then the answer is simple, we'll go straight up to the house with the gown, ask to see Mistress Westwood, and deliver it."

"At this time of the morning? Breaking in on them at dawn? With me looking like a wild woman after the trek here? Mistress Westwood is a lady!" cried Sally.

"This be a great house," he replied laconically, "If the sun is up, so they will be. This ain't no social call, Sal. We've been sent by Mistress Sophie. If they be used to dealing with Mistress Sophie, they'll be able to deal with us at this hour."

"Mistress Sophie is a lady, Will. I am but a dress-maker," she wept. "I don't know what to do."

"A dressmaker, and Mistress Sophie's partner," he replied firmly. "She sent you and your girls here for safety. They'll understand that when we tell them."

"Will you come with me then?" she asked hopefully.

"I'd not let you face 'em alone, Sal," he replied. "Come, we'll walk there right away, leaving Judith to settle the girls safe in the barn whilst we are gone."

"Oh, Will, you are so good to me! I don't know how to thank you."

"You just keep your chin up, Sal, and we'll do fine and dandy," he said bracingly, as she ran to tell Judith.

Will strolled round the side of the barn and looked about him. He could see the stables, the dovecote, smaller barns, and beyond that the house itself. "Come on, Sal," he said cheerfully, over his shoulder, as she caught up with him. "Let's see how close we can get before we are stopped."

In the event, they got all the way to the house, round to the front, and rang the bell. The sound echoed back at them, followed shortly by muttering from within and the noise of bolts being pulled back with noisy gusto. The door was yanked open abruptly. An unshaven red-faced fellow, dressed in a sketchy manner glared at them from under beetle brows. Sally took a step back.

"Be you from the Eastern Counties?" he bellowed. "If you be, you keep mortal strange hours up there!"

"No, we're from the west, from Chawcester. Mistress Sophie sent us here to be safe," Will replied boldly, not at all deterred by this welcome. "This be Mistress Rose. I'm Will Guthrie and Mistress Sophie said as how we were to hunker down here in the Great Barn 'til the trouble dies down in Chawcester. Sal—Mistress Rose—has brought Mistress Westwood's gown for the wedding."

"You'll have to bring it back later—" began the servant.

Then footsteps were heard, and suddenly Mistress Westwood appeared hurrying down the staircase. She was dressed, but it was obvious she had rushed. "Sally Rose, is aught amiss?" she cried at once. "I have been anxious all night, worrying about how they are in Chawcester!"

Such was Sally's relief at the welcome that she burst into tears, rendering her speech incoherent, so Will was forced to explain as they stepped into the hall.

"What is occurring here?" Mistress Kingscott's voice cut imperiously through the weeping of Sally, the defensive excuses of the servant, Will's patient explanations and Mistress Westwood's soothing words.

"Oh, Margery, have we disturbed you? I am so sorry," Kate responded at once. "I should have taken everyone to the parlour and not spoilt your rest."

"I wasn't resting, Kate, but at my prayers, until this hullaballoo made we wonder if the boys weren't up to mischief," Mistress Kingscott replied, stiffly descending the stairs. "I am too anxious about the events in Chawcester to rest. Why is everyone gathered in the doorway, Jenks? Why have you not invited our guests into the parlour?"

"I didn't think such folk would be—" he began, but

was cut short by a very imperious Margery.

"I am surprised you ever have time to think, Jenks ! You are forever telling me how busy you are. Well, open the door to the parlour for me, man! Good Heavens! I don't know who your last employers were, but it is obvious to me they were not people of status. Where is Jane? Oh, yes, she will be helping Bess with the boys at this hour, no doubt. Come in, Mistress Rose, and your companion—"

"This is Will Guthrie, ma'am," said Sally, hastily mopping her tears, "I do beg your pardon, m'lady, for coming here unannounced like this, but you see—you see. . ." Sally struggled to regain her composure again.

"It's like this, milady," Will interrupted hastily, as Margery stared at him with her brows raised in amazement, "I beg your pardon for stopping in like this, but Sally here is all in. She's been working full tilt for weeks on these gowns for this here wedding. Then Mistress Sophie came by last night to say she was worried with all the trouble in the town that Sal and her girls might come off worst, if they do start to riot or some such—"

Margery cut through his ramblings incisively. "So there has been no riot so far? You are sent here not because you have been attacked, but because Sophie thinks you might suffer? You greatly relieve my mind! Jenks, bring some hot food to the dining parlour at once. We'll all feel a lot better if we have something inside us. Come, Mistress Rose, stay your tears. You are amongst friends now. No further harm can come to you, I promise. We'll discuss this further as we break our fast."

"If it please you, my lady," whispered Sally, "there are above a dozen of my girls out in the Great Barn. I must see them fed and comfortable first. Most of them are young and frightened, although my helper Judith is with them now. I cannot sit to eat, and not have them settled. I beg pardon, ma'am, indeed I do."

"No, you are quite right, Mistress Rose. One must always see to our responsibilities first. Jenks, be off to the barn—no, you are in no fit state to go anywhere! Good Heavens, man, is that any way to present yourself at a gentleman's door? What if it had been our guests from the Eastern Counties?"

Will broke into the conversation again, heedless of the danger. "Begging your pardon, mi'lady. Why don't I go back to the wenches in the barn and settle them?"

"No," said Kate, quickly, as Sally cried out for him not to leave her, "No, Mr Guthrie, bring the young ladies back here. They must be tired, frightened, and they could probably do with some good food inside them."

"Indeed, Kate, you take the words from my mouth. Mr—Guthrie—is it? Pray fetch the sewing girls from the barn, whilst we organise some hot food for them. Once everyone is well fed, we can settle matters," Margery said as she set about commanding the servants to provide food for the visitors.

"Yes, ma'am," said Will promptly, giving Sally's arm a pat. "I won't be but a few minutes, Sal, so don't you fret yourself." Then with a respectful nod to both ladies he took himself off.

Sally was drawn into the hall, then Kate took her upstairs to tidy up. As she thankfully washed her face in scented water and tidied her hair Sally said, "Oh, Mistress Westwood, I am so sorry to have come here and put you all out. Mistress Sophie was most anxious that we didn't intrude upon you. She said we were to go to the barn. She said you had enough to do with all the guests, and that Mistress Kingscott wasn't as well as she had been, and so she wasn't to be troubled by us."

"If you value your life, Sally, don't suggest such a thing within her hearing," Kate said swiftly, with a smile. "Mistress Kingscott loves a bustle. It may tire her out more quickly these days, but she still likes to be at the hub of things. This wedding has been a boon to her. She'll get to see all her kinsfolk, and we are making sure she gets enough rest."

Kate paused, wrinkling her nose thoughtfully. "Now, I am afraid with the guests due almost hourly, we cannot bring you all to stay in the house, as we would wish, but we can most certainly make you comfortable in the barn, once you've had something to eat."

"Oh, ma'am, that would suit me real well. Mistress Sophie said the grooms would help us fit up tables with bales of straw and planks. I brought all my working things and the gowns, so we can carry on finishing the clothes and make adjustments. We left so quickly, that we didn't have no time to bring food with us. So Mistress Sophie said I was to speak about it to you, and to keep a tally, and that she'll settle it all up with you later, if you'd be so good as to feed us from the kitchen."

"Yes, that shouldn't present a problem. Hal, Sir Henry has been at pains to see Mistress Kingscott wasn't put to too much trouble over this wedding, which is why a lot of the guests are staying at Elmley Park, but I think he was mistaken in this." Kate added, in hushed tones. "I think she feels just the slightest bit left out of things, sort of pushed off to one side, when she is used to being at the hub of everything. Provided we can keep her from getting too weary, your arrival here might be a blessing in disguise. Now, if you are feeling a little more presentable, come, let us go down to break our fast. I'm sure your girls will be happy to see you here."

"Oh, yes, ma'am, they will. None of them will have ever been anywhere so fine as this in their lives. Most are from the town and their homes are pitiful enough, but some are from the poorhouse. They are in a sad state, some poorly with the cough, but I hadn't the heart to send them back to that misery. So Mistress Sophie sent for the French gentleman, the doctor, and he has been dosing them with one of his mixtures. They are much better now. We've been feeding them well, so I thought the fresh air out here might help, too."

"I am sure it will, Sally. Good food, and sunshine can do wonders. We must see they don't sit too long over their work, and get some gentle exercise, too," agreed Kate, a little anxiously.

"I've had to push all of them hard with everybody

wanting a new gown," sighed Sally, as they walked back along the gallery. "Good Heavens, I forgot to pack up my own gown! Oh, I can't go to the wedding dressed like this. I do believe I shall be the only one wearing an old gown, but I shouldn't complain."

Kate turned as her niece Jane entered the gallery from the far end, looking puzzled to see them at such an early an hour. "Oh, Jane," she called softly, "are the boys awake yet? We are all in an uproar. Sophie has sent her friend Mistress Rose and her girls from her workroom here to be safe from any trouble in Chawcester."

Jane whispered, "Apart from us, everyone is still asleep, which isn't surprising as Hal's boys and their cousins were up late, creating such a noise I thought they might keep Aunt Margery awake. Then I remembered she is a little deaf these days, which is a mercy. Is there trouble?" she asked, the anxiety plain on her face. "My husband, Ambrose, went to see Hal yesterday and hasn't yet returned. He said he might remain there, that Hal might have further commissions for him, but I am so concerned for them all!"

"I can't deny, Mistress Carver," said Sally curtsying, "that Chawcester is like a pot about to boil, but so far Sir Henry is keeping the peace. It was just that Mistress

Sophie thought the girls and I were in a risky situation. She was worried that with feelings running so high in all the turmoil before the wedding and if it got out of hand—like in a riot or if they were to set fire to my cottage—everyone's gown would be burnt and all my work destroyed, so she sent me here with everything, just to be safe."

"Sophie never does anything by halves," said Kate ruefully, as Jane's eyes widened in dismay to think that Ambrose, Hal and Sophie might be in danger. "When Mistress Rose says everything, she means exactly that, not just the wedding clothes, but nearly the entire contents of her workroom, cottages, and all her girls."

"Good Heavens," said Jane inadequately, "where shall we find room to—"

"That is all under control," replied Kate in soothing tones. "Now, Jane would you step along and see if Mistress Hollingshead is up and about? Her woman should be around somewhere,"

Madelaine Hollingshead strode along the gallery toward them saying, "Indeed, I am up and about Kate. I heard the noise and wondered if aught was amiss in Chawcester."

"No, thank the Lord! Mistress Rose said when they

left Chawcester last night it seemed all was well. Madelaine, dear, do go down to the dining parlour, and give Margery your support, whilst Jane and I quiz poor Mistress Rose about the situation in Chawcester, for I'd rather Margery didn't hear too much of what is going forward. She reminded us only last night that she had routed the rabble that thought to invade Westwood during the war, and so she was probably the one to deal with them now. The last thing Hal needs is another problem to add to the others."

"I'll go with Mistress Hollingshead if you will awaken Bess, so she can take care of all the boys," said Jane quickly, as Mistress Hollingshead heartily assented.

"Is Bess well enough? She seems so weary since the last babe was born, and this removal from Adamsholme to Chawcester will take what strength she does have," said Kate anxiously.

Jane nodded as she turned away, "Yes, I am concerned, too. Those boys, although they are well-behaved, they are still lively and require a lot of attention."

"She needs a nursemaid," nodded Kate. "I know she loves to tend her boys herself, but if she doesn't rest more, they'll end up motherless. Now, who do we know who would be suitable?"

Jane agreed. "Yes, you are right, but, in the meantime, we keep Mistress Hollingshead waiting, and here is poor Mistress Rose half starving. Aunt Margery is below probably terrifying her girls. Go, I'll join you in a trice."

"Sally, I am sorry to keep you waiting! It is just that a wedding seems to throw up so many other problems in its wake. Now, what were we talking about?" continued Kate, as the others descend the stairs. "Oh, yes, you have left your gown for the wedding behind in Chawcester. Now, don't fret! I am sure something can be contrived—oh, now here is a splendid thought! After Hal's first wife Libby died he locked the door to her chamber and just walked away, never going in there again. A few weeks ago, he mentioned we should have that chamber set out for Sophie to use after their wedding, but somehow it never happened. And Margery—Mistress Kingscott—and I have been talking about it, too, saying we should try to sort it out for him. Libby, as you may have heard, came from a Puritan family, so her clothes were rather plain, but of very fine quality. If you've no objection, I am thinking her gowns will be perfect for you and your girls to wear, should the wedding go forward from here, as seems most likely now. Libby was rather small, like you, so the gowns may only need minor adjustments."

Sally, rather bewildered by all this information, nodded her understanding. "Oh, Mistress Westwood, won't Sir Henry object? I mean the idea of giving the girls some decent clothes is wonderful. They'll be so pleased, poor things, they never have anything pretty, but won't he mind seeing his wife's gowns on other women?"

Kate smiled as she knocked gently and a weary-looking Bess opened the door and stared at them both in amazement.

"Good morrow, my dear, you are awake then, at this early hour, and so I fear are we. Mistress Rose here brings news from Chawcester."

"Chawcester?" Bess, befuddled by sleep, cried out in fear.

"All is well, so far, don't fret," replied Kate in soothing tones, "but I have sent Jane and Mistress Hollingshead to attend upon Aunt Margery, as they break their fast with Mistress Rose's seamstresses. Can you manage your boys and Hal's? There is Prudence to help you."

"Yes, of course I can," replied Bess, a little bewildered, smothering a yawn. "Prudence is very good with all the children, but do tell me Justin is well—and Hal?"

Sally curtsied. "Yes, so she said, ma'am. Mistress Sophie said as how Sir Henry was fixing up the shutters and making the house secure, just in case of trouble, but at the moment all was quiet. She just thought my workroom in my cottages may be a target if some of the men got drunk."

"We must go now and help Sally's poor girls. Do join us with the boys when you are ready, Bess," said Kate as she nodded to her niece and turned away retracing her steps.

"Now, Sally, where were we? Oh, yes you were concerned Sir Henry might be disconcerted to see his late wife's clothes on your girls." She gave a little chuckle, "Truth to tell, I doubt Sir Henry could bring to mind any garment any female ever wore. If, however, we remove a problem from his path by clearing out that chamber, I am sure he'll happily agree to anything," Kate nodded, well satisfied with her deliberations. They descended the staircase, and turned toward the dining parlour. "What is your candid opinion of the situation in Chawcester? Is the wedding likely to go ahead as planned in the Abbey?"

Before Sally could reply, they entered the dining parlour, to find a dozen timid girls sitting on long benches on either side of a long table presided over by Mistress Kingscott at the head with Judith next to her. At the foot sat Mistress Hollingshead, Will Guthrie and Jane.

"Ah, I see you have not waited upon us," continued Kate, smiling a little more broadly. "Come, Sally, take a place next to Mistress Kingscott—and Judith, is it?" She smiled encouragingly at the nervous young woman, "whilst I get acquainted with Master Guthrie. Margery, no doubt you've said grace? I do trust the Lord will forgive us if we say ours silently."

In sympathy with the nervous girls, Kate bowed her head quickly, then was soon chatting to Will as the table echoed to the sound of spoons clattering against bowls and the creamy oatmeal disappeared in double-quick time, followed by hot biscuits and broken meats in a delicious sauce. Will ate his fill, and smiled to see Sally replying to her companions' questions with a calm he wouldn't have thought possible a few hours back.

"So, Mr Guthrie, you are a carrier, I gather?" asked Aunt Kate, who had not wanted to disturb his breakfast.

He turned to her with a smile. "Aye, I fetch things for local folk," he agreed. "Occasionally I take goods further afield, to Oxford, and once to London itself."

"You are kept busy?" she asked curiously.

"Aye, most times. There are farmers who want goods taken to market, and those who want goods brought back, if they are too busy to go themselves. Then there are gentlefolk, like yourself, who need things sent from London collected from the nearest town."

Kate nodded, "Yes, indeed. Margery—Mistress Kingscott—had her gown made for the wedding in London—"

"And I fetched it from Oxford for her, and brought it to Chawcester, where your man picked it up," he agreed amicably.

Margery interrupted from the head of the table. "Kate, what is this Mistress Rose tells me? You are thinking of clearing out Libby's chamber? That would be a task well done, if indeed, it could be achieved. I have spoken to Sir Henry and indicated it was a task long overdue. If it could be done whilst he is from home, I feel sure he would be greatly relieved. Those Puritan gowns Libby's father had made for her have been put away for far too long, even though we laid lavender with them to stop any moths. It is an excellent plan and I am certain Sir Henry would be thankful to be spared the arduous task. I shall attend to it at once. If we can find something there to clothe these girls, Libby herself would have been pleased. She was a sweet and generous creature."

As the meal progressed toward its conclusion, they heard a man's voice in the hall and looked alarmed, thinking it news of further trouble in Chawcester. Before they had time to react, the door was thrown open, and the voice bellowed, "No, my good fellow, there is no need for a ceremonial escort, I am merely going to introduce my son to his grandam—"

"Tom!" Margery struggled to her feet in amazement. "Tom Kingscott! Is it you?"

"Indeed it is, Mother," he replied, entering the chamber, holding a tightly swaddled bundle in his arms. "Come in, Molly, don't be shy. Good Heavens! When your man said you had guests, I thought he meant Jane or Bess!" Tom stopped dead and looked about him in astonishment, then espying Margery at the head of the table, he advanced to kiss her cheek heartily, and placed his bundle in her astonished arms. "Mother, meet my new son, Henry Kingscott."

"Oh, Tom!" she gasped tenderly. "Tom, I thought it was agreed this was too far for Molly and the baby to travel, when she has so lately left her bed from childbirth!"

A rather weary Molly, was handed to a seat, which Will Guthrie had vacated with alacrity.

"Yes, but we both found that we were miserable, missing out on all the fun going forward here, and we agreed Molly could rest just as well, under your and Aunt Kate's aegis than at home, so we set off several days ago, taking an easy pace in my new carriage. We stayed last night in Adamsholme, heard all the gossip, and decided we needed to get here as soon as possible." He looked round the table and grinned broadly at the shy seamstresses. "Mind, nobody told me Hal had turned the place into an orphanage in the interim. Well, ma'am, you don't say, what do you think of your grandson?"

"I say I am truly blessed to have seen this day, and I give thanks unto the Lord for being allowed to hold such a beautiful child in my arms! Molly, are you well? I pray God this journey hasn't put any of you in danger."

"Indeed, ma'am, I am very well, although I do tend to tire easily," replied Molly smiling in delight at the vision before her. "Tom is right. We were so disappointed to think we were going to miss Hal's and dear Sophie's wedding, that we set out nearly a week ago, travelling by easy stages. Oh, thank you, my dear, that smells delicious," she added, as Jane put a plate before her, then called for the servant to bring more food. "I can't believe we thought of missing out on all this, Tom, but then we knew in our hearts that if Sophie was finally marrying Hal, it would be no ordinary affair."

Amid the laughter, Sally signaled to Will and her girls to vacate the table, and they began to file out into the hall, just as Bess, carrying her baby, was followed by the children tumbling into the chamber. Kate called them to order, telling them to go and meet their new cousin like little gentlemen, and not like a rabble. Then she turned, catching Sally's arm, her face still aglow with pleasure. "Oh this is wonderful! It will give Margery such pleasure. But I am sorry that—"

"Nay, don't apologise, Mistress Westwood," said Will. "Sally were fretting about getting on, and fixing up the barn, so they can all get back to work."

"Oh, ma'am, you have been that kind to us all, and it was so good to see Mistress Kingscott's face when she held her new grandson in her arms. Good Heavens, look at me, I am weeping myself!"

Kate embraced her heartily. "Thank you, my dear, I leave you in Mr Guthrie's capable hands. I have told our bailiff to give you every assistance. You should find him and some grooms setting out trestles for you in the barn. I'll try to visit you later to see nothing is amiss, and if you do have any further problems, you are to ask for me. Mr Guthrie, I have arranged for food to be brought to the barn at mid-day. Will you still be here, or do you go back to Chawcester?"

"I am in two minds, ma'am," he replied frankly, "I'd like to stay to see Sal settled, but then I'd like to know how things are in Chawcester. However, if I can be of any use to you I am ready to go where you need me."

"Yes, it may be useful to know exactly what is happening there, but if you should encounter hostility—"

"It's not likely ma'am," he replied serenely. "They are used to me appearing and disappearing for days on end. None are likely to associate me with Sal's leaving. I think we can be easy on that score."

"Then if you will linger until noon, and see Sally organised, I am sure we'll all be grateful to you. And mayhap you can carry messages back to Sir Henry for us."

"It will be my pleasure, ma'am," he replied. Raising his hand to his forehead in salute, he took Sally's arm and followed her girls, who were picking daisies and running through grass as they crossed the meadows.

❧

Chapter Twenty Four

Margery sat back rather wearily and considered the piles of garments piled all about them. "Well, I have to say, this has been an excellent morning's work, don't you agree, Madelaine? I don't know why we haven't tackled this task sooner."

"Possibly because we don't really have permission" suggested Kate with a smile. "If you recollect Libby's testament, she left everything to her most beloved husband, Henry Westwood."

"A few months after his return I did once ask Hal what he wanted done with all this," recalled Margery.

"What did he say?" Jane asked curiously. "I never dared to broach the subject. Until recently he clammed up whenever Libby's name was mentioned."

Margery was so happy she let Jane's lapse into the vernacular pass. "Oh, he said that I wasn't to fret over it as it was an unpleasant task, and was something he just had to do. He insisted he couldn't allow me to shoulder any more of his burdens."

"That was after you both had fallen out over Sophie. He wouldn't let us help him at all during that time," observed Kate.

"Yet, you see how I am paid out for my intransigence, Madelaine?" sighed Margery as her face glowed with sheer happiness. "Here we are eighteen months later, and I must admit, Hal was right. Sophie is the wife for him. How much pain and suffering could we have saved him in the meantime, if only I hadn't thought I knew best? Yet does the Lord punish me for being a foolish old woman? No, instead he lavishes bountiful gifts upon me, and sends dear friends to comfort me."

"I don't think the Lord wants to punish us, Margery," said Kate quickly, disconcerted by this rare display of tenderness. "Indeed, he allows us to make errors, so we can actually see our own follies. Look how foolishly I behaved over Sir Richard."

"You weren't foolish, Kate," protested Madelaine, as Jane and Bess began to put the piles of clothes into baskets. "It was plain you had your doubts from the very beginning. You said so yourself."

"No the error was all mine," admitted Margery. "I thought we should try to make a life away from Hal, and for Kate marriage was the easiest way to do so. I know we both agreed we had no true claim on him, and that it was unfair that he should have to accommodate us relics of the past, but I should never have involved you in such a folly as I did, in engineering a match between you and Sir Richard."

"Well, I agreed with you, Margery," insisted Kate firmly, as she paused wearily to sit on the edge of the bed. "And nothing has changed. We both feel it is only when we can be of use to Hal, that we really have any right to remain under his roof. Indeed I broached the matter again only last week and suggested perhaps you and I should leave Westwood, and he said quite firmly neither he nor Sophie would ever countenance it. He said Sophie was most emphatic. She insisted we two came as a package, and that if we were leaving Westwood, then the marriage wouldn't go ahead."

Margery looked concerned as Madelaine laughed. "It was only said in jest, surely?"

Kate laughed with her. "Yes, it was only in jest, of course. You know how Sophie does so enjoy a jest! But it is not, I think, as you once feared, Margery. Being flippant is more her method of dealing with things."

"Yes, I have come to understand of late that hers must have been a difficult childhood, endlessly travelling the country, as she did, poor child, with her father preaching, never sure of how welcome they would be, or where their next meal would come from. She certainly learned how to be adaptable and very resourceful, it would seem."

"I must confess I have seldom seen her at a loss," agreed Kate. "Now, don't you think you should rest for a while, Margery? I could ask Doctor Douay to look in on you, if you wish."

Looking affronted Margery said, "Kate, I am merely a little weary. I shall take a short rest, and then return to my duties. I really don't know why Hal sent that doctor here to Westwood. I am perfectly well now!"

"Hal sent him and his family here to be safe from trouble in Chawcester, Margery," replied Kate quietly. "You know how Hal has a care for all his friends."

"Indeed, I do," said Margery, "and I honour him for it, but I am in good health. Doctor Douay told me so himself, and agreed that Sir Henry had used my health as an excuse to get him and his family to safety."

Kate nodded. "Very well, but I think you would benefit from a rest. We have made excellent progress. Jane has said she will see that the clothes are taken down to Sally Rose. Now, the chamber is cleared and if the girl polishes it and makes up the bed with fresh hangings, it will be perfect for Tom, Molly and their baby."

"Yes, it is a beautiful chamber, and much better put to use again instead of locked up against time," Margery agreed. "You are right, Kate, a rest would be sensible. I have to finish the hem on the embroidery I have made for Sophie as a wedding present. I have not shown it to you yet, have I, Madelaine?"

"Indeed, you have not, although you promised you would," she replied, reaching out a hand to help her to her feet. "Why don't I come and sit with you for a while? And then you can show me. We would both benefit from a rest, I think." As Madelaine escorted her from the chamber Kate flashed her a look of gratitude.

A short while later Kate paused in the hall prior to setting off in hope of catching the church choir at their regular practise. Madelaine came downstairs and joined her explaining, "Margery has fallen asleep over the last few stitches of her beautiful work, so I crept away thinking it best not to disturb her."

"All the preparations have left her very tired. She

spares herself so little," said Kate. "I tried to suggest she left more of it to me, but I fear she was offended."

"Yes, she said her family appeared to think she was in her dotage," said Madelaine with a smile. "I told her I was happy to leave more of the running of the house to my dear Catherine, as it gave me time to pursue my own interests. Now, is there anything further I can help you with, Kate?"

"Well, I am off to the church now," replied Kate. "Hal thought it would be a nice surprise for Sophie if she were greeted by a choir singing on their return from the Abbey after their wedding, so I am going to listen in on one of the village choir practises. I don't know if you would like to join me? I would so value your opinion."

"A walk in the fresh air to hear a choir sounds idyllic. I'll be happy to join you," said Madelaine warmly.

Tom Kingscott glanced about him as he strolled out toward the Great Barn. It was a good few years since he had been at Westwood, and he was enjoying inspecting all the improvements Hal had discussed with him when they had been in company together. He missed Hal's presence, for theirs was a firm friendship cemented in more recent years. Then as he was about to return to the house, he spied the figure of the fellow, who had been present on their arrival. When Tom stepped into the parlor his own brow had furrowed a little in surprise, for he had never in his life ever imagined his step-mother sitting down to dine with what appeared to be a carrier, her dressmaker and a host of apprentice dressmakers.

The cheerful man, suddenly recognized Tom and raised his hand in greeting, then crossed the springy turf to join him. "Mr Kingscott?" he asked, putting the question a shade hesitantly. "Begging your pardon, sir, but be you lost?"

Tom laughed abruptly. "Thank you, friend! No, I am not lost, I needed to stretch my legs, to stop myself from nodding off in my step-mother's parlour."

The carrier nodded, uncertain as how to proceed. His wits had told him this was somebody of importance, but he found that far from being high in his notions, the honoured guest was of a very pleasant disposition.

"The truth is I am searching for a likely place for some players to perform a play," Tom Kingscott, said as he looked about abstractedly. "You may have heard that our journey here has been a slow progress, so as not to tire my dear wife. I must confess by travelling more slowly instead of post haste, I saw so much more, which would normally pass me by as we made our way here."

The carrier nodded his understanding. "Aye," he agreed. "The view hereabouts, be it from cart or carriage, is a very fine one this time of year."

Tom smiled. "Most times," he agreed. "Although on our journey I did miscalculate and in one village we ended up in a overcrowded inn sharing accommodation with what I can only describe as a troupe of travelling players. They were on their way to Oxford, hoping to find a crowd to play to."

"Not best company for your wife and son perhaps," agreed Will.

"I rather think they thought the boot was on the other foot," laughed Tom. "It seems my son's screams of fury penetrated even their ale-sodden dreams, and to compensate them in some measure, I invited them here to perform for us on the day after Hal's wedding. So you see me searching for a suitable venue for the venture."

"My Sal and her girls are staying in the Great Barn," said Will, hesitantly. "Mistress Sophie said they'd be safe out of harms way there. Do you want them to move?"

"No, no indeed, the house is quite full, but there is a surfeit of barns here at Westwood," said Tom easily. "I was thinking perhaps an area closer to the house would be more convenient, so my step-mother could get there without wearying herself."

"The Great Barn has huge doors that would give better light than the other barns," said Will reflectively. "It would make a grand stage for players and it holds a lot of people. Mistress Kingscott could be brought there by cart if necessary."

"I have persuaded the players to perform *Much Ado About Nothing,*" continued Tom thinking aloud as he weighed the idea. "Hal read it with Sophie earlier this the year, and I thought a performance of the play would be a gift to please them both."

"I don't know that I've ever seen a whole play of Shakespeare," Will remarked thoughtfully. "Although that bit from the one about soldiers is quite common at fairs and the like. The one where a King—blessed if I know which one it is—is standing on a barrel, like as not, telling his soldiers to fill up a hole in the wall with English dead rather than let them Frenchies in."

"That's *Henry the Fifth,*" Tom nodded sagely, and seeing Will's face remembering his enjoyment he added,

"Well, *Much Ado About Nothing* is more of a comedy, although there are a few soldiers in it."

"I reckon as my lass Sally Rose wouldn't mind moving her traps if it is for Sir Henry and Mistress Sophie," Will remarked. "She said that most of their work is nearly done now, just the last bits and pieces. Indeed Sal said one of those other barns nearby would be a bit cosier, once they're done sewing. The wind do whistle through that Great Barn at night. I could help her move, if you'd care to use it."

"Well, I must confess I had the Great Barn in my mind's eye when I invited the players," Tom admitted, "but I'd not care to incommode Mistress Rose."

"Sal's not one to make a fuss," said the carrier. "I can get a couple of the grooms to help us move It won't take us long to get it all changed about."

Tom Kingscott nodded in appreciation. "Quicker yet if we all lend a hand, once I've had a word with my step-mother, though I'm sure she will agree. I have yet to visit Sir Henry in Chawcester later today, but I'll be happier in my mind if we have set the wheels in motion."

❦

Tom Kingscott, having parted company with Will Guthrie on the outskirts of Chawcester rode past The Cross and up the High Street, turning in, as instructed by Kate, at The Greyhound. The town appeared peaceful, dozing in the languid heat of the afternoon sun.

Having handed his horse over to a groom, Tom stepped back onto the pavement, and made his way to the handsome house further along the long street. His knock on the door was answered immediately by a young lad, who was obviously in a state of great excitement as he stared at Tom's understated elegance.

"Good-day, might I find Sir Henry Westwood within?" Tom put the question mildly.

"Aye!" the boy replied, after a momentary hesitation, but made no move to admit him.

"Then can you admit me to his presence?" Tom put the question more sharply, not used to being kept waiting on a doorstep.

"Who is it, boy?" the peremptory tones from above were very familiar to Tom, who grinned, crying, "For Heaven's sake, Jack, tell the lad to admit me, will you? He obviously believes I have some fell intent."

"Tom? Tom Kingscott? Good God! Hal—Sophie— 'tis Tom! I thought it was Simon and Nick returned with Bella Craven from Elmley Park. Come on up, Tom! Boy you are an idiot! When I told you to not let anyone in at the door, I didn't mean a gentleman!" Jack scolded the bemused lad.

Tom ascended the graceful staircase to be met by Hal, who cried, "Tom, what are you doing here?" in astonishment as he hastened to the stairs in welcome.

Sophie stood in the hallway above, laughing with delight, her eyes alight with mischief. "Oh, dear, we are in such trouble now, Hal! Aunt Margery will have our blood for this! Tom Kingscott, not only here, in a country town, but in a house almost under siege!"

"You refer to Cerberus, the three-headed dog guarding the door presumably?" asked Tom, having briefly embraced Hal and Sophie. "My, you look splendid, Sophie—not the anxious bride, my step-mother predicted!"

"Sophie is up to her neck in plotting, so of course she is happy," Jack laughed wryly.

"I am about to be married to Hal. How can I be other than happy?" retorted Sophie.

"I think we are too optimistic, but come, meet our hostess, Mistress Capel," said Hal with an easy smile.

"Sir, you do my home great honour," said Susanna,

with a curtesy. "Pray step into my parlour."

"Madam, I am obliged to you," he replied, bowing over her hand and indicating she should lead the way.

"Well, how is it you are here, Tom?" asked Jack as they settled in the parlor. "I thought you had decided the wedding would be too much for Molly."

"Aye, but we pretty soon discovered that missing Hal's wedding would be even worse. So we set off about a week ago, travelling slowly with frequent rests. I am amazed you didn't hear tell of our progress, and of the devastation to eardrums my young son has left in his wake."

"He is healthy Tom?" asked Hal.

"Robustly so, it would seem," replied Tom cheerfully. "All my worry and grief is in the past. This one crept up on us, and took us all by storm, especially Aunt Margery."

"I do believe you may have secured my release, Tom," said Hal with a grin. "You have given Aunt Margery someone much more dear to fidget about."

"Now that I seriously doubt," he replied. "I have never, to my knowledge given my respected step-mother a day's worry, but you, Hal, you are ever in her thoughts."

"Well, fairly soon I shall be able to relieve her of that

chore," said Sophie, who had linked her arm through Hal's. "Only a few more days 'til we are wed."

Hal smiled down at her mischievously. "If you imagine Aunt Margery will worry any the less once we are married, my dear, you are deluded. By becoming my wife, you will get added to her list."

"Why would she worry about me?" Sophie asked wrinkling her nose. "She doesn't care for me."

"Perhaps that is so, but she knows Hal loves you, therefore she must take care that you don't injure yourself," replied Tom. "Margery is the same with Molly and baby. I heard her instructing your steward, Hal, that Mistress Kingscott was to be afforded every assistance. Indeed, her own maid is in attendance on my son. I feel I am quite unremarkable now."

"I wasn't aware I had anything quite as grand as a steward, Tom," replied Hal with grin. "Although I do have a fellow who seems to idle away his days gossiping and occasionally announces guests,"

"Well, he will have constant employment over the next few days. It seems the great and the good are converging on this part of the world. There was talk of your wedding at Stratford, where the innkeeper assured me that the King himself would be coming, although he added 'like as not,' as an after thought."

Hal laughed with everyone, then added, "I have to say His Majesty had threatened it, but fortunately he is much caught up with the Dutch, the peace treaty, and other affairs, for which I give thanks. A royal visit would be the final straw. Aunt Margery would be impossible."

As they all laughed at the thought, Adam returned from a visit to Jem, the groom, who was standing in for the Constable.

While he gave his report to Hal, Tom quietly engaged Sophie in conversation. "I have successfully completed the commission you gave me a few weeks ago," he whispered quietly. "But I have not brought your gifts with me thinking it safer, in this volatile situation, to keep them at Westwood. After all, that is where you'll exchange gifts. However, I must confess I have exceeded your commission somewhat, and bought several folios, rather than just the two you requested, as the offer was too great to be ignored."

"Indeed, oh, thank you, Tom," she whispered. "Tell me, were you able to match the binding on the covers?"

"Exactly," he replied, with satisfaction. "To the eye it will be like they were all purchased at the same time."

"I would that I could have bought the complete

works," she replied, frowning a little, "but my expenses have been vast. It is my own fault. I should have used the bridal clothes from my first wedding, but I felt they were tainted by the events which occurred, so I had new ones made. Then I had to have some repairs on various local properties, which had been impossible whilst my money was tied up. And I have yet to organise the matter of Sally Rose's apprentices."

Tom nodded. "We came upon her and her girls when we arrived at Westwood. I thought I could not believe my eyes when I first saw them in the hall. Now all the girls are working at a long table in the Great Barn. Aunt Kate told me all about your plan for Sally to take on more apprentices from the poorhouse. I had been scratching about wondering what to give you for a wedding gift then later I decided to fund two girls as apprentices, for that is what Aunt Kate thinks Sally can manage."

"Oh, Tom, thank you, you are so very kind," she cried. "What a perfect wedding gift!"

"What is?" asked Hal, overhearing her words, for he had been at pains, he thought, to give her such.

"Tom is to fund two of Sally's girls from the poorhouse as apprentices. You'll recollect I had it in mind to do so, but I have been so extravagant with my wedding clothes, that I am beginning to scratch about to cover my expenses."

"That will never do," he replied, with mock severity. "I was under the impression I was mending my fortune by marriage to an heiress. I see I shall have to take control of your finances before we are ruined."

"I wish you would. I never did have a great head for figures, in spite of all Uncle Edmund's lessons," she said with a sigh. "Oh, it will be such a comfort to be safely wed to you! I shall be able to leave all such problems in your hands."

Hal looked amazed and crestfallen. "Well, I never thought to be told that financial acumen was one of my main attributes as as future husband," he said bluntly.

"Age creeps up upon us all," agreed Tom with a grin. "Even Hal Westwood, it would seem."

"Do you stay for dinner, Tom? Or is this just a spying mission for Aunt Margery?" Sophie asked as Mistress Capel glanced to her uncertainly.

"Thank you, but, no. Much as I would love to remain here in the thick of all the excitement, I had to promise Molly, I would return, and not get caught up—as Jack, Simon, Nick and Ambrose have done—in whatever is going forward here." He sounded quite regretful.

Hal hastened to speak, "I assure you, Tom, and pray tell those at Westwood nothing is going forward here. We are being cosseted by Mistress Capel, as we wait for our wedding. True, some inmates of the town are a little unsteady, but no more than usual. All will be well, and we will all soon be back home."

Meanwhile Kate and her guest were enjoying a walk in the warm sunshine, discussing all that had gone before and catching up on news of mutual friends. Finally Kate laughed, "Sophie can exasperate and irritate beyond measure, but in truth, in the end you just have to love her. Ah, there is the Great Barn," she added as it came into sight. "At least it is a lovely day, and they can work outside in the fresh air. Some of those poor girls from the workhouse are very frail, and need all the sunshine they can get. Good Heavens, only listen to that singing! Madelaine, I think we may have found our choir!" They stopped and stood listening as the sound of a melody drifted across the meadow to them. The yard, which was bounded on three sides by barns, was open to their view, and there, in front of the largest barn, was a long cloth-swathed table, covered in fabrics, where Sally Rose's seamstresses sat on long trestles. They sang as they sewed, their youthful, melodic voices rising and falling on the soft breeze.

"A picture to take one's breath away," whispered Madeline. "Good Heavens, is this place bewitched? I have never heard such loveliness."

"This was my husband's favourite view. We always paused as we came through this copse, and looked across to past the Great Barn, with the house rising to the south. 'This is the England they fought for, the land so many never saw again, but died to preserve' he said. "

Madelaine touched her arm in sympathy. "How could any bear to leave it, even in death?"

"They don't. Once you give your heart to a place, you never leave," Kate said simply. "Henry walks with me now, even as we speak. This is where the ghosts of the past gather, to celebrate all that is good, all that is right and true—all that is England."

Madelaine nodded, "Yes, we have such a place deep in our greenwoods. My husband and I exchanged our first kiss there and that is where we took Jack on his first pony, close by where Nick and young Bella Craven used to tryst. Good Heavens, listen to us, we sound like old women! Come, we must see if we can organise this choir."

The singing died away as they drew nearer and Sally Rose came to greet them, looking so much happier and peaceful. Kate rejoiced that which had been a minor inconvenience was proving so successful for all. "Sally, we've come to see what progress you are making, and see how you are all are getting on. Mr Kingscott told me he and your friend Will Guthrey have moved you to a smaller barn. I was anxious that you are going to be comfortable there."

Sally smiled her face aglow. "Yes we are perfectly happy, thank you Mistress Westwood. The smaller barn will be more cosy with no wind creaking through the rafters. The girls are very excited to see a play, too."

"Do your girls often sing?"asked Kate.

"Singing is something we often do on good days," Sally. "It stops the girls chattering, and somehow, while singing, it helps the work go more quickly and it seems we grow closer together. It may sound foolish, but if we sing our worries seem to melt away."

"Is your task complete?" Madelaine asked curiously.

"Very nearly, thank you Mistress Hollingshead," replied Sally, with a swift curtsey. "I'd like another fitting for Mistress Sophie, but I suspect I won't get it. I do trust I have got the hem on her gown exactly right."

"Now Sally, I'm sure you have," Kate said soothingly. "I am pleased to hear you are nearly finished, for we come to you with a proposal. We have been busy ourselves, clearing out Sir Henry's first wife's chamber. We agreed that her clothes are just the thing for your girls to wear to the wedding feast. They are of good, stout quality, and hardly worn. For the most part they are rather plain, but I was thinking if anyone could give them a more modish twist, it would be you."

"New clothes for my girls would be wonderful! I was just thinking how to make us look more respectable for Mistress Sophie. She said she'd find a place for us at the feast, but new clothes—the girls will be so happy!"

"Not new, Sally, only gently worn. Libby was very careful with her things, and they are very fine quality."

"Oh, it won't matter if they are worn, so long as the fabric is sound. I'll be able make something of them, especially if I can use some of our pieces left as a trim." Her brow furrowed in concentration, as she considered it. "I know Mistress Sophie won't mind me using her bits and pieces. I don't think there will be any difficulty."

"On the credit side the gowns are not the usual black, so beloved of our sterner brethren, but just rather plain. Sir Henry's first wedding took place in high summer too, so Libby's gowns were light. There are some which are soft dusty colours, a grey-blue, a sandy shade and a colour which could be pink in some lights," said Kate. "None will know better than you, Sally how to make them suitable. And they will last. The quality is superb, and there is one especially lovely gown for you, if you won't be offended."

"No, Mistress Westwood, I won't be offended, for I doubt very much Will Guthrie will remember to bring back any gowns for me. Thank you, ma'am."

"Well, if you will come up to the house presently, you may make your own choice from what is there," said Kate, "but meanwhile, Mistress Hollingshead and I have another favour to beg."

Sally seemed to quail, then straightened her thin shoulders and lifted her chin. "Indeed ma'am, I'll be happy to help. What is the difficulty ?"

"From what I remember, when Sir Henry finally got Sophie to agree to marry him, he quoted to her a poem by Mr Christopher Marlowe."

Sally nodded, her brow furrowed, but her heart

sinking, for it sounded like another task for her. "Yes, ma'am," she said politely, but not really understanding.

"Well, as a wedding gift for her, over these last few weeks he has been assembling all the things the poem promised. Ambrose, my niece Jane's, husband, brought home a parcel from London, full of the most beautiful, strange and odd things. But the final item on the list was the promise that shepherds should sing on a May morning. I know this is a difficulty, as it is now July." Sally's brow furrowed deeper as she tried to keep pace with the conversation and Kate continued, "Hal said it didn't have to be taken too literally, so when Mistress Hollingshead and I went to listen to our village choir we were hopeful—until we heard them sing. Then we realised that they just wouldn't do. The choir was for the most part made up of very old men, who were, it seems somewhat the worse for drink."

Sally smiled faintly. "It's not uncommon, Mistress Westwood. Usually the men have to be bribed to sing. The better a choir they are, the more drunk, they be, as a rule."

Kate nodded. "As I now realise. Some of the younger men might be persuaded to stay sober and appeared to have quite reasonable voices. I was hoping you and your girls might join them to form the choir Hal wants."

Sally looked doubtful. "We have no training, Mistress Westwood. We just sing because we are happy."

"The best possible reason!" insisted Mistress Hollingshead. "We heard you as we came out of the woods. It was a beautiful sound. You need no training."

Sally blushed, unused to compliments. "Thank you, ma'am! The girls are so happy here with food, fresh air and sunshine—and they are free of fear. One of the girls from the poorhouse told Doctor Douay, when he came to physic her, that she thinks she's died and gone to Heaven."

Madeleine laughed. "On a perfect day such as this, one could almost agree with her."

Sally smiled uncertainly. "We wouldn't have time to practice, Mistress Westwood, as I do still have more work to do, and these gowns to alter."

"No, you won't need to practise," replied Kate quickly. "Hal wants the choir to sing a sort of welcome greeting for his bride as the carriages arrive back from the Abbey. So just sing like you do while you are working."

"Sing for Mistress Sophie? Oh, that be something most would want to do anyway. They think her so beautiful and kind, but what about the men from the village choir?"

"They will be the younger men. I'll send our man to organise them. He can bring them here, perhaps to fetch and carry for you, then they can sing with you as you work, and get into harmony. It doesn't have to be formal, just joyful. 'Singing from gladness,' as you say."

"Well, that be easy enough, Mistress Westwood, for I think we all are," agreed Sally. "We'll just carry on with the sewing and wait for the lads to arrive with them, shall we?"

"Yes, you and your girls seem to have impressed the steward. He said earlier he'll be happy to assist you in any way. Perhaps you have gained an admirer, Sally," she added with a smile. "I will get him to bring the young fellows to join you presently. In the meantime, I'll return to the house, and have the gowns brought to you, so that you may make the alterations."

"Goodness, Kate," said Mistress Hollingshead as they walked away. "I thought I had a busy life at home, indeed, I relish it, believing firmly it is better to be busy from morning to night, than be one of those women who settle for imaginary ailments, as the years proceed. But I see now I am almost idle compared to you."

Kate laughed. "Life is not always conducted at this brisk pace! But, in truth, like you, I prefer to be busy.

I recollect sitting by the window in my chamber, the morning my Henry's body was found, and thinking life was over for me. Then young Hal knocked on the door, full of apologies for disturbing me, but needing my help, for he had only been back in the country a few weeks, and had no idea of our customs, of whom he could talk to, or trust. He said he needed someone he could rely upon to tell him where he was making mistakes. He looked so much like my poor, dead Henry, it was like suddenly realising I had a son. Hal has been my mainstay ever since."

"And you his, I do believe, from the way he speaks of you. It is plain he holds you very highly in his affections. It seems the Lord saw both your needs, and as ever, provided," replied Madelaine, adding as they rounded a corner of the house, "Good Heavens, what are these fellows at?"

"Ah, this is the garden Hal has created for Sophie," replied Kate, pausing to watch the progress of the gardeners. "Once again, from the poem: 'I will give you beds of roses, and a thousand fragrant posies.' It used to be the old formal garden, but some of the hedges took the blight over winter, leaving gaps and Hal decided it would be a good thing to renew it. Jackson, it looks like some of the roses will be in flower," she added, pausing to engage the irascible old gardener in conversation.

"Aye, Mistress, and the lavender to edge the beds, not to mention the sops in wine, but we be having trouble with these arches to take the climbers. The honeysuckle is nearly done, and I don't know that we'll get this jasmine to flower in time."

"Well, one can't force plants to bloom out of their natural cycle, Jackson. Sir Henry knows that. Are those myrtles there? The fragrance is wonderful."

"Aye, I've had them packed in straw in my cabin, along with the orange trees. Just so long as we don't get to much heat over the next few days, they'll be safe. Sir Henry says he'll build an orangery to overwinter them."

"Did he indeed?" Kate laughed. "Good Heavens, an orangery! I've heard of them, but never seen one."

"Aye," the old man eyes sparkled with anticipation of his heart's desire. "He said he'd seen one in Paris when he were a lad there, at the palace of that French king. He said that it were attached to a wall of the house, and had a stove in to keep it from freezing in the snow and frost. He said he didn't see why we couldn't try to make something like it here at Westwood. Sir Henry says that wall over there, which is the back of the kitchen might be just the thing, as there is a fire on the inside already, which would help to keep it warm."

As Kate exclaimed in amazement at the idea, Madelaine looked interested. "Why, what a wonderful thought. I should like to hear more. I've been noticing how much more advanced your season is here compared to ours, too. The cold can be fierce in our hills, but the idea of a room tacked on to the house to keep precious plants—that is amazing!"

"Aye," the old gardener nodded his head. "I don't usually hold with what them Frenchies do. Sir Henry says they do have some passing strange ideas, but some seem to work."

Seeing this was a conversation dear to both their hearts Kate said, "Why don't I leave you here with Jackson, Madelaine, to discuss Hal's plans? I'll continue on my way to the house and get the garments organised for Sally Rose."

"Indeed, do, Kate," she replied at once. "I am perfectly happy to dog your gardener's steps and learn more, if he can tolerate me."

"Jackson will be happy to accommodate you," said Kate firmly, fixing the irascible old man with a look. "Show Mistress Hollingshead your amazing currant bushes, Jackson. He has developed them himself, and we now have currants laid down for use all year round. Indeed, Margery brewed some currant wine last autumn, which has the strength of French brandy."

With another speaking-look for the gardener, Kate hurried off to her next task, leaving her guest to engage the gardener in conversation as he went about his tasks for the next hour.

Once back inside the house, she found the reluctant steward, and organised him and two of the boys from the kitchen to transport the baskets of clothes down to the Great Barn. For the first time in a long while she began to feel confident that everything might be done in time for the great day.

Chapter Twenty Five

"Well, I have to say, if a fellow is to be married, this is the place to do it! Do you tell me this is actually the parish church?" asked Jack Hollingshead, the next evening, as he paused to admire the Abbey while he and his companions took a stroll about the town to get their bearings before joining friends for supper once again.

"So it seems. Our host at The Greyhound was telling me the worthies of the town bought it from the King, more than a hundred years ago, when all the monasteries were put down. Pretty much the way my ancestor bought my estate," said Nick Revesby.

"I thought it was one of his ministers who had the handling of all that. Cardinal Wolsey, was it? Or that other one—Cromwell, I think he was called," said Simon Craven as he glanced uneasily to a crowd of rowdy men at the tavern opposite.

"Didn't they both meet unpleasant ends?" Nick asked, aware of Simon's unease, and suddenly sharing his disquiet, as the noise level grew.

"People in the past invariably did it seems," remarked Jack, following Simon's look. "Or perhaps it is more that those who meet unpleasant ends are recorded more often than those who die peacefully in their beds. There seems to be some commotion going on over yonder. What's toward?"

"It would appear to be the usual drunken rabble," replied Simon, in disapproving tones. "No, wait, is that a young woman in their midst? No, not to worry, she is walking away from them."

"Isn't that the young woman I met at Elmley Park?" Jack asked frowning, as he recognised the slender figure. "What is she doing here, I wonder? Do you remember her? Isn't she the one who came with Hal's sister?"

"We've only just arrived. We weren't at Elmley Park with you, Jack," explained Simon as his eyes followed in the direction of Jack's troubled gaze. "I wouldn't know. I've never met Hal's sisters. Hasn't he several?"

"It *is* Mistress Howell!" Jack insisted sharply. "And I don't like the look of that mob! What on earth is she doing in this part of town?"

"Looking at the Abbey, as we are?" suggested Nick, doubtfully as he viewed the rowdy group of men.

"No, she is of the town. She would hardly—hold on the mob is following her! I don't like the way this is going," said Simon uneasily.

"She will come to grief! There she has fallen—" Jack Hollingshead wasted no time, and darted across the street as Rebecca Howell slipped on some wet cobbles. Without a word he snatched her up into his arms, in front of the group of men, who were all the worse for having drunk a considerable amount of ale. Simon and Nick watched, dumbfounded by Jack's actions, as he turned and hurried with her back toward the High Street. The mob suddenly turned with a howl of fury and gave chase.

"Come on!" cried Nick grabbing Simon's arm. "We'd best cover Jack's back. If they catch him there will be Hell to pay!"

Simon took one look at his brother-in-law, striding away on his long legs as Rebecca clasped his neck, then turned to follow swiftly as they were pelted with mud and stones. They ran past the trim timber-framed houses, past Justin's new home, heading for the upper High Street. Finally overtaking Jack, Nick hammered loudly on the door of Susannah Capel's house. The door was opened by a surprised young man, who with one glance at the roaring mob approaching up the street, gave a cry of warning over his shoulder to those within, then ran to help to relieve Jack of his weeping burden.

Given this opportunity Jack unsheathed his sword and turned to confront the motley crew of drunken louts. In a second, Nick was by his side. The scrape of steel on scabbard echoed above the cat-calls of the advancing mob, as Simon came to stand alongside them with his own sword grasped firmly in hand. Then, Hal and Ambrose, followed by Justin, spilled out of the house to stand shoulder to shoulder with their friends.

Hal advanced a step to two and thundered, "As your Justice of the Peace, I order you to cease and desist this disorderly conduct! This is fast becoming a breach of the peace, and by the power invested in me, I shall be obliged to summon troops to my aid. Go now about your business at once—or it will be the worse for you!"

"Give us the bitch as killed Capel and we'll leave you in peace with your bride, Westwood!" cried a voice from the back of the mob.

"I am Lord Westwood to the likes of you, and a Justice in this town. Get back to your business in an orderly manner, or I shall take measures to shut all the ale houses and summon the militia!" commanded Hal. "Harry!" he called, addressing the ancient ostler from The Greyhound, who stood open mouthed, slightly to one side, as if he had just stepped onto the pavement. Hal knew him to be a reasonable man, who had probably got mixed in with the mob by chance or curiosity. "Go and fetch Jem from the lock up, before this becomes a riot."

As the old man reluctantly turned to do as he was bid, some of the crowd began to melt away down the many back alleys, but the men at the front, bolder, or more drunk, cried out, saying, "What about Tom Banks' lass? She were snatched away by an Up-country man. Who knows what Up-country men be at? It be a breach of the peace to run off with one of our wenches of the town."

"Mr Hollingshead is my friend, a guest at my forthcoming wedding, and an acquaintance of Mistress Howell. He carried her away, it would seem, from a threatening crowd of drunken louts, after she tripped and fell. No doubt he feared you were about to trample her underfoot. Who is Tom Banks? And where is he?"

"He be her step-father, and he be flat on his back by

the river, having spewed his guts into it!" The cry came, which made the others chuckle, a shade shame-faced.

"Quite an edifying display of West Country manners for our Up-country guests," said Hal witheringly to no one in particular. "If I were you, I'd be gone from here before Sambourne arrives to haul you off for a night in the cells!"

The crowd gradually thinned out again leaving but a dozen there, all too drunk on ale and excitement of the moment, to see reason when confronted by it. Then as Hal stood his ground, his foot tapping impatiently, sense began to return, and a few more slipped away down the convenient side alleys, leaving a mere half dozen sragglers. So by the time Jem came hurrying up the street, hatless, with determination writ large upon his honest face, the riot he had been called to deal with had dissipated naturally.

"Ah, Jem, as you see the birds have flown. To continue celebrating my forthcoming wedding no doubt!" Hal remarked ruefully. "Touched as I am by this show of support, I feel it would be better for all, if we can confine their more drunken excesses to the actual day. Meantime, it is obvious we must make some attempt to keep the peace in the town. We must swear in some more men to assist you in this task. It hardly reflects upon us well if our guests leave Chawcester believing it to be inhabited for most part by brawling drunkards!"

Nick exchanged a quick grin with Simon, who still looked grave. Jack was more concerned with the fate of Rebecca, as he glanced over his shoulder and strode into the house.

The other men sheathed their swords and the few remaining stragglers drifted off. This left only the ring leaders, which Jem soon hauled away, assisted by a glum ostler from The Greyhound, who had been promptly seconded as a temporary constable by Hal.

As Hal followed them to see justice meted out, Nick and Simon also sheathed their swords, and ascended to the parlour, where Mistress Capel waited nervously as she readied a jug of wine for them.

A short time later Jack found his way to small chamber next to the kitchen. He was pleased he had managed to find Rebecca without the aid of anyone and entered the chamber in a determined manner. Rebecca sat with her foot in a tub of warm, scented water, and her face hidden in her hands. "Mistress Howell, I beg pardon! Do I intrude upon you?" he asked.

She looked up quickly, much flustered that he, of all

people, should find her thus in such disarray. She made as if to rise to her feet, but gasped and sank back down on the stool with a hastily suppressed cry and shielded her face again.

"You are hurt my dear Mistress—Rebecca! Do please take your ease and let me express how sorry I am that I used you so roughly earlier. When I saw you fall as that damned mob—I beg pardon, those men advanced upon you, I feared you might be trampled underfoot. I acted on impulse and I fear that the way I snatched you up, without so much as a by your leave, may have frightened you."

She looked up into his face, which expressed great concern, with an uncertain smile and said, "Sir, like you, I feared the worst. I thought in their anger they would indeed harm me, for I had rushed away from their lewd words, and then suddenly you appeared, and lifted me in your arms and rescued me from the horror of it all! Please, give no heed to my foolishness. My heart is full of gratitude to you for my prompt rescue, but I can't seem to control either my tears or my emotions."

He knelt by her side so he could scan her lovely face. Touched by her distress he said, "Pray, weep all you will. It is only natural you should feel so. You have had a nasty experience. I only regret that convention, and the fact that we only met a few days ago, prevents me from following my inclination to take you back into my arms and hold you safe again." He reddened as he realised the import of his words, and she gazed back at him in stunned amazement, thinking she must have misunderstood him in her confusion.

He broke into further speech hastily. "Mistress Rebecca, I am not without experience of broken bones. I have lots of horses and dogs at home, and they frequently take falls and damage themselves scrambling through fences and the like. Over the years my groom has often said how good I am at helping these beasts—how I seem to be able to find the source of their pain, and in some inexplicable manner ease it. I wonder, would you trust me enough to allow me to see if I can ease some of your hurt?"

She gazed back at him, only half-comprehending his words as she struggled to admit what her instincts told her he was saying. Fear of confusion that she was mistaken only made her more shy. To her dismay she was disappointed not to be able to formulate a clever or witty reply, so she only nodded and said softly, "I cannot deny, sir, that my ankle hurts. I am frightened that I am like to become a great nuisance to those who I only wished to aid. For I am aware what an inconvenience I am to everybody like this, and my sole intention was to be of assistance in this time of trouble."

Emboldened by this scant encouragement, he lifted her slender foot from the scented water and held it gently in his hands, prodding gently to see the extent of her injury. His fingers gently traced the bones and traversed the ankle, seeking out any damage. She flinched in a little pain, and considerable embarrassment at the intimacy of his actions.

He spoke confidently, "No, there is no break, as far as I can tell," he said desperately concentrating his mind on the task at hand, not on his thumping heart. "The swelling and heat indicates you do seemed to have mangled your muscles somewhat. Are you in much pain?" he asked as he glanced up at her. A sudden smile lit his face as their eyes met, and he felt his heart swell with strange emotion. Ordinarily he had compassion for any beast he found in pain, but the commonsense side of him usually assessed the situation and made a swift decision on the relative merits of what could be done and whether it was a viable proposition to keep an injured beast, or what assistance could be extended by one of his people. This, however, was something entirely new to his experience. This overwhelming desire to protect and nurture a fellow human being whom he was not responsible for, and to whom he owed no duty. He felt an almost uncontrollable urge to clasp her in his arms again, not only so that she would feel safe and no longer look so anxious and forlorn, but so that he could experience the delightful perfume that surrounded her, feel the softness of her body against his.

As he carefully massaged her swelling ankle, his mind raced. He had never experienced such a tumult of emotions as he did now. Hitherto his life had been an ordered existence. He had gone about his business, achieving his objectives in a measured manner, occasionally being gratified by the sight of his land in good form, or strangely stirred by the smell of apple blossom, of the laughter of children, but these he knew were foolish thoughts. He had mentally congratulated himself on being a steady fellow, not one to run mad over a pretty face. He had come to greatly admire Hal Westwood in the past months, but he had agreed with his mother, who deplored Hal's irrational devotion to Sophie once he was engaged. Yet for all her faults, Sophie was, he had to admit, a good sort of a female, although she still had the power to irk him by her passionate words and unchecked ability to cause disruption where ever she went.

This young woman before him was no foolish maiden, of that he was certain. She seemed to be modest and compliant and more than that, she suddenly seemed more dear to him than any female he had ever met. He now realised this truth with a sense of utter shock. He only met her briefly, danced with her twice, laughed with her almost immediately, over some nonsense, which had meant nothing. Yet now her importance astonished him. Had he been a blind fool? Was this the sort of feeling Hal had for Sophie? Its sheer magnitude stunned him. He pulled himself together and said, "I can't think that any here have thought of you as an inconvenience, Mistress—Rebecca. I do trust I am not being forward in calling you by name, but you are such a lov—"

"Jack—Mr Hollingshead! Oh, there you are!" Sophie called from the kitchen. "Hal has returned and was wondering where you were! Hal! Jack is here, with Rebecca washing her feet!"

Rebecca stammered, blushing hotly, at being discovered in such intimacy. "Mr Hollingshead has been—been—"

"I am attempting to locate the source of Mistress Howel's pain and distress," replied Jack gently surrendering her foot to the warm water. He picking up a cloth to wipe his hands, as Hal, entered the chamber rather surprised to find so august a guest in the kitchens. "I am not without some expertise in these matters. There are no bones broken, but there is inflammation and much swelling. We have found with my horses, alternate hot and cold compresses can be very efficacious in these situations." With an odd look from Hal, he got to his feet. Then to cover a sudden feeling of embarrassment, he hastily added, "I managed to save a favourite mare from being shot by such a process."

"Both you and Mistress Rebecca are to be congratulated that no such desperate measures will be required," said Hal with dry amusement. "I do hope you are not much hurt, Mistress Rebecca, although you are clearly in some distress. I would that you could be returned to your lodgings with Mistress Latham, but the streets are still very uneasy, with groups of men lingering about, even though the ringleaders have been taken away. Such are the circumstances, that I shall dispatch a boy with a note to Mistress Latham, to tell her you will remain here with us, until all danger is dispersed."

Rebecca's face looked stricken, "Oh, she will be so cross with me!" she confessed artlessly. "My mother sent a servant, with a message for me to call on her. It seems my step-father had been from home for the past two days, and my mother sent me to seek him out at the tavern and bring him home to her, which was why you found me in such an unsuitable place, sir," she said, casting an anxious glance at Jack. "Unfortunately, my step-father is not a reliable man especially when drunk. He had fallen in with some old compatriots, who saw me as an object of sport." Tears overcame her as Jack Hollingshead looking greatly displeased, exchanged glances with Hal.

"This is intolerable," he said sharply. "What can Rebecca's—Mistress Howell's mother be about, to send her daughter on such an errand, when the town is so unsteady?"

"She wanted him safe at home with her, sir," Rebecca replied quickly, before Hal could comment. "She knows that my step-father is not a rational man when in drink and thought—thought—"

Once again her emotions over came her and she wept

into her hands with such despair, that Jack knelt beside her, clasped her in his arms and uttered soothing words, much to Sophie's astonishment. She turned to Hal and her mouth dropped open to see him grinning. He met her eyes, and shrugged as Jack assured Rebecca she need not bother her head about anything again, he would attend to everything for her.

"Not exactly an easy task, Jack, as we are placed, but I do admire your sentiments," said Hal politely, with a half-laugh as he thought of the reactions of Madeleine Hollingshead and his Aunt Margery. "We thought we might hold a council of war presently, and that you might care to join us, when you are less pleasantly engaged."

Jack looked up, any embarrassment faded, and he grinned at Hal, recognising a fellow traveller. "Yes, thank you, Sir Henry, once I have settled a few things with Mistress Howell, I shall be at liberty to join you and our other companions. Pray, do not stay for me, no doubt you'll be fully occupied for sometime."

"Indeed," agreed Hal gravely. "Mistress Rebecca, I trust you'll soon find some relief from your distress."

Hal bowed and withdrew as Sophie followed him to the foot of the stairs. "Who would have thought it,

Hal?" she cried, in an amazed whisper. "Aunt Margery will not be pleased, nor Mistress Latham, although, she could hardly be irked surely, for Jack is the best possible catch! But somehow, I just know Aunt Margery will blame me for it all."

"I rather think we should concentrate on getting through the next few days without threat to life and limb. Then perhaps this matter will sink into insignificance, beside the small problem Mistress Howell might present," he replied, with a grimace.

Sophie looked thoughtful. "Oh, I think we can contrive something. After all, you have always said Jack is very much his own man."

"You might try contriving a way to get us married and all out of here, safely to Westwood first. That matter being rather more pressing than getting Jack Hollingshead settled in life."

"How can you say that, Hal? It has been Aunt Margery's task these past six months, since she failed to marry you suitably. This was to be her vindication!" Sophie retorted, adding, "But I shouldn't tease you. 'This is not the time for levity,' as Aunt Margery would say. Things look bad, Hal. What shall we do?"

He shook his head. "I am not yet certain. I am hoping

for some relief in the form of reinforcements, but with the river rising we could yet be cut off from Maucester. If that help doesn't materialise, then we shall have to take more direct action."

"Direct action usually leads to trouble," she frowned.

"Aye, and loss of life. That is something we must avoid at all costs."

"At all costs save that of our being married," she replied swiftly. "That I cannot put aside. Recollect, Sir Henry, you have made a promise and I hold you to it."

"Come Hell or high water?" he asked wryly.

"Either! I expect to be your bride come Tuesday."

"How very Shakespearean you sound," he laughed. "I see I have taught you well."

"Away with you to your council of war, I am for the kitchens to see how long a siege Susanna's cook thinks we can stand."

"Give me a kiss then, and tell her that it will harm none of us if she is frugal, in case the river cuts us off for a few days."

Sophie complied willingly. "Neither Susanna nor her cook will thank you for that thought. The river falls as quickly as it rises, once the tide turns into the channel."

He kissed her again and hurried on his way, still smiling at the thought of her transformation from a unruly girl into an accomplished young woman, a bride fit for any man.

Chapter Twenty Six

"Please do not trouble over me, Mr Hollingshead," said Rebecca quietly, as their companions' footsteps died away. "I shall be well enough here. Mistress Capel's cook has gone to make a draught for my pain. I shall do very well on my own, if you are needed elsewhere."

"I am needed more here," Jack replied firmly. "Sir Henry is no fool. He can manage the situation without my help, unless, of course, you would prefer I left you in peace?" he added in sudden doubt. "Have I been presuming too much? Now I think of it, I gave you little choice by my actions."

Rebecca shook her head as a tiny smile appeared on her tear-streaked face. "Your actions saved me from an unpleasant experience, if not real danger, and I don't know how to thank you."

"A simple yes to a question would be all the thanks I

need, but it would be unfair at this juncture, when you are so discomposed, to ask you to make me the happiest of men by becoming my wife," Jack replied, gazing intently at her.

She stared back at him, amazement writ large on her face, which suddenly flooded with colour. "Your wife?" she whispered. "You mean—marriage?"

He smiled at her amazement. "Is it beyond hope?" he asked tentatively.

She gazed at him, dumbfounded. Mistress Latham had been full of plans when Rebecca returned from Elmley Park, but she had made haste to discourage her, for she knew that another bride had been chosen for Jack by Margery Kingscott and his mother. Then as his hopeful expression faded, she quickly replied, "One must always have hope, sir, but I thought your marriage was already arranged?"

His face, which had been shadowed by doubt, cleared. "My mother, bless her, has been arranging marriages for me since I was a stripling. I always knew that until I found the perfect wife for me, I would go my own way. I have now met you, the only woman for me, and I am hoping you will make me the happiest of men, my dearest Rebecca, by consenting to become my wife."

She stared at him in amazement. "But we have only just met, sir!" she protested.

"And I knew in my heart, the moment I led you to the dance at Elmley Park, but I foolishly allowed doubts to creep into my mind, wondering if you thought me a mere acquaintance. I know this is neither the time, nor the place to ask."

Amid the sounds of the bustling kitchen nearby he paused, glanced to her hair tumbled about her tear-stained face and laughed. "Good Heavens, this is surely not the time nor place, with a mob at the door, and both of us in disarray, but will there be a better one? I love you Rebecca! I knew it the moment I took your hand, for it felt at once that it was right and natural. I want to hold tight to you, my dearest, for the rest of my life, however long that might be. I know I am being unfair in asking you now, in these circumstances, but I find such a strong desire to make you my wife, I'll use any unfair advantage."

"There is nothing unfair in it," she replied swiftly. "I too, felt as if I had found that which I had been seeking all my life. I have since wept because I knew there was no possibility of ever being with you. Any hesitation I have in giving my answer stems from the fear that your friends and relations will hold you in less esteem for your choice.”

“More fool them then,” he replied promptly. “My friends know me well. They know once I am set upon a course, little turns me from it.”

She looked into his eyes and bit her lip, as she considered his words. “My conscience tells me I should say no, because I am aware your mother and the Westwood family expect you to wed Mistress Elgar. Yet my foolish heart cries out at the thought.”

“You are utterly adorable,” he declared grinning in delight at her innocence. “There is no help for it. I am compelled to kiss you.” He did so, giving her no chance to argue further as he lifted her into his arms. She found a place of safely, which felt entirely natural.

A little later, as Jack sat in a rickety chair, with her on his knee and her head on his shoulder he asked, “So, when are we to be wed? I do feel, having made free with your lips, we should probably make an announcement of our intention of marriage.”

“You don’t think Sir Henry will be angry after all the trouble his aunt has gone to?” she asked timidly.

“Hal angry?” Jack laughed with pure joy. “The one person we can rely upon to assist us in every way is Hal.

For most of his adult life, he's had his aunts making matches for him. Yet he's eluded them since the death of his first wife. In a few days time he is due to wed his choice, if we can but stop the town from rioting."

"Yes, but what with the riot and the wedding, don't you think—

"I think I probably need to kiss you again to shock Mistress Capel's cook, who has arrived with your potion," he declared suiting his actions to his words. "Then we shall bind up your foot and take you up to join in Hal's council of war. You live in this town, so your insight will be valid and welcome."

And so it proved. She accepted the potion given her, and Jack deftly bound up Rebecca's foot, watched over by Cook, who nodded in appreciation. Once she was aware of the relationship, which had so suddenly blossomed in her quarters, she sped them on their way to the upper chamber with her blessing.

Chapter Twenty Seven

Hal glanced about the table as his friends gathered in Mistress Capel's parlour. Everyone looked strained and anxious. "Well, gentlemen, we find ourselves in a quandary. In spite of my best efforts, it would seem certain elements within this town are intent on mayhem."

"And succeeding," said Simon uneasily. "I was watching that ruinous alley opposite as we waited for you. The entire town seems to be coming and going there."

"Mistress Capel said that area is known to be a hotbed for rogues, the disaffected poor of the town, and a disgrace to honest folk who try to go about their business," said Nick, glancing through the window opposite. "It seems quiet enough now. Perhaps your words have had some effect, Sir Henry?"

"I doubt that very much, Nick," he replied. "The mob doesn't just walk away with its tail between its legs when confronted. It slinks back into the shadows, to lick wounds and plot." Then as Adam appeared in the doorway, he turned adding, "Adam, what news at The Greyhound? Oh, Mr Langley, what brings you here?

"I rode into town earlier to buy some provisions, and found that there was trouble afoot, so I came to offer my assistance, but I see you are well supplied with that."

"Yes," said Hal. "There has been some trouble with drunkenness in the lower part of the town, and a young woman whom you met at Elmley Park, found herself beset and was rescued by Mr Hollingshead. This sparked a near riot. We are gathered now to discuss how we can contain any further problems. So I asked Adam to go to The Greyhound to hear what was being said. Adam?"

"Trouble, it seems," he replied promptly. "I went to see old Harry, who used to be head groom. He says the word is that there is a foreigner behind it all."

"A foreigner?" cried Nick in astonishment.

Simon said swiftly, "Not a true foreigner, like the physician. Just one born outside of this town."

Adam grinned, set out a chair for Julius Langley, then took a seat himself. "No, in this instance I am not using the usual local meaning, but men born overseas."

Hal grimaced, as their thoughts were mirrored in

their faces. "Chawcester is so very unique in its notions, but this is not the time to discuss them. Gentlemen, we have a situation developing, which if it isn't contained could lead to serious trouble, if not loss of life. Normally in these circumstances, the suggested methods are to shut the taverns, and prevent any seditious meetings, however, in view of the proximity to my wedding, I am more inclined to seduce most of the townsfolk to our side by announcing I shall open the taverns to all."

Simon and Adam looked shocked as Nick grinned, in appreciation of the suggestion. "An excellent idea, Sir Henry! Do you think they'll take the bait?"

"Probably," he replied ruefully, "but the trouble is how do we keep them drunk enough to be amiable, and not so drunk as to become even more aggressive?"

"What we need to do is to isolate the troublemakers, those intent on riot. Most citizens are God-fearing folk. They don't truly want to cause trouble. They just get drawn in from a desire to witness a spectacle, and an excess of ale," said Simon thoughtfully.

"We should call a parley with the ringleaders in a neutral place, listen to their grievances and then arrest them for disturbing the peace," suggested Adam.

"At the moment, those deemed to be ringleaders are

in the lockup overnight, sleeping off their drunkenness. If, on the morrow, they are sober enough to see sense, we might avoid a riot. We have until then to think of a way to keep troublesome elements under control. However, nothing of a combative nature should be attempted unless we have troops at our disposal," said Hal shaking his head. "Your suggestion is a good tactic for war, Adam, but not for ordinary everyday trouble.

"This is everyday trouble? Is the West Country a law unto itself?" cried Simon.

"At the moment we are faced with a few drunken townsfolk intent on trouble," replied Hal. "My task as Justice, is to keep it from escalating to the next step, which is calling in troops. Once that happens we have gone from a little local difficulty to a major incident, which will be reported to London."

Adam inhaled sharply, disliking the inference. "Nothing wrong with Western folk. They have opinions of their own, they do, not just thoughts hammered in to their heads by clergy, like Eastern folk."

"Gentlemen!" Hal cried swiftly. "Please, let us not fall out amongst ourselves! It matters not what region surely! East, West, North or South, we are all Englishmen, and as such stand together, for Truth, Justice and the rule of Law!" He held the eyes of each in turn. "Did we not fight a bloody war to prove that we are all equal before the law? That none of us, be we so high as the King, or so low as the meanest fellow in that alley yonder, are above the law?

The door swung open and Jack advanced into the chamber carrying Rebecca saying, "Make way!"

Everyone about the table stopped arguing, and turned, to stare as Jack announced with a great flourish of satisfaction,"Ladies and gentlemen, I give you my future wife, Mistress Rebecca Howell!"

Sophie entered the room with Bella, Beatrice, Hugh St John, and Mistress Capel in time to hear his announcement and cried out in astonishment, "Good Heavens! Your future wife? So soon?"

"I am not Hal Westwood to dither, and Rebecca is not you, to endlessly dispute. We do not challenge the gods of love. We embrace their generosity! But for your whims and fancies, you two could have been married years ago," retorted Jack, carried away by his elation.

"Thank you, Jack," said Hal with a wry smile, as he helped the others to find seats around the table. "There were a few problems for us, of course, but it would be churlish to dispute you on such a happy occasion."

"If it is a happy occasion," said Sophie sharply, as ever, irked by Jack's blunt manners. "Rebecca, I have not heard your voice. Are you happy in this? You have not been overly persuaded by Mr Hollingshead? He is not a man to listen. If you have any doubts, do not agree to his proposal."

Rebecca's smile was enough to rid any doubt. "No, I do this for no one but me—and Jack of course."

"Thank you, Mistress Sophie," cried Jack as he tenderly set his beloved in a chair by her side. "If I weren't so happy I might take issue with your opinion of my character, but now Rebecca has agreed to be my wife, I don't really care."

"That's because your reputation is now in Mistress Howell's hands. She will be the keeper of your character," grinned Simon. "Jack, I am happy for you and Mistress Howell, I am glad to welcome you into the family we share.

"Thank you sir," said Rebecca blushing, and glancing at the faces, which showed various degrees of surprise. "I do hope you don't think I intrude, but Jack says that I can be of assistance."

"Yes, Hal," said Jack insistently. "Rebecca is of this town. That drunken rabble who were baiting her earlier, are her step-father's drinking companions. She'll know who they are and why they are intent on trouble."

Hal asked, "Do you have such a knowledge, ma'am, and if so, will it compromise you in any way to divulge what you know to comparative strangers?"

"I know of the men my step-father drinks with," she replied, looking troubled. "None of them are gentlemen more the lesser tradesmen of the town, which was one reason why Cousin Eunice had me come to live with her. But the others, the newcomers, I know little of them, although it would appear they are men of religion who seldom drink more than a cup of small-beer."

"Men of religion?" asked Hal incredulously. "That is surely odd."

"Never mind how odd it is!" Sophie said impatiently, "We came to join you because Susanna's boy Francis brings news. She turned to beckon the serving lad in then said to him, "Come right in, don't hover on the stairs! Francis tells me the mob is gathering again even now, down at The Cross. A man standing on the plinth is calling upon them to march for their God and Liberty! If this it is not got under control, we might well find ourselves under attack, just as you feared, Hal!"

Justin, who had just run up the stairs, entered the

room adding, "It's not like you to succumb to panic, Sophie! The man in question is one Deliverance Smithson, or to use a name perhaps familiar to you all, Harrison. He and his brothers, Persistance and Zeal, are sons of our former acquaintance, Sir Richard, who was formerly bethrothed to Hal's aunt Kate Westwood. They have come to the town intent, it would seem, on fermenting trouble. Their aim, so they claim, is to right the wrong done to their father, and they intend to call Sir Henry Westwood to book!"

As everyone looked appalled Justin added, "Before we all get into a fret, the furore is under control. I have had my eye on these men for sometime, so I sent for Constable Sambourne, who has just returned from his trip across the river. He tells me he saw all sorts of wonders there—including Mother Sandwell, who is hale and hearty in her new home. He should by now have rounded up the ring leaders and have them under lock and key. I instructed Sambourne to bind them over, to appear before you, Sir Henry, in the morning.

"Harrison?" cried Simon, as Hal looked appalled. "It was rumoured he was drowned on his journey home!"

"Swept overboard off Virginia!" Nick agreed.

"Indeed, it was widely reported," agreed Hal. "One of

Guy's sea captains brought the news to us a few weeks back. Although I thought it didn't quite ring true."

"Rather too convenient," suggested Justin. "You think it was ploy to lull you to a false sense of security, Hal?"

"No," cried Sophie impatiently, "His idea was to escape from his life which had become intolerable to him! Sir Richard Harrison spoke to me before he was exposed as a cheat and a liar and said he hated his life."

Adam looked shocked. "But as a minister, he would never have taken his own life!"

"Not taken it, no, but perhaps allowed it to slip away," replied Hal. "It seemed to me he did not react to situations, so much as go along with them, rather than fight back. I can see if he was standing on the deck of a ship in a storm, and a sudden wave swept him away, he might not try too hard to save himself."

"Possibly," agreed Simon, looking troubled. "He was a strange fellow. I escorted him to his horse as they left, and I asked him if he would be returning to Virginia. He said he cared not where he went and he might as well go to the devil, as your aunt, would not give him a fair hearing. I took him to task as a man of God, telling him it was her right, for he had been masquerading as a widower, and had engaged her affections. He replied that if he could not have the woman he loved, he despaired of life and had nothing to live for. And, as he was bound for Hell anyway, and he no care of what became of him."

Justin looked grave and said, "Well, whatever happened to him, his sons hold Hal at fault for his death. They are locked up now, but how do we deal with this matter when the town is so volatile? If you pass sentence on them in the morning, Hal, you can kiss your wedding good bye. There will be a full-scale riot, for there is still talk in the ale houses that one of your guests has abducted a local woman, and is holding her against her will."

"Jack Hollingshead, rescued your kinswoman, Mistress Howell," said Hal, indicating both who sat at the table. "Jack, walking with our other guests to view the Abbey, removed her from the danger posed by a drunken mob intent on mischief. The mob took exception to his actions and gave chase. They were pursued to this house. In the way of mobs with bellies full of ale, it took all four of us with drawn swords to convince them we weren't going to release Mistress Howell to them. Now you find us discussing how to return her to safety."

Justin frowned over the tale, which he repeated incredulously, "Bound up her ankle—Jack?"

Jack, who sat at the table next to Rebecca, shrugged his shoulders at Justin's look of disbelief and asked, "Why not? I have some skill in these matters. Why should I not use it?"

"Indeed," agreed Simon. "I don't know how many beasts he has attended on, but when I put my shoulder out after a fall, he wrenched it back for me in a trice."

Hal sat wearily, dropping his head to his hands. "I don't think he intends to give Mistress Howell back her heart. I think it is more an exchange for his, he has in mind." Hal looked up to meet Sophie's eyes, "Sweetheart, this is the point at which we discover discretion is the better part of valour, and return to Westwood. If you really hate the thought of being married in the village church, then we will summon the Rector to the house, or perhaps beg a Canon from the Abbey to attend on us."

Sophie got up and came to slip her arm about his shoulders and kiss his cheek. "Whatever you think best, Hal," she replied meekly.

As those about the table stared bemused by her uncharacteristic compliance, a shout was heard from outside the window which was suddenly lit by the flickering light of many torches.

"Too late!" cried Nick with a nervous grin, as the boy Francis burst into the room.

Chapter Twenty Eight

Hal leapt to his feet and cried in dismay, "Are they returned?"

"Aye, sir," panted the boy Francis. "When them brothers, the ones they call foreigners, were taken away to the lock up, the rest of the men went back to the tavern and fell to drinking again. I followed to listen and they were a-muttering about the Constable. He ain't liked, for they were saying as how they had a right to gather together as free-born Englishmen. And as how Sammy—that be what they call the Constable, sir—how he had got above himself, thinking as he were rubbing shoulders with the gentry—he could take a lordly air with the likes of they. I don't know how it came about, but it all blew up, sudden like. They said they were off to the lockup to let the brothers loose! That was when I thought I'd turn tail to come to warn you, Sir Henry, as you asked me to! But I got caught up in the mob, and lifted clear off my feet! I was carried along to the lockup, where they attacked poor old Sammy, who was about to sit down to his supper, and that fellow he had with him!"

"Sambourne was attacked? Were either men harmed?" Hal asked, as the boy ran out of breath.

"I don't know, my lord," the lad replied. "I wasn't near the front, but I heard him cry out. Then there were another groan when they opened the lockup. They let out the men, and another one, but he were too drunk to join in the mob. I worked my way to the edge then ran ahead and ducked down the alley, to get back to here. I have shut the gate to the alley, sir, as you bade me and put across the iron bar and only just in time, for they were hammering on it. But all the doors and windows are safe barred, as you said we must each night. No one can get in."

"Well done!" Hal nodded in approval and dismissal, then turned back to his guests. "Well, gentlemen, in spite of all our efforts, it would seem we are in a siege situation. I have made arrangements for just such an occurrence, so let me reassure you, our position is not dire. Owen, the boatman, will have taken his boat with the tide, to get help as soon as this trouble blew up. Relief will come, but it may take some while. In the meantime, perhaps we can parley with these men, and discover the source of their grievance."

"Do you think it wise, Hal?" Simon asked doubtfully.

"A show of force might answer," insisted Jack as he glanced to Mistress Capel. "How many weapons can we muster?"

"No weapons,"said Hal firmly. "Recollect these are our own people. We will talk."

"Talk as much as you care to," replied Jack. "We need muskets to hand."

"He has a point, Hal," said Justin. "By all means parley, but let some of us be armed, just in case they try to storm the house, or set fire to it."

"Pray, don't frighten the ladies, Justin. There is little chance of them doing either," Hal said sharply.

Nick and Justin exchanged looks, and left to search for firearms, followed by Hugh St John, Adam and the boy Francis, while Mistress Capel and Sophie went to find sheets and brandy.

Hal, Simon, Jack and Julius Langley stayed to discuss tactics, whilst Rebecca was forced by her injury to remain still. She nervously tried to engage the other women in conversation to divert them, but their attention was really on the discussions of the men, and the rising noise of the rabble gathering outside. By the time Justin, Adam and Nick returned with an odd assortment of weapons, some of which were very ancient, they had fallen silent, no longer able to maintain a sense of normality.

The men discussed options while listening anxiously to the angry shouts from the street below, and the sound of missiles hitting the house. The acrid smell of burning crept into the room as Hal outlined his plan to the others. After weapons were sorted and distributed, Nick crouched beneath the window.

As shouts and yells grew louder, Hal stepped forward to the open window and confront the mob. The atmosphere suddenly became very tense as Hal stood silently waiting for the noise to die down. Jack and Simon flanked him on either side, just out of sight of those gathered below. Julius Langley hovered anxiously in the background.

Finally the noise faded and all stood silently. "This is an unlawful assembly," Hal delared. "You have already been told to go about your business, and I now repeat that directive. If you have a grievance, this is not the time or place to air it. Go home to your beds, before I am forced to call in the militia to maintain the peace. If you do not obey, you will all be thrown in jail."

"You'd be set about to do that! There ain't no jail now we burned it down!" Various cries echoed back from the street below, amid gales of drunken laughter.

"Where is Constable Sambourne?" demanded Hal.

"Dunno! Depends whether Sammy got out of the lockup or not!" yelled one lout.

"Last I saw of they, he were sleeping like a babe in arms!" cried another to more laughter echoing in the smokey night air.

Hal became aware of someone behind him. Jack swiftly glanced to one side, with a puzzled look on his face and Simon shrugged.

Hal continued to address the crowd, ignoring his unease. "I have to tell you, the militia has been called out. You all know the consequences of this. Do you really want armed men on your streets? Armed men who have the right to shoot first and answer questions later?"

A swell of shocked angry shouts surged through the crowd. What had been muttering rose to irate shouts and cries of fury, "We have no care 'o them!"

The cries of different voices resounded:

"We be free men!"

" 'Tis our town, if any try to take it, we'll fight to the last!"

"We won't have them devils here, not like back in the war, we won't!"

"Then may I suggest you—" Hal got no further.

At that moment, Sophie and Mistress Capel entered the room laden with old sheets, a bowl of water and a flask of brandy, then halted in the doorway, frozen in horror. A shot rang out. Then Sophie gave a cry, and rushed forward. Hal was thrust aside by Julius Langley, then lost his footing from the force of his shove as Sophie grabbed Hal in a protective embrace. They knocked Simon over as they fell to the floor in a heap of bodies.

"What the devil!" Jack exploded in fury, bounding to the window, with no thought for his own safety. "Who dared to shoot at Sir Henry! You down there! Yes, you, the one with the red hat! Grab that man with the musket, and hold him! I hold you responsible for restraining him, and you, next to him, you with the bald pate! You are both temporary constables, by order of Sir Henry."

"Jack, Jack, do not worry, Sir Henry is unharmed!" Simon cried, extricating himself from the melee of thrashing limbs and flounced petticoats, as he helped release the furious Hal from Sophie's panicked grip. "Let go, Sophie! Let go! He isn't shot!"

"No, but Mr Langley is!" Mistress Capel cried in dismay, with a strangled cry as the man lay clutching his chest on the floor. His coat fell open to reveal a blood-stained shirt. Mistress Capel hurried to assist him, while Hal, cursing freely, got to his feet, and staggered, half-choked to the window.

"Who is there to be trusted among you?," Hal cried, angrily. "Which of you stand for law and order? Would you rather rule of the mob? Englishmen are you? Then stand for your rights now! You, each of you, know that justice is never served by mob rule! Step away from the drunk, and those drunk on a desire to overthrow the law! A man lies bleeding at my feet. One of you shot him. Will you all hang for this one man?"

Hastily the mob, suddenly sobered by the furore, stepped back, to reveal three men held by the citizens of Chawcester.

"Good evening! I take it you are the Brothers Harrison? You men who are holding them, come to the door, with your prisoners and you will be admitted." Hal stood waiting while this was accomplished, before beginning to address those remaining outside.

"The rest of you good people of Chawcester know I am to be wed in a few days time at the Abbey. Tomorrow, I expect to see everyman jack of you in your church, thanking your Maker we have not had a riot! Go home in peace now, and there will be no further repercussions. You have my word on it! Furthermore, on the day I wed my wife you may all drink our health and eat your fill in any of the inns or taverns to celebrate our marriage, provided there is no repeat of this disgraceful display."

There was a half-hearted cheer to greet this, and the odd, "God Bless you, Sir Henry!" as the crowd began to miraculously melt away.

"Mr Langley is hit, Hal," cried Sophie, who was holding a sheet over a fast-bleeding wound. "Oh, that Doctor Douay should be at Westwood!"

Julius Langley's face was almost as pale as his shirt, and he beckoned Hal closer. "Hal Westwood, come here. I cannot see you against the light. I have to tell you I've paid my debt to your father. He once saved my life in France."

"Don't speak," said Hal, dropping to his knees beside him, while trying to stop the flow of blood more effectively than Sophie. "We'll get a—"

"No time! Listen to me," he gasped, grabbing Hal's hand urgently, "Listen, I came here tonight to confess that I killed Jonas Capel. I went to The Ring o' Bells that night and brought with me a mixture made from a plant grown in Virginia and put it in his wine, when he wasn't looking. It pleased me that I should kill him using something from that place where my wife and children died. It—it was those berries that killed them—and it was all his fault."

"Why?" Mistress Capel cried, in bewilderment, as the bandage she was trying to roll with shaky fingers, dropped from her hand onto his blood-soaked shirt.

"Jonas Capel cheated me out of my lands here," he gasped as his voice dropped to a whisper. "After the war I couldn't find the money to pay the fines, so he lent it to me. But each time my harvest came in—he raised the price. There wasn't ever enough to pay him back—so we were forced to flee to Virginia and start again. There my wife and children starved, all because of his greed. I hated that man! He didn't fight, not for King—or Parliament. He just stole—" He groaned as he clutched Hal's hand blindly. "Tell Susanna Capel I am sorry! When I heard what was said about her—I never thought—"

Then the grip on Hal's fingers suddenly loosened. He paused then got to his feet and said, "I am sorry. He is dead. I doubt that Philippe could have saved him, even had he been here."

"Oh, Hal, it might have been you! That could have been you! Those evil men!" Sophie sobbed as tears filled her eyes. Weeping tempestuously she flung herself into Hal's arms, pointing to the three Harrison brothers as they were ushered into the chamber. "It was them— they could have killed you!"

Hal clasped her to him tightly. "Be calm now, Sophie, hush, hush. Be still, I am unharmed, thanks to poor Julius Langley."

Hal's sister Bella came to put an arm about her. "Come, Sophie, you are covered in blood. Shall we not go and wash your face and hands and change your gown?" With the help of the other women, Sophie and Mistress Capel left the chamber, leaving the men confronting the sons of Sir Richard Harrison.

⚜

Chapter Twenty Nine

Hal crossed to the bowl of warm water, washed his bloody hands then dried them on a piece of torn cloth. Simon and Nick carefully covered the body of Julius Langley, then everyone stood quietly with their heads bowed respectfully in silent prayer.

Simon poured wine for them all with an unsteady hand. Hal drank deeply of his, then sat down drained, as though no longer able to stand.

Jack, relieved that the crisis was over, observed Hal's sudden exhaustion and took control of the situation. "Bring forward the prisoners," he said sharply. "You men I made Constables—what are your names?"

"Saul Watson, your honour and this be Joe Crumpe," said the other nervously, with no trace of surliness.

"Until we know the fate of Samborne, you men are to be Constables," said Jack imperiously. "Your first task is to go and find out what has happened to him and the lockup. Then maintain law and order, until the Militia arrive."

Jack glanced uncertainly to Hal, who said, "I'll swear you in tomorrow," as he drank off the remainder of his wine. "Come back and report to me within the hour, and remember, you are required to remain sober at all times."

The men assented glumly and departed. Hal refilled his cup and motioned for the prisoners to come forward to the table.

"So, you are the sons of Sir Richard Harrison," said Hal in the short silence which followed. "I knew your father. Indeed most of us knew him."

"Aye," snarled the elder. "You sat in judgement on him too!"

"I do not sit in judgement of you," Hal replied. "This is not a court of law. If it were you would have representation. I have had you brought here to find out why you have caused such mayhem in this town. We want to know why you damaged the lockup, and other buildings. We want to make sure you understand that you are completely responsible for what has befallen our Constable. And finally to ask why, in Heaven's name you attempted to take my life, and instead killed another man in error."

The youngest of the three, who was bloodied, covered in soot, and reeking of smoke, spoke up quickly, "The Constable ain't dead. He were a bit battered, and choking on the smoke, like us, but we got him out. Didn't we, Persy?"

"Aye, that we did, Zeal," his brother, equally battered agreed, looked askance at the eldest brother.

"We don't hold with violence, Zeal and me. We don't! We wanted no part of this here to-do! We tried to hold 'em back but—"

He met his elder brother's eyes doggedly. "We don't hold with mob rule, we don't. We aren't responsible for the Constable. We got him out of the ruins, him, and the other one, that drunk. They might be a bit roughed up, but they were all alive when we left them."

"And the town lockup?" Adam asked sharply.

"Well, that don't be so good, on account of some fool setting fire to the thatch—but that weren't our doing, were it, Livery?" Zeal replied quickly.

"We came to call Sir Henry Westwood to account, that's what we did. That were our plan. That's why we left Virginia and set sail for England, isn't it, Livery? We didn't set no fires. We just want answers."

"Here I am," Hal interrupted. "I am Sir Henry West-wood, ready to be called to account."

Both brothers turned to their elder brother uncom-fortably. "Livery knows what's what," said Zeal confi-dently.

"Will you not ask him, Livery?" asked Persy as his brother stood silently.

"As if Sir Henry will dispense justice to the likes of us," spat the elder brother. "We'll be tried unheard by the likes of him. Just as our father was!"

"Your father was not tried at all," said Jack addressing the younger brothers. "I, indeed several of the people you see here, were present that day. We can all attest to what happened. Sir Henry merely asked Sir Richard to explain his conduct. How it had come about that a young woman was deprived of life by their greed. The other men were ready with excuses, but your father, like your brother, gave no reply."

"So, your justice only works one way, does it? You are happy to condemn me unheard, are you, Deliverance Harrison?" asked Hal, as the men stood silently again. The two younger brothers looked puzzled, clearly wait-ed for their brother to speak. Then as there was still no response, Hal added, "I assume you were told your father's garbled tale by the captain or crew members of the ship he sailed to Virginia?"

Then as the men still did not respond, Hal sighed wearily and concluded, "So, rather than seeking out those you imagined to be the architects of your father's downfall—or to discuss the truth of what actually did occur—you choose to believe all the rumours and half-truths relayed to you."

"Rumours?" Deliverance cried, finally goaded into speech. "There have been no rumours, no half-truths, just a plain story of how our father was lost to us, by the wickedness of this man." He pointed dramatically at Hal, addressing his brothers. "We know who has bought this misery upon us—how we be like the Children of Israel, wandering in the desert. How our mother has four more fatherless children to bring up, with help from none but we three."

"As a widow, could she ask for more than three splendid sons to assist her?" Hal asked. "How fares she now? Without you three, who must be her mainstay, no one of you is there to help and assist her?"

"There be Testament. He be old enough now. He turns fifteen at Lammas, he and Repentance will get in the harvest, with the help of Charity and Clemency," replied Deliverance, sullenly.

"Aye, Testament be a grand lad, and not idle, like Penty," agreed Persy.

"I am relieved to hear your mother is not alone, at this time," said Hal, "and the baby—the little girl born last winter—she thrives ?

"Piety, aye, she was well enough when we left. A comfort to our mother in her grief, that's what she be,"said Zeal, smiling at the thought of his sister.

"A grief I share," said Hal quietly. "For you must try to understand the situation which faced us all at Christmastide last winter. None of us took action against your father, save that I insisted my aunt—who is to me like a mother—was informed of the truth. She had to be told that your father was not free to marry, as he presented himself to be. His wife, your mother still lived, therefore he could not honour the contract he had entered into when he became betrothed to my aunt."

Zeal looked bewildered. "This makes ill hearing for us. That our father thought to replace our mother with another."

Hal replied earnestly, "When he was told your mother had died in Virginia and left him a widower, he thought to provide a mother for you all, and chose my aunt. She, good lady that she is, has performed a like service to my brother and sisters, these past twenty years. Your father thought he was acting in his children's best interests, in finding a mother for the younger ones."

Simon interrupted impatiently, irked by the self-righteous attitude of the eldest of the men, "Our complaint against your father, which has little to do with Sir Henry—save that he came to our assistance—was more his moral cowardice, in the face of the tragic death of a cousin of mine."

"Your father, mistakenly imagining he was a widower, entered into our society, meeting and eventually becoming betrothed to a good and virtuous woman. A simple error, it would seem, but it became more than an error once he discovered the truth—that his wife had survived. But he did not tell those he was living amongst, any more than he made an effort to return to his family. Thus he laid himself open to coercion, by those he mistakenly thought of as his friends. When the truth became known to them, they sought to involve your father in their plot and a young woman died as a result of those actions. Your father, who was a minister and had a family of his own, did not intervene to stop.

Instead he made no protest. Sir Henry discovered the truth of the matter, and challenged the men to explain themselves. Although their explanation was barely satisfactory, what they had done was not a crime in the eyes of the law, only in the eyes of society. There was nothing to charge them with in a court of law, so they were allowed to go free. But I told them they were no longer welcome in my house. Any subsequent ill that befell them was of their own doing."

"And none of it has any relevance to this town and townsfolk," said Adam sharply. "But that these are my friends, I have no interest in you, yet you have created mayhem here for your own ends. Our lockup is destroyed and a constable has been harmed. We still don't know if anyone has died. Is this all done so that you might be revenged upon Sir Henry Westwood?"

Justin interrupted, "And finally, there is the matter of Mr Julius Langley, who took the bullet intended for my brother-in-law. You cannot deny that a shot was fired into this chamber and fortunately Sir Henry was pushed aside by a friend of his father, or he might now be the corpse laid out on this floor."

"The shot wasn't to kill Sir Henry!" Zeal cried quickly. Livery shot in the air to quell the mob, which had got out of control! They were all drunk, getting up a list of those they had a grudge against and talking of setting fire to houses! But as Livery were about to shoot a warning, there were a scuffle behind us, and he were knocked forward."

" 'Tis true!" Persy cried anxiously, in agreement. "Livery said it were all going awry. The townsfolk were run mad on that Evil Whore of Liquor and he had to get them back on the Path of the Lord's Righteousness. He only wants the people to have the right to justice, like we have in our settlement."

"The people of this town have justice," cried Adam, indignantly. "We fought a long and bloody war to have justice as a right in this country! We don't need settlers from the wilds of Virginia to come and tell us what we well know! Sir Henry is our Justice, and you'll see him personally tomorrow."

Hal sighed, "I see your brothers plead eloquently for you, Deliverence. Yet you have little to say for yourself to excuse taking the life of a man, who has served his King, and was also a settler in Virginia, like yourself. He had returned to this country, after the death of his wife and children there. He was a broken man, trying desperately to make a new life for himself. Yet you express no regret, or sorrow that you took his life."

" 'Twas the Lord's will," Deliverance replied, without any show of repentance or emotion. "I did not intend to shoot the man. The Lord willed it so. I am but the hand of his Divine Power. Blessed be the Power of The Lord!"

Both brothers echoed his words, "Blessed be the Power of The Lord!"

"How do you know it was the Lord's will?" Nick cried hotly, his hackles rising. "How do you know it wasn't the Devil himself at your elbow? It so easily could have been Sir Henry you killed! That wasn't the Lord's will. It was your incompetence and stupidity in rousing a rabble of drunks and idlers! You cannot behave like fools and then blame the consequences on God!"

Deliverance Harrison stood unmoved, "Many are the slings and arrows thrown at His Chosen One. I will suffer mortification at the hands of thine enemies. Oh, Blessed Lord, but be Thou with me and I shall not fail."

"Blessed be the name of The Lord," repeated his brothers.

"And blessed be the peacemakers," Hal added wearily. "As we have lost our lockup to fire, we'll hold these men here in Mistress Capel's storeroom until the morning."

"Provided they don't eat all the stores, Sir Henry," said Adam, viewing them askance.

"If they do they shall pay for it threefold," said Jack severely. "But it may be as well if the cook gave them some supper," he added fairly, glancing to the others adding, "I don't know about you, but I am ravenous!"

Adam nodded. "If I know Susanna's cook, she'll be in the kitchen now organising food. It is her natural instinct. Watson, Crumpe, bring the prisoners! I'll see them fed, and put under lock and key, Sir Henry,

"Jack, I'll leave you to organise a rota to keep watch overnight until the militia arrive. If we take turns in pairs, the others can have some rest."

"Nick and I will take first watch," nodded Simon. "Adam is right. We should team up so there is one always to keep the other awake. Sir Henry, you need some rest, so once we've eaten, you should sleep first, then Jack and Hugh can relieve us,"

"Leaving Hal and I to take third watch,"agreed Justin. "Which should bring us nicely to dawn, and hopefully the arrival of the militia."

❧

And so as it happened, Adam knew his step-mother

only too well. In no time at all, the prisoners were fed and locked securely away, not with delights in Mistress Capel's store room, but in another small chamber.

As the table in the dining chamber was heaped with hot food they sat down to eat a late supper and discuss all that had occurred.

Morning brought relief, with the return of the temporary constables, who confirmed that the lockup was a smoking ruin, but there had been no further trouble in the town.

A body was found down by the river, Hal, convinced there had been foul play, set off with Justin and Adam to investigate, ending up at the Deeper Lode, where the body was found by a group of men.

" 'Tis Owen, the boatman, Sir Henry," called Saul Watson, as the men pulled aside the cloak which hid his face. "Aye 'tis Owen alright. He's been on this river all his life, he has. Why did he think to take a boat out with the tide, when the river was in flood?"

"Because I asked him to go down with the tide to call out the militia," replied Hal, looking grieved. "He knew there was an element of danger, but Owen was confident he could do it. He said he did it a dozen times every year."

"He were the best boatman on the river, and he won't do it no more. That river do be tricky this time o' the season, especially after rain," sighed Saul.

"I am greatly grieved his death is the result of following my instructions. Has he family, do you know?"

"No, his only daughter were took in childbed two year back, and his sister soon after," said Saul.

Hal said, "Take him to the Widow Black to lay him out. I am away to the Abbey to see about his funeral.

"But they won't have the likes of Owen in the Abbey, Sit Henry. They only take the great and the good in the Abbey!"

"Owen will be laid to rest there in good company," said Hal sharply, "In the Abbey he shall be lain, alongside Julius Langley, the friend of my father, who saved my life. Owen has saved the lives of so many others. He shall have a plaque on the wall to that effect, and an honoured place in the grave yard."

The men looked impressed, as they took up their burden and made a sorry procession to the widow's gate.

Justin and Hal followed them. "So, Owen wasn't murdered," remarked Justin quietly. "It is as well we dealt with the problem of riot ourselves. If we'd been still trapped at Mistress Capel's still waiting for the militia, we'd be in a very sorry state indeed."

Hal nodded. "I am not so confident there wasn't an element of foul play in his death, but without any proof, how can we hope to know?"

"Truth will come out in gossip in a few weeks," said Justin. "According to what I've heard, Chawcester people can't keep their tongues between their teeth. You go to make funeral arrangements, do you?"

Hal nodded and walked through the Abbey gate. "Yes, I might as well use up all my credit with the Abbey at once. I doubt I'll be very welcome."

Justin nodded, "I'll go ahead and settle up with the Widow Black. It would be good to get this matter done with before we leave for Westwood."

Justin escorted the body of the boatman to the cottage of the widow, leaving her with Owen's body and instructions to send a hand cart to collect the corpse of Julius Langley.

⚜

Chapter Thirty

Hal handed his bride into the coach and climbed in after her, shutting the door as the crowd of well-wishers thronged about them.

"Is that everyone of our guests accounted for?" Sophie asked, anxiously.

"I devoutly hope so! I left Jack organising it. What a boon he has been these past few days," Hal replied, sinking back against the squabs of the coach, with a deep sigh. "I do not know which is the more exhausting, Chawcester in holiday mood—or Chawcester in a riot."

"Chawcester is always exhausting, I realised that a few days ago, when I began to long for the peace of Westwood."

Hal glanced to her surprised and delighted, "Truly?"

She smiled. "Truly! Why do you ask?"

He let out a contented sighed. "I thought you might miss all the excitement and be miserable at Westwood, where it is all so calm and well-ordered."

"Believe me, I can't wait for a calm and well-ordered existence," she replied. "It has been the thought of Aunt Kate's peaceful manner which has kept me from being frantic."

"It is good to know she'll have organised everything, and we can enjoy the remainder of our wedding celebrations," he agreed. "I stood in that beautiful, vast nave of the Abbey, feeling totally insignificant, wondering if anything else could go wrong, or if you would decide the auguries had been so bad, you'd best not marry me at all."

She laughed. "I set out in procession to the Abbey, with Justin on one side and Adam on the other, followed by Bella Craven and Beatrice, with Nick and Hugh St. John, as sort of outriders. None of us said anything, but we were all nervous. I was expecting to be ignored, if not worse, for the High Street was deserted. Then as we got near The Cross, it seemed suddenly the whole town appeared and stood waving and cheering, throwing rose petals under our feet, blessing me and shouting out good luck to us all. By the time I got to the Abbey, I was so bewildered by it all, I wondered if the world was about to end."

"We could hear the noise inside the Abbey, and I worried it was trouble and would have left to find you, but Simon and Jack forestalled me, leaving Ned and I at the chancel steps, wondering if we'd have to make a sudden dash to Westwood. I was about to discuss it with Canon Hall, when Jack rushed back into the Abbey saying it was like a royal progress, and that we had to come and see. I thought the Canon would be vexed, but he led the way. It was a sight to gladden the heart. You, looking like a queen, walking through a shower of rose petals, with the cheers and blessings of your friends and neighbours."

"In all the noise and confusion, we nearly lost Susanna," she replied. "She had gone ahead with Jem, the groom from The Greyhound, and his sister, to collect Harry and Francis from Bess. We thought the walk might be too much for the boys, so they were waiting in the churchyard. The townsfolk helped Susanna and Bess get the boys to the front, then they joined in the procession like little gentlemen, carrying my train."

"They did so well. I saw them, as you turned in the door, for the Canon, rather ashamed of how he hotfooted it down the nave, had insisted we return in a decorous manner. I must admit I watched in trepidation, half-expecting Francis to stamp on the train, but he rose to the occasion. Libby would have been proud of them." He slipped his arm about her waist and kissed her cheek. "Thank you for including my sons."

"At last, I get a kiss, other than that chaste salute on the chancel steps!" she exclaimed.

"Sweetheart, we are still flanked on either side by well wishers. Don't you think we should keep our embraces for a later assignation?"

"At this rate I shall be dead on my feet, by seven of the clock!" she laughed. "Give me a kiss now, that I may know I am married and I'll take pot luck later."

He laughingly complied, to the delight of the last few townsfolk. Then as the houses of the town ended they drove into the countryside. "It shouldn't take much more than half an hour," he remarked, settling back with her snuggled against his side. "Take care you don't spoil your gown. It is particularly handsome. I think Sally Rose did you proud! "

"Everyone was so kind!" sighed Sophie as she leant her head on his shoulder. "Your Aunt Margery sent to London for the silk for my gown. Mistress Hollingshead sent the lace, which she procured in Nottingham. Guy got the finest Spanish leather for my shoes. I am truly blessed, Hal, not only in having you as my husband, but in having such a large, loving family. I shall never be alone again."

"That isn't always the boon you think it, sweetheart," he replied wryly. "By this time next week we might long to be alone for some peace and tranquility."

"Peace and tranquility can be had easily enough," she replied. "We'll tell Cook to put some food in a saddle bag, and then we'll ride out into the countryside."

He smiled at the thought adding, with a sigh, "You do realise I must be in London for Lammas? Will you come with me, or remain here in the country?"

"I should like to see London, but I think you would prefer me to remain here," she replied.

"Infinitely I would prefer you to remain here, but it is hardly fair that we spend the first weeks of our married life apart."

"You need have no fears for me, Hal, I am not like to be dazzled by the King, when I have you as my husband!"

"I was thinking more that we have a houseful of guests," he replied ruefully. "It is bad enough that their host should desert them, but their hostess too."

"Oh," she blushed at her error. "I thought you meant—

He hugged her closer. "Do not look so dismayed, sweetheart. You guess correctly, I do have mixed feelings about taking you to be presented to the King. Indeed, I am relieved that guests make it imperative you remain here, so it gives me an excuse to return home to you as soon as possible! Ah, the road for Westwood! Soon we shall be home."

"Home! I never had one before. Not one truly mine, where I actually had a right to be, where I belonged," she replied.

"Yes, that is something you don't have to explain to me—home," He replied. "I remember when I first came to Westwood, I had travelled through France and the Low Countries and lived with royalty, and with the next best thing to vagabonds, but the sight of Westwood, as it sits in the landscape, drew me like nothing had before.

"Here is the village," said Sophie nervously, "and there is the church. I thought I might bring my flowers to Libby's grave tomorrow, but I don't know how that would be viewed by everyone."

"Libby loved flowers as much as she loved her family. She would want to know her boys are safe and to see us happy, I am sure," Hal replied gently.

"She was kind to me, even though she knew I loved you. I feel so guilty for the pain I caused her," Sophie whispered.

"The past is the past. Neither of us acted well then," he agreed. "All we can do now is take care of her children, and her brother Justin, when he allows us. What she wouldn't want, is for us to be sad on our wedding day."

She bit her lip, smiled up at him, and confessed, "Now it comes to it, I am afraid."

He laughed. "You, afraid? Never! I have seen you confront both my Aunt Margery and armed murders! Why would you be afraid of being married?"

"Because it is so important to you—all this," she indicated the estate around them. "So it is precious to me. I might not do the things I am expected to do well."

"What matter the way the head lies, if the heart be right," he replied kissing her. "Look! Everyone has come to greet us!"

As they turned up the drive to the house, a cheer rose up from those assembled. All the servants, household, and people from the village, which had been disconcertingly deserted, stood lining the route, waving and cheering, while some threw flowers and petals. Whilst outside the house itself, stood those who had not gone to the Abbey, Aunt Kate, Aunt Margery, Molly Kingscott, Madeline Hollingshead, Jane, Cordelia, Doctor Douay and his wife, and a group of children.

Over to one side stood Sally Rose and her girls, along with boys from the village choir, singing country songs familiar to all with a mixture of sweetness and great enthusiasm.

And as they passed by the people joined in, following their carriage in a joyous procession, singing as they made their way up to the house.

Enjoy the Next Book in the Series:

Where Waves Whist

Chapter One

Hal Westwood entered the chamber to find his wife sitting at her toilette table gazing wistfully at her reflection in the mirror.

" 'Shall I compare thee to a summers day, thou art more lovely and more temperate,' " he said smiling at her reflection.

" 'Rough winds do shake the darling buds of May, and summer's lease hath too short a date,' " she replied quickly.

He laughed. "Buds of May are but a dream. It's damned cold out there."

"It looks it," she replied with a shudder, as sudden rain lashed the window. "What took you out so early, my lord, whilst I lay a sleeping?"

"The letter from the King, which arrived last evening, needed thinking on," he replied.

"And having thought, which you did last evening, whilst I was reading *The Tempest* aloud. Indeed, Aunt Kate remarked upon your silence. What is your conclusion?" she asked, brushing her long hair into a twist, and securing it with pins.

"What, no demure cap for my lady to go about her duties this morn?"

She smiled. "No, nor apron, but don't tell me if it is secret. I know I shouldn't have asked."

He nodded, and changed the subject. "I see I must take a trip to the West Country. Would you care to accompany me? Spring comes earlier the further west one goes, and I might have to go as far west as possible."

"As far west as possible? Do you speak of Virginia?" She could not keep the dismay from her voice.

"No, not that far west," he laughed. "But I would like to—some day, perhaps. No, I mean to the west of England, to Cornwall."

"Cornwall? Is that not an untamed country full of legends and wild folk?"

"Some of the King's most loyal subjects live in that land of legend," he replied, as he changed his clothes.

Sophie hastened to pour him fresh water to wash, and fetched a clean cloth.

"The battle fought at—at Lostwithial, was hard won," he added in muffled tones, "and the only church in the country dedicated to his father, King Charles the Martyr, is in Falmouth, the largest port, which also has very deep water, and a lot of space. As a result of the debacle with the Dutch last year, the King is considering various ports to dock ships, so they are not all conveniently located in one place. Our fleet will be less vulnerable to attack than last summer. His Majesty requested that I go to sound out opinion—and to look at the port—to see if the rumours of pirate raids are valid. I have also to sit at a trial in the county town of Launceston, where one of the Justices has had certain accusations brought against him by a fellow Justice."

As she puzzled over his words, he added, "It is strongly suspected that the Justices are at odds over a lady. And this is the method of the more senior of the two is using to be rid of a younger, possibly more handsome, rival. Unfortunately, it means I have to go to both Launceston—which is on the border with Devon, and Falmouth—which is at the opposite end of the county, over what are reputed to be the worst roads in the county. Part of the route is over Bodmin Moor, a place inhabited by rogues, ghosts and murderers, or worse."

"And you want me to go with you?" she asked.

"I am considering going by sea, which is thought to be the quickest and safest option. We could embark from Bristol with a sea captain of Guy's acquaintance, sail down the estuary, go ashore at one of the fishing ports on the north shore, travel by coach to Launceston, then after the Assizes, travel south to another port and from thence, to Falmouth. It could be an adventure and we would be together. If I go alone I might be away some weeks," he added.

She replied uncertainly, "Yes, of course, I shouldn't care for that at all!"

He glanced to her, a little puzzled by her lack of enthusiasm. He had been expecting her to embrace the idea with the enjoyment of one who had been confined to the house by a particularly wet and chilly winter. "Well, think about how you might like it, but I warn you, I must be gone within the next few days."

"Within a few days!" she cried in dismay. "So very soon?"

"All instructions from the King usually need urgent attention," he replied with resignation. "Come, let us go down to breakfast. Perhaps, some food in your stomach will make you look upon the project with more favour."

Some twenty minutes later, Aunt Margery stared at her nephew with an affronted expression as Hal outlined his plans. "The King sends you where?"

"Cornwall, ma'am," he replied, having broken his fast in a substantial manner, Hal felt more equal to relaying the news.

"Cornwall? Why how very odd! I had a letter come only last evening from my cousin's daughters. They live in a small village some miles from—now where was it?" Aunt Kate took up a small brocade bag she habitually carried and began searching for the stiff pages of her missive, whilst Aunt Margery expressed her disapproval of a such a foolhardy escapade as a visit to such a distant place.

"I am inclined to agree with you, ma'am," said Hal patiently, "unfortunately, His Majesty requests my assistance in this matter and, as we all know, a request from the King is not to be denied."

"Falmouth," cried Aunt Kate, looking up from her letter. "It is from my cousin's daughter, Jennifer. She and her sister Elaine have been left alone since the death of her father. He was the vicar of the parish of—oh, now where is it?"

Margery grew plaintive. "What can that signify, Kate?

Hal isn't going to Falmouth, are you, Hal?"

"Oddly enough, ma'am, I am," he replied frowning a little. "Initially I must go to Launceston, but after that, the King requests I go to Falmouth to attend to some matters and make a report on the state of the harbour there."

"What a very strange request, Hal," said Aunt Margery. "What can you tell him that others haven't already? You are aware that Madelaine and Jack Hollingsworth will be with us within weeks for his marriage to Rebecca Howell."

"I am of the opinion that the King wishes an independent assessment of the harbour," he replied. "As for the arrival of the Hollingsheads, I could hardly be unaware of it, ma'am. As witnesses to his rescue of Rebecca, and the subsequent near riot which almost upset our wedding, Sophie and I have a vested interest in seeing Jack and Becky safely married. If we leave within the next few days, we should be back in plenty of time before their arrival or their wedding takes place."

"We?" Aunt Kate looked up quickly. "Is Sophie going with you?" She glanced to Sophie who sat opposite her.

Sophie smiled. "I am a little unsure, ma'am," she confessed. "I have never been to sea, or indeed very far afield, apart from our visit to Court before Christmas."

"You enjoyed that, my dear, you know you did," said Kate, casting an anxious look at the preoccupied Hal. "You returned home full of all you had seen and done."

"And how, when that diversion palled, she took to ransacking any draper within walking distance of our lodgings," murmured Hal, his eyes on the contents of his letter, as he perused it again.

"I was purchasing supplies for Sally Rose, Hal, you know that," Sophie cried indignantly

"And you did so well with your mission, we nearly had to hire a cart to bring it home," he agreed.

"Hal, we did no such thing!" she said with a laugh. "I'll agree the coach was packed out, but—"

"I prayed all the way home we wouldn't lose a wheel, for it would have taken hours to unpack the coach, or six strong men to lift it. As it was, we needed to change horses twice," he continued mercilessly, as his Aunts joined the merriment.

"Sally was thrilled to get such lovely fabrics, you know she was and she thanked you personally, Hal, for all your trouble," Sophie said. "I grant I may have been a little enthusiastic, but only look at what she has achieved," she smiled indicating her own gown.

"Indeed! You were, of course, down to your last dozen gowns. I was forgetting," he replied humorously. "I am just praying Sally Rose doesn't require tar or whalebone from Falmouth, or we might have to hire a galleon to bring it back."

"Now you are being silly, Hal! There is no way a galleon could come up river as far as Chawcester," she replied, playing him at his own game. "Anyway, any escapades of mine palled into insignificance at Christmas, given the furore of the early arrival of Cecily's baby, in the midst of the feast."

"Now that is true, Hal," agreed Aunt Margery. "I have never seen a baby more in haste to arrive than little Noel!"

"Indeed," he agreed, laughing. "Nor a father and brother more panicked than Ned and Guy."

"We laugh now, but it was no wonder we were all afraid, given Cecily's history. Yet here we sit, thankful that both Cecily and Noel, and indeed, Jane and little Rosie are in the best of health," said Aunt Margery.

"Mmmn," murmered Hal, "although I cannot but think it unfair to call a baby boy by such a name."

"Ambrose was called so by his mother, and his father thought it built up a man's character," said Sophie.

"Well it isn't a name I would choose—"

Aunt Kate, having found her letter interrupted Hal, "It is St Medoc, two miles from Falmouth, or just across the water. Jennifer says it is situated up a creek, and has only half a dozen cottages, an inn and several farms. The church her father had was beautiful, with views out over the water. Only now they have had to quit the parsonage, as the new incumbent is due to arrive, and they are living in one of the cottages nearby. Jennifer, is betrothed to a young lawyer from Falmouth, she reminds me, that he has been taken up on a charge of piracy and has been taken to Launceston to stand trial." She looked up again, to meet Hal's eyes, "I am sorry, Hal, I interrupted you, but surely the coincidence is too great? Do you think—"

"It sounds likely," he agreed, a little bemused. "How very odd, that it should be the two places I am sent to? Although the King's letter makes no mention of any specific cases in his instructions, as is his want. I am instructed merely to go, assess the situation as I find it, and report back to His Majesty."

"I think this has happened only recently," Kate, equally puzzled, returned to her letter, her anxiety plain. "It seems Elaine thinks there is something afoot, for she has also enclosed a note."

She handed the note to Hal who unfolded, it to reveal words written in the tiny script across the length of the piece of manuscript. "Jennifer's betrothed, one Tallen Marrack, which is surely an odd name, has fallen foul of a local lawless family, though how—oh, I see. He had been to Exeter, and was returning by boat, when it was blown upon the rocks in a sudden squall on the approach to the harbour. Somehow, this young man got caught up in a fight with some pirates, who were trying to board the ship, and was knocked out. Good Heavens, I had no idea that Cornwall was so lawless! He regained his senses, it seems, to find himself in goal in Launceston, along with those who attacked them."

Kate looked up to meet Hal's eyes, her face anxious. "Hal, could you try to find out what has been going on? I know you go there at the King's command, but it sounds like a grave situation, which is out of control. I can't think Jennifer, who always comes across as being remarkably pragmatic, like her mother, would be involved with a young man of such dubious principles."

Hal who was grimacing over the note she gave him, shrugged his shoulders. "I'll happily look into it, but young women have been known to make mistakes—

young men, too," he reminded her.

"Yes, of course, but I worry that they must feel particularly alone, since the death of their father. They have no other kin but me, now my brother is gone."

"Your cousin had no other kinsfolk?" Hal asked in concern, handing the note over to Sophie to see if she could decipher the scrawl.

"We are not a large family, as you know, Hal," she replied. "In thinking back, as far as I can remember, there was just my uncle and my father. I did have another kinsman, Robert, but he was killed at Marston Moor, leaving just Polly, his sister who married Roger Walter, a minister, and they had two daughters, Jennifer and Elaine."

"Who, like Kate, lost nearly everything, once their grandfather died," sighed Margery. "It was just as well you were safely married to Henry, Kate."

"Indeed," she agreed absently. "But as the last of my generation, I must be concerned for the welfare of these young women."

"If you wish me to seek them out, Aunt Kate, then naturally I shall do so," said Hal, politely. "Two miles from Falmouth is no great distance, and it sounds like they might be company for Sophie, whilst we are there."

"Indeed, Aunt Kate, this Elaine says she thinks it is all a plot of some sort," said Sophie, who was looking more interested than previously.

"Oh, is that what she says?" Hal remarked, examining the page over her shoulder. "I found the writing impossible to comprehend, but be assured, Aunt Kate, I should be happy to meet any cousin of yours."

"They are very much of an age with Sophie, or at least the elder is. Elaine is younger I do believe. It is so difficult to remember the ages of people one has never met, although I have corresponded with Jennifer occasionally over the years since her mother died. Now I fear she is greatly distressed at the thought of her betrothed being cast into gaol, and she doesn't know whom to ask for advice." She glanced apologetically to Hal, adding, "I did tell her how wonderful you have been in the past, at getting to the bottom of awkward situations."

"I have often made discoveries," he agreed, "but I cannot, in all honesty, say my intervention has always helped people."

"It certainly helped Madelaine Hollingshead get Jack settled into matrimony, Hal, and she is very pleased about that," Margery said, a shade impatiently. "But this young kinswoman of yours, Kate, is another matter. Surely in such a situation as she now faces, she'd do better to forget the young man ever existed."

Kate looked distressed. "I don't know that she'd want to do that, Margery. From what I understand, this young man is wealthy and of a good family."

"Surely if he is of a good family, they will be in attendance on him," frowned Hal.

"It seems Mr Marrack was in attendance on his son, but he was suddenly taken ill, and they fear for his life. And that of young Tallen if he doesn't recover," said Sophie, who was suddenly making headway with the missive. "For without representation of some sort they fear he will surely be found guilty. Why on earth has she written this in such tiny script? No wonder you could not decipher it, Hal."

"They were never, of late, a wealthy family," said Kate taking the note, and holding it at arms length to peer at it. "No doubt my kinswomen are using up paper left over from their father's sermons."

"But of course, that explains it!" Hal cried. "How could I have forgotten—when we were in exile we would use and reuse every scrap of paper which came our way! Yes, this is a piece cut from the foot of one of their father's old sermons, the writing on the other side had no bearing on it at all! Well, that is a great relief, the tribulations of Job, although they might bear some similarity to the case in hand are not necessarily germane to the matter." He glanced to Sophie. "So, has this convinced you to accompany me? Are we westward bound?"

❧

www.ingramcontent.com/pod-product-compliance
Lightning Source LLC
Chambersburg PA
CBHW031449260626
47154CB00016B/1